I0662526

The Paragon Park Murders

Frank J. Infusino Jr.

The Paragon Park Murders
Copyright ©2025 Frank J. Infusino Jr.

ISBN 978-1506-914-98-5 PBK
ISBN 978-1506-914-99-2 EBK

LCCN 2025933929

March 2025

Published and Distributed by
First Edition Design Publishing, Inc.
P.O. Box 17646, Sarasota, FL 34276-3217
www.firsteditiondesignpublishing.com

ALL RIGHTS RESERVED. No part of this book publication may be reproduced, stored in a retrieval system, or transmitted in any form or by any means — electronic, mechanical, photocopy, recording, or any other — except brief quotation in reviews, without the prior permission of the author or publisher.

Other books by the author:

The Final Word

Murder at Fort Revere

The Lady in Black

We live in God's amusement park.
Dean Koontz

CHAPTER 1

December, 1957

The solitary figure trudged along the beach walkway in the face of slashing wind and sleet sweeping in off the Atlantic. He moved like a drunk staggering home after a booze filled night, two steps forward, one back, listing to his left and right.

He scrunched his head deeper into his Navy peacoat but the collar offered minimal protection from the biting cold. He cursed himself for not donning a hat, but he had just minutes to gather some belongings to escape former pals who threatened his life.

He stashed his Chevy Bel Air near a block-walled restroom in the empty beach parking lot hoping the small building would offer concealment from any would-be trackers.

Bile rose in his throat with the thought men with murderous intent were chasing him. He sought refuge in the tiny Hull peninsula expecting in the dead of winter, days before Christmas, few residents would venture out.

Confirming his belief, he hadn't seen a soul, walking or riding, since coming into town.

He lurched forward, leaning into the gale, cold, hungry and exhausted. He drove all night zig-zagging through three communities to ditch anyone on his trail. He kept his head turned away from the ocean, his face wind-burned and itchy, his hair soaked, icy rivulets of water creeping down his back.

In the gray morning light, the silhouette of Paragon Park loomed on the other side of Nantasket Avenue, the town's central thoroughfare. The park's stark, silent profile stood in sharp contrast to the bright lights, clanking rides and merriment of bustling crowds in summer.

As a teenager, the man worked on the giant wooden roller coaster, hailed as one of the highest in the world. He longed for those care-free times joking with co-workers as they started the trains on their way, teasing girls who tried to hide their anxiety with strained laughter as they hopped aboard—dreading every heart stopping hill and body twisting curve.

His former job and vacations here with relatives lured him to this town as he fled real or imagined pursuers.

Battered by the storm's relentless onslaught, he lurched toward the dim light in the windows of the Anastos restaurant a hundred feet in front of him across Nantasket Avenue. Shielding his eyes, he squinted both ways before crossing the street, but saw no cars or pedestrians as the temperature hovered near freezing.

Stomping slush off his shoes, he slipped through the door to the café. Red Formica-topped aluminum tables were arranged along the windows to his right and a soda fountain with red cushioned stools stood to his left.

Napkin dispensers and silverware place settings dotted the tables alongside white coffee mugs turned upside down. On one wall, an ad for Carnation ice cream vied with a poster for the movie, Sayonara, starring Marlon Brando.

Anastos served as the refreshment center for the adjacent, Apollo Theater, opened only during the months of June, July and August to cater to the surge of summer residents and tourists.

The man, the lone customer, chose a table where he could eyeball the front door. He raised a mug to signal for coffee to an elderly gent behind the counter and ordered bacon and scrambled eggs when the brew came. His hands trembled and his right leg shook, a reaction from the chill and fear.

He had reason to be frightened.

He drove the getaway car in a gas station robbery gone bad the night before where the attendant was shot. Surprised and angered because his companions assured him no one would be hurt—he didn't know they were armed—he took off, leaving them cursing and waving their guns in his direction.

As he sped away, one shouted, "We'll kill you, you bastard. We'll get you."

The man, twenty-nine-years old, slender, not thin, sported a full head of sandy hair parted down the middle, a style long out of favor, but one he thought cool. His blue eyes, straight nose and strong jaw, attracted the ladies though he had no current partner.

A good thing.

He was on the run with no idea when, if ever, he could return to the life he lived before last night's debacle—regretted hooking up with the unstable punks who suggested it might be fun to rob a gas station.

He shook his head in disgust. Thought it a lark until those dip-shits started shooting. He reached into his coat pocket and fingered the .38 Special he carried for protection. Reassured, though he had never fired it in anger—hoped he never would. He mustered out of the Marines after serving in Korea and wanted nothing more to do with firearms or killing. Yet, he carried a weapon; a contradiction he chose not to examine.

He peeked through the window blinds as the storm increased in ferocity. Sheets of snow blanketed the sidewalks and roads. Fearing his Bel Air would be snowed in, he wolfed down the eggs and bacon the old man delivered minutes earlier. He took a last sip of coffee, pulled up his collar, dropped a five on the table and headed into the treacherous weather.

He kept his head down while slogging back toward his Chevy, hair matted with ice, shoes and socks drenched. He scurried by the Metropolitan District Commission (MDC) Police Station with its blue light on and Funland—a miniature Paragon—with its towering Ferris Wheel.

Finally, reaching his car, he was stunned when two men burst out from behind the vehicle. He froze for an instant as one shouted his name and pointed a gun at him. Fear engulfed him like a giant wave; he felt like he was tumbling inside it, gasping for breath.

A bullet buzzing by his head took him back to reality. He rolled to his left and in one smooth motion, leaped up and darted back across the street. Caught off-guard, his assailants fired wildly as their prey dodged their bullets. A yellow snowplow with flashing lights rumbled by, the driver oblivious to the gunshots.

The man reached the chain link gate of Paragon Park, and despite his heavy peacoat, catapulted over. He set an obstacle course record for speed and agility at boot camp during his Marine training, but couldn't outrun bullets. Two pinged off the barrier, one finding its mark as it ricocheted and grazed his left shoulder. He shook it off like a bee sting and pushed on.

The fence slowed his would-be killers enough for him to increase the distance between them. He leaped through the accumulating drifts like a kangaroo, but with no tail to steady himself, fell headlong into the white powder. He cursed. His footsteps and the outline of his body would lead his hunters straight to him. But as he struggled to regain his footing, a plan took shape in his mind. If he could reach a higher perch, the trail could be used to his advantage.

And from his experience working in the park, he knew just where to go—the "Flying Scooters," whose platform stood fifteen to twenty feet off the ground providing an excellent view of the surrounding area. The metal scooters were in storage, their supporting cables hanging lifeless like downward pointing arrows.

The man veered off the concourse, darted between the Caterpillar ride and the Lindy Loop—two attractions with cars traveling a circular, undulating, wave-like track—and climbed the stairs to the elevated platform.

He side-stepped a cable and dove into the accumulating snow lying flat, waiting—a disciplined, expert marksman occupying the high ground with the element of surprise.

He yanked his .38 from his pocket, supported it with his left hand, aimed with his right, hair sopping wet, hands and feet numb. Hatless, he blinked often as snowflakes blinded him. He forced himself to remain still and block out the cold as if in Korea preparing for the screaming Chinese hordes to storm his position.

His hunters were not soldiers, though, and followed his trail like lemmings, heads down as they moved within range of the .38. Oblivious to danger, they never looked up. Single rounds struck both in the upper torso slamming them backwards, arms and legs splayed, guns flung from their hands.

The shooter jumped to his feet and rushed down to stand over his victims. His body convulsed and tears came to his eyes. "Why? You dumb bastards?" he screamed into the wind and driving snow. "Why?"

Gaining control of his emotions, he debated his next move. In Korea, he would have finished his attackers off with head shots. But this wasn't combat and he was no killer.

He tossed their weapons onto the track of the adjacent midget racers and ran toward the main gate, glancing back at the corpses lying on the snow-covered ground, blood saturating the area. They would soon freeze to death if not already gone.

He thought of calling the police from a phone booth to alert them of the men in the park but rejected that notion. If alive, he feared they would implicate him in the robbery and murder of the filling station attendant in Hingham, a town northwest of Hull. He saw the man fall, believed they killed him. His cronies, no friends really, might turn on him, blame him for everything.

He couldn't risk it.

He kept running into a nightmare future where he became the target of revenge and the investigation of this killing uncovered drug dealing, police corruption and exposed the criminals responsible for one of the greatest bank heists in Massachusetts history.

CHAPTER 2

Patches of ice still dotted the ground in shaded areas of Paragon Park. Three consecutive storms since December battered the New England coast. Massive snow drifts clogged roads and highways from Cape Cod to Bar Harbor, Maine—thousands of motorists stranded for days.

Five people trapped in their autos died from carbon monoxide poisoning, emergency vehicles unable to reach them. Relentless high-tides pounded the seawall along Nantasket Beach leaving gaps up to four feet. Chunks of concrete littered the sand. Steel rebars pointed upward and eastward as if chastising the ocean for its callousness.

Eighty-mile-an-hour winds ripped through Paragon Park blowing out windows in the Carousel canopy and uprooting a wooden fence on the Red Mill, a pseudo "tunnel of love." Ten support beams from the Giant Coaster tore loose and cluttered the concourse. An arcade sign dangled from its anchor bolt.

The lighthouse on the miniature golf course blew against the coaster and lay in pieces. Three aluminum light-posts bent in-half as if bowing to the power of the wind. The temperature hovered near fifty degrees on April 2nd 1958, when maintenance crews began the annual ritual of preparing for a May opening.

Paragon Park, the Disneyland of its day, opened in 1905 touted as a mini-World's Fair. Its highlights included an interior saltwater lagoon navigated by gondoliers from Italy, camels and camel drivers from Egypt who toured visitors around the grounds and an authentic Japanese village populated by Tokyo natives. The centerpiece was a 150-foot electric tower, a beacon seen from miles away. Thousands of tourists arrived daily during the summer months by steamboat, trolly and railroad.

The glory years didn't last, though, a victim of multiple mysterious fires and financial shortfalls. Eventually, wooden planks covered the lagoon and the Italians, Egyptians and Japanese returned to their native countries. The electric tower toppled in high winds in 1916.

Despite these setbacks, the park remained a premier tourist destination on the Massachusetts South Shore into the 1950s. Carnival rides and arcades with pinball machines and other games of chance replaced its once stunning attractions—the landscape, concrete and steel instead of a man-made lake.

On special days, dare-devil high-wire artists dazzled onlookers and wrestling matches featuring the popular Haystack Calhoun and Gorgeous George enticed men and women fascinated by mayhem. Hated villains like Dick the Bruiser goaded crowds into a frenzy. Staid elderly ladies, wild-eyed, faces contorted in anger, spittle spewing from the corners of their mouths, threw folding chairs into the ring to express displeasure if one of their hero's was manhandled.

The park opened a few weekends in April, weather permitting. Maintenance crews hustled to scrub the grounds, inspect each attraction, lubricate and/or replace worn out parts and paint anything that didn't move.

This season's grueling winter with its attendant destruction left much to be done putting an early opening in doubt—the effort further complicated by the discovery of two dead men sprawled amidst the debris. One six-man team, the first to stumble onto the remains, stood cowering and immobile until their foreman screwed up his courage to check the bodies.

The victims lay side by side, arms akimbo, shock etched on their discolored, bloated faces. One man's left leg was twisted at a right angle pinned under his other leg. A cursory inspection by the crew leader revealed they were, indeed, dead. The cold and snow had preserved their bodies though decomposition had begun.

Loath to touch the corpses, the boss backed away, rejoined his group, and dispatched one man to the administration offices located at the rear corner of the park, in the shadow of the bumper cars, to alert the cops.

In a quirk of official jurisdiction, the Metropolitan District Commission assumed legal authority at Paragon Park, not the locals. They patrolled designated waterways and highways in the state along with Revere and Nantasket Beaches. The worker directed to contact the police, not aware of these intricacies, called the Hull PD. The desk officer forwarded the distress call to the MDC Station, a small white stucco building, a block away from the park.

In the 1950s, the MDC, known as the Metro Police, or just, "The Mets," was the third largest law enforcement agency in New England with over six-hundred officers. Its detective division investigated felonies within its bailiwick. Two detectives dispatched from Boston would handle the murders since the small Nantasket Substation lacked an investigative unit.

An "old-hand" and a rookie, caught the case, two men different in temperament and physical stature. Sergeant William "Bill" Wilkinson, a fifteen-year veteran in his mid-forties, stood five-feet nine inches tall. He sported a pencil thin moustache and fought a receding hairline. Though slight of build, an emerging paunch pressed against his belt. To many of his colleagues, he resembled a silent film villain, a circumstance that made him the brunt of crude jokes—behind his back, of course.

Wilkinson paused near the cadavers, pushed his cream-colored fedora back on his head and scowled, arms folded across his chest. A Camel cigarette dangled from his lips; the fingers of his right hand yellowed from his two pack a day habit. He viewed the killings in this Podunk town as a nuisance delaying his chance to move up the chain of command. It interrupted his daily lobbying efforts to ingratiate himself to the higher echelon. Some less than charitable fellow detectives labeled him a brownnoser.

His partner, twenty-eight-year-old, Anthony James Gallo—AJ to his friends and family—a patrol officer for five years with Metro, promoted to detective just two months earlier. On the street, he earned a reputation for honesty, dedication and toughness.

His size didn't hurt.

The physical opposite of Wilkinson, he stood—in military jargon—four clicks over six feet, weighed two-hundred twenty pounds with a bull neck and bulging biceps; his black hair cropped jarhead style. No wrestler of the day would enjoy stepping into the ring with him.

His off the shelf, maroon blazer strained against his massive chest; his tie loosened. A thrice decorated Korean War veteran, he relished the challenge of his first murder investigation.

Wilkinson stepped back from the decomposing corpses, wrinkling his nose. He took a drag on his smoke to obscure any stench and ordered his young counterpart to search them.

The former Marine, no stranger to death, patted down the victims and uncovered wallets for each. Their driver's licenses identified them as Dustin Rose and Donald Berger, both thirty years old, living in the adjacent town of Cohasset but not together. Rose had a nasty scar on his right cheek, now blue-green in color. His billfold bulged with cash.

While searching the men, Gallo flashed back to Korea. On the battlefield, he rifled through the uniforms of dead North Korean and Chinese soldiers, at the behest of senior officers, looking for anything of military value. More often than not, he found creased and faded pictures of loved ones or carved Jade charms believed to bring luck and protection to the holder. The faces of those poor souls—if they had one—resembled those of Berger and Rose, twisted in disbelief, eyes wide, unseeing.

Shaking off the memory, Gallo swiped his left fore-arm across his forehead to rid the sweat formed there despite the cold. He handed the identifications to Wilkinson, who gave them a cursory glance and returned them. As he did so, one of the members of the repair crew, who wandered over to the track of the midget racers, yelled, "Sir," pointing at the older detective, "guns over here."

No one saw the man wipe the weapons clean with his gloved hands.

Sergeant Wilkinson didn't budge. "Bag those as evidence along with their ID's and anything else relevant, Gallo," he directed, acting more like the rookie detective's commanding officer than his partner. "Then contact the families and the Cohasset Police," he continued. "The local coppers may know these turkeys and can run interference with friends or relatives who try to stonewall us."

Wilkinson flipped his used butt into a spot of snow and lit another from a silver Ronson lighter he carried. A wracking cough doubled him over before he lurched further away from the corpses and turned his back on them. "You assume the lead on this, rook," he said, over his shoulder, eager to flee the scene. He viewed himself more as a manager or director, dispatching his squad to crime scenes rather than working them firsthand. Bodies nauseated him, like the present ones beginning to bloat.

"I'm needed back in Boston," he said, "to wrap up a couple of other cases. I'll ask the Hull Police to spare officers to secure the area. Keep me informed of your progress."

As he skulked away, the white medical examiner's van—blue stripe painted on the sides and back, light bar flashing—rolled up. A Mets patrolmen, walking in front, escorted it through the back gate to guide it along the concourse. Two white jacketed lab assistants wearing blue rubber gloves, alighted the vehicle, one carrying a new Polaroid Land Camera.

The shorter of the two spoke to Gallo. "Sorry we're late. Traffic was a bitch and a fender bender clogged things at the rotary in Hingham."

Gallo laughed. "I hate rotaries. Never know who is supposed to enter first."

"Apparently those drivers this morning didn't know either," the man said, and guffawed, his substantial belly shaking.

His partner a tall, thin dude with coal black hair holding the camera, jumped in. "We got the call the same time they notified you boys. We'll take pictures of the bodies from all angles, and anything else you think important, then load the men into the van. Hate to say it, but the M.E.'s staff is overloaded right now—Irish gang war in Southie—so the report will take a while, I suspect."

"Understood," Gallo replied. "I know you can't determine much just by observing the corpses. We know they were shot. What I'd really like to find out is how long they've been lying here and if the gunshots killed them or they froze to death."

Tall guy shook his head. "The M.E. makes that call. We can't speculate."

"How about an educated guess?"

"Sorry pal. I need this job."

Gallo dipped his head in resignation. He thanked the attendants for their help and let them get to work.

Wilkinson saw the M.E.'s van arrive but didn't stop his retreat. He bolted away happy to be free of the stench of the decaying bodies.

Gallo, angered by Wilkinson's choice to abandon him, thought it a chicken-shit move. No Marine gunnery sergeant worth his salt would have done that. He fought to control his rage as his neck muscles bulged and his massive fists opened and closed as if preparing for a fight.

He thought Wilkinson might be setting him up to fail. The two did not mesh well. The older man appeared to resent Gallo's youth and Gung Ho attitude and the deferential treatment the former war hero received from their colleagues, seasoned coppers—some World War II and Korean War vets.

AJ, for his part, deferred to the man's experience, but did not respect him and did little to conceal his feelings. They had investigated two previous cases, neither a homicide. In those, he was treated less like a partner than as an errand boy, his thoughts not solicited or expected; tolerated because the brass assigned them to work together.

Nevertheless, Wilkinson left him in charge, and he resolved to make the most of his opportunity. And as a Hull boy, he felt added pressure to succeed.

Being a "Hull Boy" in the 1950s often brought disparaging comments from residents in the adjacent towns of Hingham and Cohasset, some of whom traced their lineage to the Mayflower. They thought Hullonians beneath them. Their ancestors described the barren, remote Hull peninsula as a "moonscape." That view carried into the present despite the lure of the town's popular beaches and amusement centers.

These elitists overlooked the fact many Hull boys filled the rosters of their school athletic teams and became stars—Hull did not have a high school of its own. AJ, a football and baseball legend, received college scholarship offers from top schools and was tendered a minor league contract by the Boston Red Sox.

But Gallo, mesmerized by the heroic exploits of the Marines he watched on movie theater newsreels, spurned the colleges and the local professional baseball team, and enlisted in the Marine Corps in 1948 on his eighteenth birthday. He left without telling his girlfriend, an omission he would later regret. His parents were supportive though nervous.

They had a right to be.

In 1950, the young, idealistic Gallo shipped out with the first contingent of Americans to Korea in what President Truman called a "police action." He distinguished himself at the Chosin Reservoir during a surprise attack by the Chinese Communists. The vicious clash in sub-zero weather and slashing blizzards lasted seventeen days. The survivors earned the nickname, the "Chosen Few."

Gallo hobbled away from the battle with multiple wounds and the Navy Cross but his injuries forced him out of the military in 1952. He joined the Mets as a patrol officer after recovering; his idealism shaken but his sense of right and wrong stronger than ever. He would do his job, and do it well, with or without the help of his sergeant and supposed mentor. He had something to prove; to himself and to those watching.

After Wilkinson's abrupt, unexpected departure, Gallo dispatched a patrolman to retrieve paper evidence bags from the MDC Substation. He placed the weapons and wallets in separate containers using a pen to preserve fingerprints. A set of keys found on Rose puzzled him. To his knowledge, no one had recovered the victims' car. How did they get here? Did they ride with the shooter, have a falling out and the killer bolted with the auto? That didn't make sense since Rose held the keys.

So, what happened to the car?

He jotted the question in his notebook and turned to the pages where he had listed, "Tips to Solving a Crime," garnered from his introductory course in investigative procedure; basic stuff but would serve as a reminder of his next steps.

He left a page for each of five components: Motive, Speak to Eyewitnesses, Find Suspects, Gather Evidence and Put it all together.

Motive was unclear and baffling—the victims were armed, not innocent bystanders. Something brought them to this unlikely place for a meeting or confrontation; something that sparked an argument and subsequent shoot-out. He left a question mark on this page.

He shook his head. Like motive, speak to eyewitnesses, would present a challenge. The bodies lay undiscovered for an unknown period—days, weeks, months? Nobody reported seeing them until the work teams showed up today. Businesses bordering Paragon Park remained shuttered at the time the park was closed. Except for the occasional sightseer coming to gawk at the Atlantic's crashing waves, the beach parking lot across Nantasket Avenue would also have been deserted.

How could he find anyone who might have seen the killing? Grasping at straws, he thought if the incident occurred during the winter storms, maybe a snowplow driver saw something out of the ordinary; but if he did, why didn't he report it? Discouraged, Gallo concluded eyewitnesses were doubtful. He wrote none at this time on the page.

Finding Suspects offered some hope. Statistics showed that individuals killed often knew their assailant—sometimes a family member or spouse. If not either, they could identify enemies of the murdered men and suggest a motive. They would be the first to be interviewed after the maintenance guys now on site.

Gathering Evidence and Putting it all Together completed Gallo's inventory of tips. So far, evidence consisted of the guns and wallets, which revealed the names of the victims and their addresses; a good start. But he would have to fill in many of the gaps to complete these sections.

He snapped his book shut, and laughed aloud, the sound ricocheting through the near empty park. He felt like a schoolboy reviewing his study-guide prior to an upcoming test, except more was riding on the outcome than a grade. If he screwed up, a killer might walk free.

Tempted to curse Wilkinson for leaving, he dismissed that as a waste of time and went to work. He grabbed two patrolmen to assist in scouring the area for anything missed earlier that might help. He drew a crude diagram of the crime scene in his book. Rectangles represented the surrounding rides, an "X" the location of the bodies.

To Gallo, it appeared the men had been taken by surprise, ambushed, if the stunned looks on their faces were any indication. His military training taught him the best place to accomplish an ambush was from high ground—like the raised platform of the Flying Scooters.

He climbed the stairs and walked out on the platform. Its height and position provided an excellent "field of fire," a concept drilled into him by his platoon sergeants. Though time and the storms erased any evidence here, he circled the Scooter rectangle as the probable site used by the gunman. Considering his next moves, he recognized he hadn't searched where the killer and victims could have come into the park.

There were three possibilities: the central entry off Nantasket Avenue, a rear access near the miniature golf course from Rockland Circle—the medical examiner's van entered from there—and a narrow walkway from Park Avenue.

Taking a patrol officer to assist, he walked to the Nantasket Ave entrance—once ornate in its glory days with twin towers resembling a medieval castle—now secured by an ordinary ten-foot-high chain link fence.

A quick inspection of the barrier revealed a coarse piece of cloth stuck to the inverted V-shaped steel wires at the top right. Using his height and the upper crossbar for leverage, he leaped up and snagged the remnant. Dark blue in color, it might have been ripped from a jacket, coat or pair of pants. It didn't belong to Berger or Rose dressed in brown Bomber jackets and khakis.

He brightened with the thought the cloth belonged to the shooter until the patrolman suggested it might have come from a maintenance worker. Deflated, he sent the cop to check the other two gates while he questioned the work crew that stumbled onto the scene.

That proved futile.

All but the foreman were part-time help and he didn't work during the park's dormant period except for periodic walk-through inspections. He confirmed he conducted his last inspection in early December before the storms hit; today was his first day back since then.

Neither he nor any of his men wore blue clothing to match the scrap found on the entrance gate. He donned a brown canvas coat and tan pants; his people wore black or brown overalls with plain brown or plaid shirts; some paint spattered. They could be wearing different attire than on the night of the shootings, of course, but why would they show up here if they were guilty?

He didn't think a search of their homes would be productive. If they noticed their torn clothing, and had committed the crime, he suspected they would have been smart enough to get rid of the evidence.

The man who found the guns on the midget racer oval was not with the group, a last-minute addition provided by personnel, the boss explained; never met him before. Didn't know what happened to him.

Gallo nodded and dismissed the men. He wrote a note to himself to check with administrative staff on the absent employee.

The cop he sent to the other entrances reported finding nothing, discouragement reflected on his face. But AJ clung to the belief the recovered tattered bit of clothing could be a vital piece of evidence in the long run. And he had a mischievous side to his personality seldom displayed. He employed it now to lighten the mood. He smiled at the trooper, eyes twinkling. "You know, if I was Sherlock Holmes, I'd be able to tell from the cloth we found how old the guy was, whether he was short or tall, where he lived and what he wore."

The cop guffawed and joined in the light-heartedness. "Yeah. All you need is a crooked pipe and a funny hat."

The cop's reaction improved AJ's morale. Since the corpses had been loaded into the medical examiner's van and removed, he returned to the MDC Substation to call ahead to enlist the support of a Cohasset Police Officer to help interview the victim's families. As Wilkinson had pointed out, the officer might be able to lessen the blow to family members hearing about the deaths of a loved one for the first time. In a small community like Cohasset, the cop might even know them personally.

Gallo commandeered a blue and white Plymouth Metro radio car for the trip, his transportation until he retrieved his Ford coupe from Boston Headquarters. The journey to Cohasset would revive a memory Gallo had long suppressed.

CHAPTER 3

Detective Sergeant Bill Wilkinson parked curbside in front of the nine story MDC Headquarters Building at 20 Somerset Street, Boston. He experienced a brief pang of guilt for deserting his young partner but pushed that aside—*the kid would be all right*.

He opted to take the staircase to the homicide bureau on the fourth floor, eschewing the elevator. Pestered by his wife about his emerging gut, he tried to exercise whenever possible. He negated these efforts by chowing down on pasta and pastries at the many Italian restaurants in the city's North End.

Laboring up the four flights of stairs, coughs racked his body. He bent over, hands on knees, to catch his breath before entering the squad room, which didn't improve his breathing.

Smoke hung in the air as three men filling out reports puffed on cigarettes while banging away on Smith-Corona typewriters.

Like "bull-pens' in cop houses everywhere, the mahogany desks were well-worn, the tops cluttered with files, stained coffee cups and butt filled ashtrays. A yellowed picture of Jayne Mansfield, with dart holes in strategic places, adorned one wall.

Two of the cops had pulled their wide-brimmed felt hats low like characters in a Raymond Chandler novel. None acknowledged the sergeant as he knocked on the closed door of Captain Martin Kellum, Chief of Detectives.

"Enter," a deep voice commanded, though his Boston accent sounded like "entah."

Wilkinson stepped into a twenty-by-thirty-foot room with a rectangular oak conference table on his right, black leather chairs positioned around it. His boss sat at a department issue metal desk smoking a Chesterfield cigarette. A silver, flip-top lighter, lay beside an ashtray with several snuffed butts. A smokey haze hung in the air shrouding the captain's head, halo-like.

But Kellum was no angel.

He rose to his present rank through treachery and deceit in an organization riddled with corruption. He slipped illegal payments to snitches for prior warning of crimes about to go down so he would be first on the scene. He took bribes to look the other way when it suited him; stole documents, forged others or misplaced crucial pieces of evidence when it advanced his schemes and helped his pals.

Kellum celebrated his fifty-fifth-birthday a week earlier. His once round, boyish face revealed stress lines etched around his eyes and mouth, no doubt hastened by his constant smoking and the pressure of walking a tight-rope between law enforcement and law-breaking. His chalk-like complexion that of a man who seldom ventured outdoors. He dressed in a starched white shirt, sleeves rolled up, red tie askew.

Behind him a bank of windows overlooked the emerging skyline of downtown Boston. One office wall displayed a collage of national, state and city leaders with President Eisenhower's picture above the others. Below Ike, in a semi-straight line, hung photos of Governor Foster Furcolo, Mayor John Hines and MDC Superintendent, Bob Fisk.

Kellum motioned for Wilkinson to sit at one of two padded chairs in front of his desk. When he did so, the senior detective craned his neck to look up. The captain had raised his desk so he hovered over those sitting before him. The sergeant stifled a smirk. His boss would take any advantage to be on top—a dangerous man to cross.

"So, Bill," the Chief began, "let's have an update on Nantasket Beach. Wouldn't expect murder there at this time of year or any time for that matter."

Wilkinson laughed. "Wild place in the summer, though."

"True," Kellum conceded. "Massive crowds, lots of booze, women parading in postage stamp bathing suits." He moved his eyebrows up and down in a sneer perfected by Groucho Marx, a popular TV personality.

Wilkinson grinned.

"I've ridden the roller coaster at least a hundred times," Kellum continued, "and love the wrestling matches and acrobats."

He glanced away a moment in thought, then jolted back from wherever he had gone. "Forget that. Tell me about the murders."

"Two guys, age thirty. Been lying in Paragon Park unnoticed, maybe for months. We won't know for sure until we get the M.E.'s analysis. A work crew discovered them. One victim carried a wallet stuffed with cash. Two guns lay about twenty feet or so from their bodies. Best guess is whoever killed them tossed the weapons. We might be able to pull fingerprints off-a-them, though doubtful. The terrible weather would have wiped them clean if the killer didn't."

"Not model citizens, eh?"

Wilkinson scoffed.

"They have a shoot-out with someone?" Kellum asked.

"Seems so. Can't figure out what they were doing in the park or how they got in. It's buttoned up tight in the off season. The town is not a destination for visitors at that time."

Kellum stroked his chin, and took a drag of his Chesterfield, sending a plume of smoke toward the ceiling.

"You trust Gallo alone on this? I don't want us to blow the investigation, Bill. The press will hound us daily and the townspeople will be looking over our shoulder. I don't need to tell you homicides are high profile crimes."

"Gallo's eager, Captain. He'll do the grunt work. I'll step in at the appropriate time."

"Okay. Don't wait too long. A screw up will not help you become a lieutenant."

"Rest assured, sir, I'll bring in reinforcements if necessary. Hogan and Hawkins are standing by."

Kellum still voiced concern. "As I said, Bill, we'll be under the microscope on this. My reputation's on the line too."

Wilkinson squirmed in his chair but held Kellum's glare.

Appeased for the moment, Kellum reached into his middle desk drawer, pulled out a manila envelope and slid it across to his sergeant, who raised his eyebrows. "What's this, sir?"

"Open it."

Wilkinson did so and discovered a copy of the civil service exam given to lieutenant candidates in the MDC as well as in other law enforcement agencies.

He gawked.

"I usually charge a hundred dollars or more for one of those, Bill," the Chief said, then smiled. "But I want people like you on my team, you understand. I'll expect payment later. Right now, I want your loyalty, is all."

Wilkinson, dumbfounded and nervous, feared this might be a bizarre test of his honesty. He hesitated, his face a mask of fear. This was either his ticket to promotion or a boot out the door.

Kellum had seen the same doubt on the faces of others he provided similar documents to and said, "Bill. This is what it seems. I need people I can trust to move up in this organization. Officers loyal to me. Are you one of those men?"

Wilkinson, still skeptical, took a leap of faith. "I understand, sir. You can count on me. Thank you, sir."

"Okay, get your ass out of here and keep me updated on the Nantasket thing."

Wilkinson grabbed the manila folder with the exam copy and bolted from the room, his heart racing. In a daze when he stumbled to his desk, he peered around as if every detective in the squad room knew what transpired in the captain's office. He thrust the envelope in the middle drawer of his desk and locked it, something he never did.

His hands shook and sweat dotted his brow.

He sat back, wiped his forehead with the handkerchief he always carried and considered his options. Only two came to mind—neither great: return the envelope to Kellum prior to the test, incur his rath and kiss his promotion goodbye, or report him to the superintendent.

He couldn't make a move without evidence if he chose the second option. No way to prove the captain provided the exam to him in the first place. Hell, he could have stolen it himself.

No dummy, he rehashed his conversation with Kellum and remembered one telling thing he said: he charged a lot of money for a copy of the test and would expect payment at another time. He needed men loyal to him. That meant others in the squad owed him for favors like he did now. He wondered how many? He knew for sure one man was not beholden to their boss; Anthony Gallo.

To get out of this mess, the rookie was the only one he could trust. *Would he help after he treated him so badly? And what would he ask him to do anyway?*

He had no answers.

After his sergeant left his office, the Captain spun around in his chair and looked out at the Boston skyline. He smiled. He'd bought Wilkinson's allegiance and enhanced his criminal empire within the Metropolitan District Commission Police.

Three years earlier, Kellum made keys to sneak into the Massachusetts Department of Personnel Administration, on the sixth floor of the MDC Building; the division that maintained law enforcement tests along with the answers.

Kellum sold the exams for as much as one-to-two hundred dollars, not just to Metro cops but to those in other departments in neighboring cities who could aid or cover up his nefarious activities in their jurisdictions.

And Kellum's cheating went beyond stealing. He broke into the offices where completed tests were stored and raised the outcomes of men loyal to him and lowered those of his rivals.

He hadn't yet determined his end game. At some point, he wanted a big score. His job brought him into contact with countless unsavory characters including Irish mobsters who were raking in dough from gambling and horse racing. He established some contacts inside their organization with the idea of somehow using them in the future to further one of his schemes.

Like in Las Vegas, he amassed as many chips as possible, so when he moved, he would have the resources to do so—Wilkinson was a chip to be played when needed.

Pleased with himself, Kellum opened the right-hand bottom drawer of his desk and removed a brown, leather-wrapped steel flask. He unscrewed the cap and took a long, slow swig of Johnny Walker. He sensed the heat in the back of his throat and outward in his chest as the liquid coursed through his body. He shivered and felt invincible, on top of his game.

He should have known better.

Puffed up by his own machinations, Kellum forgot he was also a chip being played by someone higher in the Mets pecking order—his rabbi—a senior officer, mentor and protector.

He would not have been able to develop his criminal network without the man's guidance and protection. No one in the Metro organization knew of this unique relationship; both took stringent precautions to ensure it stayed below the radar.

The "rabbi" would play this chip when it suited him.

CHAPTER 4

Leaving the Paragon Park crime scene, AJ Gallo turned onto Nantasket Ave from the MDC Substation. He skirted the now shuttered entertainment district, all asphalt and cement.

Packed side-by-side on the boulevard were joints hawking pizza, hot dogs, fried clams and saltwater taffy along with "penny arcades" featuring pinball and skeeball machines—a far cry from the late eighteen and early nineteen hundreds when the town, a tourist mecca, attracted partygoers from around the country and abroad.

Back then, in its massive wooden hotels and bars, booze flowed, gambling flourished and prostitutes plied their trade with impunity—cops being on the take.

Major crimes at the time were pickpocketing and rigged games of chance on the boardwalk. Assaults were rare—often scuffles between drunks—murder non-existent. All of this on a tiny peninsula settled as a fishing village by the Wampanoag Indians who called it Natascot, "at the strait or low tide place."

Gallo's memories of the town did not extend beyond his youth, though the last of the grand hotels, **The Nantasket**, was just torn down the previous year. As kids, Gallo and his pals, Lenny and Chet, ran barefoot with sandy feet through its elegant lobby infuriating the staff and upsetting patrons. They bumped into no movie stars or famous politicians as they might have in the town's heyday. Presidents Grover Cleveland and William McKinley summered there.

As he drove by, AJ glanced toward the beach where the hotel once stood and shook his head, remembering the fun, not its history.

He continued by a closed Howard Johnson's and struggled with the lumbering Plymouth as he climbed Atlantic Hill. He passed several aging and weathered landmarks of his youth: the town hall/police station, Cochrane's candy store, and Saint Mary's of the Assumption Church, where his career as an altar boy began at age eight.

He maneuvered through the hardscrabble Gun Rock area, which stretched about a mile between the ocean to the east and Straits Pond to the west. Often buffeted by winds and inundated by ocean surges, homeowners jacked up some of the houses on metal stilts to avoid destruction. In Gallo's mind, the zone reflected the struggle many Hull residents faced against the elements.

He stopped at the intersection of Jerusalem Road and Forrest Avenue, both leading to Cohasset. He studied the hill in front of him, once the site of an unspeakable personal tragedy. The memory flooded Gallo's consciousness and sent chills down his spine.

In his sophomore year of high school, two youngsters in a Ford Super Deluxe coupe, challenged by two classmates in a modified Buick Roadmaster, raced to their deaths, seventeen-year-old AJ Gallo a passenger in the Buick.

At 11:00 p.m., on a Friday night, the massive Birch, Maple and Elm trees shrouding Forrest Avenue formed a foreboding tunnel. Oblivious to any danger, the young drivers, fueled by alcohol, pushed their cars forward, careening over the roller-coaster terrain, sparks flying as their front ends scraped asphalt.

Though they knew the roadway ended in a sudden drop, neither driver slacked off. The boys in the coupe whooped as they snaked ahead and took the last incline pushing seventy-miles an hour. They lost control, sailing through the air, and plummeting headlong into a stone wall separating the roadway from a rocky beach, their vehicle bursting into flames, incinerating the unconscious kids.

Inexplicably, AJ's companion had slowed at the crest of the hill and wrestled the swaying Buick to a stop about twenty feet past the smoldering wreckage. The boys sat immobilized, nauseated and shaking. Thick black smoke enveloped them as the roaring flames threatened to spread, gasoline seeping toward the Buick. Realizing they could not help their pals, and afraid to face probing questions from the police and the wrath of their parents, they drove away, guilt ridden and sobbing.

Gallo and his classmate never spoke of the incident. His friend dropped out of school, joined the army and died on a desolate promontory in Korea.

Flashbacks of that horror tortured AJ for years and still disrupted his sleep. He imagined hearing the screams of his friends in the blazing coupe; but they died instantly. He thought himself a coward for fleeing the scene and vowed never to run from trouble again. A promise he kept in combat and would do so again in future life-threatening situations.

Casting the memory aside, Gallo turned left onto Jerusalem Road, a narrow two-lane highway, which snaked along the scenic coast to downtown Cohasset—a drive with pricey homes flanking both sides and offering a panoramic view of the Atlantic and its ancient lighthouses.

Like many coastal New England towns, Cohasset reflected native American influence; inhabited first by the Wampanoags and then the Massachusett in the 1600s. The town's name came from the Massachusett word, "Conahasset" which, in one interpretation means "long rocky place." That description described Gallo's coastline route.

At Cohasset Police Headquarters, he picked up Officer Vincent Russo who would act as liaison to the families of the murdered men. The twenty-six -year-old patrolman wore his brown hair buzzed at the sides, flat on top, boyish face radiating enthusiasm. His blue uniform clung to his toned body—a poster boy for police recruitment.

After shaking hands and identifying themselves, AJ hit the young cop with a surprise question. "Any recent accidents on Forrest Ave?"

Russo gave Gallo a quizzical glance. "Yeah! At least one a year. Often around prom or graduation. Kids drinking. Joy riding. The flashing lights at the crest of the hill signaling danger don't slow them down. Punks think they're indestructible. Why the interest?"

"I was one of those punks. Lost a couple of friends on that road back in the day. Think about them from time-to-time."

"We don't have the manpower to patrol it much, Russo said, his eyes downcast. "If I'm on duty and there's a major event at the high school, I cruise it, do what I can to discourage the idiots."

Gallo dipped his head, kept silent, glad somebody cared.

"You working the case alone?" the cop asked, noting the absence of a Metro side-kick for the young detective.

"Nah. My partner, a sergeant, was recalled to Boston. Should meet up with us soon."

Two miles later, Russo directed Gallo to a residence on North Main Street, a single story, white clapboard house with an unattached garage about thirty feet back from the road. A faded green Hudson Hornet rested in the gravel driveway; cords of wood stacked against a wall of the garage.

"Berger's mother-in-law, Estelle Ochs, owns the house," Russo said. "The Berger's live in a room there. Money is tight. Estelle, no fan of Donald's, thinks her daughter, Amy, an elementary school teacher in town, married beneath her. Don's been in and out of trouble most of his life. Always between jobs. He stayed as an overnight guest in our lock-up more than once."

"Thanks for the heads up, Vince. Are they aware of the nature of our visit?"

"Nope! Your job, brother."

"What did you tell them?"

"That we had information about Donald. Amy filed a missing person's report with the department a couple days after her husband disappeared either prior to or after Christmas; can't remember the exact date.

She's called many times since seeking updates. With Donny's reputation, our guys didn't spend much time looking for him, sorry to admit; and we were overwhelmed by the aftermath of the storms."

Gallo thought the last part of that sentence an attempt to justify the PD's inaction, didn't press it. He was also intrigued. If Berger went missing sometime around Christmas it would help pinpoint when he was killed.

The two men strode up the gravel walkway to the front door, which opened before they knocked. Russo, not surprised, spied someone watching from a window as they approached.

Amy Berger, a petite woman with short brown hair and matching eyes, wore a blue poodle skirt cut two inches below the knees and a white blouse. She steeled herself for bad news based on her husband's checkered past and the stern expressions on the faces of the men facing her.

Russo began. "Amy, this is Detective Gallo from the MDC Police in Nantasket. May we come in?"

Berger stepped aside as the two men walked into a spacious carpeted parlor with a six-foot long sofa flanked by two multi-colored wing-backed chairs. A stone fireplace—with a nautical painting above it off to their right—burned a log, no doubt from the pile outside.

Mrs. Ochs, a broader version of her daughter, a clump of grey hair twisted into a bun on top of her head, wearing a shapeless flowered housedress, stood when the cops entered.

"Sit down, please," she said, pointing toward the couch. Russo took off his cap and sat beside Gallo. Ochs plopped into one of the wing-backed chairs while Amy pulled up a chair with a latticed back.

AJ broke the silence. "Mrs. Berger, my name is Anthony Gallo. I'm a detective with the Metro Police in Nantasket. Sorry, I have distressing news."

"Get on with it," Ochs interrupted. "Never good when it involves Donny. What did he do now? Is he locked up someplace?"

"Mother, please," her daughter protested. "Donny's a decent man, just needs a break."

Ochs grunted.

Gallo, despite his military background, had no experience comforting relatives about a loved-one who had been killed. In Korea, an officer and chaplain performed that grim task.

Though this was not a combat death, he struggled to find the right words. "I'm afraid Donald is dead," he blurted. "A work crew discovered his body this morning in Paragon Park."

Amy stammered, "What? How? What was he doing there at this time of the year?"

Before Gallo responded, Berger said, "I can't believe he's gone. He was young. Strong. This can't be."

She slumped back in her chair, tears cascading down her cheeks.

Russo offered her a handkerchief, which she took and pressed to her eyes. AJ made a mental note to carry one in the future. He continued into uncharted waters. "Mrs. Berger. Uh! I'm sorry to say, Donald was murdered."

"Oh my god," she shrieked and slumped forward.

Russo sprang up and caught her before she fell to the floor. He lay her down on the sofa as Gallo stretched out her legs. Russo placed his heavy blue duty jacket over her and pulled it up to her neck.

AJ spotted the concern with which the officer covered the woman and the anxiety reflected in his eyes.

He had affection for her.

"I'll fetch some water," Mrs. Ochs said, and fled the room.

Prior to Ochs return, Amy Berger sat up, pulling Russo's jacket tight. She blinked multiple times and gazed around the room as if getting her bearings. "I'm so sorry," she said, choking out the words. "I expected something bad when Donny went missing for so long, but not this."

Her mother came back and handed her daughter a tall glass of water. She sat down beside her and draped an arm on her shoulders, made no further disparaging comments about her now deceased son-in-law.

"Can you tell us what happened?" Amy whispered, having difficulty speaking.

"We're not sure," Gallo answered. "Donald and another man, a Dustin Rose, were shot. Their bodies may have been in the park since the storms began in December, we're not sure."

Amy shuddered. "Oh my God," she blurted, again. "He's been gone since then, December twenty-third to be exact. He sometimes stayed away for a few days, but when he didn't come home for Christmas—his favorite holiday—I panicked and filed a missing person's report the next day. The date is etched into my memory. We didn't know he left with Dusty. They were classmates at Cohasset High School, worked together."

Mrs. Ochs scoffed and received a withering stare from her daughter.

Gallo wrote the information in his notebook, then said, "Did you know Donald owned a gun?"

Amy, dazed, fell back on the couch, shaking her head in disbelief.

Mrs. Ochs was speechless.

"What about enemies?"

"He didn't always get along with people, I'll admit. No one who would want to kill him, though. That's horrible, unbelievable." She dabbed at her eyes with Russo's handkerchief.

"Did he pal around with anyone beside Dustin?" Gallo asked, making an effort to keep his voice calm, understanding.

"Billy Cooper and Johnny Goodwin, football teammates with Don, practically lived here. A Bradley Evans came by a few times. Seemed pleasant enough."

"Do you have their addresses by any chance?"

"Yes, for Billy and Johnny. No! for Bradley. All I know is he lives in Hingham."

She paused, glanced from Russo to Gallo. "Do you think they might be involved?"

"No. No. We're just starting the investigation. Looking into those close to Donald. It's procedure."

Once clear Amy and her mother could offer nothing more, and in deference to Amy's emotional state, Gallo stood and gave them his business card. "I'm sorry for your loss, Mrs. Berger," he said. "We'll do our best to find out who did this. If you can think of anything that might be of importance, please call me at any time."

Russo took both of Amy's hands in his. "I'll come by to check on you from time to time, if that's okay?"

Berger smiled. Ochs beamed her approval.

As the detectives were leaving the house, Amy called out. "Wait. Another man came by once or twice. His father owned a gas station in Hingham. Dustin worked there part time."

"Do you remember his name?" Anthony asked.

"I'm sorry I don't. I believe the station is the one near the Hingham rotary. The one robbed and the attendant shot."

"Thank you," Gallo said, "that's helpful."

Russo smiled at Amy and pulled the front door closed. As he did so, they heard Mrs. Ochs say, "Told you Donny was no good."

They couldn't hear Amy's retort.

The men walked back to the patrol car, each with his own thoughts. Gallo wondered if he had done okay in dealing with the grieving relatives. Russo reflected on his interaction with Amy Berger and planned to contact her to check in from time to time as he said. He pushed any romantic ideas aside—for now.

Both lawmen had similar notions of Donald Berger, one of those forgettable people who brought grief to those who loved them. While his wife would grieve, he wouldn't be missed by many, let alone his mother-in-law.

One of the vagaries of life. Some destined—through hard work and perseverance—for success and prominence, others, through bad decisions or chance, fated to fail. Even in the investigation of his murder, Berger would play a secondary role to his partner, though neither Gallo nor Russo knew that on this day.

CHAPTER 5

Four months earlier
December 23, 1957

Fleeing the Paragon Park murder scene, the man retrieved his car and crept behind a snowplow on George Washington Boulevard, a route out of town. Driving was treacherous. Weathermen on the radio warned southeastern New England would be ravaged by the heaviest snowstorm of the year. They cautioned travelers to stay off the roads. The man shook his head. What choice did he have but to be on the highway?

But freed from the terror of being pursued by killers, he believed it safe to return to his rented room in nearby Hingham. The less than thirty-minute trip, took ninety and not all side streets were plowed.

Forced to abandon his car, he trudged through knee-high snow drifts and fierce winds to reach his destination, a house owned by Virginia Summers, a kind woman who took in boarders to make ends meet.

A physical and emotional wreck—he shivered as much from fear as from the cold.

He shed his wet shoes, socks and peacoat in the enclosed mudroom and stepped into an expansive parlor/dining room warmed by a fire raging in a stone fireplace. A lighted Christmas tree stood in front of a double-paned picture window.

Mrs. Summers, shocked by the man's appearance, sat in a multi-flowered stuffed chair knitting. "Land sakes," she said, "you're chilled to the bone. Come sit by the hearth while I make you a cup of hot chocolate."

He opened his mouth to protest but his landlady put up her hand. "Do as I say, young man," she said, and got up and headed for the kitchen. She didn't provide meals to her boarders but made food available to them. They kept a tally of what they ate, which was added to their monthly rent—an honor system everyone abided by.

Mrs. Summers returned in ten minutes with cocoa and a blanket. The man sipped the drink, wrapped the covering around his shoulders and fell asleep; exhausted after driving all night the evening before, fighting for his life then battling a blizzard to get here.

He woke up alone at midnight with the log reduced to embers. He climbed the stairs to his room and tumbled into bed wishing he'd dreamed the last hours. The pain from the bullet that grazed his shoulder reminded him it was all too real.

Once awake, he reviewed in his mind the events which shook him to his core. Though no expert on crime, he doubted anything in Paragon Park could tie him to the dead men. He touched the weapons wielded by Rose and Berger when he tossed them aside, but believed the heavy snowfall would obliterate his fingerprints. And since the park didn't open for months, the bodies, he hoped, wouldn't be found until spring.

He resolved to carry on his life, yet memories of the episode troubled him day and night. He thought many times of turning himself into the police and explaining what happened.

Not completely innocent, though, he participated in a robbery where the attendant, to his knowledge, died. That made him an accessory to murder, he supposed, not understanding the intricacies of the law or the court system. Better to let the investigation play out. If they never traced the killing back to him, so be it. If they did, he would deal with it, though he had no idea how.

As things would "play out," his name surfaced as a suspect. He became the object of a police manhunt as well as a target of a vengeful stalker.

CHAPTER 6

Detective Gallo and Officer Russo returned to their car after speaking with Amy Berger, wife of Donald Berger, at the home in Cohasset she shared with her mother.

"Noticed the concern you took with Amy," AJ teased, a playful smirk on his face.

"We're friends. Went to school together," Russo replied, face flushed.

"Right."

Russo changed the subject. "Let's visit Rose's family. They live on Pond Street, close to the high school, not far from here."

"Lead the way."

The two men rode in silence until they pulled up in front of the Rose house.

"Let me bring you up to speed on a couple of things before we go inside," Vince said.

"I'm listening," AJ answered.

"Dustin lived with his sister and brother in their childhood home. They all moved in three years ago to care for their mother who was fighting cancer. She died last year."

Gallo grimaced. "So, another blow."

"Yeah. They took their mother's death hard."

"Another thing," Russo added. "Dustin and David are, were, twins."

Gallo's eyes widened. "Glad you told me. Might have freaked seeing a ghost."

"You may still be spooked. They were identical. Pranked us all the time in high school. Wore each other's clothing, exchanged classes, dated the same girl and didn't tell her."

"Yikes. Kind of cruel."

"Yes, it was," Russo said, then pointed. "Pull over. We're here."

The two story, brown shingled house sat back from the road with a long stone walkway to the front door, grass springing up between the stones. Three huge oak trees stood as sentinels on the property. Guards that couldn't stop cancer.

They walked single file to the house, Russo leading. He rang the doorbell answered by David Rose, the mirror image of Dustin—without the scar on his cheek. Recognizing Russo, he stepped aside for the men to enter. He directed them to a gray sofa with two matching stuffed chairs on each end angled to face a dormant fireplace.

A young woman standing in the middle of the room extended her hand to Gallo and introduced herself as Linda Rose. She wore a pleated green skirt and white pull-over sweater. Her dark hair fell to her shoulders. She smiled and hugged Russo.

Brother and sister sat in the two chairs flanking the sofa. They moved them to face the lawmen.

Vince presented AJ and informed them they had bad news about Dustin.

"Figured as much after all this time," David said. "He in jail somewhere?"

"Afraid it's worse, Dave. He's dead, murdered."

Linda cried out. Her brother scooted his chair to sit close and leaned over to wrap an arm around her. They embraced for a long time, their heads touching, fingers interlaced, their labored breathing the only sound in the room.

David, in shock, blinking to fight back tears, broke the awkward silence. "How did it happen?" he asked, directing his question to Russo, who deferred. "I'll let Detective Gallo explain."

Gallo cleared his throat and said, "Not much is known at this point. A work crew in Paragon Park found him this morning beside another man, Donald Berger."

"Donald too," Linda wailed. She held one hand to her mouth, moisture forming at the corners of her eyes. David pulled her to his chest.

AJ waited for the woman to compose herself, then ran through the litany of when, where and how they were discovered. He added the fact both carried guns. He studied their reactions when he asked the inevitable, "Did Dustin have any enemies?"

"My brother—our brother—" David said, "could be difficult. Lose his temper if he thought someone wronged him. Had his scrapes in high school and at work. Didn't hold a job very long. I can't think of anyone angry enough to kill him, though."

He glanced at his sister who kept shaking her head, unbelieving.

"How did he get the nasty scar on his cheek?" AJ asked. "Appears to be a knife wound."

"He refused to tell us. A misunderstanding he claimed," David said. "He was drinking a lot then."

"Pretty serious misunderstanding."

David shrugged, so Gallo changed direction. "Were you aware he owned a gun?"

David said no—too quickly, Gallo thought. Linda gave him a curious glance and turned away.

AJ didn't pursue it, but asked, "How long has Dustin been gone?"

The siblings looked at each other. "Around Christmas time last year," Linda said. "We filed a report. Vince could tell you exactly when."

"I can check," Russo said.

Gallo again shifted the focus. "Would you mind if I went into Dustin's room. Might be helpful."

Linda dipped her head and escorted him to the room on the first floor, opened the door, and walked away.

The room was small for a big man, no doubt his as a child, thought Gallo, no more than ten by ten. A grime covered window overlooked a sprawling back yard with a rusting swing set engulfed by foot tall weeds. A picture of the Cohasset football team decorated one wall. Dustin and Donald stood together in the back, grinning, arms dangling by their side.

Except for the bed, an end table with a lamp perched on top served as the lone piece of furniture. Gallo slid the center drawer of the table open and found a fistful of change, a three by five-inch notebook, a pack of Camel cigarettes, a matchbook from the Red Lion Inn downtown and car keys.

The keys peaked AJ's curiosity. He removed a set from Dustin's pocket when he searched him. *Were these a back-up or did they fit another vehicle?*

Some questions for his siblings later.

He chose to thumb through the notebook—empty save for the names: Mitch Smith, Jerry Morris, Bradley Evans and Bobby Moran— a phone number for Evans, no address. Nothing for the others.

Finished with his search, Gallo strode back to the living room where Linda and David Rose engaged in a subdued conversation with Russo.

AJ interrupted: "Dustin's notebook contains four names and his desk drawer some car keys," he said, and held them up. "Is this a second set because he had keys in his pocket when he was found?"

Linda squirmed at AJ's words: "when he was found."

"No. The Ford Fairlane in the driveway is his," David explained. "He left the house with someone else, didn't see who. Maybe Don? Didn't need his keys."

Gallo then showed them the book. "Know any of these people?"

Linda scanned it and answered. "Bradley Evans hung out with Dustin. They worked together on a couple of construction jobs. Jerry managed the Hingham gas station where Dustin served as a mechanic from time to time. Smith is the owner's son, I believe. Never heard of Bobby Moran."

"Don't know him either," Dave chimed in.

"Anyone else pal around with your brother?"

"Classmates from school, Billy Cooper and Johnny Goodwin. They're always under foot. Can't tell you much about Evans."

"When can we bury our brother?" Linda asked, choking up.

"I'll notify you when the coroner releases his remains and when you can assume control," AJ said.

Linda blanched at the use of the term 'remains.'

AJ flushed, realizing his insensitivity. He didn't know of a less objectional way to refer to a dead body. He'd run it by Wilkinson if he ever turned up.

With no further questions to ask, he was relieved when David escorted them to the door and closed it behind them.

Linda grabbed her brother's arm, when the lawmen left. "Why did you lie about the gun?"

David raised his eyebrows, didn't answer.

"And you own one too!"

"What difference does it make? "

"You lied."

He ignored her reproach and began pacing the room. "Got a bad feeling about that guy Evans" he said, opening and closing his fists.

"What do you mean?"

"Didn't like him. May pay him a visit."

"You're scaring me, Dave."

He drew his sister close. "Don't worry, hon. Blowing off steam is all."

She didn't see the look of hatred on his face.

Once outside the Rose house, Gallo went to the Ford Fairlane and opened it with the keys he grabbed without Dave and Linda's permission or knowledge. They never asked about them. A good thing because AJ wanted to compare them to those in Dustin's pocket. Snatching the keys was illegal, something he knew, yet took the chance. Anything recovered in the vehicle could not be used in court, if it came to that.

Gallo realized since these keys opened the Fairlane, the other set in Dustin's possession belonged to another vehicle.

Where was that car?

The thought perplexed him as he continued to search the Fairlane—nothing pertinent to the murders turned up.

The lawmen returned to the Cohasset Police HQ.

Once there, AJ asked Russo to contact the two classmates of Rose—Cooper and Goodwin. He hoped interrogating them at the station would lend a bit of angst to the two and encourage them to answer questions truthfully.

Besides the mystery of the keys, another thing bothered him. Linda's reaction when he asked David if he owned a gun. He suspected

Dustin's twin lied about that and Linda knew but didn't challenge him in front of the detectives.

Did both brothers own guns?

Strange to possess a weapon in a quiet town like Cohasset. Only three reasons he could think of—protection, intimidation or to use in a crime.

Did someone threaten them? If so, who and why? And could it have something to do with Dustin's murder?

David downplayed the fact Dustin's aggressive behavior might have made someone angry enough to kill him.

The scene at Paragon Park gave the lie to that belief.

CHAPTER 7

At 10:35 a.m., at Cohasset Police Headquarters, the day following their interviews with the families of the slain victims, Gallo and Russo dismissed Billy Cooper and Johnny Goodwin, friends of Berger and Rose, as suspects in their murder. Their alibis appeared solid.

As the lawmen walked to the reception desk, a teletype bulletin came in from the Hingham Police seeking information about a Dustin Rose and Donald Berger, sought in connection with a gas station robbery in that town in December, 1957.

The station attendant, now recovered from a coma suffered in the theft, identified the two assailants from past association. They didn't wear masks. He couldn't identify a third person who drove the getaway car. Claimed he didn't remember much about the day other than the identity of the gunman who shot him.

Gallo thanked Russo for his help and using a phone provided by the desk sergeant, contacted the Hingham Police to inform them they needn't continue to search for the now dead robbery suspects. He asked for and received permission to talk with the recovering station attendant and agreed to have one of their detectives join in the interview.

It was a short drive to Hingham on Route 3A. The town lies to the south and west of Hull and is part of the region known as "The South Shore." Like the adjacent towns of Hull and Cohasset, the Wampanoag Indians roamed the area before they deeded it to English settlers in 1655.

Named "Bare Cove" by the first colonizers, the town was incorporated as Hingham after its namesake in the English countryside from where most of the first colonists came, including Samuel Lincoln, an ancestor of Abraham Lincoln.

A statue of President Lincoln stands in a small park near downtown. The police department is located at the intersection of Lincoln Street, which runs past the park, and Route 3A. Gallo had driven by many times on his way to and from Boston; he found it with no trouble.

The detective handling the gas station robbery, assigned to assist Gallo, gaped, awe-struck when introduced. AJ recognized the look: "I'm not a hero pal, just an ordinary Joe trying to do a job."

"Not in these parts," Jeff McCrory said, like a character in a John Wayne western. "Silver Stars, Navy Cross, Purple Heart. I went to Hingham High two years behind you. Didn't play sports—book nerd. Kids idolized you, a star in football and baseball."

"Ancient history, man. Can we just do our jobs?"

McCrory nodded, but his eyes remained wide. They traveled together in Gallo's MDC cruiser, McCrory snatching glances at his hero.

The gas station attendant lived on Beal Street, in Hingham, in a two-story gray house with blue shutters flanking the windows. A two-tone Ford Edsel sat in the driveway. AJ thought the car ugly but kept his observation to himself as McCrory admired it. "Like it. Can't afford it," he said, as he rang the doorbell. AJ hoped McCrory's judgement of people better than his assessment of cars.

An older, heavy-set woman in a flowered housedress, graying hair pulled back in a bun, opened the door. She gave the two men the once-over, her mouth twisted into a frown. Crossing her arms over an ample bosom, she declared, "You can talk with him for five minutes," her voice tinged with contempt. "I'm his mother, Estelle. His wife's working. Someone's got to put food on the table."

A slap at her son?

She escorted the two detectives to a room on the first floor, pushed the half-closed door open and repeated, "Five minutes."

McCrory glared at her; kept silent.

She never asked for identification. The Hingham Police called ahead to set up the meeting. She assumed the two men at her door were cops—a dangerous assumption under different circumstances.

Jerry Morris lay in a hospital bed with the back elevated to a sitting position. He sipped a liquid through a straw from a plastic cup; his head not bandaged. A white streak on his left side traced the path of the bullet that almost killed him. His face was gaunt, his eyes dark and recessed, his fingers boney. If it was Halloween, he wouldn't need a costume to play the part of a Ghoul.

"Thank you for meeting with us, Jerry," McCrory said, in a sympathetic tone. "Must be hard. How are you?"

Morris set his drink on an adjacent end table and offered a weak smile.

"I'm Detective McCrory, Hingham PD. This is Detective Gallo, MDC. He's investigating the murders of Rose and Berger whose bodies were found in Paragon Park."

"So those bastards are really dead," Morris crowed. "Good."

He didn't ask how they wound up in the park.

"Do you have any idea who might have killed them?" Gallo asked.

"Nope; but they deserved it," he said. "Thought we were friends."

Gallo met Morris' eyes, sensed the man was hiding something. Though a rookie investigator, he guessed two reasons armed robbers would not wear masks. Either they planned to murder their victim or the victim participated in the scheme. In this instance, despite the guy's injury, he believed the latter. Something wasn't right.

"Why didn't Berger and Rose cover their faces, Jerry. You could identify them."

"That's why those dipsticks tried to kill me."

"Why would they do that if you were pals?"

He teared up and sniveled, "I don't know. I don't know."

"You didn't expect it, did you?"

Morris reached for his cup and took another sip, his hand trembling. "Course not," he said.

"Because you helped plan the heist, didn't you?"

"I, I," he sputtered. Tears ran down his cheeks. "They were my friends. My friends. The bastards."

The lawmen eye-balled each other. No doubt Morris took part in the robbery scheme. His buddies double-crossed him, perhaps choosing to split the stolen money two ways instead of three.

"I'm going to arrest you right now, Jerry," McCrory threatened, "unless you tell us everything."

He did.

"Dustin's idea," Morris confessed. "Hated the boss for firing him, though he deserved it. Always jawing at customers. Almost got in a fist-fight once."

A tear formed at the corner of his left eye, which he swiped away struggling to regain his composure.

"The boss works until six and I close at ten. We have a small safe hidden in the service bay. I stash the day's profits there after my shift and he takes it to the bank every three or four days. We keep a hunnert for change and stuff."

He took a deep breath then sipped his liquid. His eyes darted around the room as if he expected Dustin Rose to burst in at any moment. He was startled when the door opened and his mother stuck her head in.

"Five minutes are up," she said, staring at the lawmen, again crossing her arms. "Leave now."

McCrory's face turned crimson. He snapped, "This is a murder investigation, ma'am. We are not finished. Unless you want us to arrest you for obstruction; you leave."

Estelle Morris motioned as if to object, thought better of it and retreated, slamming the door behind her.

Jerry dipped his head, embarrassed. "My mother's very protective."

"How about over-bearing," McCrory said, his voice dripping with sarcasm.

Morris snickered, then continued his tale.

"Dustin knew the location of the safe and that I could open it. Four days receipts were in there. He promised to tie me up, make it appear like a real robbery. We'd split the take when things calmed down. I didn't want to do it, ya unerstand. I like my job, but I needed cash. My wife and I struggle to make ends meet; the reason we live here."

He paused, sighed and resumed his story. "Should 'a never trusted Dustin. I was scared a' him. He had a scar on his face from a knife fight. No telling what he might do."

"Like shoot you," Anthony interjected.

Morris swiped droplets of sweat from his lower lip clearly uncomfortable.

"Go on," McCrory ordered.

"I opened the safe and without warning, Dustin pulls a gun. Shoots me. I don't remember anything after that. I swear."

"And you never saw the getaway driver?"

"No, sir."

"Who else did Rose hang out with?"

Morris looked away for a moment as if in thought. "Two guys came around sometimes. A guy he went to school with, Johnny Goodman and a Bradley something. Never caught his last name. Don't think he gave it."

Amy Berger mentioned a Bradley Evans as did Linda and Dave Rose. AJ found him listed in Rose's notebook. He dismissed Goodman as a suspect though this information he palled with Dustin at the station changed his outlook. They should give him another look, he thought.

"Could Evans or Goodman have been the wheel man?" Gallo probed.

Morris shook his head. "Could 'a been. Never saw him, like I told ya."

"Ever heard of a Mitch Smith or Bobby Moran?" AJ continued.

Morris blinked several times. "Mitch is the bosses son. Don't know Moran," he lied.

"Smith come around much?"

"Nope. His father canned him."

"What about the night of the heist?"

"No, sir."

"He know about the safe?" Russo asked.

"Yes, sir."

Morris being so polite unnerved AJ, but he understood the man's terror. Jerry's next question confirmed it. "Are you gonna arrest me? I don't know nothing about no murders."

"Okay," McCrory said, not convinced Jerry told them all he knew. "When you're well enough to leave the house, you call us right away. We'll take you down to the station. Charge you with accessary to robbery. You may be able to claim intimidation, coerced by Dustin Rose. Might buy you a lighter sentence or probation."

Morris cringed; tears flowed.

"Doubt you'll ever work at the gas station again," he added, not the least bit sorry for the man.

The two detectives left the house under the stern eye of Estelle Morris. Once outside, McCrory proposed, since their cases were intertwined, they collaborate to find the murderer of Berger and Rose. "Will have to clear it with our chief, though."

"Okay by me," Gallo responded, "and I'll need to do the same with the sergeant I'm supposed to be working with."

McCrory raised his eyebrows at Gallo's use of the word "supposed" when referring to his relationship with his partner, chose not to comment. He continued to ogle the Edsel.

Gallo shook his head, had a deeper reason for the gesture than what he considered McCrory's poor taste in automobiles.

He questioned whether his own inexperience resulted in missing a vital piece of information—that Johnny Goodman spent time hanging around the gas station with Dustin Rose. He and Cohasset Officer Russo eliminated him as a suspect in the Paragon Park shootings because his alibi was solid, spending the holidays with his friend Billy Cooper's family. The Cooper's confirmed it.

But a new question now surfaced. Did Goodman leave at any time—say on a cold night a few days before Christmas?

And what kind of a guy was Johnny Goodman?

CHAPTER 8

When he got back to the MDC Building in Nantasket, AJ called the Cohasset PD to speak with Officer Russo. The desk sergeant informed him he was on foot patrol. He used one of the blue call boxes positioned around town to check in every thirty minutes. Russo couldn't contact him because the boxes were on a dedicated police line. AJ asked the sergeant to have him do so when available. He spent the next two plus hours reviewing his investigation notes.

The motive was still unclear, possibly a clash over the money from the gas station robbery. Morris was an eyewitness to that, not the murders. No one in Hull or affiliated with the park had come forward, nor were they likely to do so. And few tourists visited the town in the winter unless it was to watch the churning Atlantic surf; the blizzard ensured no one would be around for that.

They did have suspects: Evans, Smith, Goodman and the phantom, Moran, who everyone claimed not to know. Linking any of them to the murder was problematic. Guilt by association didn't cut it. Frustrated, Gallo was about to give up and leave the station, when Russo called.

"Vince. Thanks for getting back to me."

"No problem. What's up?"

"It might be nothing. I found out Johnny Goodman spent time with Dustin Rose at the gas station that was robbed. The attendant says he hung around a lot."

"What are you thinking?"

"That he drove the getaway car in that heist."

Russo laughed. "I can see him being convinced by Dustin to participate in the robbery. He idolized the man. But no way would he shoot anyone, no matter what type of argument they had. No way."

Gallo sighed. "Understood. I'm new at this detective business. I don't want to find out I missed an important fact or suspect. Can you check with the Cooper's and verify he never left their house during the holiday?"

"Sure," Russo said after a short pause.

"Thanks pal. And by the way, what kind of a guy was Johnny. You went to school with him, right?"

"He was one of those guys you instinctively like, funny, carefree, smooth talker—a rules breaker, not a great student. Joined the army after graduation. Served in Korea. Rumor has it he received a dishonorable discharge for striking an officer. I don't believe it. He never got into fights near as I can remember."

Didn't sound like someone who would shoot his friends, yet Gallo wasn't ready to cross him off the suspect list. "Thanks, Vince. Keep me updated on what you find out from the Cooper's as soon as you can."

"You bet," Russo answered. "I'll drop by there after work tonight."

The call over, Gallo leaned back in his chair, confused. Despite Russo's assessment of Goodman, a trained infantryman, could have made the shots that killed Berger and Rose—and if he did strike an officer, he was no longer the boy Russo knew. Could he have been goaded into killing his friends?

Yeah! If they chased and tried to kill him. But why would they pursue him in the first place if he drove them. Did they argue and he jumped out of the vehicle taking the keys. Again that didn't make sense if Dustin had them in his possession.

Then it dawned on him. If the killer left the keys, he escaped in another car leaving the one Dustin and Donald came in behind.

It came back to his original question: What happened to the car?

CHAPTER 9

One of the maintenance men who discovered the bodies in Paragon Park leaked the news to the newspapers, prompting brief articles in the Quincy Patriot Ledger and Boston Globe. More detailed reports were promised once the investigating detectives had been interviewed. The desk sergeant at the Nantasket Station diverted information requests to the MDC HQ, Boston.

Captain Kellum, Chief of Detectives, fielded the inquiries. Though loath to talk to the media, he recognized the benefit of controlling the narrative about the murders and he liked getting his name and photo in the papers if it would show him leading the charge to solve a heinous crime.

He set up a press interview with Wilkinson and Gallo in Nantasket on Monday, April 7th, at 8:00 a.m. to give reporters an opportunity to meet their evening deadlines. The gathering would be staged at the entrance to Paragon Park, an appealing backdrop for any photos.

After setting things in motion, the Captain summoned Bill Wilkinson to his office. He stood gazing out the window at the Boston skyline, hands locked behind his back, when his veteran sergeant entered the room. Without turning away, he said, "I love this view, Bill, love this city."

"I feel the same way, sir," Wilkinson said, as he slipped into a chair in front of the captain's desk.

Kellum turned, sat and lit a cigarette, one of his favorite Chesterfields. "We're going to meet with the press on Monday in Nantasket, provide information about the murders."

Wilkinson was shocked knowing the boss's aversion to speaking with newsmen. He picked up on the word "we're" and asked the boss if he planned to be there.

47

"Damn right Bill. I want no screw-ups on this. We have to control info going to those vultures."

"And Gallo?"

"You and I will field the questions. We'll prep Gallo before the interview. Have him bring us up to speed on his progress. You will NOT reveal the kid has been on his own. Understood."

"Yes, sir."

"Good. Our reputation and the department's rests on a quick resolution to the case. We need to find the bastards who killed those men. I hope Gallo is the right point-man to do it, war record aside." It was a back-handed slap at Wilkinson for letting the rookie run with the investigation and an intimation if things blew up, the sergeant would be held accountable.

Wilkinson did not miss the warning.

CHAPTER 10

The entrance to Paragon Park served as the setting for the press conference. Reporters from the Boston Herald joined those from the Globe and Patriot Ledger along with their photographers. The Hull-Nantasket Times was represented by its managing editor.

A mobile TV van from Chanel 4, Boston, was also present; a boxy camera on a tripod positioned on a platform extending from the rear of their vehicle.

Gallo and Wilkinson, in sport coats and ties, flanked Captain Kellum, in full dress uniform and cap with gold braid on the visor. Wilkinson wore his gray felt fedora and smoked a cigarette. Gallo, bare headed, stood with his arms at his side, the awkward giant towering over his colleagues, both under six feet tall.

Kellum quieted the gaggle of reporters by clearing his throat several times and addressing the group. "On April 2nd," he began, "a work crew sprucing up Paragon Park for an intended May opening made the gruesome discovery of two bodies. Evidence suggests they lay in the park undiscovered since before Christmas. They were shot to death. They have been identified as Donald Berger and Dustin Rose, of Cohasset. Their families have been notified."

A hand thrust up from a Patriot Ledger reporter. "We've heard both were armed. Any comment?"

Kellum debated whether to tell them the two men were believed to have been involved in the Hingham gas station robbery. He decided to do so—and did.

That tidbit led reporters to write furiously on their scratchpads and shout other questions.

"How did they wind up here?" a Globe journalist probed.

The query was never answered because the Patriot Ledger guy who began the questioning interrupted. "We understand Detective Gallo from Hull, a war hero, is spearheading the investigation. Is that true?"

Gallo shuffled his feet and reddened, as Kellum replied. "He's working the case with senior Detective Wilkinson here," he said, gesturing to the man on his left.

"What progress have you made Detective Gallo?" the same man asked, ignoring Kellum's attempt to deflect questions away from him.

AJ dipped his head, shot a sideways glance at the chief, didn't respond. He learned in the Marines never to embarrass a high-ranking officer.

Kellum responded, irritated. "We're just beginning our inquiries. We can't release specific details at this time."

"I'd like to hear from Gallo sir," the man persisted as the others voiced their agreement.

Clenching his fists to control his anger, Kellum retorted. "Look people. Right now, updates on the progress of the investigation will come from my office to ensure continuity in what is publicized. These detectives will submit daily reports to me."

The reporter, not appeased, pressed the issue. "Why don't you want Detective Gallo to talk, Captain? The public deserves information from the men doing the actual investigating. What are you hiding?"

Kellum, his face crimson, lost his composure. He bellowed, "We're not concealing anything. We want to speak with one voice, is all. You know what we know, or can release, at this time."

"Why can't that voice be Gallo's or Wilkinson's?" another journalist chimed in. "They would know more than anyone about what's going on."

While the reporters continued to badger Kellum, he paused, pulled a pack of cigarettes from his pocket, lit up, took two deep drags, expelled the smoke into the air and said, "Now boys. That's not how it works. We will provide you updates on the investigations as soon as we can, mindful we don't reveal details to tip off the perpetrator or perpetrators."

"So, there might be more than one killer?" the TV man broke in, setting off another barrage of questions.

Disgusted, Kellum shook his head and silently berated himself for agreeing to this inquisition. Any positive outcome he hoped to achieve was lost. "Gentleman," he said, "thank you for coming this morning. This interview is over."

Three more reporters hollered out as Kellum, Gallo and Wilkinson strode off to the MDC Building. Gallo walked on his toes like the athlete he was, ready to dart left or right as the situation required.

That ability would later save his life.

Once the press conference broke up, the TV newsman turned facing his camera and said, "That's all the information we have now on the brutal murders here in Nantasket Beach. Join us tonight for more up to the minute coverage of this horrific event."

The other newsmen drifted to their cars in the lot across from the park, some writing in their notepads others scrambling to find a pay phone to file a report.

One reporter who filed from a phone in Anastos restaurant didn't leave town, determined to publish an article about AJ Gallo.

The lawmen, reeling from the bombardment of questions from "the fourth estate," entered the MDC Building and climbed the stairs to the cramped office above. Kellum grabbed the swivel chair behind the wooden desk while his subordinates stood. Smoke polluted the air as Kellum and Wilkinson lit fresh cigarettes and took deep drags.

"That pack of wolves will never be satisfied," Kellum said, as he leaned back. Neither Gallo nor Wilkinson commented.

"I'll tell you one thing," he added, staring at AJ. "We got to keep a tight lid on this and solve it pronto, understood?"

"We've just begun, sir," Gallo cautioned. "It will take time."

Kellum took three pulls on his Chesterfield and expelled fumes into the air. "I know this. I do. Don't want corners cut, mistakes made. Do your job as best you can. Bill will help, as will I. We'll send you some more assistance if you feel it necessary."

"I don't sir, not yet," Gallo said, perhaps too quickly. He snatched a glance at Wilkinson to see if he was offended. The sergeant's face remained impassive, shrouded in smoke.

"All right then. Find the murdering scum," Kellum shouted, pounding the desktop, his face red.

Gallo stepped back surprised by the rage displayed by his boss.

After a few additional puffs on his cigarette to calm himself, Kellum left the building to drive back to Boston. Wilkinson slid into the chair he vacated, found an ashtray in the middle drawer of the desk and snubbed out the remains of his Camel.

Gallo, still standing and leaning against the doorway to snatch a breath of fresh air, hoped it was the end of the chimney of fumes released into the office. Wilkinson dashed his hopes by lighting up again.

Between drags, he said, "Sorry I haven't been with you on this. Been tied up with the upcoming lieutenant's exam and a couple of cases that need to be closed. I can ask the captain to send another detective to help if you want."

"Not necessary, sir. Hingham Detective McCrory and I are making good progress"—an overstatement but one he hoped the sarge would accept.

Wilkinson, satisfied, left after getting briefed on the status of the case.

Bert Jones, the lone crime reporter for the Patriot Ledger, and one of those who pestered Captain Kellum, called in his story from the pay phone in Anastos. He had parked his Volkswagen bus in the lot across from the MDC Substation jotting notes for his next column.

A recent graduate of Boston University's School of Journalism, he was happy to be with the Ledger, which covered the twenty-six communities south of Boston, referred to as the South Shore. The tabloid, once the hometown newspaper of President John Quincy Adams, was founded in 1837. The former president became a prolific letter writer to the editors after he left office.

John Quincy wasn't on Bert's radar. His grandfather and father were longtime members of the Ledger's board of director's. Bubbling with enthusiasm and self-confidence, he dismissed that circumstance as unrelated to his getting a position with the paper. He felt he would succeed no matter where he landed. He intended his current post as a stepping stone to a prominent daily like the Boston Globe or Herald, even the New York Times, if the gods smiled upon him.

The murders in Nantasket, among the few such incidents on the South Shore, gave Jones the opportunity to burnish his reputation. That a Korean War hero was involved in the investigation added to that prospect. A biographical article on Gallo would be an eye-catching lead into subsequent stories.

All he had to do was convince the man to cooperate.

Screwing up his courage, the five-foot ten, pudgy reporter, sauntered across Nantasket Ave to the police station in time to see the older detective leave.

Super, he thought. As the senior guy on the case, he, no doubt, would try to dominate an interview, if he allowed one at all.

Jones entered the stationhouse and encountered the desk sergeant who appeared in an ill mood. He scowled before the newsman introduced himself.

"I'm Bert Jones, of the Patriot Ledger," he said, a slight catch in his voice. "I'd like to speak with Detective Gallo."

The sergeant glowered, his jaw tightening. "Got an appointment?" he asked, knowing Jones didn't.

"No," Jones admitted. "I have some information to share regarding the murders at Paragon Park."

The veteran sergeant recognized the bluff. "Sorry pal. Call and make an appointment."

His enthusiasm waning, Bert turned to leave, when Gallo tromped down the stairs. Jones gasped at the imposing bulk of the man. Before the sergeant reacted, Jones stepped in front of AJ, hoping the detective wouldn't crush him with a massive fist or pick him up by the collar and throw him out the door.

With a quivering voice, he stuttered, "Detective, ah, ah, Bert Jones of the Patriot Ledger, may I have a word?"

"Mr. Jones," Gallo said, feeling sorry for the cowering reporter. "If you were at the press conference today, you're aware any information about the murders must come from Captain Kellum."

Jones broke into a Cheshire Cat grin. "I don't want to discuss the case. I want to write an article about you. Hull boy makes good, that sort of thing. Review your time in Korea and how you signed on with Metro."

Gallo, mindful of undermining his boss and bending Wilkinson's nose out of shape, demurred. He didn't want to rehash Korea or play the hero.

"Bert, again, I appreciate your interest, but any information about me or the investigation must be approved from above. I'm a rookie, can't afford to appear to be grandstanding. Clear it with the boss and I'll be happy to talk to you."

Jones, discouraged, did not persist. He had laid the groundwork for his profile having set up interviews with Gallo's former classmates at Hingham High, his football coach and a couple of teachers. Gallo's Marine buddies stonewalled him when he tried to meet with them.

The military bureaucracy was deep and unyielding.

"Thanks for your time, detective," Jones said, shaking Gallo's hand. "I'll arrange an interview through Captain Kellum."

"Good luck with that," Gallo said, eying the sergeant, who rolled his eyes.

Bert Jones exited the building rubbing his right hand. Though he knew the detective hadn't purposely hurt him, the man's grip was viselike.

He ignored that with the prospect, however unlikely, of interviewing Gallo.

CHAPTER 11

The man sat in a window booth in Pages Diner in Hingham Harbor on Route 3A, a road that led to Cohasset, Scituate, Plymouth and other communities south. The setting was picturesque. He gazed across the highway where boats moored at the marina bobbed in the waves and a family of four picnicked on the grass bordering the bay.

He looked but did not see; his mind focused elsewhere.

He'd just read an article in the Quincy Patriot Ledger about bodies recovered at Paragon Park in Nantasket. The reporter, a Bert Jones, noted no suspects had as yet been apprehended though detectives speculated the dead men had staged the robbery of a Gulf Station in Hingham in December, 1957. Rumors hinted a disgruntled co-conspirator murdered them.

Anyone with information was requested to call Detective Anthony Gallo of the Metropolitan District Commission Police—the number posted at the end of the piece.

The man was not surprised. A pal had tipped him off when the repair work for the new year was scheduled to begin and he joined a crew masquerading as a worker. It was an opportunity to see if he left any evidence behind to incriminate himself. He was the guy who "found" the guns on the track of the midget racers and surreptitiously wiped them of fingerprints.

The man had long ago disassembled his .38 Special, scattering its parts in Hingham Bay and the Atlantic. He had also discovered a tear in the blue peacoat he wore the night of his confrontation at Paragon Park and dropped the garment off at a Salvation Army store in Boston; accepted no receipt for his donation.

He knew the gas station attendant and relatives of Rose and Berger would identify him as a friend, but he took pains to stay in the car during the robbery. He believed he couldn't be seen from inside the garage.

Nevertheless, he remained nervous. He hung out with Berger at his house in Cohasset and met his wife and mother-in-law. But Donald had other friends; no reason for him to be singled out, same was true of Dustin.

Hashing these things out in his mind, he jolted back to the present when the young waitress, dressed in the uniform of the day, pink dress, white scalloped apron and a nurse's style hat, asked if he wanted more coffee. A refill cost five cents.

He said he would.

Drinking his brew, he understood he had few options. He suspected the police would find out about him during interviews with family members of Rose and Berger. Would he lie if questioned? If he did lie, and they discovered it, would it prove his guilt?

His other choice was to turn himself in and claim self-defense. They did try to kill him. Their guns would show they had been fired. His shoulder wound would reveal he had been hit. Two against one, an unfair fight, right?

Still grappling with what to do, he came to no decision. He left money on the table, smiled at his server and pushed open the door to the outside. As he did so, two men in sport coats and ties slipped by him and entered the diner.

His heart skipped a beat. Sweat formed on his brow. He recognized Detective Gallo and turned his head away to avoid being identified.

He needn't have worried. The last time Gallo had seen him he was wearing work coveralls splattered with paint, sunglasses and a Red Sox cap pulled low shielding his face.

He took a chance then. Would he take another soon?

The two detectives occupied a window booth behind the one the man had vacated. They ordered black coffee from a young waitress and waited until she left before speaking.

"How did the press extravaganza go?" McCrory asked, a smile creasing his face. "Didn't see the paper this morning."

Gallo laughed. "A disaster, in my opinion. The captain cut questions short, ticked off by the rudeness of the reporters. We fled the scene like we had something to hide."

"Glad it was you and not me, pal."

Gallo smirked. "The boss was spooked, wants daily reports and a quick resolution. I'm afraid he might pull me off the case if we don't show results soon. Can't count on Sergeant Wilkinson to have my back."

"What's his deal?"

"Not sure. Resents me for some reason. You'd think he'd want a win since he's angling to be a lieutenant."

"Let's give him that, then," McCrory declared, thrusting his jaw forward and pounding his fist on the table. The outburst drew disapproving glances from two elderly ladies who sat across from them.

Gallo raised his arms in a sorry gesture toward the old gals though pleased by McCrory's enthusiasm. Nevertheless, he didn't like their progress so far despite what he told Wilkinson. "Not much to go on," he said. "Foul weather obliterated any useable evidence from the crime scene. Lab couldn't pull fingerprints from the guns though it's obvious they belonged to Berger and Rose. The killer may have wiped his own prints since he tossed them away from the bodies."

"Yeah. These guys were armed," McCrory said, "didn't go to Paragon Park to ride the coaster."

He continued after a brief pause. "We now know they robbed the gas station and were likely killed the same night, probably by a co-conspirator I suspect was the getaway driver."

"Who Morris says he never saw."

"Not sure I believe it."

McCrory laughed. "Really? You don't trust the guy?"

Gallo's turn to laugh. "My theory is that, for some unknown reason, Berger and Rose had a falling out with the wheel-man. They went to Hull—again for some strange reason. The man bolted into Paragon Park, they chased him, and got killed for their effort."

"Makes sense."

"And I believe the shooter ambushed them from atop the Flying Scooter platform. No proof, but it's what I would have done. Good 'field of fire' and the high-ground as my gunny sergeant pounded into my head."

McCrory waited until the waitress brought their coffee and took their order— bacon and eggs for both— before responding. "The gas station guy named 'a Bradley someone' who hung out with Berger and Rose. He could have been the getaway driver in the robbery, and our possible shooter. They argued about splitting the loot. Argument turned violent."

"Morris also said a classmate of Dustin's, a Johnny Goodman, was at the station a lot. I interviewed him at the Cohasset PD," Gallo said. "His alibi at first seemed solid. But I requested Cohasset Officer Vince Russo to further check it."

"Yeah. I heard Morris mention Goodman," McCrory said.

Gallo took out his memo pad and reviewed his notes.

"Amy Berger identified a Bradley Evans who hung around with her husband. Gotta be the other guy Morris mentioned. Said he lived in Hingham, didn't have his address. His name also turned up in a notebook Dustin kept with a telephone number next to it, no address."

"Let's go back to the PD after breakfast and call him," McCrory said.

Before Gallo could respond, the waitress returned with their food.

The conversation energized Gallo. He enjoyed working with McCrory, a man closer to his age than his Metro partner, Wilkinson, and easier to talk to. Still, he needed to break him of his "idol" obsession.

He thought less and less of Wilkinson as the days passed. He couldn't sever their connection, though. Captain Kellum would never allow it. He wanted Metro to get the credit when the case was solved, not share it with anyone from another police agency.

"A reporter came sniffing around my office yesterday," Gallo said, as they finished their meal. "Claimed he planned to do a human-interest story on me."

"Ah! The hometown hero. Gonna do it?"

"Not unless the brass clears it, and not then if I have a choice."

"Be careful with reporters. They're snakes. What you say is not always what they report. They can make you look like a jerk as well as a star."

"Never happen. Doubt the captain will clear it."

McCrory scanned the bill, showed it to AJ and they contributed an equal share, adding a ten percent tip.

CHAPTER 12

Sergeant Bill Wilkinson was being dragged into the dangerous world of his boss, Captain Martin Kellum, the cost of accepting a copy of the lieutenant's exam he would take in two weeks. He felt trapped; regretted his decision.

At 10:30 a.m., on a Thursday morning, Wilkinson and Kellum met with Roger Newman and Patrick Duffy, at McShay's in Quincy. The diner had Burgundy leather swivel chairs lining a wraparound counter and booths with matching Burgundy bench seats. The group took a booth for four at the back of the restaurant away from the dwindling breakfast crowd.

Roger Newman, a shade over six feet tall, broad shouldered, brown hair cut short, military style, wore a gray suit, maroon tie, and spit-shined brown wing-tip brogues. A lieutenant with the Quincy PD, he was among the lawmen being groomed by Kellum for his expanding criminal network.

Patrick Duffy, five-ten, slight build, black hair slicked back, face unshaven, sat next to Newman. He donned a black motorcycle jacket with multiple zippers and a narrow black belt, the cuffs of his blue dungarees rolled up.

Duffy, a convicted bank robber and safe cracker, hadn't held a legitimate job in years. He spent much of his youth in a reform school for habitual truants in Tewksbury, Massachusetts.

Rumors connected him to Somerville's Irish mob and to its current leader—Bobby Moran, who was standing in for his incarcerated boss, Buddy McClean. Reporters nicknamed McClean, the Irish King of Winter Hill; a Somerville neighborhood where the gang originated.

This was Wilkinson's first foray into Kellum's nefarious world, and he was nervous; hadn't been briefed on the nature of the meeting. He was wary of Duffy whose eyes kept darting around the room as if worried someone might recognize him and pounce. After scouring the diner for the umpteenth time, Duffy spoke, leaning in close to Wilkerson and Kellum. "So, Captain. Are you ready for a huge score?"

Kellum smirked. "What do you have in mind?"

Again, Duffy surveyed the room. "The Quincy Savings and Loan, Memorial Day weekend."

Wilkinson gasped. A bank job? He wasn't naïve and no saint. As a patrol officer and detective, he had nailed scumbags by planting evidence and skimmed cash from a drug dealer's stash. He took bribes to rip up traffic citations and once forced a prostitute to perform a sex act on him in return for not hauling her in—a situation he regretted and never repeated.

He wasn't alone, of course. Corruption was rampant within Massachusetts police agencies and its political leaders; bribes accepted practice. Even a former Mayor of Boston served time in the '40s for mail fraud and still ran the city. Negative role models could be found from top to bottom in law enforcement and the political realm.

But a bank robbery would bring in the Feds with the odds of success never good. He didn't think Duffy ranked with John Dillinger, the most famous bank robber in U.S. history; who tallied 40 bank robberies until shot down in the street by FBI agents.

Wilkinson kept his mouth shut, intending to express his concerns later to Kellum. A promotion to lieutenant might not be worth the risk?

Yet, what were his options?

To Wilkinson's relief, Duffy provided few details of the robbery scheme. If he backed out now, he might not be considered a liability, somebody to be eliminated. He had no doubt if this plot had mob backing, his, and his family's, lives might be in danger. He squirmed in his seat as the other men ordered breakfast.

He stuck to coffee.

When the meal ended, Duffy and Newman left about five minutes apart, leaving Kellum to settle the tab. The Captain, in no hurry to leave, lit up a Chesterfield enjoying the semi-solitude. When he finished his smoke, he snuffed it out on one of the glass ashtrays provided, dropped two ten-dollar bills on the table and nudged Wilkinson to exit the booth.

The two lawmen left together; Wilkinson nursing a queasy stomach like the one he got when approaching the first hill on the Giant Coaster at Paragon Park.

This was a ride he should never have taken and one he planned to jump off; he just didn't know how.

CHAPTER 13

Three days after his visit from the cops, Jerry Morris felt better. He closed the door of his bedroom, so he wouldn't be overheard by his mother, picked up the phone on his nightstand and dialed a familiar number answered after two rings.

"Those yahoos almost killed me," he said, without identifying himself.

"What are you going to do about it?" the man responded. "They're dead."

"Serves 'em right."

"You under arrest?"

"Didn't charge me. Blamed it on Dustin."

"Good. He can't point the finger at anyone else. But I checked the safe. The stuff is missing."

Morris gripped the receiver tighter, his upbeat mood vanishing. "Yeah. That could come back to bite us in the ass. The cops who grilled me didn't ask about it. Berger and Rose must have stashed it somewhere."

The man laughed. "Think about it. Word is they were killed the same night of the robbery. Didn't have time to do that."

"Where is it then?"

"You better find out."

Morris shuddered. Didn't like the implied threat in the man's tone. His palms sweat. If the thugs they were working with thought they had been stiffed, they would look for someone to blame.

He scrambled for an answer.

"Two possibilities," he said. "First, I never got my car back. Stuff could be there and the cops didn't discover it—or the guy who shot them took it."

"Find out," the man repeated, his voice dripping with venom. "The people we're dealing with will not take kindly to us losing product."

With that, the man Jerry called hung up, slamming the receiver down. Jerry swiped the sleeve of his right arm across his forehead to wipe away beads of sweat; his armpits moist.

What had he gotten into?

The man Morris contacted was Mitch Smith, son of Gavin Smith, owner of the gas station robbed by Rose and Berger. Mitch, needing cash, masterminded the robbery. He amassed serious gambling debts and got sideways with the Irish gang out of Somerville, Massachusetts. They controlled the rackets in the greater Boston area: ran numbers, made loans with exorbitant interest rates, hijacked trucks and fixed horse races.

In addition, they sent donations to the IRA (Irish Republican Army) and, it was rumored, conducted the occasional contract killing. Their leader had the reputation as one tough bastard.

This petrified Smith, who feared the gangsters would come looking for him if he didn't pay up. He couldn't go to his dad for money, though he was one of the wealthiest men on the South Shore. He owned a string of gas stations from Cohasset to Boston, along with two thriving local car dealerships. He banned Mitch from the family business because of his "slothful ways" as he had put it.

Mitch's betting through the Somerville network hooked him up with a young guy named Whitey Bulger, who he hoped might help him join the gang and let him work off his debts or, better, forgive them. To his chagrin, Bulger was arrested in '56 and out of contact.

Mitch did the next best thing to save himself, at least in his mind. The mob dabbled in the distribution of cocaine and heroin. He talked them into letting him supply customers on the South Shore. He stashed his hoard in the safe at the gas station robbed by Rose and Berger. He assumed they grabbed it along with the money.

Whoever knocked them off, now had both. This put Mitch in a double bind. He lost needed cash and now had nothing to sell to get more. The mob would brook no excuses. In deep trouble if he didn't recover the drugs, he vowed to find the guy who killed Rose and Berger, and take him out before he could muscle in on his territory.

He figured the killer was the getaway driver, either Johnny Goodman or Bradley Evans. They hung out at the gas station and were pals with the dead men.

Goodman was a flake; Evans more intelligent, more mature. Goodman sucked up to Dustin, could be manipulated into participating in a robbery. Yet in his gut, Mitch felt those guys would trust Evans more.

So, in his mind, he pegged Evans as the wheel man, who, for some reason had a falling out with those dumbbells, killed them and now had possession of his coke.

Evans was a dead man.

CHAPTER 14

The man sat bolt upright in bed. He wrestled with his predicament all night, unable to sleep. In the end, he made a decision to go to the police rather than wait for them to come to him. He would not claim self- defense. He would disavow everything about the killing of Berger and Rose—no witnesses, no evidence to tie him to them.

They don't even know the exact time the shooting occurred. It took months for anyone to discover the bodies. He would concede knowing the two men. Friends and their families had seen him with them. Beyond that, he'd admit nothing.

He glanced at the clock on his nightstand next to the bed; 6:30 a.m. Time to get ready for work in Quincy, about twenty-five minutes by car from Hingham, half that time by train. Later, he'd call the MDC Detective leading the investigation, arrange to meet, confident he could pull this off.

In his mind, he was innocent of murder.

He took his time dressing before his drive to Pages Restaurant in Hingham for his usual breakfast. After his meal, he'd hop the train to his job at Sears in Quincy, unaware he was being stalked by a man intent on killing him.

Four days later, at 10:00 a.m., on his day off, Bradley Evans dialed the number for the MDC Police Station in Nantasket listed in the Boston Globe story about the bodies found in Paragon Park. He called from a phone booth in the downtown train station and asked for Detective Gallo, who came on the line in about two minutes.

Evans hesitated, gave his name and identified himself as a friend of Dustin Rose and Donald Berger. "I expect you may want to talk with me," he said.

"Mr. Evans," AJ said, ecstatic. "Thank you for your call. Yes! We'd like to speak with you soon."

"I'm off today. I can be in Hull in about an hour."

"Look, Mr. Evans. I'm working this case with a Hingham Detective because we believe the murders are related to a gas station holdup there. And, my office here is cramped. Can you meet with us at the Hingham Police Department, in say, two hours?"

After a brief pause—Gallo worried he might have spooked him—Bradley replied, "can do, sir."

"Perfect. See you then."

When the call ended, Bradley fought to control his fear. He hoped his ploy of preempting their search for him was the wise thing to do; and not a prison sentence or worse.

Bradley Evans (the man) wasn't sure how he wound up in this predicament, having shot two men once considered friends. The easy answer was that he chose the wrong friends. But life was more complicated than that, he knew.

He exited the train terminal after the call and sat at a wooden bench outside. Across the street was the white clapboard St. Paul's Catholic Church, with its ornate multi-colored spire. He hunched over, holding his head between his hands.

Once a devout Catholic, he hadn't been inside a church since high school—an act of rebellion against the iron grip of his parents who insisted he attend mass every Sunday. He was beginning to think his current mess was a continuation of that struggle.

He grew up in Amherst, a college town in western Massachusetts. His father was a professor at the private, Amherst College, downtown, which frequently touted its most famous alumni, former President, Calvin Coolidge. His mother served as a librarian at the University of Massachusetts, a ten-minute drive from their home.

Their plan was that he enroll in either institution—he had the grades in classes they selected—and enter the field of education after graduation from high school.

Their plan, not his.

Thinking back on it now, he joined the Marines when the Korean War broke out to flaunt his independence from their stifling control, as he saw it. He was on his way to boot camp at Parris Island, South Carolina, before they knew he had enlisted. The draft age after WWII was eighteen-and-a-half to thirty-five.

He was nineteen.

His father tried his best to terminate his enlistment, traveling to South Carolina to confront Marine Corps brass. They rejected his dad's effort since Bradley fell within the new draft guidelines though he had not been drafted but volunteered.

The confrontation between his father and the general in charge of recruit training, degenerated into a shouting match, with the young Bradley in the room, outwardly looking mortified but glad to see his father get his comeuppance.

Brad was shipped to Korea when he completed training. He participated in the famous Inchon landing which gave the United States momentum against the North Koreans. That success was blunted when the Chinese entered the conflict and a stalemate ensued.

He wrote no letters home like most of his comrades. He feared their return missives would contain ugly comments about his betrayal of their wishes.

After his release from service, he further angered and alienated his parents, by settling in Hingham instead of Amherst. His uncle, his father's brother, lived in Hull where the young Bradley spent wonderful summers going to the beach and Paragon Park.

He saw it as being liberated.

He met Donald Berger and Dustin Rose when he serviced his car at the Gulf Station near the Hingham rotary. He wasn't an outgoing personality, had few friends. They massaged his ego by showing an interest in him, though they had little in common. They did odd jobs together until Brad secured a permanent position with the Sears Store in Quincy.

His participation in the robbery was an impulsive act he immediately regretted; another subconscious act of rebellion against his parents, perhaps. He never expected Rose to shoot the attendant since they were buddy's with the guy and had planned the heist with him and Mitch Smith.

Shaken after he was forced to kill them, he sought counsel from his uncle, Phil, in Hull, who was estranged from Bradley's parents. His uncle, after hearing details of what happened, persuaded him to keep silent, believing what his nephew did was self-defense. Though it may have been, it troubled Bradley daily and led him to call Detective Gallo.

Evans arrived at the Hingham Police Station five minutes after twelve. The desk sergeant escorted him down a small hallway dotted with vintage pictures of the town like the Old Ships Church circa 1861, and Loring Hall circa 1852, one of the few movie theaters in the area still open.

He lingered by the photos, fascinated, before being ushered into a conference room dominated by a six-foot-long oak table with padded black chairs arranged around it. Two men wearing white shirts and ties sat on one side. A carafe of coffee and a dozen donuts rested on the table in front of them. They stood as Evans entered, shook hands, and motioned him to sit opposite them.

AJ introduced himself and McCrory and opened the conversation: "Thanks for contacting us, sir. You saved us time looking for you. Mrs. Berger, Dustin's brother and the gas station attendant did mention you as a friend of Donald and Dustin."

Evans smiled at the use of Berger and Rose's first names, an effort to make him more comfortable and lower his guard. Not going to fall for that, he thought.

"I wouldn't call us friends," he responded. "We did a couple of odd jobs together until I got a permanent position at the Sears in Quincy."

"How did you meet?" McCrory asked.

"We answered a newspaper ad for some carpentry work at a building site in Hingham. The foreman needed semi-skilled labor and hired us on the spot. We hung out during the job, split up when it ended. I first saw them when I got gas at the station where Dustin worked."

"When was that construction job?" Anthony asked.

"Oh! last fall sometime, in September or October. When I read they were killed, I couldn't believe it."

"Did they appear dangerous? Capable of robbery?"

"Not to me."

"Did you know they had guns?"

Evans thought short answers to their questions would be best. Leave little opportunity for him to screw up. "No," he said.

"Do you own a gun?"

Evans, prepared for this question, said, "No, sir. Haven't held a weapon since Korea."

"You served?" AJ asked, not surprised. Many men his age did.

"Yes, sir. 7th Marines. First Marine Division."

Anthony reached across the table to once again shake Evans' hand. "5th Marines. You at the "Frozen Chosin?"

Now relaxed, Evans nodded. "Good to meet another Jarhead—and a hero to boot. Read about your exploits."

McCrory watched their interview focus coming apart. He jumped in.

"Do you know if Berger or Rose had any enemies?"

"Wouldn't know. But Rose was quick to anger, got into several beefs with guys on the construction job."

"Got any names?"

"No. The foreman might; Abe Shuman, who owns the company, South Shore Builders. You can find them in the phone book, I'm sure, or check their Ad in the Patriot Ledger. I don't have the number."

McCrory wrote down the name of the company, then asked, "What about Berger? He violent?"

"Never seen him angry. Everyone liked him. Don't understand why he palled around with Rose. Guess high school ties are hard to break."

"Speaking of high school ties, do you know Johnny Goodman?"

"Not well. He hung out with Dustin and Donald sometimes."

"Could they convince him to join in the robbery?"

Evans suppressed a smile. He could push them in that direction but thought it best to be non-committal. "Above my pay grade," he said, a phrase familiar to both McCrory and Gallo.

Gallo seemed satisfied with Evans's responses, yet McCrory pushed ahead. "Do you know the attendant at the Gulf Station in Hingham? The man who was shot?"

"Met him once. Didn't speak to him though."

The man was cool. His answers clear. McCrory still sensed something off about him. Nothing specific. He ended his questioning.

With that, he and Gallo pushed back their chairs and stood to signify the interview was over. With handshakes all-around, they released Evans. The donuts remained untouched.

Evans walked out of the police station and took several gulps of fresh air. He congratulated himself on his preemptive move to get dropped as a suspect in the Paragon Park shootings. The comradeship he shared with Detective Gallo helped, he suspected. The Corps was a brotherhood, forged in bootcamp, honed in combat. Once a Marine, always a Marine, the mantra they shared—Semper Fi.

The cops may have dismissed him as a suspect—his stalker didn't.

"What do you think?" McCrory asked, when Bradley Evans left the conference room at the Hingham PD. Gallo rubbed his chin and leaned back in his chair. "We have nothing linking him to the crime. Guilty people don't turn themselves into the police. He admitted knowing Rose and Berger and meeting Jerry at the gas station."

McCrory knew gut feelings weren't evidence. "So where do we go from here?"

"Let's wait for the report on Johnny Goodman. In my mind, he's another candidate to have been the wheel-man in the gas station hit. In the meantime, we contact Abe Shuman at the South Shore Builders. See if he can give us the names of the men who beefed with Rose. Maybe one of them joined Rose and Berger for the gas station job."

Gallo fingered an abrasion on his neck, a souvenir from Korea. "You know, it's curious," he said. "Whoever killed them didn't take the cash from Rose's wallet. If money caused the falling out, why leave it?"

"Guy panicked, spooked by what he'd done," McCrory reasoned. "And why do you think it was over money?"

"What else?"

"Don't know. Something serious enough to have a shoot-out over."

"And another thing," Gallo persisted. "If it was a shoot-out, the killer defended himself against two guys trying to kill him."

"So now our guy's a hero?"

"Not saying that. Good defense though."

McCrory shook his head, unconvinced.

Gallo changed the subject. "Maybe the autopsies will reveal something helpful."

"Hope so. In the meantime, let's go see Abe Shuman."

Neither detective anticipated the post-mortems on the murder victims contained a bombshell that threatened to change the focus of their investigation.

CHAPTER 15

Captain Kellum devised the robbery scheme to include a police chief, at least three officers from the Metro ranks and the Quincy PD, and two career criminals, Irish gangster Francis X. "Frankie" O'Brien, and master-safe cracker Patrick Duffy. Bill Wilkinson would serve as Kellum's liaison to the group, although he didn't know it yet.

The price of his lieutenancy.

On a Wednesday morning, around 10:00 a.m., Kellum drove to Wollaston Beach, Quincy, and parked in a vacant space facing the ocean. Five minutes later, Duffy arrived on his motorcycle. Both men moved to sit on the four-foot-high concrete wall, their backs to the clouds hovering over the water. The crisp air smelled of algae, fish and crab. Gulls circled in hopes of a meal. A woman pushing a baby carriage along the walkway smiled as she strolled by. No one else was within earshot on the deserted beachfront.

Before a word was spoken, Lieutenant Newman ran across the highway and joined them.

"Sorry I was late, he said, department meeting."

Duffy shook his head but Kellum understood, familiar with such bureaucratic responsibilities and how meetings often droned on. "No problem. Let's keep this brief."

He dipped his head toward Duffy, who filled them in on the scheme's progress. "Got a guy eyeballing the alarm system and ways to neutralize it. He's also checking on the security, whether off duty police or rent-a-cops. We're looking at the Memorial Day weekend when the bank and all the businesses around it will be closed. Most people will be celebrating. We can operate without interference. Should post someone outside keeping watch, though."

"I'll handle that," Newman volunteered, "and check into the bank's security detail. Some of our guys could be working there on their days off. We don't keep a record of that."

Kellum stood, signaling the end of their meeting. "We'll meet again beginning of May. I'll notify you when and where. Turning toward Duffy, he said, "any complications contact me."

Duffy grinned. He'd never pulled off a caper with cops helping. He knew Kellum had contacts on both sides of the law. He didn't know how or who, didn't care. Everything promised to go without a hitch with lawmen watching his back. He got on his motorcycle and headed north on Quincy Shore Drive for the twenty-five-minute ride back to his home in Whitfield. He was a black streak on his bike, hunched over to cut the wind resistance.

Duffy, a skilled bank robber, but no mastermind, relied on Captain Kellum and his Mafia cohorts to ensure no major snafus in the operation. A man as devious and unscrupulous as Duffy, manipulating people to his own advantage, should have known the ranks of law enforcement agencies were riddled with leaks and informants.

Back in his office after the beach rendezvous, Captain Kellum summoned Bill Wilkinson via intercom. He entered with not much enthusiasm. Ever since the gathering in the Quincy diner with the motorcycle freak, he was wary of what his role in the robbery might be. He sat before Kellum in his usual chair waiting for the ax to fall.

He didn't have long to wait.

"Bill," said Kellum. "Time to ante up. I don't dole out favors without expecting something in return, capisce?"

Wilkinson, afraid to speak lest a tremor in his voice betray his anxiety, just stared at his boss.

Kellum ignored the silence. "Something huge is going to go down soon and you will liaison with the people who will pull it off. It will be a hefty payday for all of us. I promise you won't get your hands dirty. Can I count on you?"

Wilkinson nodded. But felt himself being pulled down a rabbit hole, powerless to stop the fall. The queasy feeling he experienced after the meeting at the diner in Quincy returned.

Back in the bull-pen, typewriters clacking, smoke filling the air, he popped two Tums tablets in his mouth. It wouldn't be the last time he'd use them to calm his fear.

Alone after Wilkinson left his office, Captain Kellum lit up his umpteenth cigarette of the day and leaned back in his swivel chair, expelling donuts of smoke into the ceiling. He worried about Wilkinson but believed his subordinate didn't have the balls to betray him. Enjoying the solitude, he was startled when his phone rang. The bureau sergeant notified him a reporter from the Quincy Ledger was on the line.

"Should I tell him you're unavailable?" he asked.

Most times, Kellum would tell the officer to do just that, still reeling from the debacle in Nantasket Beach. But buoyed by the prospect of a big payday ahead, he told the officer to put the man through.

The line buzzed again and he said, "Kellum here."

"Sir, Bert Jones, Patriot Ledger. How are you today?"

At least the man exhibited a modicum of courtesy, Kellum thought. "Fine, and how's your day going?" he responded, wary of the newsman's motives.

Jones, happy his call hadn't been dismissed outright, pitched his case. "Sir, my day will get better if you grant my request to speak with Detective Gallo in Nantasket. I'd like to do a bio piece on him, human interest, if you will, war hero, Hull native, leading a murder investigation; won't press him for details."

Before Kellum could say no, Jones said, "Wonderful publicity for Gallo and for the Metro Police. Cops could use favorable press these days."

Kellum thought Jones might be referring to the latest scandal in the Boston PD; patrolmen on the take from pimps to allow prostitution in some upscale neighborhoods in the city like Beacon Hill in the shadow of the statehouse.

The commissioner was under fire, politicians and citizens demanding his ouster. Kellum also knew Globe reporters were probing for corruption in the Mets. Although a longshot, their snooping might uncover the robbery scheme. A positive article on Gallo could deflect that.

"You know what Bert," he said. "Let me think about this. I promise to get back to you in a couple days. Give me your number."

Jones was ecstatic. "Yes, sir. I appreciate your consideration. I'll wait for your call."

After he hung up, Kellum lit up a Chesterfield, got up from his chair and stood by the window appraising the view he enjoyed so much. He felt like the master of all he surveyed.

Like Duffy, he should have been more wary.

CHAPTER 16

Unaware his boss, Captain Kellum, might agree to the unthinkable, an interview with the press, Gallo continued to work with Jeff McCrory on the Paragon Park murder case. The two detectives opted to contact, Abe Shuman, owner of the construction company where Rose and Berger once worked. It was two days after their meeting with Bradley Evans.

Gallo drove to Nantasket and parked behind the two-story white stucco building that served as MDC Headquarters. The cramped structure housed only a few officers during the winter and spring months. An elevated reception counter was just inside the front door and two ten-by-ten holding cells in the back.

Upstairs held a compact office for the sergeant in charge and an eight-by-ten room with two cots for officers staying overnight. A narrow bathroom was jammed between the two rooms. The bunks were not used except in summer when the force doubled to handle the rowdy revelers visiting the beach and the park. Most of the regular MDC detail assigned here lived in Hull or nearby towns giving them a short commute to work.

As Gallo entered the front door, the desk sergeant handed him a manila envelope. "The autopsy reports for the two dead guys," he reported.

"Thanks," AJ responded, and bounded up the stairs to the small office and took a seat in the wooden swivel chair at his department issue desk. Though eager to see the report, he worried he might not be able to decipher its medical jargon. An experienced partner would help. Wilkinson's continued absence fueled Gallo's disdain for the man; he preferred working with McCrory.

The M.E. did not couch his report in medicalese. He wrote most of the commentary in plain English using medical terms only for specific organs. He listed the cause of death for each man as a gunshot wound to the upper torso, close to the heart; the wounds caused by rounds fired from a .38 Special revolver. The angle of entry indicated they were discharged from above. Both men died instantly, the cold notwithstanding. The bodies likely remained in the park buried under snow and ice for months—he couldn't determine with certainty the exact time frame.

Gallo smiled. The M.E. didn't have to nail the time period. He had already discovered through interviews with family members, the murdered men had been away from their homes since December 23rd, 1957, and hadn't been seen since.

Before he could gloat, a bombshell in the report stunned him—cocaine residue was present in the bodies. Damage to their nasal passages indicated frequent use.

AJ leaned back in his chair and rubbed his neck. This information threatened to alter the focus of their investigation—turn it toward the result of a drug deal gone bad. Maybe Berger and Rose robbed the gas station to pay for their habit.

It still didn't explain how they wound up in Paragon Park and why they got involved in a gun fight that cost them their lives. He doubted anyone would use the shuttered park to deal drugs; unless it was an employee, which he dismissed as improbable. He questioned whether laborers would have the money or contacts to distribute or consume narcotics.

Who then?

Gallo called Bill Wilkinson at the MDC Boston Office and shared the autopsy results. Wilkinson expressed surprise at the cocaine discovery but otherwise seemed disinterested. He advised Gallo to follow up and keep him apprised of progress.

AJ fumed. His sergeant blew off a major twist in the case. He respected the chain of command and wouldn't go over Wilkinson's head to complain. Besides, he was comfortable working with Jeff

McCrory and buzzed him at the Hingham PD to divulge the autopsy findings.

"Holy shit, Anthony," McCrory said. "This changes things. The murders might be the result of a drug deal gone bad, nothing to do with the robbery."

"My thoughts, also," AJ said, "but the getaway driver in the heist may still be involved. Perhaps he was the one who supplied Berger and Rose with the coke."

He didn't offer the idea that the seller could be a park employee.

"I don't know, AJ. Why rob the station at all?"

"For cash to buy the drugs which aren't cheap. Berger and Rose weren't rolling in dough working part time jobs."

"Makes sense."

AJ laughed, changed the subject. "Are you interested in walking the crime scene at Paragon Park with me? M.E. confirmed the shots that killed Rose and Berger came from above as I suspected. Only place that could be is from the Flying Scooters given the bullets angle of entry and the position of the bodies. I checked it out with a patrolman, but another pair of eyes might find something we missed."

"Sure," McCrory said. "Give me an hour."

"Meet me at the MDC Station. We can walk over."

The entrance gate to Paragon Park hung open while workers toiled in their massive cleanup effort. A carpenter was suspended from ropes as he labored to replace missing or broken support beams on the Giant Coaster. Another specialist replaced the glass on the Carousel.

The lawmen flashed their badges to workers still sweeping up debris and walked down the concrete concourse and veered off to where the bodies of Dustin Rose and Donald Berger had lain. A faded white chalk outline of the men remained.

They looked up at the Flying Scooters. The popular ride consisted of a center post with gondolas suspended from cables which whipped around causing the cars to fly outwards. Each gondola, or scooter, was equipped with a large rudder, allowing risk-takers to "snap" the cable arms sending the scooter into an almost uncontrolled in and out zigzag.

McCrory smiled. "Rode that sucker many times as a kid. Buddies and I thought we were real daredevils making the cables snap as we flipped the rudder back and forth."

Gallo laughed. "Know what you mean. All of us did the same thing. Tempting the fates. We didn't know any better. Let's go up."

They walked up the stairs and dodged the steel cables hanging from the top of the ride which held the "scooters" (bright red and yellow metal painted shells(gondolas) that resembled race cars without the wheels. They stopped on the edge of the platform and looked down on the chalk silhouettes of Rose and Berger.

"Perfect place for an ambush," Gallo remarked.

"Yeah. Someone with military experience would seek out the high ground—like Bradley Evans?"

"He's not the only guy who served," AJ replied. "Johnny Goodman was in the army. And you don't have to be a vet to recognize this would be a great spot to shoot from. Any hunter would know that."

"Agreed. But Evans is still a suspect, right?"

"Can't eliminate him. Though the cocaine residue in Rose and Berger opens up a lot of possibilities. Drugs could have sparked the fight Rose had with the two construction workers on the job in Hingham. The owner may be able to help us with that."

"A longshot is that the drug seller works in Paragon Park," McCrory said. "That would account for why they were here."

Gallo laughed. "My thought too but I'm not ready to accept that scenario. You rob a gas station then plan to meet your supplier at an amusement park in the dead of winter. Even if the dealer worked here, doubt he'd arrange to link up in his workplace. And what employee here would have the money to buy and sell coke. Most are part-timers."

"Valid question," McCrory said.

They searched the Flying Scooter platform for about twenty minutes, found nothing helpful and walked back to the MDC Building. The desk officer uncovered a listing for South Shore Builders in a Hingham telephone directory and Gallo made an appointment to talk with foreman/owner Abe Shuman that afternoon.

Was Shuman the key to unraveling the drug mystery or another detour in solving the crime?

Gallo and McCrory drove separately to Hingham and located parking spaces on North Street across from a two-story gray clapboard building with South Shore Builders in black block letters on a placard over a downstairs door.

They went inside the building and encountered an immense, well-lighted, open workroom. Incandescent lights were suspended from the ceiling and high windows dotted the back wall. Lumber was stacked along the side walls; mostly 2x4's for framing houses and 4x8 plywood sheeting used in roofing and flooring. Circular table saws and routers stood unused in another area of the room. Gallo liked the fresh, earthy smell of cut wood; it was somehow comforting.

A man studying blueprints spread out on an angled architect's table turned as the two men entered. He walked over to greet them; hand extended.

"Welcome," he said. "What can I do for law enforcement today?"

"We're interested in two men we believe worked for you, Dustin Rose and Donald Berger," Gallo said.

Abe Shuman, in his early fifties, the length of a roofing nail shy of six feet, smiled. His calloused hands were those of a man who labored hard for his daily bread. His broad shoulders hefted many a piece of lumber. His dark hair was graying at the temples, his moustache following suit. His tanned skin was not earned by lying on a beach, but by toiling in the scorching sun.

"Read about their murders and their involvement in the gas station holdup here in town," Shuman said. "Station is just around the corner from here."

He shook his head from side to side and frowned. "Wouldn't have guessed it." He made a tsk tsk sound with his mouth then asked, "But how can I help you?"

"What can you tell us about them?" AJ asked.

"Not much. They worked for me a short time; you understand. I hire part-timers when needed to supplement my regular guys. Pay's good, $2.16 an hour, so I receive a lot of applications. Young guys, some ex-military."

"We appreciate that. Anything at all you can disclose about Berger and Rose would be helpful."

Shuman dipped his head. "Good workers. Rose more skilled, carried his own tools, but not reliable. Let him go when he missed two straight days of work. Couldn't tolerate that. Bad example for my permanent employees. Berger stayed on until we finished the job."

"Heard Rose got into a squabble with a couple of your men."

"That he did. Pushing and shoving. Rose picked up a hammer, seemed ready to use it. I intervened and sent him home. He had a threatening look, but backed off."

"Any idea what caused the ruckus?" Anthony asked.

"Rose claimed one of the guys stole a tool from his work belt."

"Could drugs have been involved?"

Shuman scoffed, ran a calloused hand through his unkempt hair. "Hell no. I don't tolerate nothing like that. Suspended a guy once when he came to work reeking of marijuana. Last time that happened, to my knowledge."

"Did either Berger or Rose have any enemies you know of?" McCrory asked.

"Didn't know them long enough to make a judgement about that. Rose had a short fuse. Wouldn't doubt he rubbed quite a few people the wrong way on his journey through life. Berger was quiet, easy going."

McCrory was impressed by Shuman's *journey through life* phrase. The old man was an amateur philosopher. He chuckled to himself. "Do you have the names of the men who fought with Rose?" he asked.

"I do. But I wouldn't call it a fight; stopped it before it got out of hand."

"I'm sure you did, sir," Gallo said. "But we still need those names?"

"Right," Shuman said, walked over to his well-worn wooden desk, opened the middle drawer with one of the keys on his large key-ring and pulled out a bulky ledger.

He flipped to the third or fourth page, ran his finger down to the bottom and wrote two names along with their addresses on a notebook page with South Shore Builders stenciled in black on the top.

He gave it to Gallo who said aloud, "Brian Burke and Joseph Maloney."

"Yep," Shuman said.

"Thanks for your help, Mr. Shuman," AJ said and handed him a business card. "If you remember anything else that might be helpful, please give me a call."

"Will do," Shuman said, putting the card in his shirt pocket as he returned to the blueprints he'd been examining when he was interrupted.

Gallo and McCrory stood on the sidewalk in front of the South Shore Builders office. They now had two other individuals to check out even though they seemed like a longshot to have been involved in the Paragon Park murders—but you never knew.

"What do you think?" McCrory asked.

Gallo looked pensive. "Well, how about this scenario? One of the guys who tangled with Rose didn't hold a grudge. He contacts him at the gas station—a kindred spirit—fellow hot-head. They chew the fat, have a beer, and Rose talks him into participating in the robbery, to act as the getaway driver. He needs more cash than the $2.16 an hour he gets working at South Shore Builders."

McCrory nods along as Gallo continues. "They pull off the robbery but Rose shoots Morris, who appears to be dead. The guy wants no part of murder, takes off, flees to Hull—who knows why—with Burger and Rose in pursuit trying to keep him from going to the police."

McCrory is skeptical but doesn't interrupt.

"The dude goes into the park, attempts to lose them among all the rides and buildings. Decided his best chance was an ambush. Scared, he leaves their bodies lying on the ground. Lucked out when the storms barreled in and they weren't found for months. So my money's still on the getaway driver from the holdup as having killed Berger and Rose. Someone who's new to our suspect list."

Gallo's face lit up: "Left a cold trail for us to follow."

"Very punny," McCrory said. "I'm impressed."

"Couldn't resist. I do impersonations, too."

"Spare me, please," McCrory said, stifling a laugh, unwilling to give Gallo the satisfaction.

Shifting gears, he said, "Something else. Each man was shot once. Not multiple times. The shooter could have put several more slugs into them, didn't. Not a professional or a hardened killer.

"He didn't call the police either," McCrory continued. "Rose and Berger might have been saved if he did."

"M.E. believes both men died instantly from their wounds—close to their hearts, by the way. Shooter wanted to get away fast."

"So, what now? We follow up on the names Shuman gave us—Burke and Maloney?"

"Got a better idea?"

"Nope."

The lead was a dead end as expected. Burke was celebrating the Christmas holidays with family in Florida; left on December 10th. A phone call to them from Gallo verified that.

Maloney was injured on a construction job in Weymouth; fell from a fifteen-foot scaffolding onto a skip loader, breaking both legs, several ribs and suffered a concussion. He spent all of December recuperating.

"We're running out of options" McCrory said, as they sat in the conference room at the Hingham PD frustrated by another dead end.

"We still have a couple of viable suspects," Gallo assured him. "Rose, a hot head, made enemies. Bradley Evans hung out with him. We need to press him a little harder on who those people could be. He might be one himself. And I'm still waiting on a call from Cohasset Officer Russo about Johnny Goodman."

"Evans came forward on his own," McCrory reiterated, not commenting on the Goodman situation.

"Yeah! But he may have held back for some reason," AJ said. "Had a beef with Rose. Didn't share that because it would shift suspicion to him. And we do have some other possibilities; Mitch Smith, and Bobby Moran, for instance. Guys who were listed in Dustin's notebook."

Gallo paused, rubbed his chin, a reflex he found himself repeating often. "You know. Perhaps the guy Berger and Rose chased—assuming that's what led up to their killing—fled to Hull because he lived there. Knew his way around town, worked in the park."

"So? Where does that leave us?"

Gallo smiled. "A search of the park records of its employees?"

McCrory's mood brightened. "Might include Evans or Goodman or the others."

"Or introduce someone new," Gallo said, an impish grin on his face.

McCrory groaned.

CHAPTER 17

Detectives Gallo and McCrory opted to pursue the idea that one of their suspects lived in Hull and had worked at Paragon Park. AJ contacted the owner, Larry Stone, who agreed to meet them the following day at the administration office at 10:00 a.m.

When they arrived at the designated time and place, Stone was standing in front of the red brick admin structure with an older gal dressed in a black skirt and blouse, black stockings and shoes, a black wide-brimmed hat and glasses attached to her neck by a gold chain.

A great Halloween costume, Gallo thought—*or she really is a witch*?

Stone, slender, about six feet tall, wore a blue sweater, brown penny loafers and gray slacks. He shook hands with the detectives and introduced Myra O'Donnell, records/personnel clerk. She nodded, did not offer her hand.

Stone unlocked the building, entered, turned on the lights and led them to a small office at the end of a narrow corridor. A time clock and a board holding time cards was attached to the wall next to Myra's office.

She unlocked the door which opened into a windowless room furnished with a wooden desk, wooden swivel chair and four metal file cabinets. The walls were adorned with black and white photos reflecting a history of the park, some dated back to the 1930s; in one, older men with tool belts stood smiling in front of rides no longer part of the park's offerings.

One picture showed two dare-devils navigating the highest hill of the Giant Coaster, checking to make sure the track was safe. They wore t-shirts and Red Sox caps; no safety harness.

"We maintain employee records for five years for income tax purposes; the rest are shredded," O'Donnell said. "We have over thirty-per cent turnover each year. High school and college students seeking summer work fill many of our jobs as do travelling "carnies." Some return, others don't. Doesn't bother us. We have more applicants than openings. We retain names and phone numbers on file since a few ride operators also leave during the season."

"We'd like to see the logs and the wait list," Gallo said.

Myra retrieved a thick notebook and a thinner one from one of the metal cabinets and handed them to AJ.

"You can use a desk in my office to peruse them," Stone said.

Gallo thanked him and the men entered a room twice the size of O'Donnell's, with a window to the outside, though its view was of two-and-three story homes which had seen better days; a couple were boarding houses where park workers bunked.

A plaque honoring Stone's contributions to the Hull Chamber of Commerce adorned one wall alongside a picture of Stone with dignitaries neither Gallo nor McCrory recognized.

They pulled up chairs to a polished mahogany desk and rifled through the ledgers. AJ took the larger employee log and McCrory the wait list. Stone busied himself with paper-work that probably didn't need attention.

After an hour of scrutiny by the lawmen, neither book revealed the name of Bradley Evans, Johnny Goodman, Dustin Rose, Donald Berger or their other suspects. Discouraged, they returned the books to O'Donnell, thanked her and turned to leave when she said, "I have a photographic memory, by the way. If I wrote down the name of someone you're looking for, I will remember it."

Astonished, and irritated that good old Myra hadn't told them this at the beginning of their search, Gallo asked in a voice he hoped didn't reveal his irritation, "How about Bradley Evans or Johnny Goodman?"

She closed her eyes—as if she were a fortune-teller conjuring up long gone relatives for anxious loved ones—sat for a minute or two, then said, "Yes. I believe those boys worked here. Don't recall the years."

Gallo was ecstatic. He pushed his luck. "What about a Dustin Rose or Donald Berger?"

Myra went through her ritual again, shook her head. "No, I'm sure neither of them was employed here."

The lawmen thanked Stone and O'Donnell, left the offices and strolled into the sunlight.

"So?" McCrory asked.

"We know Evans and Goodman knew the park layout. Either could have led Rose and Berger into an ambush. Both were capable of making the shots that took them out."

As they hustled back to the MDC Building, McCrory recommended one more option to find out if their suspects lived in Hull as well as having worked there—voter registration lists.

Gallo agreed—he should have thought of that earlier—retrieved his cruiser and drove up Atlantic Avenue to the town hall. He parked in the semi-circular driveway in front. The façade of the red-brick building had massive white Doric columns supporting a short-peaked roof that offered minimal protection to those who entered in foul weather.

From the outside, the structure appeared to be two stories, but AJ knew a meeting room and basketball court were located above the windows. Christmas parties for the kids were often held there. A four-cornered clock—that never seemed to work—with a weather vane perched on top, capped the building's exterior.

There was no reception desk, although the Hull Police Department shared the building with other government agencies. Their office was to the left of the entry doors. Gallo stuck his head in, introduced himself and asked for the records clerk.

He was directed to the second floor.

The lawmen walked down the tiled hall to the stairs. As they did, McCrory stopped, shocked by Swastikas embedded in the floor tiles.

"What the hell, AJ?" he said, incredulous.

AJ, as a Hull kid, knew of the controversy surrounding the emblem. He explained, as town officials had, that the tile was put in the building long before the Nazi's appropriated the symbol. It was used for thousands of years before the Third Reich came into existence and stood for, among other things, "good luck." Despite a storm of protest during World War II, the town lacked the funds to have the flooring replaced.

McCrory shook his head, unconvinced. "Should have found some way to get rid of it."

"Shows how good intentions can be twisted into something bad," AJ said. "No problem until 'der Fuhrer' came along."

"You talking from personal experience?"

Gallo's good intention, as he saw it, was leaving Hull without telling his high school sweetheart that he had joined the Marines to spare her grief if he had been killed or wounded. They hadn't spoken or seen each other since. "Forget it, man. Just a thought."

McCrory fixed him with an inquisitive look, didn't pursue it.

They reached the second floor and found the records office three doors down on the right. Gallo knocked and a voice from inside bid them to come in. A portly man of about fifty, gray hair, glasses, stood as they entered. "Roy Hobbs," he said, extending his hand. He was dressed in a white shirt and tan pants, a red tie loosened at the collar.

Gallo introduced himself and McCrory and explained what they were after—the name Bradley Evans as a registered voter. Johnny Goodman lived in Cohasset. They dismissed him as a possible Hull resident.

Hobbs went to a file cabinet and extracted a folder labeled 1958. He scanned the list, found no Bradley Evans. "I've resided in Hull most of my life," he said, "and I don't remember a Bradley Evans. Of course, I don't know everyone."

He paused, then said, "Two Evans families are listed though. A Mr. and Mrs. Ralph Evans on Rockland Circle and a Mr. and Mrs. Stephan Evans on Valley Beach. They could be related to this person."

Gallo requested Hobbs jot down their addresses, thanked him for the help and left the office with McCrory. They clomped down the stairs, exited the building and returned to their car parked on the semi-circular drive in front. McCrory made no further comments about Swastikas.

Before they got in, McCrory asked, "What's this going to prove, AJ, if we do find he lived here? We know he worked at Paragon Park. Isn't that enough?"

"You think the 'supposed' photographic memory of an old woman is proof he was an employee? Without written evidence, we'd be laughed out of court if we offered what she said as a part of our case against him—if it ever came to that."

The Hingham detective scoffed. "We don't need proof. It's a lead to follow up. We can always ask Bradley himself. Wasn't something that came up when we met him."

"You think he'll tell us the truth?"

"We believed him before. Why would he lie now?"

"Let's just dot our i's and cross our t's, okay. Won't hurt to know for sure he lived here."

McCrory put his hands up in surrender and moved to grab the car door handle. Gallo stopped him. "Hey. Valley Beach is just across the street. Why don't we walk. Get a little exercise."

McCrory feigned being offended, stood sideways, sucked in his gut. "You saying I'm fat?"

AJ laughed. "A slender fellow like you. Nope. I like to walk or run every day. Keep fit."

McCrory raised his eyebrows and poked fun at his friend. "A slender fellow like you?"

They shared a laugh and jogged across Atlantic Ave to avoid the non-existent traffic. They found the Evans house about a block down at the corner of Maple Way and Valley Beach, a two-story grayish blue clapboard structure, storm windows, no shutters, no yard to speak of. Stairs, painted white and blue, rose to a first floor above a cement cellar.

Gallo took the stairs two at a time and rang the bell to the left of the door. After a moment or two, the door cracked open. A gray-haired man, late fifties to early sixties, about five-ten, wearing a Boston Bruins sweater with the logo on the front and the number 66 on the left sleeve, peered at the two detectives. Gallo pulled out his badge, held it up and introduced himself and McCrory.

The man sized up Gallo from head to toe, his facial expression registering surprise. He opened the door wider and stood aside. They emerged into a gray carpeted living room with a flowered blue and white couch and matching stuffed chairs. A woman, about the same age as the man, sat in one of the chairs, a cup of hot brew next to her on a mahogany end table. She did not get up when the men entered, but nodded and smiled.

Two nautical prints decorated one wall of the room. On the other, a watercolor of a Bruins player, number 66 on the back and sleeves of his jersey, raising his hands in victory after scoring a goal captured one's attention. "Our son," the man said, noticing Gallo admiring the painting. "Spent five years in the NHL."

"Impressive" Gallo said, eliciting a broad smile from the man. "Never had the coordination to play hockey on a team," he continued. "Skated on Damon pond up the road with a bunch of guys a few times—fell through the ice more than once."

The man chuckled, his midsection rising and falling. "Our son started there, played at Weymouth High and B.U before being drafted by the Bruins. Happiest day of his life and ours."

"Can imagine," Gallo said. "Not many make it that far."

The pleasantries out of the way, the man introduced himself. "I'm Stephan Evans, with a Ph," he emphasized. "This is my wife, Judith. Have a seat on the couch, for goodness' sake, and tell us how we can help the police. And excuse my rudeness," he added. "We don't get many visitors. Can we offer you anything to drink; water, coffee, tea, soda?" He sounded like an airplane stewardess.

Both lawmen declined and Gallo said, "We have a couple of questions sir, we hope you can assist us with."

"Of course."

"Do you know a Bradley Evans?"

The old man smiled, and despite a wary look, launched into a brief overview of the boy's youth. "Bradley. Yes. He's my nephew. My brother's son. Used to spend summers with us when he was a boy. Rode his bike all over town, went as far as the Village once or twice. Made a lot of friends. Worked at Paragon Park as a teenager."

He paused in his story to snatch a glance at his wife, who frowned, smoothed her dress and looked away.

"We lost touch when he graduated from high school, way out in Amherst," Evans continued. "Heard he joined the Marines. My brother and I don't talk much anymore, family issues. My fault as well as his."

His wife sighed and pursed her lips, obviously agreeing with the fault part of her husband's tale. Evans shook it off. "He in some kind of trouble?"

"No sir. We've just come from Paragon Park. Investigating the murder of the two men found there and are talking with anyone who may have known them—a Donald Berger and Dustin Rose," he lied.

"A murder in this town—unbelievable. Never heard of such a thing. It's quiet here in winter; beach area noisy in summer. Rowdy motorcycle gangs. A few fights is all," Evans said, shaking his head. "Can't say as I ever heard of those boys you mentioned. Read their names in the paper though."

"What about you Judith?" he asked his wife after a pause.

She shook her head.

Gallo and McCrory had what they needed. Brad Evans spent summers in Hull, rode his bike everywhere according to his uncle. He would know the town inside and out. Might seek refuge here if being pursued.

The two lawmen stood. Gallo thanked them for their help. Mrs. Evans smiled and her husband led them to the door. When they had gone, he gazed at his wife, grimaced and went to the phone on the wall in their kitchen. He dialed a business number, asked for his nephew. When he answered, Stephan made one brief comment: "The police are investigating you."

He hung up, not waiting for a reply.

Bradley Evans rubbed his chin, worried that his ploy to cut off the investigation of him for the Paragon Park murders had failed. He considered running, had nowhere to go and that would certainly cement his guilt. He fell back on his first thoughts. They had no evidence and no witnesses. They were only doing their "due diligence" questioning his aunt and uncle. He'd stay the course, unaware he had more to fear than the police.

Once back on the street after interviewing Mr. and Mrs. Evans and walking toward the town hall, Gallo said, "Okay. One more piece of the puzzle making Evans familiar with Hull and Paragon Park."

"And proving nothing," McCrory said, still skeptical of the importance of that information.

Gallo didn't comment as they again trotted across Atlantic Avenue on the way to their MDC cruiser. Traffic had picked up and they scooted to avoid cars coming both ways. Reaching the other side, McCrory dodged running headlong into an historical marker—a gray metal placard with the dates 1630 and 1930 flanking the name Hull at the top. It celebrated the three-hundredth anniversary of the town's official settlement by the Puritans and its origin as a fishing station inhabited by the Wampanoag Indians who called it Natascot.

Gallo walked by the sign many times on his way to Saint Mary's church as an altar boy and rarely took notice. Most Massachusetts natives, in towns along the coast from Boston, were familiar with such markers heralding the founding dates of their communities.

After reading the sign's inscription, McCrory poked fun at his counterpart. "AJ. You may be part Indian. Ever think of that?"

"No. But I might scalp you if you keep this up. Can we just focus on our case?"

"You have no sense of humor, pal."

CHAPTER 18

Back in the MDC Substation, AJ Gallo collapsed hard onto the wooden swivel chair behind the desk reserved for the sergeant in charge. With Wilkinson absent, Gallo was the man. He sat back, resisted the temptation to light a cigarette, and thought the investigation was moving in the right direction; not fast but moving.

They had confirmed that Bradley Evans and Johnny Goodman had worked at Paragon Park and that Evans had summered in the town as a kid. That alone proved nothing, as McCrory reminded him. Evans came forward and didn't offer either nugget but they didn't ask. And there was no update on the whereabouts of Goodman at Christmas.

Nevertheless, Gallo sensed that Bradley Evans had played them. He and McCrory were inexperienced, should have asked about Paragon Park and living in Hull. He worried he was blowing the investigation. In his mind another black mark against his Mets partner, Bill Wilkinson, who he disliked but whose experience would come in handy. Pride kept him from calling him and Captain Kellum and asking for help.

Frustrated, he snapped off the end of his pencil writing a note in his book. With no sharpener in sight, he rummaged through the desk drawers to find another pencil or pen. No luck, but he discovered a manila envelope at the bottom of the left-hand drawer with Wilkinson's name across the top. Curious, he peered inside hoping Bill had left some notes relevant to the murder investigation.

He slipped out the contents of the unsealed envelope. As he did so, a small folded paper with "Quincy Savings & Loan" written on it, fell on his lap. Since Wilkinson lived in Quincy, Anthony assumed it was a reminder to go to the bank.

When he further examined the envelope, he found some sheets of paper clipped together. He was stunned and glanced around expecting to be surprised by someone at any moment. He recognized the civil service test given to prospective lieutenants. AJ took a similar one for detective. This was the actual exam, not a study guide.

Confused and upset, he stuffed the exam back in the folder, returned it to its place in the drawer and lurched down the office stairs to the street. He sprinted across Nantasket Ave to the concrete walkway that paralleled the beach and stopped at a rusted iron railing. The low-slung white bath-house was on his left.

He stared out into the Atlantic and wrestled with the dilemma. A flock of gulls flew in formation a few feet about the water. Others pranced along the beach. A brisk breeze blew in carrying a refreshing mist from the breaking waves. The sea had soothed him since he was a child; its vastness comforting.

He needed that reassurance now confronted by his partner's dishonesty. Having a copy of the lieutenant's qualifying exam was a clear ethics violation, which he should report to their boss. He couldn't understand why Bill would do it. He had been a sergeant for many years, didn't need help to pass the test. So what if he had a leg up on other candidates? None of his business, didn't affect him. He ran back across the road, disappointed but determined to do his job.

As he walked back into the station, the desk officer gave him a note from Vince Russo. Johnny Goodman hadn't spent the entire holiday with the Cooper's. He went to his sister's a couple of days before Christmas to deliver presents for his niece and nephew, got stranded by the storm. He returned to the Cooper's two days later; sister and brother-in-law confirmed this. While info from relatives is always suspect, Gallo had no reason to discount their story.

That narrowed the list of suspects in the Paragon Park murders to Bradley Evans, Mitch Smith and the elusive Bobby Moran. They hadn't interviewed either Smith or Moran.

The drug discovery raised the possibility that unknown dealers could be in the mix. That, and the newfound knowledge that his Metro partner, Bill Wilkinson, was scamming the system, left Gallo reeling.

To clear his head, he drove his used 1949 Ford coupe on Nantasket Avenue to the end of the Hull peninsula, passing landmarks like Strawberry Hill with its distinctive water tower on top and the bayside playing fields with the Memorial School in the background.

At Pemberton Point, the recently opened high school now stood on the site of the once majestic Pemberton Hotel, a landmark during the town's heyday as a renowned tourist attraction. In the 1880s, the hotel was located near a steamboat landing and railroad station. Remnants of the pier still existed—the railroad tracks long gone.

You couldn't drive any farther through town or you'd wind up in Hull Gut, a narrow deep-water channel between Pemberton Point and Peddocks Island, an old military outpost.

Gallo parked on gravel facing the Gut. Winds sweeping through the area rocked his vehicle. He sat for five minutes debating whether to brave the gusts, when a woman standing on the shore attracted his attention. She wore a brown knee length wool coat with those barrel-type buttons down the front, her collar turned up and a multi-colored beany pulled down over her ears.

A shock reverberated through Gallo's body. It was Susan Lawrence, his high school sweetheart, the girl he'd left behind to join the Marines. He started the ignition to flee before she saw him, but flipped it off moments later.

He gripped the steering wheel, heart pounding, beads of sweat forming on his forehead—the fight or flight reaction. He couldn't avoid her forever now that he was back in town. Screwing up his courage, he grabbed his overcoat from the backseat, exited his car and shuffled down the small embankment to the waters' edge.

Lawrence, battling the wind, often forced backward on her heels, focused on skimming rocks over the water, didn't see him until he stood about five feet away. Startled, she pulled back before recognizing him. "AJ, is that you?" she exclaimed, not having seen him since graduation nine years earlier. He was a man now, an imposing figure.

He nodded searching for the right words. He chose, "Hi Susan. How've you been?" It sounded dopey even to him. He could imagine what she thought.

She studied his face for a minute or two, then replied. "I'm good. No complaints."

He didn't know if that was a rebuke or not, so he just said, "Glad to hear it."

She offered a tightlipped smile, and unsure whether to hug or not, settled for an awkward handshake. "When did you get back in town?" she asked, folding her arms across her chest—not a welcoming sign.

"I'm staying with my parents for now, working a case. I'm with the MDC Police."

"A cop?"

"Detective actually."

"You're involved in that murder at Paragon Park? That's awful. Makes one want to be sure to lock your doors at night."

"Always wise, even in Hull."

"True," she said. Then, flashing a look of disapproval, asked, "So, why are you here?

"Came to think."

"Great place to do that," she said, bent down and picked up a flattened rock and flung it into the raging current. It skipped several times before sinking.

"Nice throw," Anthony said.

She waved him off. "Been doing that as long as I can remember."

"It shows!"

"Are you flattering me?"

"Is it working?"

She smirked.

"I'll take that as a yes," AJ said. Then, not to be outdone, he chose to demonstrate his own prowess at skimming rocks

He grabbed one, turned it over in his huge hands, let it fly. To his dismay and embarrassment, the rock splashed and sank without so much as one flip.

He reddened. "Out of practice."

"Sure," Susan responded, a tight-lipped smile creasing her face.

AJ glanced at his watch. "Hey! Five o'clock. How about a beer?"

She shook her head. "I don't drink during the week. I teach third grade at the Memorial School. Lots of busy-bodies would be shocked to see a teacher drinking a night before teaching their little darlings."

"I doubt there will be any busy-bodies imbibing at a pub at this hour. And if there are, they wouldn't talk about it."

"Why not?"

"Because they'd have to explain why they were in a bar and not home caring for their "little darlings" as you called them."

She laughed.

The former sweethearts drove in AJ's car the short distance to Darcy's on Hull Bay. No one had raised concern about a gin-mill located close to the high school. And the bar was there first. The school didn't open until September, 1957, the bar in 1952.

At any rate, it was a curious place for a school.

Locals suspected the landowners greased the palms of the town's leaders to select this site at the tip of the peninsula. A more favorable location championed was the Hall Estate, a tree lined park at the beginning of town near the borders of Hingham and Cohasset. It was more accessible to visitors and sports teams and less susceptible to the ravages of flooding and damaging winds off the Atlantic. The excuse used for rejecting the estate was that the owners wanted their name on the school rather than the town's—Hall High instead of Hull High.

Gallo and Lawrence, Hingham High grads, gave little thought to the high school's location or name. They sat in the semi-darkness at Darcy's sipping their beers in silence.

Darcy's was located in the basement of the home of Jack and Josephine Darcy. Patrons were locals or enlisted men from the Point Allerton Coast Guard Station, a stones-throw away. Few outsiders, except during the summer months, opted to drive the length of the peninsula to buy a beer.

Others, taking the boat ride from Rowes Warf, in Boston, stopped in for a brew and caught the next commuter after enjoying a view of the bay and the sight of small outboard motor boats churning up the surf.

Nautical memorabilia covered the cramped walls of Darcy's Bar. Only two other people imbibed at this hour. Susan took off her beanie and let her auburn hair fall to her shoulders. Her pale skin had a reddish blush from the wind and cold outside, her green eyes, wide and inquisitive.

She appeared to be evaluating Gallo, perhaps trying to see the impressionable boy who courted her in high school, then disappeared leaving her heartbroken and imagining all sorts of calamities that may have befallen him..

He gawked.

"What?" She asked, noting his intent stare.

He fumbled for an appropriate response, not a fawning comment unlikely to be well received by this intelligent woman. He shook his head. "Remembering our school days, is all."

"A long time ago. You're a detective and a war hero. I'm a third-grade teacher struggling to keep little minds interested in learning."

AJ took a sip of beer, then said: "No hero. Just lucky."

"And modest too," Susan said, unwilling to allow him to downplay his bravery. Even in school, he never touted his athletic prowess.

AJ worked up the courage to take advantage of this reunion of sorts. "I always admired you."

She didn't let him off the hook. "Not enough to look me up after Korea," she said, a bitter edge to her voice, scolding, reproachful. "No note. No call. No letter. You left without a word, disrespecting our history—disrespecting me."

AJ sat back as if slapped. He deserved the barb. He had shown callous disregard for their relationship even if they were just kids. He couldn't explain it to himself, let alone someone else—least of all the girl he once loved. Still did.

He gave a weak rejoinder. "There hasn't been anyone since you, Susan. Korea messed me up. Trying to find my way, I guess. Can I make it up to you?"

She shook her head, her hair swirling left and right, at once covering her eyes, then revealing them again, as if playing hide-and-seek. She crossed her arms and answered his question. "Don't think so. Been a long time. We've both moved on. At least I have."

The comment cut him to the quick but he had no suitable response.

She got up, struggled into her wool coat, pulled her beanie down over her ears, thanked him for the drink, told him she preferred to walk back to her house and left.

Susan's abrupt departure and rejection stunned him. His hope for a reconciliation dashed, though their meeting was not planned.

To settle down, he set aside his beer and ordered a Johnnie Walker Red. He downed the Scotch, the pleasant warming sensation engulfing him as he signaled for another. After finishing the second, he called for the check and leaned back in his chair more confused than ever about his feelings for Susan and his partner, Bill Wilkinson.

Coming to Pemberton Point to clear his head had been a colossal bust.

Ambivalent about whether to trust Wilkinson—the discovery that his senior partner possessed a purloined copy of the lieutenant's exam—further undermined his confidence in the man and magnified the fact that the investigation appeared stalled. Their inquiries uncovered no solid suspects other than Bradley Evans, who came forward of his own accord. Not the behavior of a guilty man.

But perhaps a cunning one.

He reached into the inside pocket of his jacket and pulled out the notebook taken from Dustin Rose's room. Of the four men on the list he compiled, two had been interviewed: Evans and Jerry Morris. Mitch Smith and Bobby Moran remained. He had a handle on Smith because of Morris' confession but Moran was a mystery.

Also, under the names, he had scribbled the word cocaine with two questions: Who supplied it? Could drugs be the motive for the murders?

Now, sitting in Darcy's, he added "missing car" to his notes. Rose had car keys in his pocket, yet none turned up near Paragon Park after the murders, at least none reported. Rose's assailant didn't take it; not without the means to drive it. Did the killer escape on foot or did he have his own vehicle as they suspected? If he did either, what happened to the car driven by the victims?

That gnawed at him.

So, with two more people to interview and a lost vehicle to track down, his mood improved, though his meeting with Susan was still troubling. As naïve high school sweethearts, they made plans for after graduation. Both considered college. He received scholarship offers in football from Boston College and Syracuse. She would attend Bridgewater State. They would eventually marry.

Then, he destroyed those ideas and sabotaged their relationship, opted for the Marines—left without talking with her. Even now he couldn't explain that. Once, he told himself that if killed or wounded, he didn't want her dealing with that. Even as he thought it, he realized it was lame. Deep down, he knew why he made that decision. Had always known.

It had nothing to do with Susan and everything to do with a cowardly act by a teenager on a deserted road.

Susan Lawrence left Darcy's walking home, pummeled by the wind and stung by the cold, her eyes watering. She pulled her beanie tighter over her ears and put up the collar of her coat.

The meeting with AJ upset her; surfaced memories long suppressed. Why had he showed up now? Why couldn't he just leave her alone? Their encounter had been unplanned, but it still riled her. What did he want? What did she want? She was dating a wonderful man, a fellow teacher. They were mature adults. Would probably marry.

That's what she wanted. AJ was a chapter in her life now closed. She wouldn't open it again.

Sometimes decisions like this can't be kept.

CHAPTER 19

The Monday after his interlude with Susan at Darcy's Bar, Gallo asked the desk sergeant about any cars towed from the beach area during the winter. The grizzled officer, a burly man with greying hair and puggy fingers, plunked an enormous three ring binder on the counter and paged through, stopping after four pages.

"Yeah! Middle of March, when the snow melted. If memory serves, our guys found a car parked near the bathroom building in the parking lot, doors locked preventing access. They ordered it towed to Neal's Service Station at the corner of Atlantic Ave and Nantasket Ave. They obtained a receipt from the station owner, Haig Neal, and noted the Massachusetts plate, 46435. The receipt and license number are attached to this page."

Gallo's face reddened, his fists opened and closed, neck muscles bulged. "Unbelievable," he bristled. "No one thought to notify me or Sergeant Wilkinson?" About to explode, he ratcheted down his temper by taking deep breaths—no sense directing his anger at someone else. He should have followed up on the missing vehicle earlier.

The sergeant recoiled, face flushed, fearful the giant detective would pummel him. "We got the station's number on file," he said. Hands shaking, he retrieved a small green covered book from a shelf below the counter, opened it, and pointed.

Gallo pulled the desk phone to him and dialed. Robert McNamara, co-owner of Neal's, answered. "This is Mac. How can I help you?"

"Sir, this is Detective Anthony Gallo of the MDC Police. Do you still have a car on your property dropped off sometime in March, License 46435."

"Three cars are still here. Let me check my records."

McNamara came back on the line after a brief pause. "Yup. Car's here. Belongs to the guy shot during that robbery in Hingham. Heard he was in a coma. Haig and I held off trying to reach him. And no family member called us. Things were hectic in the storms. We didn't follow up. Is he asking about the car? Newspaper said he just recovered from his wounds."

"No sir. He hasn't asked, to my knowledge. I'm investigating the shootings in Paragon Park. I suspect the men who robbed that station in Hingham and the two killed at the park, drove it."

"Wow," McNamara, exclaimed sounding like a kid who discovered a bike under the Christmas tree. "Why do you believe that?"

"Can't go into that right now, sir. I'd like to come to your place and search the vehicle. I should be there in about ten or fifteen minutes."

"Come ahead."

Gallo thought about notifying his partner, Sergeant Wilkinson, of this development, instead called Hingham Detective McCrory, who agreed to meet him at Neal's but couldn't get there for another hour or so. Gallo notified McNamara he would be delayed getting there.

An hour later, Gallo waited in front of Neal's Mobile Station with co-owner, McNamara, to await McCrory who drove up in an unmarked police cruiser. He turned off Nantasket Ave and stopped near the two closed service bays. He exited his car, introduced himself to the older man and shook hands.

McNamara, a short stocky man, wore a brown hooded jacket with the Mobile label over the left breast pocket. He led the detectives around the right side of the station and stood beside a two door 1953 Chrysler DeSoto.

"This is it," he said.

"Open it for us, please," Gallo asked.

"It's locked."

"No doubt. I'm sure you can access it."

"Shouldn't we call the owner first? Get permission?"

"This is a murder investigation sir. We're authorizing you to open the car door."

McNamara dipped his head, went back to his office and came out with a thin metal wire with a loop on the end. He forced it through the seam between the door and frame, encircled the lock button and jerked it upward. Once it opened, he stepped away.

"Thank you, sir," AJ said, and offered a Cheshire Cat grin. "We'll take possession now and contact the owner after we complete our search."

"The guy owes us a storage fee," McNamara said, a sheepish look on his face. "But since we didn't call him, because of the, uh situation, I'm sure we can work something out."

"Sounds fair. Detective McCrory and I will talk to him. Shouldn't be a problem."

McNamara, satisfied, left as a car pulled up to one of the pumps.

AJ opened the driver's door and leaned in when McCrory grabbed him by the shoulder. "Do you have rubber gloves?"

"No, should I," AJ answered, feeling foolish, knowing the answer.

"If you don't want to contaminate everything."

"Crime scene investigation 101, huh?"

"Yup. Use mine. We don't need both of us rummaging around in tight quarters."

AJ took the gloves and searched the glove box, felt under the passenger seat, then did the same for the other side when he touched something. Leaning down to examine it, he screwed his head to the side, reached in and pulled out a gray, linen bread bag secured with a cloth tie at the top. He untied it, discovered a white substance and held it open for McCrory who eyeballed it.

"Possibly cocaine," McCrory said. "But I'm no expert. In fact, I don't know squat. Not much drug activity in Hingham. We're a white-collar town, for the most part, conservative."

AJ stuck his finger inside the bag and sampled it. "Coke all right. I'll send it to our Boston lab to confirm."

McCrory stared at him, questioning. "How can you be so certain?"

AJ could see the wheels spinning in McCrory's mind. "Let me tell you a story. Take the stuff and walk over to my car. I don't want anyone to overhear us."

Once ensconced in the MDC cruiser, AJ asked. "You serve in Korea?"

"Nope. Joined the army reserve, spent time at Fort Devens, up north in Shirley. Never got out of the state."

"Okay. I'm going to give you a brief history lesson. Bear with me. Some of it I learned from a Navy doctor on Okinawa where I recuperated from my wounds. Some I picked-up first-hand in combat and recovering from a drug addiction."

McCrory raised his eyebrows and shifted in his seat. "You were an addict?"

"Just listen, please."

McCrory's face reddened, like a schoolboy being scolded.

"The doctor filled me in about the record of drugs in the military. He saw too many guys in Korea like me. He accessed some classified documents in the War Department, never revealed how and I didn't ask. He discovered that as far back as the Civil War soldiers got high on opium and morphine. And in the so-called Great War, French and German pilots used coke as a stimulant. The British even issued a medicine to the troops labeled "Forced March" containing cocaine, which they hyped as a "miracle drug" to offset combat fatigue and to encourage fearlessness in the trenches. Other medicines they handed out contained coke and heroin."

McCrory's face contorted in shock as if learning for the first time there was no Santa Claus. "Jesus. That's horrible. I never heard about this. How did that affect you?"

"Have patience. I'll get to it."

"Sorry."

"In World War II, the Germans developed "Pervitin," an amphetamine that stimulates both the central nervous system and chemicals in the brain. The pills energized the soldiers, increased alertness and, for many, gave them a mindset of invincibility. Think blitz Krieg."

McCrory, ready to interrupt, was waived off.

"Not to be outdone," AJ continued, "Great Britain and the U.S. distributed Benzedrine pills (bennies) first to bomber crews then to the infantry to stave off sleepiness."

McCrory's eyes riveted on Gallo.

"In Korea, our government issued us Benzedrine to help us stay alert for long hours. They distributed millions of pills. Some creative grunts mixed bennies and heroin they dubbed 'speed balls,' which produced an intense high; the cold disappeared; the danger forgotten. Helped many of us endure the misery of Korea."

"Unbelievable," McCrory exclaimed, his expression animated.

"Just before the Chosin Reservoir battle, I began speed-balling. I don't remember much about the attack. I was wounded and medevacked out on a tank; corpsman gave me morphine to ease the pain. That, coupled with my speed-balling, pushed me over the edge.

I was sent to Camp Hansen on Okinawa to detox. I begged for morphine which kept me high until the Navy doctor recognized what I was doing. He made me tough out the pain without drugs and brought in a psychologist to work with me."

"Jesus."

"None of this is on my military record, of course, because our government got me, and thousands of others hooked in the first place."

"Never heard about any of this," McCrory said, again.

"And you never will."

"Why are you telling me now?"

AJ twisted his mouth into an awkward grin. "Two reasons. I can tell you read about my wartime exploits, the Navy Cross, Silver Stars. I'm no hero. Most of what I did is a blur."

McCrory kept silent.

"And second, I saw your expression when I tasted the white stuff and identified it as coke. You thought I must be an addict."

"Didn't know what to think. Thought you learned about and sampled drugs in your police training or something."

AJ laughed. "Did you?"

McCrory dipped his head. "No."

"My reason for the little history lesson. Didn't want that in the back of your mind. I've been clean since my rehab."

"Thanks. I appreciate you opening up. Does Wilkinson know?"

"No one in the department does. My military record is spotless. I'm a hero."

"You are in my book," McCrory stated unequivocally. "Nobody does what you did because of drugs alone."

AJ didn't argue. It would be futile.

Gallo assessed the evidence they now had as they sat in the Mets cruiser.

"A lot of coke in that bag. More than enough for two men."

"Think they were dealing?"

"Most likely. And the next question is, who supplied it?"

"You got an idea?"

"Perhaps. Heard the Irish Mafia in Somerville is peddling drugs now among other things. We've got some people eyeballing them; undercover stuff. Very dangerous. You don't want to get sideways with those boys."

McCrory, still reeling from Gallo's report on his drug use, was confused. "You're thinking the murders of Rose and Berger were a gang hit, a drug deal gone bad?"

"I'm speculating. I don't see Berger and Rose as big-time criminals. This whole notion might be way off. How would they have a link to the Mafia or anyone else who pushes drugs?"

"So, who supplied them?"

Gallo's expression turned thoughtful. "Maybe no one. Maybe they just took it? Maybe the stuff was in the gas station safe along with the cash receipts. Someone was dealing out of the station which gets a lot of traffic. People coming and going at all hours wouldn't raise suspicions. We need to go back and squeeze that pump-jockey, Jerry Morris. He knows more than he admitted. And that would mean Mr. Morris is involved in this up to his eye-teeth."

McCrory smiled. "Let's go talk to the weasel."

They caught the "weasel," as McCrory referred to him, stepping out on his front lawn to fetch his newspaper. They convinced him it served his best interest to accompany them back to the Hingham Police Station for a friendly chat.

In the interview room, Morris flicked his eyes from side to side. Sweat droplets formed on his forehead, his right leg pumped up and down like a piston. He constantly rubbed his hands, resting on the table.

"Jerry," McCrory said. "New information has come to our attention about the night of the robbery. Can you go over the details again?"

"Sure! Sure!" Morris stammered as he retold the story of that night.

"Well, Jerry," Gallo said, "that doesn't jibe with evidence we recovered from your car."

"My car? You found it? Where?"

"Doesn't matter now," Gallo said, annoyed. "What does is what we discovered in the car?"

Morris wiped his forehead and scrunched his face as if he had bitten into a lemon. "What? What did you find?"

"A bag containing cocaine. Quite a bit. Enough for distribution. Possession of drugs and selling them, Jerry, is a felony. You're looking at hard time, my friend."

"Me? It's not mine. I swear."

McCrory jumped in. "It was in the safe at the station along with the money you stashed there, wasn't it?"

Morris bowed his head. His leg bounced with greater gusto. "Belongs to Mitch Smith. He sells cocaine to cash customers. I couldn't do anything about it. He's the boss's son, for Christ's sake. Threatened to get me fired if I snitched. I was scared a' him. Still am."

"Who supplied Smith?"

"I never asked, but he hinted he worked for a gang. Mafia types."

"So, Berger and Rose took the coke when they snatched the money during the robbery?"

"Guess so. I was in a coma for months, ya know. But I suspected they did because you guys didn't ask me about it the first time you talked to me."

"And you didn't volunteer that information."

Morris teared up, didn't respond.

"Have you spoken to Smith?" AJ probed.

Morris dropped his eyes to the table, his face a mask of fear. "I called him after you left my house. Told him you didn't mention drugs. Told him I thought the bag might still be in the car. But with Donald and Dustin dead, I didn't know where that could be."

"We're going to step outside for a few minutes, Jerry. Sit tight."

In the hall, McCrory advocated not arresting Morris now. With him in custody, Smith would guess he spilled his guts and take off.

"Can we trust Morris to keep his mouth shut if we release him?"

"Prison terrifies him. He'll button his lip long enough for us to track down Smith."

"Good. Let's go in and tell your friend, "the weasel," he's free for now. And might stay that way if he continues to cooperate."

McCrory laughed. "My friend, huh?"

McCrory drove from the HPD, after being dropped off by Gallo, to the "Ye Olde Mill Grille" in Hingham Harbor. Like many New England buildings, the Grille dated back to 1643 when it was the town grain mill. The no frills restaurant had a bar by the front door and padded booth seats on both sides extending to the rear. McCrory took a window seat midway down the aisle.

Not much of a drinker, he needed one now. Gallo's history lesson about drugs in the military, and his use in Korea, shocked the young detective. His idea of combat was garnered from old World War II and Korea newsreels shown between feature films at Loring Hall. He marveled at the bravery of the soldiers and Marines, knew nothing of their personal struggles with cocaine and amphetamines, provided by our government no less. He felt like a naïve bumpkin.

The story didn't dissuade him from idolizing Gallo, his hero since high school. His admiration for the man only increased. Gallo put his life on the line and received shoddy treatment from the country he had sworn to defend. He was prouder to work by his side now than he had ever been.

He shared with his girlfriend Ruth, his high school sweetheart, stories about working with Gallo. She, too, was impressed. As classmates, they had cheered Gallo as he led the Hingham Harbormen to the league football title.

He and Ruth were engaged and planned to marry when both earned enough money to get their own place. But they weren't close. She worked as a sales clerk in Talbots clothing in Hingham—known as the little store with the bright red door. Her salary was meager. They were saving, but their goal was still elusive. McCrory wouldn't consider marriage until he felt financially secure—a bone of contention between them.

Another irritant, was that they lived with their parents, in the room they had occupied since childhood. McCrory's father was an Episcopal minister; his mother the church secretary. Having Ruth stay the night was out of the question.

The same held true for Ruth. Her father managed a dry-goods store in Quincy; her mother stayed at home. Though they weren't particularly religious, their views on couples living together before marriage mirrored the mores of the day. They wouldn't hear of it.

McCrory's reverie was interrupted by a forty-something waitress in a too short skirt and a soiled apron. She took his order as if he were interrupting her day. He asked for a bottled Schlitz beer, no glass, and a hamburger with French fries.

As he waited for his food, he reflected on the case he and Gallo were investigating; a gas station robbery turned double murder. Crime in Hingham was low and the likelihood of his working a homicide almost nil. It was both thrilling and frustrating. The murders of Berger and Rose unraveled who committed the robbery, but the investigation of their deaths was convoluted, going off in several different directions. Now drugs were involved and possibly Mafia gang types.

When the waitress appeared with his beer, he took a long swig from the bottle. He shook his head and wondered what would come next.

He didn't anticipate more killings—not in his quiet town.

CHAPTER 20

Afrer interviewing Jerry Morris and dropping McCrory off at the HPD, Gallo returned to the Nantasket MDC Substation. He planned to review the information they now had about the Paragon Park murders. The picture was more muddled than when they thought they were dealing with the murder of two gas station robbers. The presence of drugs in the systems of both Berger and Rose and the discovery of the bag of coke in Morris' car, opened up more possibilities.

His puzzlement was short-lived. As he entered the stationhouse, the desk officer notified him Captain Kellum had called. He was expected to return it ASAP. His gut churned. A call from the Chief of Detectives was rare and unnerving.

He climbed the stairs to his office, legs heavy. He sat for a few moments collecting himself, then dialed Kellum's direct number.

"Kellum here," the Captain answered, his jovial voice reverberated over the airways.

"Sir. Detective Gallo reporting as ordered," he said, sounding like a Marine boot instead of a lawman.

Kellum smirked. "Gallo, you're not in the military anymore, relax."

"Yes, sir," Gallo said, unable to shake old habits.

"Listen, AJ, I've considered the request of a reporter from the Quincy Ledger to write a human-interest piece about you and the Mets—good PR for you and the department. What do you think? You up for it?"

Gallo's stomach flipped. He didn't want publicity for himself, given his tenuous relationship with his partner, Bill Wilkinson. Averse to the spotlight, he threw the decision back to the boss to lessen Wilkinson's anger when he found out. "I'll do whatever you think is best, sir."

Kellum had made up his mind. "OK. I'll set it up with one ground rule. I'll need to be present during the interview."

Gallo, still skeptical, responded as expected and not above a little flattery. "You know best, sir."

Kellum recognized the fawning, didn't care. "All right. I'll schedule it for the next day or two in Nantasket."

He clicked off without waiting for a response.

After the dispiriting call from Captain Kellum, Gallo left the office and drove to his parent's house in the Kenberma section of Hull, the lowest geographical part of the town sandwiched between the Atlantic and Hull Bay.

Many summer cottages, now empty, dotted the area. Though he shared an apartment in East Boston with two other Mets officers, he thought it best to stay locally while working on the Paragon Park case.

His mother, like mothers everywhere whose sons no longer lived at home, preserved his room as a shrine to his youth. The walls were covered by school banners and awards heralding his high school athletic achievements. A framed display of his military medals competed for wall space.

The exhibits elicited opposite responses in AJ. Pride when he envisioned himself racing past would be tacklers on the football field and sadness when visualizing his buddies eviscerated by gunfire in combat. In nightmares, he felt the sting of bullets ripping through his own body and often awoke from a sound sleep, awash in sweat and imagined pain.

The top of a small roll-up desk, his father purchased at a bankruptcy sale, displayed a photo of AJ in his letterman's jacket and Susan in her cheerleader regalia. The picture, intended to make him feel welcome, stirred feelings of loss and regret, which he didn't confess to his mother, who meant well.

Another reason he didn't visit much.

He lay on his bed staring at the ceiling unable to sleep. The aroma of the lasagna dinner his mother had prepared still lingered and wafted into his room. Memories of his youth flashed, plates piled high with spaghetti, and meatballs as big as a fist. That, and the photo on the desk, took him back to the time he dated Susan.

They had been boyfriend and girlfriend, not lovers. As Catholics, they didn't cross the line, but experimented with everything short of intercourse. AJ, humiliated, confessed impure thoughts to his priest, skipped the details. He never asked Susan how she handled it.

His drink with Susan at Darcy's saddened him. She told him she had moved on, not interested in pursuing their former relationship. Mired in the murder investigation, he doubted he could do anything about that now—but wanted to. With reflections of Susan intermingled with those of the murders, he got little sleep that night.

The next day, the smell of bacon frying and coffee brewing welcomed him as he rolled out of bed. He had vowed to concentrate on his job, but wondered if he could. His resolve during Lent to refrain from intimacy with Susan when they were high schoolers never worked. He longed for that affection now.

After breakfast, he put on a pair of Marine sweats and Converse tennis shoes, and sprinted along the beach to Allerton Hill and back—about a mile—a practice he had employed to keep himself in shape for sports in high school.

His physical fitness and athletic prowess enabled him to fly over the obstacle course at Parris Island in recruit training and finish at the head of the pack on the morning five mile runs. It also helped him heft his .50 caliber machine gun over the granite hills of South Korea.

Thoughts of these experiences flashed through his mind as he pumped his legs along the beach, leaving footprints in the moist sand; his forehead dotted with sweat, his running suit saturated.

When finished, he stripped to his shorts and plunged into the frigid Atlantic, feelings for Susan Lawrence pushed aside for the moment.

CHAPTER 21

When he got to the MDC Building at 9:00 a.m., Gallo climbed the stairs to the small office. Bill Wilkinson sat behind the desk, a manila envelope laying on the desktop in front of him. AJ knew it contained a copy of the upcoming lieutenant's exam Wilkinson would take in two days.

The sergeant made no comment on the test, instead directed a question to Gallo about the investigation. Gallo gave him an update on their progress to date, filled him in on the discovery of cocaine in the car used by the victims and their suspicion, confirmed by the gas station attendant, that Mitch Smith, son of the owner, supplied the drug. And he got it from a gang—possibly the Irish Mafia.

He and McCrory intended to interview Smith today. He emphasized they had no concrete proof to tie him to the drugs, only the word, shaky at best, of Jerry Morris, the station employee.

"You don't believe Morris?"

"Oh, we believe him, all right. It's doubtful a jury would. He'll fold like an accordion under questioning from a defense attorney."

Wilkinson smiled at the reference to the musical instrument that no one played anymore except on variety shows like Ed Sullivan. He said: "I'd like to accompany you boys to talk with Smith."

AJ, surprised, had no choice but to acquiesce. "Yes, sir. It's your case as well as mine."

"You've done a remarkable job, Anthony, and you may have to continue to carry the load. This will help me get a better picture of how things are going. I've been preoccupied by the lieutenant's exam coming up."

AJ blanched at Wilkinson's reference to the exam, made no comment. "Understandable sir," he said. "I'll call Detective McCrory and tell him we're on the way to pick him up."

"Let's do it," Wilkinson said, sounding more enthusiastic than he was. Smith's involvement with the Irish Mafia, possibly selling coke, would complicate Captain Kellum's robbery plans and undermine his own ambitions to advance through the ranks.

Blinded by those aspirations, he didn't imagine his life might be in danger.

Mitch Smith lived on Sherwood Road, Hingham, in a one-story, white clapboard house with black shutters flanking the windows, not far from the country club where his father was part owner. His dad also owned the house where Mitch resided, a circumstance Mitch resented, but could do nothing about given his wretched finances; a result of his out-of-control gambling.

The three detectives pulled into the driveway of Smith's home where a bright red 1954 Buick Skylark rested in front of a detached garage. They admired the car as they exited their government issue Plymouth cruiser. McCrory had called Smith ahead of this visit and apprised him about their quest to learn more about the gas station heist.

Wilkinson let the other men take the lead as he studied Smith's reaction. Still standing, McCrory opened the interview. "Thanks for your willingness to answer some questions, Mitch."

Not impressed by McCrory's effort to make him relax, Smith wrapped his arms across his chest and retorted, "Did I have a choice?"

McCrory ignored the hostility in Smith's tone and asked to sit down. They were in an expansive parlor with two couches, three matching chairs and a dormant brick fireplace. Smith, clearly annoyed, waved the men to the couches and sat opposite them. He didn't offer anything to eat or drink.

"So, how can I help you?" he asked, facing McCrory. His body language reflecting a less than helpful attitude—arms crossed, jaw set, eyes darting around the room.

"We've come across some disturbing evidence, Mitch."

"What evidence?"

"A pouch of cocaine in the car driven by the robbers, Dustin Rose and Donald Berger. The autopsy showed they ingested the drug at some point and were frequent users."

"Nothing to do with me. I don't even know those guys."

McCrory shook his head. "Rose's family said he hung out with you from time to time."

"Don't remember doing that."

McCrory switched tactics. "Jerry Morris says the stuff is yours."

"That weasel would say anything to save his ass."

Gallo and McCrory glanced at each other with Smith's use of the term 'weasel' to describe Morris.

Gallo stifled a laugh he disguised as a cough.

Silent till now, Wilkinson broke into the conversation. "Do you know a man named Bobby Moran?"

Smith said no, blinking and looking away. A mannerism recognized as a "tell" for people lying.

Gallo and McCrory were dumbfounded when Wilkinson mentioned Moran and confused when he didn't pursue that line of questioning.

They were startled when the Mets sergeant stood up and terminated the interview. "Thank you for your cooperation, Mr. Smith," he said, and retreated toward the door.

Blindsided, and with no other choice, the two detectives followed him out.

Once outside, AJ challenged his partner about the abrupt ending of their probe. "Bill," he said, a hard edge to his voice. "We were just starting to question the guy."

Wilkinson dismissed his concern. "We've got no evidence linking him to the drug. Can't even get a search warrant of his home based on a flimsy connection to the gas station safe and the testimony of an unreliable witness."

They couldn't dispute Wilkinson's reasoning, yet both wanted to squeeze Smith about his knowledge of this Moran character. They had his name but no idea who he was. Smith gave a hinky response when asked if he knew the man. And it was clear he lied about not knowing

Dustin Rose. The Rose family named him as someone who palled around with their brother.

Gallo, uneasy about Wilkinson's behavior, had nothing to put his finger on. And Wilkinson interrupted his thoughts as they drove back to the Hingham Police Station to drop off McCrory. "Not sure this drug angle is going anywhere," he said.

McCrory caught Gallo's eye and raised his brows. He wondered if Wilkinson was trying to steer the investigation in another direction? If so. Why?

Wilkinson, noticing the silent exchange between Gallo and McCrory, gazed out the window to hide his embarrassment. He rationalized accepting the copy of the lieutenant's exam with the knowledge other officers in the department had done worse. Some accepted bribes by mobsters to lose evidence or not show up for court so cases would be dismissed. Others submitted fraudulent slips for overtime shifts not worked or solicited sex from prostitutes in return for not busting them.

The examples were endless.

Wilkinson convinced himself his transgression was minor compared to those. But the upcoming bank robbery would put him in the company of those most corrupt. And undermining his rookie partner was unconscionable. He was caught between the proverbial "rock and a hard place."

When he sought help, it was too late.

CHAPTER 22

Bill Wilkinson passed the lieutenant's exam as expected. His boss, Captain Kellum, wished he hadn't received such a high score though, which sometimes drew scrutiny from internal affairs.

Wilkinson sat in Kellum's office at Mets Headquarters basking in the unwarranted glow of his success. Kellum, more interested in the report of the investigation of the Paragon Park murders and the dangerous direction it was taking under young Gallo, opted not to pop his balloon

"So, Gallo found cocaine in the getaway car? And the autopsy revealed traces in the bodies of the two men murdered?"

"Yes, sir."

"How did Smith's name come up?"

"The gas station attendant confessed that Smith kept the drugs in their safe with the daily receipts. He hinted Smith got the supply from the Irish Mafia. That he was their dealer on the South Shore."

That revelation shocked Kellum. He opened the right-hand drawer of his desk, took out his flask of whisky and drained two long belts to calm his nerves. He didn't offer Wilkinson a swig.

One he regained his composure, the Captain asked, "And Gallo and this Hingham detective confronted Smith?"

"Yes, sir. I joined them. Smith stonewalled us and I steered the inquiry away from the drug angle."

"Good thinking. Will Gallo back off?"

"Too early to tell."

"Dammit Bill, this threatens our plans."

"Do you want me to take a more direct involvement in the investigation, sir?"

Kellum lit a cigarette, leaned back in his chair and spun it to survey the Boston skyline. He took several drags on the Chesterfield as smoke crowned his head. When he swiveled back, he answered Wilkinson's question. "Not yet. But order the kid to give you written daily reports and send copies to me. We're moving forward with the Quincy Plan and I don't want any hiccups."

Wilkinson nodded, stood up and retreated from the office. The glow of having nailed the lieutenant's exam dimmed by the minute. He longed for a Camel.

As soon as Wilkinson left, Captain Kellum dialed the number of his contact with the Irish hoodlums. He gave the man a stilted account of their investigation into the Paragon Park murders and the connection made to Mitch Smith.

Kellum did not offer much detail, keeping his conversation brief. A department phone call could be overheard by staff, either by mistake or by design. Kellam hadn't risen to his position by being careless.

He put the receiver down, lit another cigarette, got up from his desk and scanned the Boston skyline as he did several times a day. He marveled at the sight of the Customs House, with its 496-foot tower, the tallest building in the city.

He tried to forget his information may have been a death sentence for Mitch Smith. He opted to concentrate on something he expected to be a positive for himself and the department.

He dialed up Bert Jones, the Patriot Ledger reporter, and arranged an interview with himself and Gallo two days hence.

Gallo was peeved. The interview with the news-hound would stall his movement on the murder case and he was still reluctant to bring attention to himself. Wilkinson would resent it and other men in his squad might regard it as grandstanding. No choice though. Captain Kellum wouldn't listen to any excuses. Gallo expected a disaster in the making.

He was wrong.

Jones had interviewed five former classmates of Gallo's at Hingham High, talked with teachers and coaches and even the principal. He maneuvered through the Marine Corps bureaucracy and found two men in Gallo's company in Korea. He tried to contact a couple of Mets detectives, but they begged off, fearful of incurring the wrath of Kellum if they said the wrong thing. Wilkinson kept his remarks brief and focused on the case, not revealing specific details.

Without exception, Gallo's teachers and coaches praised him. To teachers, he was a quiet, respectful, studious boy. His football coach believed he had the potential to be a star in college. His Marine buddies said Gallo's heroism saved their lives on more than one occasion and the lives of men in their entire unit.

No one had anything negative to say about him.

Jones weaved most of these statements, and those of Kellum, into the profile. A Ledger photographer took photos of the Captain and Gallo separately, and a few of them together, one inside the Nantasket Stationhouse with Kellum standing on two stairs so Gallo wouldn't dwarf him.

Wilkinson was not in the pictures. Gallo was supportive of Hingham Detective McCrory, but Jones omitted his observations in his article, preferring to keep the spotlight on Gallo and the Mets. He praised the over-all leadership of Captain Kellum aware that the story would not have been published without his support.

While the Ledger would ordinarily have placed the piece in its Lifestyle or Entertainment sections, because it highlighted a local hero working on a murder case, they carried it on the front page. And to Bert Jones' delight, the Boston Globe and Boston Herald, with permission, picked up the story and published it under South Shore News.

Captain Kellum was delighted. The Gallo profile, despite the best efforts of Jones to limit them, included more quotes from him— Kellum—than the true subject. It also painted the MDC Police in a positive light, which brought kudos from the superintendent.

Kellum was riding high, more confident than ever that the Quincy robbery would go off without a hitch and his role never discovered.

He should have known better.

CHAPTER 23

The Hingham telephone directory, like all phone books, listed people alphabetically including their addresses. The stalker searched for a Bradley Evans, located his name and address, and pinpointed it on a Triple A road map.

He staked out the house for three straight days and noted Evans was a creature of habit—breakfast at Pages Diner, then a short drive to the train station to leave his car and board a north bound commuter toward Boston. The man didn't follow him once he boarded, didn't care about his destination.

He planned to intercept him in town.

The stalker eyed the diner from his position across the street, smiled as his prey left the restaurant, got into his car and drove to the downtown train station, parking in his usual place on Fearing Road across from the stately Saint Paul's Catholic Church.

Bradley Evans was distracted and unnerved by the call from his uncle that the police were delving into his background; perhaps reconsidering him as a suspect in the Paragon Park murders; sweat formed on his brow.

Oblivious to his surroundings, he grabbed his briefcase from the backseat, locked his door, gave a perfunctory glance both ways for traffic, then stepped off the curb. As he did so, a car double parked at the corner of Fearing and North Streets, accelerated toward him.

Evans, paralyzed by fear, didn't move as the speeding auto caught him flush, throwing him over the right side of the hood and onto the pavement. His head cracked on the asphalt, blood spewing from his nose and mouth, his left arm twisted at an unorthodox angle. His briefcase spiraling several feet in the air and flattened under the tires of an oncoming town maintenance truck. The driver slammed on his breaks and gaped at the prone body sprawled in the street.

The car that mowed Evans down did not slow as it fish-tailed up Main Street, tires screeching and sped away. A seventy-year-old woman descending the steps of St. Paul's after the morning mass witnessed the incident. Her screams attracted other parishioners who ran to support her as she convulsed in panic, clutching her heart.

Father Robert Ryan, who conducted the sunrise service, drawn by the woman's screams, joined the group, assessed the situation, and hurried back into the church to call the police. A patrol car, siren blaring and lights flashing, arrived ten minutes later along with an ambulance. The attendants loaded Evans into the bay of their van and rushed him to the nearest hospital, South Shore, in Weymouth, twenty-five minutes away.

Not close enough.

Evans died on route.

When the officers responding to the incident returned to headquarters, they reported to the desk sergeant that a witness, herself needing medical attention, believed the automobile deliberately swerved toward the pedestrian, never slowed. She couldn't tell whether the driver was a man or a woman.

Detective Jeff McCrory, advised of the woman's statement, was stunned to learn the victim was Bradley Evans, now the primary suspect in their murder investigation. Based on the eyewitness account, the driver targeted Evans.

No believer in coincidences, McCrory called Gallo to report Bradley Evans had been run down in the street and that he suspected it was related to the Paragon Park killings.

Gallo, likewise, wondered why someone would want to shut Evans up? Did he lie about his involvement in the murders and the gas station robbery? Was he a partner of Donald Berger and Dustin Rose who, for some reason, had a falling out? Over drugs? Over splitting the loot from the robbery? Over something more personal?

And if Bradley Evans killed Rose and Berger, who killed him, and why?

Mitch Smith came to mind. Angered by the loss of his coke, did he run down Evans assuming he stole the drug from the gas station safe?

Although that didn't seem plausible—wouldn't killing him eliminate the possibility of recovering his stash—you never knew what went through the brain of a druggie.

Why was Brad Evans intentionally run down?

For Gallo and McCrory the answer lay in whether he was involved in the Paragon Park murders.

All but written off, this new development, coupled with the information he once worked at Paragon Park and summered in Nantasket with his aunt and uncle, earned him more scrutiny.

He may have snookered them by coming forward without being summoned. A smart move and a rookie mistake.

Worse, AJ lamented, irresponsible and unprofessional.

He called McCrory. "Jeff. We need to dig deeper into Evans. His preemptive action threw us off. It was calculated and I fell for it."

"Both of us did, man. Can't blame yourself."

Gallo was thankful for McCrory's attempt to lesson his guilt, but it still hurt. "Let's start with where he lived," he said, in an effort to move on.

Evans address was listed as 403 Water Street, Hingham. They parked by the curb and trudged up an inclined stone walkway to the front door and rang the bell. In under two minutes, an elderly woman wearing a white knitted shawl around her shoulders opened the door. She appeared to be in her sixties.

She smiled at the two young men standing before her. "Yes, how may I help you gentleman?"

McCrory held up his identification and introduced himself and Gallo.

"Oh my," she said, as tears formed at the corners of her eyes. "Are you here about poor Bradley?"

"Yes, ma'am. May we come in please?"

"Yes! Yes! Of course. Poor Bradley. Such a dear man."

She led the men through the mud room and into a spacious living room where a woman in her twenties sat on a six-foot long sofa. She stood as the men entered.

"This is Mya, one of my other boarders. She and Bradley were friends," the woman said.

Gallo and McCrory shared a glance. "Boarders?" McCrory said. "So, you are not related to Bradley?"

"Land sakes, no. He is one of five tenants who live here. I rent out my rooms to young people. Keeps me invigorated by their energy and dreams and helps pay the bills. Been on my own since George, my husband, died, oh, six years ago now."

"What can you tell us about Bradley?" McCrory asked.

The woman shook her head, took a white handkerchief from the pocket of the multi-colored sweater she wore and dabbed at her eyes. Her voice cracked as she said, "A quiet young man, bright, had a job in Quincy. Kept to himself. Don't know much about his background. Paid his rent on time."

"May we check his room please, Mrs. . . . ?" McCrory asked.

"Summers. Virginia Summers." She paused, then said, "Mya? Would you show the officers to Bradley's room?"

The search turned up nothing of significance except four articles cut from the Patriot Ledger and Boston Globe reporting on the murders at Paragon Park and the gas station robbery in Hingham. Gallo discovered them on the bottom of a green footlocker in the closet, just like the one Gallo owned. The Marine Corps supplied them to troops to store their belongings when travelling.

He showed the cut-outs to McCrory. "Doesn't prove anything," he said. He admitted knowing Berger, Rose and Morris."

AJ agreed and they went back downstairs to find Mya, Mrs. Summers and three other people huddled together in the living room: two young men and a young woman. They all turned out to be college students who barely knew Evans. Their schedules varied and they came and went at different times.

The detectives thanked everyone for their cooperation and Mrs. Summers escorted them to the door. "Never knew anyone murdered before," she said, her voice cracking. "I worried about that young man sometimes, though."

"Why was that, Ma'am?" Gallo asked.

"A few days prior to Christmas, he came in wet and cold from the first storm that hit us. And he appeared frightened."

"Are you sure about the time?" Gallo pressed.

"Oh yes! I remember it because I had just wrapped some presents and put them under the tree."

Gallo patted Mrs. Summers on the shoulder, told her she had been very helpful, and left the house along with his partner. Once outside, they discussed the revelation. "He comes home wet, cold and scared at the time we believe our boys were killed," Gallo said.

"Circumstantial but convincing."

"Gotta be him. Hung out with them. Even Morris met him. Goodman's not a suspect anymore as far as I'm concerned."

"I agree," McCrory said and described a possible scenario. "Here's how it might have played out. Evans is living in a boarding house, keeping his nose clean. He's not a criminal. He makes friends with Donald Berger and Dustin Rose on a construction job and hung out at the gas station with them from time to time. They talk him into the gas station robbery—God knows how. He panics when they shoot Jerry Morris and takes off. They chase him to Hull to shut him up. A gunfight ensues. Evans wins. Self-defense; two against one as you said before."

Gallo rubbed an old wound on his neck. "I like that story; makes sense with what we know. Still conjecture though. If the beef at Paragon Park just involved those three, who killed Evans? And why?"

McCrory had an answer for that, too. "My money's on Mitch Smith who blamed him for the loss of his coke."

"Why kill him? Wouldn't he just want the stuff back?"

"Smith's a user too. Not the best decision-maker."

"That's plausible. But there's someone else who could be angry with Evans."

"Who? We've just come to the conclusion Evans killed Berger and Rose, haven't told the chief or announced anything publicly."

"Not ready to say yet."

McCrory threw up his hands in frustration. "You're going to hold out on me. Why?"

"Jeff. If we bring another suspect into the equation now, it may undermine our focus. And I may be off-base. I agree we should concentrate on Mitch Smith now. We can always pivot later to this other person."

"Okay, man. But so you know, I'm not happy. We need to trust each other."

Gallo nodded, chastised. "Understood."

The following day, Jerry Morris put down the newspaper and sighed. Bradley Evans was run down in the street. Morris shuddered and his heart raced. He'd lied to the cops.

In what was surreal at the time, before he descended into a three-month long coma, he glimpsed Evans behind the wheel of the getaway car speeding away from his gas station. Berger and Rose cursing him. He didn't tell the detectives because he feared retribution from Evans, who he believed had killed Berger and Rose and might not hesitate to come after him.

It was clear to him now. Donald Berger and Dustin Rose grabbed his car and chased Bradley. That's how the car turned up in Nantasket with coke in it.

But who killed Bradley? Would they now come after him?

Jerry went to a cabinet where he kept booze. He poured two-fingers of Jameson and sat in his recliner debating his next step. He had two options as he saw it: go to the cops and tell them everything or run.

But he had no place to go.

He and his wife lived here with his mother. His father was dead and Jerry was estranged from his family, two sisters and a brother, all of whom resided on the Cape. He couldn't go to his former boss who knew Jerry participated in the failed robbery of his gas station. That left the two cops who interrogated him. Perhaps they could protect him until Evans' killer was caught.

Jerry downed his glass of whiskey and poured another. The drinks settled his nerves. He had only one play. Go to the cops.

He fell asleep in his chair.

Jerry went to Hingham Police Headquarters two days after his drinking bout and confessed to Detective's McCrory and Gallo that he had, in fact, seen the driver of the getaway car during the gas station robbery.

His admission validated their theory about how the events at Paragon Park played out and that Bradley Evans killed Berger and Rose in self-defense as they chased him. Mrs. Summers statement that Brad had stumbled home wet and exhausted three days before Christmas cinched it.

The Plymouth County District Attorney recommended to a judge that Jerry Morris be placed on one year probation for his role in the robbery, advocating leniency because of Morris' cooperation in the matter.

Hingham Chief Taylor agreed to put out a joint press release with the MDC declaring the Paragon Park murders solved and identifying Bradley Evans as the culprit. Both statements praised Detectives Gallo and McCrory for their work in cracking the case and mentioned Bill Wilkinson as a "senior supervisor" in the matter.

Not one to miss an opportunity for good publicity, Mets Homicide Captain, Martin Kellum, brought Gallo and Wilkinson into his office for a photo shoot with Boston's leading newspapers, the Globe and Herald. He presented the men with a framed commendation for their efforts in solving the first murders in the town of Hull in recent memory.

No questions were entertained.

Bert Jones of the Patriot Ledger was invited to the ceremony along with his photographer. Jones was miffed that the Hingham Chief had put out the press release without first notifying him. He realized, though, he could follow up his bio article on Gallo with a report of this award and slip in details of how the Nantasket killings were resolved. He also saw an opportunity to wangle his way into the inquiry of the hit and run that killed Bradley Evans.

Bill Wilkinson appeared unashamed by the accolades heaped on Gallo and himself, though he contributed little to the investigation.

Gallo, already uncomfortable with the Bert Jones profile piece, chose not to make waves. As a consolation, he convinced Kellum to allow him to work on the murder of Bradley Evans, although it did not occur within Metro's jurisdiction. He hinted to his boss that the killing might be drug related and lead to the unveiling of a major pusher, a big win for the Mets—or so he thought.

This worried Kellum, given his association with the Irish, but he thought it the best way to keep tabs on the investigation. He believed he could warn Moran and reign in the rookie if warranted. He ordered daily reports and gave Wilkinson the job of monitoring the situation. Wilkinson's stomach churned with no choice but to follow orders.

Neither he nor Kellum seemed concerned about the danger to Gallo if he strayed within the gunsights of Mafia thugs.

CHAPTER 24

Gallo left the ceremony in Captain Kellum's office and returned to Hull, his partner, Bill Wilkinson on his mind. The man bent like a tree in the wind, swaying in any direction that enhanced his career, taking credit for the work of others, and using a pilfered test to move up the chain of command.

And why did he warn them off Mitch Smith so fast?

Gallo didn't have many confidants. His parents wouldn't understand and McCrory served in another department. He couldn't reveal Mets problems to an outsider. Only one person emerged as a possible confidant. The woman who scorned his romantic interest but was still a friend, he hoped.

He opted to contact her when classes let out around three in the afternoon. He drove down Nantasket Avenue to M-Street, turned left at the Bayside Theater on the corner and circled the playing fields. He veered left again on Central and parked to have an unobstructed view of the exits.

Hull Memorial School opened in 1950, after AJ graduated from Hingham High. Four concrete pillars capped by a white domed clock tower dominated the entrance to the impressive red brick edifice. It had two upper floors and a basement level. The building was one of the newest in town. Some classroom windows faced Central Ave which ran parallel to the front. Others overlooked "L" and "M" Streets on the south and north sides.

From his vantage point, Gallo viewed the main entrance/exit and one to his right. The building obscured another on the far side. He felt foolish. He should have gone into the office, asked what room Susan taught in and went straight to it. But he didn't want to interrupt instruction, scare her or spark rumors of why an MDC detective wanted to speak to a teacher. So, he sat in his car hoping for a chance meeting.

At three o'clock, a bell rang and children exploded through the exit doors screaming with delight. Parents on the sidewalks greeted the younger kids while older ones scrambled into yellow busses awaiting them. Those who lived within walking distance, ran, danced and skipped down roads bordering the school, chasing each other, lunch pails flying at their sides. Some rushed across Central and leaped onto swings and slides, part of the school's playground equipment. Gallo marveled at their energy, wondering if he ever possessed such carefree enthusiasm.

As he pondered this, Susan Lawrence came out the front door with four students. One held her hand, another grasped her blue dress and two just ogled her. She smiled as they stepped gingerly down the concrete steps. At the bottom, she said something to the kids and they scurried off in different directions. She was smiling when AJ intercepted her on the sidewalk.

"AJ," she said, her face registering surprise and a bit of annoyance. "What's a celebrity like yourself doing here? My mother bought five copies of the Ledger with your profile in it. Made sure relatives got a copy, and that they knew we once dated."

AJ sensed the resentment in her tone. "I'm sorry Susan. The article was not my idea. I'm here because I need to talk to somebody I trust."

Her eyes widened and she said, "okay," stretching out the word into more of an exclamation.

"Let's take a walk. We can speak privately on the bleachers overlooking the baseball field."

Lawrence agreed and they strolled down "L" street. A couple of boys in uniform threw a ball around in the outfield.

They moved up to the last row of seats and rested their backs on the wooden guard-rail which prevented people from leaning back and falling off the otherwise open stands.

"What's on your mind?" Susan asked.

"I have a dilemma at work and need an opinion on how to proceed."

"I'm an elementary school teacher. I know nothing of the law or police politics."

Gallo smiled. "It's not a legal question, Susan. Just want another person's take on something. I value your input."

Lawrence didn't seem convinced but urged him to continue.

He told her about finding the lieutenant's exam and Wilkinson's apparent effort to undermine their questioning of a suspect. "Should I confront the man or take it to a higher administrator?" he asked.

Lawrence scrunched her face and gazed out onto the baseball field. She cradled her chin in her hands, elbows on her knees, deep in thought.

Gallo was struck by her clean-cut attractiveness. She wore a faint amount of lipstick, hair pulled back in a pony tail, face scrubbed. His heart skipped a beat as he longed to hold her.

She sat up straight after three or four minutes. "AJ, my dad gave me a bit of advice a long time ago. He said, 'if you have a problem with someone, go to them and share your concerns. Ask a third person to intervene as a last resort.' Have you talked to Wilkinson?"

AJ hadn't, not sure why. Perhaps because Wilkinson was the veteran and he a rookie. Maybe he feared for his job, which made him feel like a weak-ass jerk. Not the thinking of a fearless war hero.

He smiled. "Thank you—or your dad—for the sound advice. My first move should have been to talk to the man. I didn't do that."

Susan stood up. "That proved easier than I thought. I worry about you, you know."

Gallo said nothing, afraid he would spoil the moment, happy she thought about him at all.

He continued the fantasy of a reconciliation.

Gallo walked Susan Lawrence back to her car and returned to his vehicle, encouraged by her sensible guidance, discouraged because he already knew this and for some reason held back, unusual for him. On the football team in high school, he rolled over defenders when necessary or scampered away when it wasn't. In baseball, he broke up double play opportunities by taking out infielders with vicious slides.

On the battlefield, he faced the enemy without fear. At the Chosin Reservoir, while shielding retreating comrades, he fought off swarming Chinese with his machine gun until his ammunition ran out, then engaged in hand-to-hand-combat before withdrawing from the battle under cover of darkness.

His citation for the Navy Cross estimated he killed at least a company of soldiers. It reminded some World War II holdovers of Audie Murphy, the intrepid young 2nd lieutenant who battled an overwhelming German force from a burning tank destroyer and repelled many assaults on his position.

Murphy received the Medal of Honor.

Drugs did not fuel Gallo's bravery, as he intimated to McCrory to discourage the man from idolizing him as a hero. He did his job. His fearlessness resulted in multiple wounds and an early exit from the Corps. He didn't give it a second thought. That's why he chastised himself for being tentative in dealing with Wilkinson.

This situation was not life or death—or so he thought.

Blinded by his obsession to win Susan Lawrence back, Gallo overlooked another friend he should have consulted for advice. In fact, he should have been his go-to-guy. Lenny Pierce, a boy he grew up with, went to school with, joined the Marines with, who lived two streets over from his parent's house at the corner of Manomet Ave and Revere Street in Kenberma.

Once inseparable, they drifted apart after the Korean fiasco. Actually, not a drift, but an abrupt separation. While AJ survived the war despite multiple injuries, Lenny suffered a life altering wound—paralyzed from the waist down.

Not until he returned to Hull, did Gallo learn of Pierce's injury. He had encouraged his pal to join the Marines and could not face him—ignoring entreaties by his parents. He beat himself up many times over this.

Driving home after his confab with Susan, AJ did not turn onto Massasoit where he lived, but continued on to Manomet and parked near, but not in front of, Pierce's house—like that of his parents, a converted single story summer cottage. It now stood out for two reasons: an L-shaped ramp that could facilitate a wheelchair descending from the front door and a room addition on to the back.

The site of the ramp sent a shiver down AJ's spine. It drove home the truth his boyhood friend was paralyzed, despite how much he might wish otherwise. He wondered if the reason he put off seeing him was to delay acceptance of that reality.

In the hospital on Okinawa during his rehab, he bunked beside amputees and other disabled Marines. It didn't hit him in the gut as this sight did now. Lenny would never walk again, ride a bike, throw a football or baseball around, chase him into the surf.

Were these regrets for himself or his buddy?

Maybe both. He vowed to man-up and visit Lenny. A tear trickled down his cheek as he drove off.

Their reunion would be short-lived, though. Fate intervened as it often does.

CHAPTER 25

Bobby Moran met with his top advisors in his hangout in the back room of the Shamrock Bar and Grille in Somerville. He was the temporary boss of the Irish Mafia. The founder and leader of the group, Buddy McClean, was in prison serving two years for illegal possession of a firearm.

Moran did not have the reputation as a vicious street fighter like McClean, but was no less dangerous. He took out two members of their Charlestown rivals who tried to muscle in on their rackets. Sitting with him at a round table with draft beers in front of them were Patrick Duffy, Frankie Obrien, Shamus "The enforcer" O'Rourke and Billy, "White Shoes," Dolan.

Moran stared at each man in turn as he spoke. "We have a caper coming up in May. Should net us a tidy sum. Patrick is leading the way on that. But one of the people distributing our product on the South Shore lost some. That don't fly with me, boyos."

He paused to take a gulp of his beer. "Shamus! I want you and Billy to visit this bloke. If he's trying to stiff us, you know what to do. Our reputation is on the line here."

O'Rourke, at five-nine, two-hundred pounds, and ripped from daily workouts at a local gym, served as the gang enforcer. With his red hair and freckled, pale skin, he looked the part of a typical Irishman. Quick to anger, often after quaffing several beers, he pummeled even his buddies when they angered him. His fists could be lethal. Everyone gave him a wide leeway.

Dolan, a string bean at six foot one, weighed one-hundred thirty-five pounds. As partners, Billy and Shamus reminded comics readers of characters, Mutt and Jeff, though there was nothing comical about either of them. O'Rourke did his damage with his knuckles while

Dolan wielded a switchblade when confronted. He concealed the knife in one of his high-top white sneakers.

After the meeting, Moran waited an hour, then drove further downtown to a pay phone. He made weekly calls to the number he dialed, left brief messages and hung up. He never used the same phone twice.

When the Mafia toughs appeared at the front door of Mitch Smith's home in Hingham a day after Moran's order, and gave him one week to either produce the "lost" coke or ante up the cost, Smith, too frightened to speak, stood mute.

He closed the door and stumbled back into his living room, fell into a stuffed chair and lit a cigarette after several failed attempts to strike a match. He had few options, find out where the stuff was, retrieve it, or plead with his old man for the cash.

If these didn't work, he planned to bolt.

CHAPTER 26

Gallo's botched attempt to visit his disabled pal hit him hard, raised the same feelings of cowardice he felt driving away from the accident on Forrest Ave in Cohasset years earlier. He was determined not to let these emotions stand in the way of winning his high school sweetheart back despite her rejections.

He screwed up his courage and walked up to the entrance of St. Mary's of the Bay Church at 9:00 a.m., Sunday, pulled open the immense door and stepped inside. There was only one Sunday mass during the spring and winter at St. Mary's before the summer residents descended in June.

The service had already begun, conducted by Pastor James Sullivan, a tall, silver haired man with a regal bearing and stern countenance intimidating to youngsters learning Latin, AJ knew from experience. The priest wore a white chasuble with a cross design.

Sullivan pivoted toward the congregation and uttered the Latin phrase, Dominus vobiscum—the lord be with you. The altar boys answered as trained—Et cum spiritu tuo—and with your spirit. The exchange echoed through the church as the veteran prelate turned back to the altar.

AJ had obsessed over Susan Lawrence ever since their chance encounter weeks ago at the edge of the Hull Gut and his meeting with her at the Memorial School. Though she dismissed his interest in her, he hoped to change her mind. Surprising her in church would catch her off guard. She would understand he was serious in renewing their relationship.

Instead, he was the one surprised.

He spotted her halfway down the center aisle, sitting in the middle of a pew, her mother on her right and a man on her left. A foot or two

136

separated mother and daughter but the man and Susan touched shoulders, a sign of intimacy.

AJ took a seat in the back and watched them for five or six minutes. In that time, the two gazed at each other with affection as the mass proceeded. His plan to sit with her during the service and reestablish their closeness unraveled as he saw how invested she was in this man.

He slipped out of his pew, opened the entry door and stumbled down the hill to his car parked in a dirt lot overlooking a field with clumps of grass interspersed with barren patches. A blocking sled stood at the far side closest to the Atlantic. The high school football team used the pathetic mud-hole for practice.

A cool breeze swept the area as winds often did on the tip of the peninsula. He considered crossing the field and slamming the machine to dissipate his anger. But, in retrospect, he recognized his wrath was misplaced. He abandoned Susan without a word. Did he expect her to pine for him forever?

And he had no right to feel betrayed. He had not been faithful to her memory while in the Marines. A solicitous nurse on Okinawa during his rehab from wounds suffered in Korea took him to her bed. They carried on a torrid affair until he shipped back to the U.S. They corresponded for a time but a long-term relationship didn't pan out. He later discovered she was married.

Shaking his head and bemoaning the folly of life, he calmed down, slipped behind the wheel of his car and sat for several minutes before backing out of his spot and heading toward downtown. Moisture filled his eyes. He swiped his arm across them to clear his vision.

He didn't know it then, but Susan would soon seek his help as a detective.

CHAPTER 27

At three fifteen on the Monday after AJ Gallo's ill-fated venture to Saint Mary's of the Bay Church to surprise Susan Lawrence, the final bell rang at the Memorial School. Children poured out of the exits, down stairs to waiting busses, into the arms of parents, or to the start of their walk home.

Lawrence sighed as her energetic third graders left for the day. Her students knew better than to run from her classroom, though. They exited single file, row by row, starting with the one nearest the door.

Her classroom stood next to a tiled ramp which led to a splendid auditorium where plays were performed and where they held eighth grade graduations. Susan was working on a short production with her class on the Boston Massacre. They rehearsed a couple of times a week with the help of volunteer moms. Today was not a scheduled rehearsal.

Susan's fiancé, Michael Callahan, taught seventh-grade on the floor above her. Most days he came down to visit and they took a walk, hand-in-hand, down L-Street, and across Nantasket Ave to the beach. In warm weather, they took off their shoes and clomped through the deep white sand to the water's edge, playfully splashing water on each other, drenching their clothing.

Susan glanced up from her desk and noticed Michael leaning against the door jam, perpetual smile creasing his face. "Hi, babe," he said, in the soft voice that sent chills down her spine. She smiled and turned her head to the side, a gesture Callahan thought endearing. She got up and went to the closet beside the chalkboard and slipped on a light jacket—not a barefoot on the beach day.

"Ready, hon," she said, locked her classroom door and they strolled down the hall past the Hull Superintendent of Schools Office and out the front door. As they sauntered down L-Street, several colleagues driving by tooted their car horns and waved. A parent standing on the stoop of her house with her daughter by her side gave a nod and a smile. The recognition made Susan feel comfortable. She slipped her arm between Michael's and snuggled closer.

She should have been content, but despite her efforts, affectionate thoughts of AJ kept intruding. She tried to push them from her mind, knew at some point she had to confront them. Michael was unaware of his fiancé's emotional struggles.

When the happy couple returned from their walk, it was Michael's turn to deal with a traumatic issue. They had parked their cars side-by-side in the area reserved for teachers behind the school.

Lawrence observed the damage first. "Oh my God, Michael, your car," she shouted.

For the second time in two months, the windows of Callahan's Chevrolet Impala were smashed. The tires slashed. The two-door blue Impala was Callahan's pride and joy next to Susan.

"This is horrible, Mike. This is more than a prank. This is malicious. Who would do this?"

Callahan thought he knew, didn't voice it to his fiancé, didn't want to frighten her. "Kids," he said.

Susan put her arms around him and held him close. "They all love you, Mike. I can't believe any of your students would do this."

"They're seventh graders, Sue. Who knows what goes through their minds."

She remained adamant. "This is unacceptable. You have to tell Mr. Damon and file a police report this time."

Callahan stood, hands on hips, shaking his head, surveying the damage. "Okay, hon," he said, resigned. But if the truth came out, as he suspected, broken glass and slashed tires might be the least of his worries.

Susan, shaken by the repeated vandalism on her fiancé's Impala, was surprised by his reluctance to notify the principal or go to the police. He loved that car. Something troubled him. She didn't know much about Mike's past. He never spoke about it. She feared these incidents had something to do with those years but she couldn't imagine anything horrible. He was a nice, loving man. If the culprits were not discovered by the Hull cops or the principal, she knew who to contact though Mike might balk at that idea.

CHAPTER 28

Jeff McCrory and AJ Gallo, sitting opposite each other, met in the conference room at the Hingham PD with notes scattered on the table in front of them. Cups of black coffee and the remnants of half-eaten donuts also graced the table-top. Gallo, unable to focus, found his attention straying to Susan Lawrence. He couldn't let go.

McCrory noticed AJ's vacant stare but before he could comment on it, the door opened and Chief Raymond Taylor walked in. He motioned for the detectives to remain seated. Taylor, a man of about fifty with hair graying at the temples, wore his blue uniform with three stars on the collar, a starched white shirt and blue and red striped tie securely fastened.

"Thought I'd share some information," the Chief began. Might help with your investigation." He took a seat at the end of the table between the two men.

"Attended a meeting of police chiefs yesterday in Boston conducted by the FBI," he related. "One topic of discussion was the proliferation of gangs in the Metropolitan area. Not real shocking. The Italians and Irish have vied for control of the city for years. One tidbit the Fibbies shared might interest you. The Irish have delved into the distribution of drugs, unlike the Italians who continue to resist getting involved with narcotics. They're concerned they may have reached into the South Shore but there's no concrete evidence of that as yet."

The Chief paused, then continued. "A fellow out of Somerville, a Bobby Moran, is the current leader of the mob, also called the Winter Hill Gang named after the neighborhood where it was founded. The agents who ran the conference, claimed 'The Hill,' as they referred to it, was made up of the most murderous mobsters they had ever run up against."

The detectives stared at each other at the mention of Moran. Taylor caught their exchange. "Thought you might find it interesting. I've seen that guy's name on the list of those you wanted to talk to regarding the Paragon Park murders. I didn't know if he would still be of interest now that you have your man."

McCrory spoke up. "Chief, as you know, we uncovered a stash of cocaine in the vehicle driven by the murder victims, who robbed the gas station. Jerry Morris, the attendant, swears the drugs belonged to Mitch Smith, who got them from the Irish boys."

Taylor nodded; kept silent.

"I believe Smith murdered Evans. Blames him for stealing the coke from the station safe. No one else to blame since Berger and Rose are dead."

"Anything to back that up?"

"Nothing solid. We intend to question him again. The info you provided will help convince him we know more than we do."

"You concur Gallo?" the Chief asked.

The Mets lawman hesitated, not wanting to undermine his fellow detective. "I agree with Jeff. Smith is our number one suspect in Evans murder, but think we should pursue other leads as well."

McCrory glared at AJ.

The Chief stood, felt the tension in the room, didn't inquire further. "Right. Keep me updated. And, be careful before you tangle with this Moran fella. He's a former longshoreman in Charlestown and East Boston. Worked alongside the founder of the gang whose now in jail. He has the reputation as a stone-cold killer but nobody's been able to pin anything on him.

The detective's facial expressions reflected concern, but they said nothing.

When Taylor left and closed the door behind him, McCrory challenged, "So who are our other suspects?"

Gallo took a sip of coffee, now tepid, then answered. "What would you do if someone murdered your brother?"

McCrory's face registered shock and disbelief. "David Rose? He didn't even know we suspected Evans until we publicized it after the hit and run."

"That is a problem and may discount him as a suspect, but he's the one other person with motive—revenge."

McCrory kept shaking his head. "You're grasping at straws pal. Mitch is our guy. We can't make a case for pursuing Rose."

"Let's find something then."

"How?"

"I'll get Cohasset Officer Russo to snoop around. He knows the Rose family. He can ask questions without raising suspicions."

McCrory relented.

Gallo then shifted gears, and rubbed his chin. "We have this Moran fellow's phone number. Maybe he also blamed Evans for the stolen coke."

"Doubt it. He had no way of knowing Evans involvement."

"You don't think Smith would offer him up to save his own ass?"

McCrory raised his eyebrows. "We've got to be careful if we approach that dude. We might be stepping on the FBI's toes. You understand how much they value local cops. They've got the means to crush us like grapes. Do we want to give them a reason to do so?"

Gallo relished the idea of doing battle with the Feds though concerned about dragging McCrory into the fray. And as a rookie detective, he could find himself out on his butt if he offended the Metro brass or Bill Wilkinson, the partner he didn't trust.

In the end, he opted to move forward. "As they say in the Corps, lock and load. Let's go after Smith."

McCrory offered up a wan smile in the face of Gallo's bravado.

He feared minefields ahead.

McCrory didn't imagine one of those minefields might disguise itself in the person of an intrepid Patriot Ledger news-hound.

Bert Jones couldn't believe his luck, or Karma, as he chose to look at it. No sooner had he been hired as the paper's crime writer, than the double murder at Paragon Park occurred. Then the deliberate hit and run slaying of the man who committed those murders took place in Hingham Square. And he heard from a source in Metro his star Detective, AJ Gallo, would also be involved in investigating that killing along with Detective McCrory.

Jones pictured himself as a sleuth as much as a reporter. He decided not to approach either lawman, yet. He opted to stake out the Hingham Police HQ and follow them around. That decision put him in the cross-hairs of some very bad people.

CHAPTER 29

The robbery crew met at Duffy's residence in Whitfield, about thirty minutes from Somerville, to prepare. Duffy, the master safecracker, Shamus O'Rourke and "White Shoes" Dolan helpers to do the grunt work of breaking through walls to access the bank vault.

Duffy had amassed the tools needed for the caper and stored them in his garage: power drills, an acetylene cutter, dynamite, a rope ladder, canvas bags to cart away the loot and three, two-way radios to maintain contact with Lieutenant Newman of the Quincy PD who would patrol outside to shield the gang from discovery.

Duffy's alarm expert, Buster Grimes, would bring a bypass box to neutralize the system. Grimes made several trips to analyze the set-up and prepare the device.

As Duffy met with his crew, Bill Wilkinson drove up and parked on the street. Captain Kellum ordered his lieutenant to keep him apprised of the gang's progress.

Wilkinson, nervous and hesitant, strode up to the front door and rang the bell startling the conspirators assembled inside. Duffy gestured for quiet, went to the window next to the door and peered out. He rolled his eyes when he glimpsed the man standing there in a brown suit and matching fedora. He thought he looked like a vacuum cleaner salesman and laughed to himself. He didn't like the man, consented to his participation in their scheme at Kellum's insistence.

Duffy swung the door open and motioned with a sweep of his arm for Wilkinson to enter. "Waddya want?" he challenged.

"The captain ordered me to see if you needed anything."

Duffy grimaced. "Everything's on schedule and going as planned, pal. I don't need a babysitter, ya unerstand?"

Wilkinson, not surprised by the chilly reception, hankered to flee the house fast. "Okay. Just following orders," he said. "I'll give the boss the good news."

He turned, opened the door and left without waiting for a response. All but running to his car, he sat for several minutes to calm his nerves. He feared Kellum would order him to take part in the heist, which he was loath to do, unsure how to avoid it.

Paralyzed by indecision, two options struck him: Go along and risk capture or go to the captain's superiors and blow the whistle on the exam scam and the robbery plot. Such a move might save his job—if the higher-ups weren't being paid off by Kellum—but cost him his life. The captain was aligned with some bad dudes. He imagined what would happen to a snitch.

He fought back tears as he pulled away from the curb. Frantic, he thought of his rookie partner, a war hero, and formulated an idea so outrageous it had no chance of succeeding, even if he could persuade Gallo to participate.

Desperate men take desperate measures—and some of those backfire.

CHAPTER 30

After Chief Taylor left, Gallo and McCrory remained in the conference room of the Hingham PD to plan their next moves. But before they did, McCrory addressed the elephant in the room. "What's up?" he asked. "You seem to be on another planet."

"I'm okay."

"Bullshit."

Gallo was taken aback. McCrory seldom used profanity. He dropped his guard. "Woman troubles."

"Know the feeling, man. You don't talk about your personal life. I sensed something troubling you"

"Not much to tell. I like this woman. She's moved on. I can't."

"Mind if I ask who?"

"Gal I dated in high school. When I joined the Corps, I didn't tell her or keep in touch. My fault. Thought I might be hurt or killed. Didn't want to saddle her with that."

McCrory shook his head. "I can understand that, but to leave without any explanation was harsh. Left her to imagine all sorts of things."

Gallo grimaced. "No excuse."

"You screwed up, pal."

Gallo nodded and mumbled, "Saw her in church with another guy. They acted like sweethearts. I can't mess up her life twice."

"So, you're going to give up? Mister war hero."

"Stop with the hero stuff. It's embarrassing, and as they say, the real heroes never came home."

McCrory, though chastised, didn't ease up. "You're pathetic. Either forget her and move on or do something to win her back."

"What?"

147

"You'll have to seek guidance on that score from a higher authority. I'm no expert on affairs of the heart. Just ask my fiancé."

"Big help, pal, big help."

McCrory smiled and raised his hands in surrender.

While their conversation about his love life went nowhere, Gallo felt a spark of anger and energy. He hadn't put up much of a fight to entice Susan back. His emotions were on a roller coaster: do something; don't do something.

At McCrory's prodding, he made up his mind to change that indecision, though he had no idea how.

For now, he and McCrory needed to plan their next steps in their investigation of the murder of Brad Evans. They had three viable suspects: David Rose, Dustin Rose's twin, Mitch Smith, thief and drug dealer and Bobby Moran, drug supplier and leader of a formidable gang.

McCrory pushed for Smith while Gallo leaned toward Rose. Neither desired to take on the mob kingpin. There were roadblocks to pursuing him even if they wanted to.

Gallo spelled them out.

"The Mafia is based in Somerville. We lack jurisdiction there. We'd need clearance from your department, mine and the FBI. Not much hope of that with our meager evidence to connect Moran to our investigation."

McCrory agreed. "That's a non-starter. Understand your thinking regarding David Rose's motive to kill Evans. Again, he couldn't have known Evans was the killer before we announced it. Even if he somehow found that out, to my mind, we have more reason to go after Smith, and he might drop a dime on Moran if pushed hard enough."

"Okay. I give up," Gallo conceded. "But, let's contact Cohasset Officer Russo who went to school with the Rose twins. He can shed more light on David's history."

"No problem as long as we focus on Smith."

"You have a plan?"

"We shook Mitch boy up on our first visit. If he did buy his stash from the Irish mob, they won't take kindly to anyone who lost it.

Especially if that person can't make it good by replacing the value with cash. Another meeting with us may push him over the edge; encourage him to throw the goons under the bus to save his own butt."

"His dad is loaded. Couldn't he borrow from him?"

"Not from what Jerry Morris said. His father canned him from the company business. Doubt he'd front the money if his wayward son confesses what he needs it for. Mitch is in a tight spot. We can make it tighter if we put the screws to him."

Gallo smiled. "Let's go talk to Mitch."

Once again, the lawmen drove out to Mitch Smith's house on Sherwood Road, Hingham. The drive took them through the center of town and tree lined streets typical of New England. The detectives, who grew up in the area, did not take note of the bucolic scenery which tourists paid thousands of dollars to see in the fall when the foliage changed colors; the brilliance of the gold, red and brown of the maple, birch and ash trees. Not as breathtaking as in Vermont, perhaps, but still worth seeing. Gallo and McCrory were not sightseers. Their focus was on their expanded murder investigation.

When they pulled up to Mitch Smith's house, his red Buick Skylark was not in the driveway. Nevertheless, they approached the front door and McCrory rang the bell—received no response. Gallo peered through a window; closed blinds blocked his view. He circled the house with the same result. Frustrated, the men met up and headed back to their unmarked patrol car.

As they did so, they became aware of a muffled sound from the garage; an engine running. They went over to inspect and flipped up the unlocked door.

The engine of the Skylark was engaged, with a garden hose attached to the exhaust pipe, which extended into the driver's side window. McCrory rushed over to wrench the car door open, gagging from the escaping fumes, his lungs filled with smoke; his eyes watering. He hauled Smith's body out and dragged it onto the cement driveway.

Gallo, shielding his mouth and nose with his right arm, raced in and turned off the car's ignition. He stumbled back out, coughing, and joined his partner, doubled over, dry heaving.

Gallo, trained by the Red Cross in the newest artificial respiration procedures, kneeled over Smith and initiated the process. He raised Smith's arms to cause expansion of the chest, then he folded them on the chest and applied pressure. He repeated this ten times..

McCrory, recovered from the inhalation of carbon monoxide, called in to the nearest Hingham fire station for a rescue unit. Gallo continued his chest pumps until the firefighters arrived within fifteen minutes.

Gallo waived them off. Smith didn't make it.

Though it appeared Smith committed suicide, the detectives were suspicious. When Hingham Police Chief Ray Taylor drove up, they shared their misgivings with him.

"Any proof?" Taylor asked.

"No, sir" McCrory answered.

"It seems too convenient, sir," Gallo chimed in. "We wanted to question him about the Evans murder—someone shut him up."

The Chief, unconvinced, rubbed his chin and glanced around as if waiting for some evidence to leap out at him.

"Okay," he said, his questioning tone reflecting doubt. "I'll call Smith's father, Gavin, bring him up to speed, ask him to come by and let us into the house. Won't inform him of your concerns over the phone. I'll station a couple of uniforms here to secure the area."

The firefighters checked Smith's vitals and confirmed Gallo's assessment. They placed him on a gurney, draped his body with a sheet and moved to place him in the rescue van, which had followed the firetrucks. Chief Taylor intervened, asked them to wait until the man's father arrived.

As they waited, neither Gallo nor McCrory eyeballed the 1956 Chevy, 4-door sedan crawling by driven by Billy, "White Shoes," Dolan. They didn't know Dolan or the man with him, so their presence in the area didn't raise suspicions. They also didn't spot the man in a Ford Fairlane parked across the street, three houses down from Smith's. Had they seen him, the killer of Bradley Evans would have become apparent.

Gavin Smith showed up at the scene thirty minutes after the call from Chief Taylor. He came up from his dealership in Cohasset. He drove a 1957 cream colored Cadillac Coupe de Ville with swept back fins and dual rear lights resembling rockets. He stepped out wearing a pin-striped blue suit with a wide red tie. His black hair, parted on the left side, was cut and shaped by a professional—the image of a successful businessman.

Taylor greeted him with a firm handshake and gently gripped his right shoulder guiding him away from his son's shrouded body.

"My god, Ray," Smith said, his strained voice reflecting fear and uncertainty.

"I'm sorry Gavin, Mitch may have taken his own life."

Gavin's hazel eyes bore into the Chief. "What do you mean, 'may have'? Is something else going on here? If you hold back on me, I swear I'll have your head."

Gavin Smith was used to wielding power. A member of the Elks and Kiwanis, he participated on the Better Business Bureau and was on a first name basis with city council members and town fathers throughout the South Shore.

Taylor, not the least bit cowed by Smith's bravado, recognized the man's grief. "Gavin," he said, in a calm, gentle tone. "Those two men—he pointed to McCrory and Gallo—"are investigating a homicide and wanted to question Mitch about it."

"What?" Smith exclaimed, his face reddening, the veins in his neck bulging. "My son wouldn't be involved in something so vile. Can't say I liked his choices, but…" His voice trailed off.

Chief Taylor again moved to placate the elder Smith. "The man run down in Hingham square was the primary suspect in the killing of the two individuals who robbed your gas station. Mitch knew them and their killer. The detectives hoped he could provide some background information on them. I'll be blunt: your son's suicide seems too expedient; might have been staged. I'm sure you'll want us to pursue every avenue if Mitch was murdered. We need access to Mitch's house to search for clues. It's standard procedure."

Mollified, Smith reached into his pocket and produced a key. He turned and walked several feet away, his body trembling, tears streaking his face, wetting his shirt.

Regaining his composure after a four or five minutes, he pivoted back to Taylor, got in his car, and drove off.

Gallo and McCrory entered Smith's home, not sure what to look for. They searched inside kitchen cabinets and drawers, under couch cushions, the base of lamps, between the mattresses and bedsprings in the master bedroom and a guest room, behind pictures in a narrow hallway to the bedrooms, found nothing.

They then moved to a room Mitch used as an office. It held an oak roll-top desk, with a black Naugahyde swivel chair in front, a wooden three-drawer filing cabinet and a multi-colored stuffed chair next to a floor lamp. Gallo took the desk, McCrory the cabinet.

The roll-top had a key-lock, but wasn't secured. Gallo flipped it up and faced the usual cubbies. Two contained unpaid bills. Two others pictures and several unsealed envelopes with letters. Gallo ignored the bills, sorted through the pictures. None proved useful for their investigations. One photo showed Mitch in a Hingham High football uniform, another him posing with school cheerleaders and one of him in a Halloween costume; all undated. His father sent the letters rejecting Mitch's appeals for money. A possible reason he turned to selling drugs for cash?

The middle drawer of the desk and the one on the left were empty. A faux double drawer on the right held three folders, only one of which contained anything of note—a three-ring binder with photos of the 1958 new cars from Ford and Chevy, and a 3" by 5" notebook with scribbling Gallo couldn't decipher; the numbers 131518114 followed by ten letters: FAGFCECCEF.

"Hey, Jeff," Gallo called out. "What do you make of this?"

McCrory glanced at it and raised his eyebrows. "Could be a code of some kind?"

Gallo brightened. "That's it. Let's take it back to the station to interpret it. Bring in the Chief."

"Worth a shot," McCrory said. "The filing cabinet contained nothing but auto magazines going back to 1950."

The two men, buoyed by the prospect they found something critical to their investigation, drove back to the PD.

Plucky reporter, Bert Jones, observed the commotion at the Smith house. He had ditched his Volkswagen bus for his sister's less noticeable Chevy Bel Air coupe. Monitoring an illegal police scanner provided by a cop he befriended, he arrived at Smith's in time to watch the rescue van/ambulance drive off, lights not flashing, siren muted. A sign, Bert knew, if they were transporting someone, that person was likely dead.

He also spotted the arrival of Gavin Smith, who he recognized from newspaper photos, and watched Detectives Gallo and McCrory enter the home. His antenna shot up. He sensed a sensational story, envisioning the opening lines though he had no details of whatever incident had occurred.

He assumed the ambulance was headed to South Shore hospital, so he sped off in that direction intending to pick up information from the staff or police on the scene. He thought of the quote by Yankee legend, catcher Yogi Berra, famous for his mind-boggling sayings as his on-field prowess. Adages like "It's amazing how much one can hear just by listening." Or as Bert thought, chuckling to himself, how much one could see just by watching.

When the ambulance turned onto the South Shore Expressway heading toward Boston rather than Weymouth and the hospital, it confirmed Jones' suspicions that a critical incident had occurred.

The other man who had parked near Mitch Smith's house in addition to Bert Jones, now took up another position on Beal Street, Hingham, across from the Morris residence, the former gas station attendant.

He had surveilled the house for several weeks, off and on, and determined Morris lived with two women, his wife and an older gal— Morris' mother or the wife's. He doubted an unemployed pump-jockey could afford a housekeeper.

The stalker saw no reason to hurt either lady, so he tried to determine when, or if, Morris would be alone or if he left for a job. So far, it didn't appear he found work. If forced to eliminate him in or near his home, that would complicate his planning. He wanted it to seem like an accident—not like running down Evans. He hadn't thought that through.

As a train whistled by the area; he smiled.

CHAPTER 31

Gallo began to think he served as a member of the Hingham PD. He spent more time there than at the Mets Substation in Nantasket or the bureau in Boston. He worried Captain Kellum would become aware and pull him off the Evans and Smith murders. To avoid that, he vowed to keep their Chief of Detectives in the loop every step of the way...and grudgingly, Bill Wilkinson.

He and McCrory sat in the conference room at the Hingham PD with Chief Taylor, who felt sorry for Gavin Smith for the way his son died. The father of two boys himself, he could imagine the pain Gavin experienced since his son's cause of death was not yet determined. They sent his body to the Boston medical examiner for an autopsy, which would not be available for several days. Suicide or murder. It would make a difference to a father.

Gallo and McCrory sat opposite each other at the conference table with the Chief between them, ensconced at the end; Mitch Smith's notebook opened to the page with the undeciphered code.

Taylor concluded it was a simple alphabet/numerical substitution code. The numbers represented letters, while in reverse, the letters stood for numbers. They tackled the numbers first, 131518114, with 1 representing A, 3, C etc., and were stymied. All had yellow pads in front of them and the resulting, ACAEAHAAE, made no sense.

The Chief rubbed his chin, then recommended they tackle the letters, FAGFCECC.

That proved easier when the numbers that emerged—6176663311—appeared to represent a telephone number.

McCrory slipped out to retrieve a directory from the desk sergeant. When he came back smiling, he pointed to the prefix for a city starting with 617—Somerville, Massachusetts.

"Guess who lives there?" he asked, with a smirk.

"Moran," Gallo shouted, as if answering the final winning question on a quiz show. His passion surprised the Chief.

Their discovery led them to try different letter combinations for the numbers. When they substituted 13, for 1 and 3 alone, it generated an "M." But putting 3 and 1 together and getting 31 didn't work with only 26 letters in the Alphabet.

So, through trial and error, combining some letters and using others by themselves, they determined 13151814 revealed a name—Moran—a triumphant moment. The code spelled out the name and telephone number of the Irish Mafia leader but Gallo contained his exuberance this time, having seen the Chief's look of concern at his previous outburst.

Their satisfaction turned sour as Chief Taylor dampened their enthusiasm. "You know, this doesn't prove anything. Moran can claim anyone could have his number. He's a popular guy."

AJ sat back in his chair and ran a hand through his hair. "You're right, Chief. But it does give us a thread to pursue at least for the supply of drugs if not for murder."

"You still have jurisdiction problems unless the FBI can be brought in, which I don't see happening," the Chief stated. "My courses with the Feds taught me federal drug cases are reserved for trafficking across state lines or cultivating or manufacturing illegal substances. Can you prove the gang does that in obtaining their stuff?"

"They must. Doubt they have the ability to manufacture it themselves," AJ answered.

"The consequences are severe if you can uncover proof. The Narcotics Control Act of 1956 increased the penalties for possession and distribution. Sale can get you five to ten years."

"What about involving the state police?" McCrory asked.

"Same problem as getting the FBI involved," Taylor said. But after a pause, his demeanor changed. "But the Federal Bureau of Narcotics (FBN), operating out of the Treasury Department, might jump at this."

"Never heard of them," Gallo said.

"They're overshadowed by Hoover and the FBI. They're the agency tasked with spearheading federal drug enforcement," the Chief explained. "The commissioner of the FBN is a crusader, name's Henry Anslinger. Claims Communist China is flooding the U.S with heroin to corrupt our youth."

McCrory grunted. Gallo lifted his eyebrows.

"Of course, he also asserts Lucky Luciano is controlling the trade from Sicily, part of an Italian Mafia plot."

Gallo got up and paced back and forth. "If Anslinger believes in the Italian Mafia hawking drugs, he'd probably buy into the Irish, the Winter Hill Gang, or whatever you call them, doing likewise."

The Chief raised the same issue as earlier. "The FBN boys will jump at the chance to get drugs off the street, but they'll need evidence. The name of Moran on a pad of paper won't cut it."

"With Mitch's death, we're up shits creek," McCrory said.

Gallo paused in his movement, picked up some chalk from the blackboard and wrote: Jerry Morris.

Taylor and McCrory looked dumbfounded.

"Why not," Gallo lobbied. "He knew Smith possessed cocaine and sold it. Had to know where it came from."

"I'm not sure he's that savvy," McCrory said. "And what if he did know, we only have his word?"

"We'll, like the Chief says, the FBN is leading a fight to stamp out drugs and those who sell them. They should listen to us."

"Okay," McCrory conceded, "but we still have to convince the weasel to tell us what he knows."

"Might be your best hope on the drugs," the Chief agreed. "But aren't you losing focus here? You're supposed to be trying to find out who killed this Bradley Evans fella and Mitch Smith. Drug enforcement isn't our job."

"What if the murders and drug dealing are tied together?" Gallo stressed. "At least the killing of Smith."

"Prove it," the Chief said and left the room.

With the Chief gone, the two detectives sat back mulling over his challenge. Gallo broke the silence. "How about some coffee? We need to review where we stand on the focus of this investigation, determine if we've been sidetracked?"

"I'll ask the desk sergeant to put on a fresh pot," McCrory said. "We have a small kitchen down the hall."

When McCrory returned about five minutes later. Gallo stood at the blackboard built onto the wall at the end of the conference table. "Let's go back to the beginning and trace the line to where we are now," he said.

"Sounds like a plan," McCrory agreed.

On the left side of the board Gallo printed, using white chalk, under the heading <u>Victims,</u> the names Berger, Rose, Evans and Smith. Beside Berger and Rose, he wrote in parentheses (Killed by Evans). Next to Evans and Smith's name he put a question mark.

"Okay," he said. "This started with two dead bodies in Paragon Park. We know those guys robbed the gas station near the Hingham rotary and were killed the same night. Jerry Morris I'D them. Later, after lying, he admitted seeing Bradley Evans driving the getaway car. Our theory is that Evans was spooked when his co-conspirators shot Morris. He fled to Hull because he had lived and worked there."

Before Gallo could continue, the desk sergeant knocked and entered the conference room with a carafe and two blue mugs with the Hingham PD logo painted on the side. "Coffee is served," he said and bowed. The detectives laughed and thanked him with Gallo offering a slow clap.

McCrory poured them both a steaming mug and urged Gallo to resume.

"Okay," Gallo began. "From here on much of this is speculation. Berger and Rose took the cocaine from the garage safe where we found it later in Morris' car, which they used to chase Evans to Hull when he deserted them.

Evans thinks he's in the clear after volunteering to meet with us. And he did throw us off. Then he's run down in Hingham square by an unknown assailant. Maybe someone who thought he absconded with their cocaine. We suspect Mitch Smith, who peddled the drug and needed to make good on the stash he lost."

Gallo paused to take a swig of coffee and McCrory jumped in. "This is where our speculation goes south, in my estimation. As I said before, why kill Evans without trying to retrieve the drugs? Witnesses say the car that struck Evans kept on going. The driver didn't get out to take Evans's briefcase, which he carried at the time, and could have contained drugs."

"Maybe Smith kills him because he's angry, not thinking straight." Gallo speculated.

"And risk the wrath of Bobby Moran's boys when he comes up empty handed and can't repay them in cash."

Gallo shook his head, "You're right. Doesn't seem probable."

"No, it doesn't."

"So where does that leave us?" Gallo asked.

"With two unsolved murders. Although we can connect the dots and guess the mobsters realized Smith could never make good—took him out as a lesson to other dealers who might try to stiff them."

"Okay, that gives us a rationale for following the drug line to the mob but doesn't account for Evans? Let's pause for a moment. We're going on the assumption Smith was murdered. Still possible he killed himself. We need to wait for the autopsy results before charging ahead."

"Says the Gung Ho Marine."

Gallo laughed and raised his coffee cup in a salute.

They agreed not to move until the autopsy report came in.

They didn't have long to wait.

Four days later, Hingham Police Chief Taylor received the results from the Boston Medical Examiner's office. The M.E. determined Smith died as a result of blunt force trauma to the back of his head—dead prior to being hooked up to a hose from his car's exhaust—not suicide.

Chief Taylor summoned McCrory and Gallo to his office to share the findings. Not surprised, McCrory shook his head. "Another murder in our quiet town."

"Not so quiet anymore," Taylor mused. "We need to bring in the state police. This is beyond our resources. No reflection on you boys," he added, seeing the looks of dismay on the two young men.

"Chief," Gallo protested. "Jeff and I have been on this from the beginning. My partner, Lieutenant Wilkinson, is looped in. The Mets is the third largest law enforcement agency in New England. We have a detective unit of more than two dozen officers. No question these murders are connected to the Paragon Park slayings, which originated in our jurisdiction. I can tap into all of our investigative services which include agents on the Governor's drug task forces and detectives who liaison with the FBI. We have a great advantage over any outsiders. We'd waste time bringing them up to speed."

McCrory jumped in: "He's right Chief. The Staties would start from scratch and, if history is any yardstick, like the FBI, they'll freeze us out. We have a perfect justification for keeping this in house. We can make the case there is a straight line from the Paragon Park murders through Bradley Evans to Mitch Smith. Lieutenant Wilkinson will work with us. We have a good relationship."

Gallo raised his eyebrows—a stretch, but the Chief didn't know that.

The double team worked. "Okay. I'll buy that" Taylor conceded. "But when word leaks of Mitch's murder, and it will, the press will go nuts. They'll want answers we don't have; his father will lead the charge."

"Can we meet with Mr. Smith?" AJ asked. "Convince him releasing the report will alert the killer who may go to ground, which is true. If the guy thinks we bought the suicide, he'll let his guard down."

"I'll talk to Gavin," the Chief said. "Get him to back off for a time—a short time."

"Thanks Chief," Gallo said. "We'll start with Jerry Morris. He lied to us once. Good chance he knows more about the murders."

"Let's hope so," the Chief said.

Jerry Morris walked more now trying to clear his head and build up his strength to look for work. The months in a coma sapped his energy.

And, he needed to get out of the house away from his mother's constant harangues and his wife's meek compliance.

The solitude of a walk while sucking in fresh air helped his mental state. He often trudged as far as the South Shore Country Club and stopped at the bar for a vodka tonic before trekking back home. He'd cross the railroad tracks and cling to the side of the road, no sidewalks in that part of town.

On this day, Jerry began his hike at 4:35 p.m. in a good mood. He struggled to whistle, couldn't manage it—never could. A rush of air all he got for his effort, that and some spittle on his chin. He shook it off and a smile creased his lips as a cool breeze energized him. He had a spring in his step as he anticipated the vodka tonic awaiting once in the country club bar.

Fords and Chevys whistled by, augmented by at least one Studebaker, a Buick, a Cadillac and a Nash Rambler. Jerry guessed the Ford's and Chevy's would outnumber all other brands. He liked to keep track in his head as he sometimes did at the gas station when bored; the Edsel he owned his mother's idea. And if the traffic was any indicator, not very popular.

The sun was setting as Jerry reached the club at the golf course. He took a seat at a table in the bar overlooking the eighteenth hole, where the last foursome wrapped up their round. Jerry expected them to change in the locker room and make their way to the lounge. He didn't know their names, though he saw the same group on two or three other visits.

The waitress brought him his vodka tonic without him asking. He puffed up his chest and felt part of the scene although he'd never golfed in his life—couldn't afford membership or a Tee time. Ten minutes later, he waved to two of the men from the last clique of golfers as they entered the bar and sat at a table two removed from Jerry's. He wasn't aware of the man sitting behind him with a Calloway golf cap pulled low over his forehead.

Jerry ordered another drink, quaffed it down, dropped two fives on the table—an extravagance but he liked the waitress—and dipped his head to her as he wobbled toward the door.

Giddy, his gait unsteady, he shuffled through the parking lot out to South Street. Cold air enveloped him as darkness fell. The roadway was not well lighted, but the glow from windows in the houses along the way marked his route home. He stumbled into the road a couple of times before recovering and returning to the dirt shoulder.

The man in the Calloway golf cap left ten minutes after Jerry, got into his Ford Fairlane and drove five miles an hour onto South Street. He planned to strike Jerry with his vehicle, throw his body into the trunk, then dump him on the railroad tracks to be pulverized by the commuter train; an unfortunate accident.

He didn't count on a kindhearted waitress spoiling his fun.

As the stalker accelerated toward his unsuspecting victim, red and blue flashing lights reflected in his rearview mirror—a Hingham Police cruiser. Fearful he violated some traffic rule, the man pulled to the roadside, only to see the cops sail by and stop alongside his target.

The thoughtful waitress at the country club bar, aware Jerry walked home, worried he would stray into traffic. He had never downed consecutive vodka tonics before, left a large tip and appeared unsteady on his feet. She notified the police and a patrol unit in the area was dispatched to search for him.

Her concern saved Jerry's life. At least for a short time.

CHAPTER 32

The morning after Jerry Morris escaped death, Detectives Gallo and McCrory showed up at his house. He answered the doorbell, his mother nowhere to be seen.

"Mother's out shopping. Went to a meat market in Quincy," Morris said, when he noticed the men looking behind him. "Expect you'll be happy about that," he said, a smirk creasing his face.

Neither man responded as they slipped past him into the house. Truth be told, they were pleased not to encounter the old shrew.

Jerry didn't offer them a seat. Annoyed by once again being harassed by the cops, he asked in a condescending tone, "What now?"

"We just want to tie up some loose ends," McCrory said. "You've been very helpful so far."

Morris crossed his arms, his back stiffened. "Told you everything I know."

"Let us judge that, okay," Gallo said.

"Make it quick. I'm busy."

Doing what, AJ thought, but didn't say; drinking and sitting in your armchair. "We need to clarify an important point about where the coke came from that Mitch Smith kept at the garage."

Morris blinked several times, turned away, scared. "Don't know nothing 'bout that, he said, his voice quivering.

"We can't protect you Jerry, unless you tell the truth," McCrory said.

"You're a dead man without us, Jerry. The dealers don't care if you talked or not. You're a liability," Gallo pointed out.

Tears ran down Morris' cheeks. He hugged himself to stop shaking.

Gallo slipped him a handkerchief. He began carrying one after he saw Officer Caruso hand one to Amy Berger while consoling her after her husband's murder.

Morris wiped his eyes and moved to sit in his recliner. The detectives sat on the couch opposite. It took about five minutes for him to get control. "I don't know nothing for sure, ya 'unerstand, just what Mitch told me."

"And what did he say?" McCrory asked.

"Mitch needed money; couldn't get it from his dad, who canned him. He couldn't find work, though I don't think he tried hard."

Morris blew his nose into the handkerchief Gallo slipped him causing AJ to wince.

"He ran up a big gambling debt with the Irish Mafia and couldn't repay it. He was desperate. Some guy in the mob, Whitey something, arranged it so he could work off what he owed by selling drugs."

"You know this for sure?" McCrory pressed.

"No! I told ya. Only through word a' mouth."

"Would you be willing to testify to that in court?"

"No, sir! No, sir!" he whimpered.

"We can protect you, Jerry," Gallo said.

Morris, agitated, rubbed his hands together, glanced around the room as if mobsters might be lurking in the house. "Won't do it. Won't do it. I'll take the Fifth. You can't make me."

"Okay Jerry, okay," McCrory said. "Calm down. Just think about it."

The lawmen left the house discouraged—pushing Jerry further wouldn't be productive.

Quincy Patriot Ledger crime reporter Bert Jones followed the ambulance from Mitch Smith's house in Hingham to the office of the medical examiner at 720 Albany Street, Boston. He watched as the attendants removed a body shrouded in a white sheet and wheeled it into the building. He was aware that, among the Boston M.E.'s duties, one was to perform autopsies on suspicious deaths. He would confront the men when they returned to their van and see what info he could squeeze from them—in a diplomatic way, of course.

CHAPTER 33

Mike Callahan reported his car's vandalism to principal, Leonard Damon, a balding, genial, understanding leader but one who brooked no nonsense. He was the descendant of John L. Damon, who founded the Atlantic House, one of the town's largest hotels in the era when Nantasket was the pre-eminent tourist attraction in New England. He owned a three-story home overlooking the ocean where the Atlantic House once stood.

Town residents, unaware of this connection, respected him for his school leadership and his involvement in the community. He directed the MDC's beach clean-up crews in the summer. When he learned of Callahan's predicament, Damon, furious, scolded the student body over the school's intercom and threatened dire consequences if the damage to a teacher's car continued. He brought troublemakers into his office and grilled them until sure they took no part in the vandalism. He warned them to inform him of anything they heard on the "grapevine."

None of these efforts succeeded, nor did the report to the Hull Police, who assigned Officer Paul Franklin to the case. Parents called the cops concerned such behavior might escalate and somehow harm their children.

Franklin lectured seventh grade classes on the legal consequences of this kind of mischief. One kid in Callahan's class reported seeing two men walking around the schoolyard one day. He couldn't remember what day, and couldn't describe, them except to say they had red hair. Franklin asked if they could've been parents. The boy didn't know.

Callahan let the principal's efforts go forward and the police follow up he believed would be futile. No kids vandalized his car. He suspected the adults seen by one of his students were old acquaintances, not friends and not people to be trifled with.

The red hair clinched it.

That said, he didn't know what options he had. The guys who damaged his car were capable of violence. If he did nothing, and the attacks continued, Susan could be at risk.

Frightened, Susan Lawrence feared her fiancé was holding back. Though upset by the vandalism of his car, he didn't appear motivated to stop it. She had to prod him to report it to the principal. She suspected he knew who did it, but was unwilling, or afraid, to confront them. She loved Mike and didn't want to go behind his back, yet she longed to do something.

She sat in a chair in her home next to the table that held their telephone. A phone book rested on her lap with a page opened to the number for the MDC Station in Nantasket. She picked up the receiver, hesitated, then dialed.

The desk officer answered. She said she was friend of Detective Gallo and asked to speak to him. The sergeant, leery of such calls, asked if he could have him return her call.

"Please," she pleaded. "Tell him it's Susan Lawrence."

The sergeant, still wary, placed her on hold and punched Gallo's extension on the off chance the woman was a friend of Gallo's. He remembered the detective's reaction when he discovered he hadn't been notified of a car towed across from Paragon Park after the storms.

"Yeah," AJ barked, annoyed, when his intercom buzzed.

"Sorry to bother you detective. A lady on the phone says she's a friend of yours, a Susan Lawrence."

Gallo's heart skipped a beat. "Put her through," he managed to say, his hand shaking.

When his line lit up, he picked up the receiver and said, "Gallo."

"AJ, this is Susan."

"What can I do for you?" he asked, curious why she would contact him after stating they had no future as a couple—curious but hopeful.

"I need your help," she cried, her voice cracking.

Her distress got his attention. "Are you okay?"

"Yes. But I want to speak with you face to face."

Alerted to the anxiety reflected in her tone, he offered to meet with her later that evening or early the next morning.

"Tonight, please, your office about eight-thirty."

Startled, and sensing her grief, Gallo blurted. "Okay. That works."

After speaking with his former sweetheart, Gallo, shaken, spent five-or-six minutes wondering what had unnerved her so much she felt it necessary to contact him. Uncomfortable, but setting aside his concern, he took the remainder of the afternoon reviewing his notes. Around five, he called Cohasset Officer Vince Russo on his home phone. Russo had given it to him and said, "call anytime."

"Sorry to bother you at home Vince. I need your help again. We should make you an honorary detective."

"Forget the 'honorary' shit.' Tell my chief what an asset I've been."

"Promise I will when this mess is over. Now, I need more information about David Rose. You went to school with him. What can you tell me about him?"

"I told you he and his twin were pranksters—fooled girlfriends and teachers by switching identities."

"Did you ever see him lose his temper, be violent with anyone?"

"I do know he could hold a grudge if crossed. Wouldn't talk with that person for weeks. He got in a scuffle once when a player on the football team started pushing Dustin around. The kid accused Dustin of missing a block on purpose."

Gallo scoffed. "I know a few guys in high school who took a dive rather than hit someone. Happens all the time."

"Yeah! But David was irate the guy attacked his brother—the one time I've seen him angry. Here's the thing, though. He waited a couple of days, then blindsided the kid after school, sucker punched him when he was walking home. Sent him to the hospital."

"Good to know, Vince. Thanks for the insight."

"No problem. Now about that honorary promotion."

AJ laughed and ended the call. The information about David getting incensed when a classmate pushed his brother was significant. And having the patience to wait several days to retaliate was also a critical piece. If he somehow found out Bradley Evans killed Dustin, he waited for an opportunity, saw him alone, ran him down. Which means, if he did it, he stalked him. Doubt he just happened to see him in downtown Hingham.

The question remained. How did he find out before the news release that Evans was the culprit? Did they have a leak—in the MDC or Hingham PD?

That was worrisome.

AJ left the office after his conversation with Vince Russo and walked down to the Anastos restaurant for dinner. He got a cheeseburger, fries and a vanilla milkshake, killing time to meet Susan Lawrence at eight-thirty that night.

While he ate, something occurred to him that should have a long time ago. He waved the guy behind the counter, Joe Mancuso, over. "Want something else, AJ?" the old man asked.

"Some information, Joe. Did you open a couple days before Christmas?"

Mancuso looked away for a minute or two, thinking. "Yeah," he said, after his brief pause. "About three hours in the morning on the 22nd or 23rd, I think. Closed up when the storm hit hard. Lucky to make it home."

"Did you have any customers?"

The old man rubbed his forehead. "Come to think of it. Young fella. Nervous sort. Kept looking at the door, working his leg like a jackhammer."

Gallo kicked himself for not coming to the restaurant before; assumed there would be no witnesses outside the park, except the plow crews. He was astonished the shooter stopped at Anastos'.

"Would you recognize the man if I showed you a picture, Joe?"

The old man ran his fingers through his hair, scrunched his face, looked out the window. "Not sure. I remember he parted his hair down the middle. Not many guys do that anymore."

AJ nodded. Brad Evans was one of the holdouts who did just that. "Thanks Joe," he said. "I'll come back with the photo. What's the damage for the burger and milkshake?"

AJ returned to the station surprised to see Susan and a man sitting on the bench opposite the desk sergeant. They both stood as he entered. Susan spoke first. "AJ, thank you for meeting with me. This is my fiancé, Mike Callahan."

Callahan was about five-ten, broad shouldered, brown hair cut short, what the barbers of the day called a regular man's haircut. He appeared small compared to Gallo, not unusual. He presented a full mouth smile of perfect white teeth.

"Nice to meet you," Gallo said, and shook his hand, resisting the urge to use a vice-like grip. "Let's go up to my office, such as it is."

AJ led the way and set up two folding chairs. "Sorry about the accommodations," he said. "Not the Taj Mahal."

Susan and Mike laughed—a forced effort by Callahan.

"Mike is here against his wishes, I'm afraid," Susan said. "He agreed at my insistence."

"Okay," AJ said, turning toward Callahan, who took the hint.

"My car has been vandalized twice in two months. I didn't report the first one but did so this last time when Sue persisted."

"More like nagged," Susan added.

Gallo kept silent. He remembered how tenacious Lawrence could be even as a teenager.

Mike continued. "The first thought, of course, given we teach at an elementary, junior high, was kids, in retaliation for some unknown transgression on my part. I let the principal and the police think that. Something I'm ashamed of. I'm pretty sure I know who's responsible and it's not students."

Gallo held back, letting Callahan finish his narrative.

"I grew up in Somerville, palled around with a bunch of boys who later formed a gang the press now calls the Winter Hill crew, mostly Irish."

Gallo perked up, stayed quiet, eager to hear the rest of the story.

Callahan glanced sideways at Lawrence. She indicated by the dip of her head that he should continue, which he did.

"Many of them dropped out of school. We drifted away from each other. They kept trying to drag me back into the group, which began shaking down kids for money and stealing from convenience stores. Now as adults, they're running numbers, controlling gambling and horse racing, hijacking trucks. God forbid killing people though I have no proof of that."

He paused, held Susan's gaze for a second or two, then plowed on. "I got farther away from them, went to Northeastern, earned my teaching credential, moved here, met Susan. Two guys, the O'Rourke brothers, never let up trying to force me back into the gang. The vandalism of my car is their not-so-subtle pressure to do so. I believe that because a student reported seeing two men with red hair, near the school when my car was damaged. The O'Rourke's are red-headed."

Gallo tried not to show his interest in Callahan's tale now that he mentioned the Irish Mafia. He said: "I'm a Metro Detective, Mike, I don't have jurisdiction in the town of Hull, just within the Nantasket Reservation as the state calls it."

Susan, crestfallen, choked up. Mike accepted the news with a shrug. He started to get up.

"But there is a way I may be able to help," AJ said.

Both Callahan and Lawrence brightened.

"I can't go into particulars, of course, but the Irish hoodlums you describe are on our radar as part of an ongoing investigation. We could use some inside information on the gang— might help us, and you, though I can't promise anything now. Would you be willing to meet with me and my partner? What I have in mind could be dangerous."

Callahan struck a side-ways glance at Lawrence, who paled. "Sure," he said. "Tell me where and when."

When they left his office, Gallo couldn't believe his good fortune. The vandalism of a car in Hull might enable him to penetrate the Irish gang, find out if they were involved in the murder of Mitch Smith.

His idea was unorthodox, risky and not strictly legal. He couldn't go through the normal channels to execute his hastily put together plan—not a plan, really—more like a hope. It all hinged on a one-time gang member and the fiancé of his former girlfriend.

The Fate's, seemingly smiling on him now, would later cast a pall on his life and shake him to his core.

CHAPTER 34

Reporter Bert Jones greeted the two ambulance attendants leaving the Boston medical examiner's office with a smile and a bag of Dunkin Donuts. He flashed his Patriot Ledger ID and intimated he worked in the lab, returning with a treat for the technicians. He said he had plenty and gave them a choice. The tired men, happy to take a break and enjoy a snack, leaned against their vehicle and enjoyed the raspberry jellies they both selected.

Again, acting as if he was a morgue employee, Jones swiped his hand across his forehead and said with a weary voice, "Been a busy day in Boston for dead bodies."

"Our guy's not from the city. We came in from Hingham," one of the men said, then wiped his mouth with a napkin Jones provided.

"Something special about him?" Bert asked.

The attendant sneaked a look around as if afraid of being overheard. "Probable suicide. The cops wanted an autopsy to be sure. His dad has a lot of juice in the town, friend of the chief of police, I heard."

"Loved ones want closure and the cops want to eliminate foul play," Jones said, a sympathetic look on his face.

"Suppose so," the man agreed, finished his donut and signaled to his partner they had to go. "Thanks for the snack, pal," he said and hopped into the cab of the van. His co-worker followed.

Bert waived, opened the door to the M.E.'s office and pretended to enter. When the van was out of sight, he jogged back across the street to his car. He couldn't believe his good fortune. His instinct proved right in following the ambulance. The dead man was Gavin Smith's son. And if he committed suicide or had been harmed in some way—murdered—it would be a scoop for him. Like the man said, "Gavin had a lot of juice in the community."

Jones practically clicked his heels together in jubilation. He'd impress Gallo and McCrory with his findings and press them for more info.

Bert didn't understand that inserting himself into a murder investigation might not be the wisest of ideas.

CHAPTER 35

Each passing day brought the conspirators closer to the bank robbery and Bill Wilkinson closer to despair. His use of a pilfered test, courtesy of Captain Kellum, opened him to blackmail. To resist Kellum's orders would end his career. He was screwed. He had a stay-at-home wife and two sons in junior college. If the scheme failed, and he was arrested, what would happen to them?

He sat at his desk in the bull-pen, elbows on the desk-top, head in his hands, seeking a way out of his predicament. He had run the options in his mind, and narrowed them to two as he saw it. One, gather evidence against the captain and turn him in or two, somehow force him to call off the robbery.

Oddly, his thoughts drifted to his idealistic partner, a Gung-Ho Marine. The name Bobby Moran, turned up in Gallo's reports. He and a Hingham detective were now searching for the man who ran down the suspected killer of the Paragon Park victims.

If he pointed them towards Moran, it might put heat on the gangsters, press them to lay low, cancel the Quincy heist and relieve him of the danger of arrest.

He took out a pack of Camels and leaned back in his wooden swivel chair. He took two deep drags and blew the smoke into the ceiling. It calmed him for the moment, though his predicament didn't disappear. Any attempt to throw suspicion on Moran for the murder in Hingham was sure to raise Kellum's hackles; a man dangerous to cross.

Wilkinson crushed out his cigarette and took a bottle of aspirin from his desk drawer. He popped two in his mouth and washed them down with a cup of stale coffee. He tried to push the mess from his thoughts.

He wasn't successful.

Wilkinson ruminated on his dilemma for most of the day, then left a message for AJ Gallo to meet him in Nantasket the next day to review the investigation of the hit-and-run in Hingham. His plan was to use this time to propose they investigate Bobby Moran. If that failed, he had an even bolder scheme in mind.

He was a desperate man and desperate men took risks; risks that might end his life and those recruited to help him. Moran was a killer and Kellum not to be underestimated. Much depended on his rookie partner. He knew the kid didn't trust or respect him. He'd all but abandoned him during the Paragon Park murder investigation. An appeal to his "better angels" was Wilkinson's best hope. A long shot by any standards.

Any attempt to gather evidence about Kellum's illegal activities was precarious, would take time, and probably prove futile. Wilkinson doubted the captain foolish enough to put anything incriminating in writing. And, even if he found such documents, he didn't consider going to the FBI or Kellum's superiors—no telling how many were ensnared in his boss's net. Distraught, he fingered his .38 Special, another way out of this mess, if he had the courage.

The following day, Wilkinson met Gallo in the cramped upstairs office of the MDC Building. "Let's take a walk," he said.

Gallo nodded, surprised when he got the message about the lieutenant coming to town. He was an absentee partner in the recent murder investigations starting with those at Paragon Park and extending to the deliberate hit-and-run of the culprit, Bradley Evans. Wilkinson didn't know about Mitch Smith's death. Why the sudden interest?

"Yes, sir," he said.

"AJ, you don't need to call me sir. We're partners."

"Yes, sir," Gallo said, a mischievous gleam in his eye.

Both men laughed.

"Let's go out on the pier for privacy," Wilkinson directed.

The old steamboat landing, repaired several times after devastating fires, still operated in the summer. Once, during the town's hey-day as a tourist and gambling mecca in the late eighteen and early nineteen-hundreds, thousands poured across its surface daily with boats arriving hourly. Now, only three or four a day, primarily on weekends, dropped off beach goers and Paragon Park enthusiasts.

In the off-season, men and boys fished off the dock's wooden planks, propping up their lines and hoping for a nibble. On this day, a father and son sat unmoving at the tip of the wharf, a bait pail squeezed between them. They both wore woolen jackets and Red Sox baseball caps.

The two lawmen crossed George Washington Boulevard and stopped half-way out on the dock to guarantee privacy. Wilkinson peered out on the water, arms folded, for two to three minutes. The bay was calm, boats lay still at their moorings. The brown shingled houses on Sagamore Hill looked down on the scene as they did every day, regardless of season.

Still gazing into the distance, Wilkinson spoke. "What I'm going to tell you will sound unbelievable, AJ, but I promise it's true."

He turned toward his partner to gage his reaction. The younger man remained impassive, so he continued. "Over the Memorial Day weekend, the Quincy Savings & Loan will be robbed."

This news braced AJ but he kept silent, waiting for the man to elaborate.

"The robbery will be carried out by people associated with the Irish Mafia, or Winter Hill Gang as some newshounds call them. They will be aided by law enforcement officers from several departments."

Gallo, stunned, rasped, "How do you know this?"

"Members of our department are involved."

"What? Who?"

"Can't tell you."

The veins in AJ's neck bulged, his face reddened. He balled his fists. "Why are you involving me. I'm a rookie. What can I do?"

Wilkinson took a step back, tried not to appear intimidated. He kept his voice just above a whisper. "I have a plan to stop the scheme you alone might be able to pull off."

AJ shook his head, unbelieving. "Bill. We have no jurisdiction in Quincy. Notify them."

"Can't. A high-ranking Quincy officer is involved. Maybe others from that department."

Gallo stood back, stunned, growing angrier by the minute. Though not naïve, the thought of lawmen brazenly participating in a robbery was hard to accept. It would tarnish everyone who carried a badge.

As if reeling from a blow, he stumbled away from Wilkinson to the edge of the highway. A 57 Plymouth Belvedere, its undercarriage rusted from the salt used to melt snow on roadways, whizzed by followed by a blue Ford F-100 pickup in better condition. Both were speeding.

Gallo ran his fingers over an abrasion on the right side of his neck, as he did when confronted by unusual or difficult situations—the healed gash a souvenir from Korea. He had others on his legs, left side and right shoulder. Nausea engulfed him as he bent over at the waist, hands on his hips—like the dry heaves he experienced before combat.

Was he about to do battle again?

Fuming, he strode back to his partner, grabbed Wilkinson by his jacket lapels and lifted him off the ground. The lieutenant's eyes grew wide, his face red, fear emanating from every pore. He couldn't speak until AJ lowered him to the pier.

Relieved Gallo hadn't pummeled him or thrown him into the bay, he straightened his jacket and pulled his tie away from his collar. He fumbled for the right words, trembling.

"I know this is a shock, son," he said.

Furious, AJ said, "A shock? It's preposterous. And don't you dare call me son. You're my lieutenant; nothing more."

Chastised and afraid, Wilkinson thought it best to tell the story before Gallo attacked him. "I know when the scheme is going to take place and where the robbers are going to split the loot if they pull it off—a house in Whitfield."

"And I suppose you can't contact cops there for the same reason as Quincy?"

"Yes."

"Then what the hell do you expect me to do Bill," he roared, loud enough to attract the attention of the father and son on the wharf, who craned their necks toward the sound of the voices.

Harnessing his fear, Wilkinson blurted, "You and McCrory are investigating the murder of Bradley Evans, right?"

"Yes, sir," AJ said, spitting out the words.

Wilkinson raised his eyebrows at the use of the word "sir," did not correct his partner this time, unsure of Gallo's state of mind. He said. "You have two names on your list of suspects—Mitch Smith and Bobby Moran."

Gallo had a quizzical expression on his face, still furious.

"And you found cocaine on the guys killed in Paragon Park?"

AJ stood transfixed, wondering where this was headed.

"The drug came from the Irish gang out of Somerville I mentioned earlier. If your investigation leads you to that outfit, no one will guess I intervened. And if you put the screws to Smith, threaten him with a long stretch in prison, he might give up Moran and his boys."

Gallo smirked. "You tried to sabotage our interest in Smith before. Why the sudden change?"

"I'm being pulled into the robbery and want nothing to do with it. This is my last resort—as crazy as it may appear."

Gallo shook his head. Wilkinson's idea was out of date. "I haven't sent you my latest report, Bill. Mitch Smith is dead, murdered, made to look like a suicide."

Wilkinson ran his fingers through his hair, looked into Hull Bay, his knees weak, heart racing.

Composing himself, he stepped close to Gallo and whispered, "Any way you can still trace the coke back to the Mafia?"

"Maybe! McCrory and I are investigating Smith's murder. We have a witness who says Mitch told him he got the drug from the Irish, but he refuses to testify to that in court."

"Put the screws to him."

"Not going to work. The guy's too fragile. Might bolt. Claim the 5th as he's threatened."

"Shit."

Gallo crossed his arms, glanced away for a minute or two, then returned his gaze to his partner. "Look, we know the coke came from Moran's outfit. He may have had Smith killed as an example to others who tried to stiff him. We can also say an anonymous source pointed us in his direction. And, we found his name on a coded sheet of paper in Smith's home office."

For the first time since their conversation began, Wilkinson relaxed. "AJ, that's perfect. Put that in your report to me ASAP. I'll show it to Captain Kellum."

"Something else," Gallo said, and paused, not sure if he should share it; decided to give him the bare minimum. "We may have a way to infiltrate the gang."

Wilkinson looked surprised, but hopeful. "Why didn't you tell me this before? How?"

AJ jumped at the chance to take a jab at Wilkinson's secrecy. "I'm not free to say right now. Like you, I can't reveal names."

Wilkinson tensed; knew he couldn't press the issue. "Just keep me in the loop as best you can. Okay?"

"I can do that, 'as best I can,' as you say. Also, I assured Chief Taylor of the Hingham PD, who wanted to bring in the state police, by the way, that the Mets had the manpower to further the investigation of Smith's murder and we would do so."

Wilkinson, ecstatic, gushed, "This is better than I could have expected."

"Can you convince the captain to agree to let us continue investigating wherever it may lead, and give us more men and resources?"

"Absolutely," Wilkinson promised.

His confidence would soon be dashed.

The two lawmen walked back to the MDC Building in silence. The older man drove off without saying anything more. Gallo climbed the stairs and plunked down in the wooden swivel chair in the small office. Elbows on the desk-top, he cradled his head in his hands, eyes closed. He didn't like his partner, didn't trust him, viewed him as playing the system. But his story was so absurd, he believed him. And the one in-house officer capable of putting pressure on Lieutenant Wilkinson was Captain Kellum, their immediate superior.

AJ had a difficult time processing the bombshell dropped on him. If Wilkinson's story was true, their profession was riddled with bad guys. He was already disillusioned by his tour in Korea. Communists weren't swarming American streets as politicians had warned; a ploy to rile the nation and send young patriots like him to their deaths.

His buddies sacrifice had been for nothing. Wilkinson's tale made him feel that, as a cop, he was again being duped. They told him he was part of a thin blue line keeping society free from criminals, except some of those who preached that were crooks themselves.

Memorial Day weekend was about three weeks away—not much time to decide. He couldn't believe he would even consider doing what Wilkinson proposed. He got himself into it; let him get out of it.

He considered blowing the whistle on the scheme but that would put Wilkinson in a vice. He didn't dislike the man enough to end his career or endanger his family. He sat back in his chair and shook his head. Maybe Mike Callahan would be a game changer. He wasn't quite sure how, though. And did he want to risk the safety of his former girlfriend's fiancé, an innocent civilian, to crack his case?

Bill Wilkinson returned to Boston with renewed hope. If AJ followed through and sent him the update on the status of their investigation, he believed he could persuade Captain Kellum to warn the Irish to postpone or cancel the planned robbery.

He was wrong.

Two days later, Captain Martin Kellum was apoplectic when he received Gallo's report that he and his Hingham partner were zeroing in on Bobby Moran as a suspect in the now confirmed murder of Mitch Smith. He was pacing his office when his lieutenant reported in after being summoned.

"Bill," he blustered, waving a piece of paper in the air. "Did you know about this?"

Wilkinson blanched in the face of Kellum's fury. "What? What is it, sir?" he asked, knowing what it must be.

"This latest update from Gallo."

Wilkinson's face flushed as he lied. "Haven't had a chance to read it, sir."

"An autopsy verified that this Mitch Smith character was murdered. Gallo believes the Irish boys were involved."

Wilkinson replied, a tremor in his voice, "I understand he and McCrory are trying to find the source of the drug in the car driven by the gas station robbers."

Kellum slammed the report down on his desk, shaking his head, face red. "Gallo expects us to provide support for his inquiry into Moran?"

"I believe so, sir," Wilkinson said, at a loss for words. This wasn't going the way he expected.

"What do you mean, "you believe so," sir? We have no proof. An anonymous tip. A name on a piece of paper. If Bobby thinks we're selling him out, no telling what he might do?"

Wilkinson, desperate, saw his opening. "Maybe if we can convince him to back off the Quincy heist for now, we can slow Gallo and McCrory down. Figure a way to steer them in a different direction."

Kellum fumed. "This is a goddamn mess, Bill. I trusted you to control the kid. Any attempt to put the robbery off now will undo months of planning. Not going to happen. Fix it Bill. Goddamn, fix it."

Bill Wilkinson slinked out of Captain Kellum's office a beaten man. He'd persuaded Gallo to forge ahead with the investigation of Moran and to send the report to their boss. He even promised assistance by supplying additional man power to the case. Gallo was a straight arrow. He'd hate being manipulated.

He and McCrory suspected Moran had Mitch Smith eliminated as a message to other dealers who stiffed him. But, as Kellum said, they had no proof of that. They still hadn't figured out who killed Bradley Evans. Moran would have no reason to be involved in that. Someone else had to have murdered Evans and maybe Smith. If he agreed to get more help for that possibility, would it deter Gallo from pursuing Moran? He had no choice but to try. His career and, perhaps his life, hung in the balance.

CHAPTER 36

Jerry Morris, shaken by the visit from Detectives Gallo and McCrory, and unaware he had been a target on his last stroll, needed to clear his head. No way he wanted anything to do with Irish criminals. If they killed Mitch Smith, they wouldn't hesitate to snuff him out.

A brisk walk and a vodka tonic at the South Shore Country Club would lift his spirits. His mother, due home any minute, no doubt would harangue him about finding work. He slipped on his jacket, almost skipped down his walkway, and turned south on Beal Street, earlier than his usual afternoon jaunt. Clouds blocked the sun and a chilling breeze braced him as he walked. No matter. He felt energized.

Jerry surprised the man stalking him by starting his trek early. The man considered taking him out but there were many potential witnesses around. A man and woman walking their dogs waved to Jerry as they passed and traffic was continuous, some drivers waving as they roared by.

The man knew from previous surveillances that it would take his target an hour to reach his destination. He would linger for another two hours after that watching the golfers and downing his drinks. By then it would be darker, with the low cloud cover; a safer time to act. He drove ahead to the country club. A few pick-me-ups would reinforce his courage.

At the country club Jerry took his favorite seat by the window, to watch the golfers finishing their round on the eighteenth hole; some pumping their fists when they sank a putt or doubling over in frustration when they missed. His mood fluctuated between joy and sadness as he empathized with the men. He had never participated in sports as a kid. He could see in their reactions how much the players enjoyed the game. He regretted never having tried it, though that was a fantasy. He didn't have the money or time.

Behind Jerry, his stalker, wearing his Calloway golf cap pulled low to obscure his face, slipped into a chair two tables away. He ordered a Jameson's on the rocks when the waitress came to his table and kept his face averted whenever possible.

As both men looked out onto the course, dark clouds swept down the hill carrying rain that pelted the windows. Thunder roared like cannon in the distance. Lightening pierced the sky above the trees as golfers scrambled across a narrow bridge to safety in the clubhouse.

Jerry was mesmerized by the scene, not concerned about his walk home. The fickle New England weather produced downpours one minute and bright sun the next. He ordered a hamburger and another vodka tonic determined to wait out the downpour.

After two hours, the skies did not clear and the rain intensified. Jerry decided to call his wife. He signaled the waitress for the bill. When she arrived, he told her he intended to use the phone in the locker room to call home. He had mingled with the golfers once or twice acting as if he was one of them.

The stalker, overhearing the conversation, and seeing an opportunity, jumped up. "Hey, pal," he said, "I'm leaving now. Can I offer you a lift?"

Startled, Jerry at first refused, but the stranger persisted. "My car's right outside. No trouble to help a fellow golfer."

Jerry smiled. "Oh! I don't play. Come here in this pleasant environment to watch and enjoy the scenery."

"Same for me," the man said. "I'm a duffer. Go out occasionally, happy when I break a hundred."

Jerry knew nothing about golf scores, assumed that breaking a hundred was good. The guy seemed nice. He relented.

"I live on Beal Street not far from here."

"Great. I'm parked a few slots over from the entrance."

They both settled their bills with the waitress who was pleased to see Jerry make a friend. He often appeared lonesome; drank his vodka and left.

The stalker was ecstatic. This couldn't have worked out better. He could take care of Jerry in his car, away from prying eyes, then dump him on the railroad tracks. That should have been his plan from the beginning. Running him down and struggling to stuff him into his car unseen was problematic—anyone driving by could have seen him and called the cops.

He smiled as they half-walked, half-jogged toward his car to stay dry. They were a few feet away when an Edsel roared up cutting them off. The driver, a woman, rolled down her window and shouted. "Jerry. I thought you would be here when you weren't home. Get in."

Jerry turned to the stranger and sighed. "Sorry, man. The wife."

The man pulled his cap lower to shield his face, and shuffled to his Ford Fairlane as Jerry and his wife drove off. Once inside his car, he smashed his fist against the steering wheel and cursed; the second time a bizarre circumstance foiled his plan to kill Jerry Morris.

He vowed not to give up. In his twisted thinking, the bastard deserved to die.

CHAPTER 37

AJ Gallo was in his office at the MDC Nantasket Station when Bill Wilkinson called. "Got bad news, I'm afraid," he said. Gallo kept silent, so his lieutenant continued. "The boss says we don't have enough evidence to pursue the investigation of the individual we discussed." He didn't mention names on the department line, wary someone might be listening.

When AJ still hadn't responded, Wilkinson plowed ahead, frustrated. "You and McCrory haven't pinned down who killed Bradley Evans. I have to agree with the Chief. It's doubtful our guy pulled that off."

Gallo fumed. He'd sent the investigative report to get his partner out of a jam. Now the man was backing off, no doubt under pressure from Captain Kellum. This confirmed, in Gallo's mind, that their Chief, possibly in cahoots with the Irish mobsters, was blackmailing Wilkinson into participating in a robbery. Bill's problem, not his. He was angry at being a pawn in Wilkinson's outrageous plot to save his own ass.

"So! You don't want to pursue what we discussed?"

"That's right. I'm ordering you to concentrate on finding the murderer of Bradley Evans and Mitch Smith. Only if hard evidence implicates our other suspect should you go in that direction. Understood?"

"Yes, sir."

Wilkinson smirked as Gallo continued to call him 'sir.' "Okay. I'm sending you two other detectives to assist. I'll tell you soon who they are."

"Understood," Gallo said, and terminated the call, angry at being jerked around. He was glad, in a way though, to avoid being sucked into the Quincy robbery scheme. He debated whether to let it happen or notify the FBI to head it off. For now, he'd concentrate on finding the killers of Evans and Smith.

If the evidence led to Moran, so be it.

Two days later, two Mets detectives showed up at the MDC Station in Nantasket. Both were twelve-year veterans. Gallo had seen them in the bureau in Boston, hadn't worked with either on a case.

Brian Hogan was tall and thin, hair cut short, going to gray, a wad of gum puffing his right cheek. His eyes darted around the small upstairs office where AJ sat in a wooden swivel chair.

His partner, Christopher Hawkins, was squat, with broad shoulders and a bull neck, cropped brown hair, green eyes. He was a veteran of the battles of Guadalcanal and Iwo Jima during World War II. His claim to fame in the Mets was being with Gunnery Sergeant, "Manila John" Basilone, when the Medal of Honor winner was killed on the sand at Iwo Jima. He spun the story often in the bureau to the delight of colleagues and in bars where he could count on at least one free beer. Both men stood since furniture in the room was minimal.

Gallo retrieved two folding chairs from the hall and beckoned them to sit. He forced a smile, not overwhelmed by their arrival. "Glad to see you guys. What do you know about the case?"

Hogan spoke first. "Not much. Just the two murders in town here were followed up by the killing of your main suspect."

Hawkins took out a pack of Marlboro's and lit up, saying nothing.

"I've been working with a Hingham detective because the other homicides took place there—out of our jurisdiction," Gallo said.

Neither man asked why Wilkinson wasn't more involved; not really surprised. They had him pegged as more of an admin guy who avoided the field whenever possible.

"Okay," Gallo continued. "We use the conference room at the Hingham PD to discuss the investigation. This office would put a closet to shame."

That elicited a chuckle from Hawkins and a knowing glance from Hogan.

Reporter Bert Jones' trek to Boston following the ambulance carrying the body of Mitch Smith had been successful. The attendants revealed the corpse they ferried to the Medical Examiner's died under suspicious circumstances. They disclosed the death was presumed a suicide but, in such situations, the police often requested autopsies.

Not news to Jones who now had a more difficult task—to discover the findings of that postmortem. He doubted he could gain access to the morgue with his press credentials, and even if he did, suspected the official would stonewall him. He decided his better option was to approach McCrory and Gallo—not sure how to accomplish that.

In the conference room at the Hingham PD, the introductions made, the four lawmen settled around the table, a carafe of coffee between them. AJ and McCrory sat on one side and the Mets detectives on the other.

"Jeff is going to take the lead on this," Gallo said, "since the last two murders took place in this town but, I think Jeff will agree, there is not a chain of command here, unless it's Chief Taylor, who has been involved. We feel comfortable working informally."

McCrory agreed, then brought them up to speed on their progress. He outlined how Bradley Evans came forward to throw them off but the testimony of Jerry Morris put him as the getaway driver in the gas station robbery. His late-night arrival at his boarding house on the night the men were killed, disheveled and cold as his landlady described, convinced them of his guilt.

The discovery of coke in the car driven by Berger and Rose led them to Mitch Smith who, again according to Morris, sold narcotics supplied by an Irish gang. He was a primary suspect in the killing of Brad Evans, perhaps believing Evans had stolen his stash. His own murder altered that thinking.

McCrory ended his spiel, took a sip of coffee and opened it up for questions.

"So, it's possible Smith did Evans and an as yet unknown person, did him?" Hogan speculated.

"Yup," McCrory said.

Gallo jumped in. "Because of the drug connection, we theorized that a banger knocked Smith off as an example to other dealers."

Hogan rubbed his chin, gulped some java, and sat back in his chair. "Seems like a lot of theorizing going on."

"Can't disagree with that," Gallo said. "Maybe we're too close to the case to see the big picture."

"What about an addict?" Hogan continued. "Angry he couldn't get his stuff from Smith when he needed it. Thought the guy was jerking him around."

McCrory smiled, impressed by Hogan's thinking. "That's something we hadn't thought of," he said, and glanced at Gallo.

The point made, Hogan then asked, "Okay what do you want us to do?"

Gallo and McCrory had discussed this so McCrory gave out the assignments. "AJ and I want to reinterview the families of the murdered guys, Donald Berger and Dustin Rose in Cohasset. We should probe deeper into what they may know about Bradley Evans. Rose had a twin. We dismissed him as the killer of Evans. We might need to rethink that. And, we'll talk to Evans' landlady again here in Hingham where he rented a room. Probably a dead end; but worth a shot.

Second, your point about a disgruntled customer of Mitch Smith's needs to be followed up. We searched Smith's house once and came up with a coded paper with the name of Bobby Moran—the honcho of the Somerville mob. We've been ordered to back off that strand for now."

Hogan and Hawkins shared a knowing glance. They were aware of the shenanigans that went on in the MDC organization and even in the detective bureau—neither was involved.

At that moment, a knock on the door brought the conversation to a halt as the desk sergeant stuck his head in. "Detective Gallo. A Mr. Callahan is in the office; said you asked him to meet you here. He's waiting in the reception room."

"Great sarge. Would you walk him back?"

All eyes turned toward Gallo. "I'll explain as soon as he comes in."

The sergeant knocked on the door, opened it and Michael Callahan walked in. Gallo indicated he should sit at the end of the table between the four detectives. He did so and nodded to everyone.

"Gentleman. This is Michael Callahan, a teacher in Hull. Seems his car has been vandalized twice while parked at the school."

This brought surprised expressions from all and questioning glances at Gallo.

"AJ," McCrory said, before Gallo put up his hand.

"I haven't lost my marbles. Mike grew up in Somerville with many of the men who are now members of the Winter Hill Gang as they're called. He knows the leader, Bobby Moran. To make a long story short, Mike ran with the crew as a kid and suspects a couple of those boys committed the vandalism trying to drag him back in. A calling card if you will."

Hogan scoffed. "Strange way to entice someone back."

"These guys aren't subtle," Callahan answered.

"I'm still confused," McCrory said. "You have a plan, AJ?"

"Yes! One that's unorthodox and dangerous for Mike. He's agreed to go back to Somerville to challenge the gang bangers about the damage to his car. At the same time, he thinks he can find out if Moran or some other thug in the group killed Mitch Smith."

"That's risky man," Hawkins said, addressing Callahan. "Any idea how you're going to approach that?"

"Thought I'd work that out with AJ."

Hawkins looked surprised but he stayed mum. As a combat vet, experience taught him even the best plans went to shit when the bullets began to fly. Making up a plan without a lot of thought was a recipe for disaster. AJ knew that too and was perhaps underplaying what he and Callahan would do when they encountered the gangsters. At least he hoped so.

Gallo stood. "I wanted you to meet Mike. I'm going to be nearby when he goes in; provide back-up."

"Count us in," Hawkins said, volunteering his partner.

"Appreciate it. But we need you to follow other leads. I'll work with Mike. Notify you when it's going down."

When Callahan left the conference room, McCrory spoke up. "Putting a civilian in danger is not kosher, AJ. Something happens to him; the blowback will be fierce. For all of us. Chief Taylor will be livid and I imagine your boss won't be thrilled. We could wind up walking a beat or worse."

"Agreed," Gallo said. He also had some misgivings. But he forged on. "Mike wants the vandalism to his vehicle to stop. He's going to Somerville with or without us."

Hogan and Hawkins both shrugged as they were late comers to the investigation. McCrory raised his hands in a surrender gesture.

He should have fought harder to derail the idea; the behavior of gangsters was not predictable.

CHAPTER 38

The situation involving Mike Callahan unsettled McCrory. He feared Gallo was going rogue but didn't voice his doubts and turned the group focus back to the investigation. "We need to speak further to our pal, Jerry Morris, about Bradley Evans," he said. "Conduct another search of Smith's house, too. Perhaps he had a list of customers. And maybe Jerry knows about that too."

"Okay, Brian, Chris," Gallo chimed in. "If you guys talk to Morris, and comb through Smith's home, you may gain a fresh perspective. Kind 'a late today. Why don't we hit it first thing tomorrow?"

The two Mets detectives stood to leave.

"By the way," McCrory asked, "are you staying in Boston or someplace down here?"

"We both have families, with school-age kids," Hogan said. "I live in Jamaica Plain. Hawk lives in Milton. Better if we come down each day."

"We could come by train, if one of you can pick us up and provide a ride," Hawkins said.

"Either way works," AJ said. "Call to let me know what you've decided."

"Done," Hogan said. "I expect at first, we'll drive. We have a department car."

"Okay. Let's do it," McCrory said, and the meeting broke up.

The murder of two men in Nantasket was spiraling in a direction no one would have anticipated.

The next day, the Mets team drove out to Mitch Smith's in Hingham greeted by Gavin Smith, who still held the keys to his son's place. Chief Taylor had informed the elder Smith that his son had not committed suicide but had, in fact, been murdered. Taylor recounted Mitch's drug dealing and that he might have been a victim of the mob when he lost his consignment of cocaine.

Gavin, flabbergasted to learn Mitch's latest misadventure, accepted the news with resignation. Like many fathers, he blamed himself for pushing his son too hard, but couldn't forgive his fall into drug use and his involvement with gang scum. Nevertheless, he wanted his killers brought to justice. He gave the detectives the keys and asked they return them to Chief Taylor at the Hingham PD. He drove off with a screech of rubber.

"Nice wheels," Hogan said, admiring the Cadillac Coupe de Ville.

"Dream on brother," his partner said, turned and let them into the house.

The two men spent over three hours combing through the residence, examining cupboards, turning over furniture, checking kitchen drawers and under the sink. They scoured the desk in Mitch's office. Their search mimicked Gallo and McCrory's and proved just as fruitless.

They finished in the garage and were ready to quit when something puzzled Hawkins: "Hey," he called out. "Why does someone who is not a professional painter keep ten cans of the stuff?"

Hogan scrunched his face. "Good question."

Smith had lined up five paint containers on a work bench now covered in dust—another five rested on the floor. Some had drippings on the side in various colors, while others appeared unused.

Hogan lifted an opener from a pegboard hook above the workbench and unsealed a can clear of drippage. Inside the clean interior, he uncovered three sheets of rolled up paper, with headings: Hingham; Cohasset and Hull. Opening the other unspoiled cans, he retrieved papers headed: Scituate; Plymouth and Bridgewater. A date was noted on each. Ten to fifteen names, phone numbers and addresses filled out the rest of the documents. Beside the name was a quantity: grams or ounces; Eightball (3.5 ounces); or Teener (one-sixteenth of an ounce).

Hawkins whistled. "Looks like we discovered old Mitch's client lists."

"Pretty good hiding place," Hogan said, impressed by Smith's ingenuity. "Can't blame Gallo and McCrory for missing it."

"Won't make them feel any better."

"No doubt. If they recognize any of these people, it may ease their disappointment. Let's go back to the PD."

"How about going over to the gas station attendant's house first?" Hawkins advocated. "Map shows it's a couple of miles from here."

"Okay. Might be some friends of his on these lists."

"Maybe. But we can't show them to him. Just read off the names."

"I'm good with that," Hogan agreed.

Having learned from the ambulance attendants that the death of Mitch Smith was considered suspicious, reporter Bert Jones, on a hunch, staked out Smith's home again. Sitting across the street from the residence, he spotted a Metro Police cruiser roll up and park in the driveway. Two men got out when a flashy Cadillac pulled up; Gavin Smith behind the wheel. The two lawmen met the elder Smith, accepted a key from him and entered the house. Bert settled down in his one-man surveillance team and waited.

When the men emerged three hours later, he followed. The road was smooth here, but potholes lay ahead for Bert.

The two Mets detectives changed plans, decided to secure their evidence at the Hingham PD before going to the home of Jerry Morris. They spent the morning reviewing the investigation notes compiled by Gallo and McCrory and revealing to the Chief what they found at Smith's. Taylor didn't recognize any of the names, surprised by the number of people taking drugs in his town and nearby communities. He was disheartened by the realization he didn't have the manpower to use on drug enforcement, obviously a growing challenge.

To improve his mood, Taylor, an inveterate story teller, regaled his captive audience with tales of going to Paragon Park as a teenager and winning a contest with his buddies to see how many times in a row they could ride the Giant Coaster without getting sick. His challengers either quit or barfed their guts out, according to Taylor's version.

Hogan and Hawkins listened respectfully but were eager to talk to Jerry Morris. The Chief seeing their fidgeting, ended his tale excusing himself to attend to department business.

When the Mets detectives pulled up in front of the Morris house, they encountered a woman entering a car parked in the driveway. She stopped when they approached, introduced themselves, and asked to speak with Jerry.

"He left on a walk over an hour ago," Jerry's wife explained. "He should be at the South Shore Country Club downing his first vodka tonic." Her scowl reflected annoyance with that circumstance. The lawmen thanked her, asked for directions, and returned to their cruiser to chase down Morris.

Jerry's wife watched them drive off, shaking her head, wondering when this robbery stuff would end. She and Jerry married a month after high school. Neither of their parents approved, believing that with only secondary educations, the newlyweds faced an uncertain future. To some extent, they had been right, though Sheila entered a nursing program in Quincy and became a registered nurse.

Jerry bounced from job to job until landing the attendant position at the Gulf filling station. By living with Jerry's mom, they scraped by. Now, after her husband's stupid decision to participate in a robbery, his prospects were nil and he didn't seem eager to look for something else. Since they had no children, it would not be difficult to move out, something she considered every day.

Hogan and Hawkins ambled into the South Shore Country Club and attracted stares from the patrons. In their sports jackets and grey fedoras, shoulder holsters visible, they could be either cops or thugs. Not knowing what Morris looked like, they asked a waitress at the bar who was placing drinks on her carry tray. "That's him sitting with the character in the beard, Calloway hat and shades," she said, motioning with a nod of her head. "Thinks he's a movie star or something, hiding from his fans behind wrap-arounds."

The two investigators shared an understanding glance.

Jerry and his companion tensed as the men approached their table.

"Hi Jerry," Hawkins said, as he reached out his hand. "Sorry to bother you here. I'm Detective Hawkins. This is my partner, Brian Hogan. We're with the Metropolitan Police helping to investigate the murders of Bradley Evans and Mitch Smith. Have a couple of questions, if you don't mind?"

Morris wanted to tell them to kiss off, but didn't want to cause a scene and embarrass his new friend. "Sure. Enjoyed our chat, Dan," Jerry said, indicating his newfound chum should leave.

"No problem pal," the man said as he stood. He dropped a ten-dollar bill on the table for their drinks, and twisted away in an awkward effort to keep his face averted and strolled out of the lounge.

"Thanks for the drink," Jerry called after him.

The man raised his right arm in recognition of the comment—kept walking

"Let's talk outside," Hawkins said.

The three men walked out with all eyes on them.

Furious, Jerry's companion strode to his Ford Fairlane parked by a strand of trees at the periphery of the country club lot. Once again, his attempt to take Morris out failed.

He had backed into his slot to have a panoramic view of the parking area. He couldn't miss the blue and white Metro squad car positioned by the entrance. *Guess they didn't worry about getting ticketed,* he snickered.

Jerry, glowering, marched out between the two larger men. One guided him into the back seat of their vehicle and slipped in next to him. The stalker thought they might release Jerry to resume his walk, but they chatted with him for about ten, fifteen minutes, then drove off. The man followed as the lawmen glided to a stop in front of Jerry's and let him out. They stayed until he disappeared inside.

Frustrated, the man executed a U-turn and headed back through Hingham center to link up with Route 3A south. He fingered the Colt 45 Pistol in his lap. Through playing games, he vowed, the next time he spotted Jerry, he'd put a bullet in his head.

Unaware of the discovery made by the Mets team in their search of Mitch Smith's, Gallo and McCrory left the Berger residence dejected. Berger's wife had no new information about Bradley Evans—only met him twice. She knew he worked with Donald on a construction project; that was it. The same was true at the boarding house in Hingham which the detectives visited first because of its proximity to the HPD. Mrs. Summers and her student boarders wanted to be helpful but reiterated what they said previously. Bradley kept to himself; friendly but not gregarious.

Leads into Bradley's slaying were drying up, though Gallo was encouraged by the info from Cohasset Officer Russo that David Rose had shown anger when Dustin was bullied in school and waited days to retaliate—a big leap from that to murder, but something to pursue.

"Let's go back to talk with Rose's brother and sister," Gallo proposed. "I think his twin lied to us about owning a gun. May have lied about other things?"

They pulled up to the stately house on Pond Street and parked in front. McCrory's first visit; AJ came with Caruso the first time.

As they walked up to the door, Gallo noticed that Dustin's Fairlane was not on the side of the house as it had been when he first came to tell David and Linda the bad news. He rang the bell. Linda, hair drawn back in a pony-tail, wearing a gray sweater and blue skirt answered, surprise on her face.

Gallo introduced McCrory.

"Why are you here?" Linda said, a bitter tone in her voice. "We know who killed my brother."

"I'm sorry I didn't come personally to tell you both," Gallo said, his eyes downcast.

The woman crossed her arms over her chest, didn't invite them in.

AJ understood her resentment, another rookie mistake among many he'd made in the investigation but couldn't let it deter him. "May we come in? Just for a few minutes," he said.

Linda relented and moved aside; didn't offer them a seat. AJ ignored the slight. "I came to see Dave. I don't believe he was telling the truth about owning a gun when I asked him about it and I think you know that."

Linda's demeanor changed. Tears ran down her cheeks, her shoulders shook and she appeared unsteady on her feet. Gallo put his arm around her waist and guided her to the couch. He pulled a handkerchief from the inside pocket of his jacket and gave it to her. Tears flowed as she fought to regain control. She doubled over, dabbing at her eyes and sat silent for several minutes. She spoke between sobs. "David does own a gun. And it's not in his room. I'm afraid of what he might do—what he's already done."

The men eyed each other. "What do you mean?" Gallo asked.

"David hasn't been home much. He comes in late at night and leaves early in the morning. We haven't spoken in forever. He's missed work too. His boss called three days ago, angry. Threatened to fire him if he didn't come in."

"Where is he employed, Linda?" McCrory chimed in.

"Hingham Lumber."

McCrory wrote it down but needn't have bothered. Hingham Lumber was the largest such company in the area. He had been there many times for home repair stuff.

"What's going on?" Gallo probed. "What do you mean when you say you're afraid of what he's already done?"

That question led to another bout of sobbing. She gasped as if having difficulty breathing. A guttural sound escaped her.

Minutes passed while she composed herself. When she did, she stammered, "David not only lied about the gun. He knew who Dustin was meeting the night he didn't come home."

She paused, blew her nose, wiped her arm across her eyes and said, "Bradley Evans."

Another glance and raised eyes between the two lawmen. "You think Evans may have joined in the gas station robbery?" Gallo asked.

"Not sure, only that they were going to join up."

"Are you afraid David is the person who ran Bradley down?"

"God. I don't know what to think. He didn't like Bradley for some reason. If he thought he killed Dustin…?" her voice drifted off and the water works began again.

Gallo waited until she regained control. "But he never said anything about that?"

She shook her head.

"Okay, Linda. Thank you for your honesty. Would you please call us when your brother comes home again?"

She nodded and the detectives left the house.

"Does that put David at the top of our list of suspects in the Evans murder?" McCrory asked once outside.

"Gotta be. He knew, or suspected, before we did, that Brad was the getaway driver in the robbery because he was supposed to meet Dustin that night."

"But David owns a weapon, according to his sister, why didn't he just shoot Evans?" McCrory wondered.

"Wanted it to look like an accident?"

"Still circumstantial but we need to find him—fast."

CHAPTER 39

David Rose now moved to the top of the suspect list in the hit and run of Bradley Evans. Nevertheless, the Irish mob were suspects in the murder of Mitch Smith. A visit to their hangout might shake them up. Gallo and Mike Callahan headed to Somerville in a Metro unmarked cruiser. Mike intended to confront his former buddies about the damage to his car. The two men peppered the hour and a half drive with small talk about their lives and careers.

"So how do you know Sue?" Callahan began.

"Went to Hingham High School together; dated some. As Catholics, we were in the CYO. Lost touch."

"She never told me that."

"Wasn't important."

"You joined the Marines after graduation. Read about your exploits."

Gallo sloughed that off, turned the conversation around. "What about you? How did you and Susan meet?"

"I attended Northeastern University in Boston, as I mentioned in your office. Got my teaching credential and wanted to get as far away from Somerville as possible. My parents had a summer cottage in Hull. I remembered the town as a nice place with a great beach; Paragon Park; quiet in winter. Was hired to teach at the Memorial School; met Sue there."

"How do you want to play this with the gang?" Gallo asked, to avoid a deeper probe into his relationship with Susan.

"They do business in the back room of a bar. The bartender and staff know me from my time hanging out there. Moran is around most days. My vandalizers should be there too. I plan to confront them, don't expect trouble. I'm not going in upset. I'm offended, not angry."

"Just walk in?"

"Yup!"

Gallo surprised, said nothing further as he was directed to downtown Somerville. He parked opposite the Shamrock Saloon and Grille. A leprechaun adorned the facade. Callahan exited the vehicle and jogged across the street to enter the grille's front door.

AJ gave him about ten minutes, then entered the tavern, a typical no-frills joint. Three long wooden tables with unpadded stools were placed in the center of the room. Four booths with green cushioned seats and backs lined the wall on his right. A low bar with additional stools was positioned adjacent to the booths.

It was eleven-thirty in the morning. Gallo scanned the room. Two men sat at the bar while a couple occupied a middle booth. He strolled to the bar and took a seat at one end next to a door he believed led to the back room—a position from which he could rush in if needed.

He ordered a draft beer, hamburger and fries to kill time, unsure how long Callahan's gamble would last; or if he'd come out unscathed.

AJ had a .38 Special strapped to his right ankle should the need arise. Though he acted unconcerned, having just stopped in for a burger, his size attracted sideways glances from the men at the bar and the couple in the booth. His presence prompted the bartender to push a button under the bar activating a blinking red light in the back room to alert the gang of trouble.

Callahan strolled into the back room unannounced drawing rapt attention from the ten men sitting around tables. Moran held court at one, engaging in an animated discussion with the O'Rourke brothers. When Bobby saw Mike, he jumped up, rushed him and wrapped him in a bear hug. "Michael, my boyo, my long-lost brother. Good to see you."

"Same here, pal."

Moran stepped back and scrutinized his friend. "What is it that brings you home? Something important?"

"I came to see Devlin and Shamus; ask them to stop harassing me."

"What are you talking about, laddie?"

Moran infused his language with words and phrases from the "old-country" to remind his brethren of their heritage. And to give the impression he had been born in Ireland, not South Boston, his actual birthplace.

Michael pointed at the O'Rourke's sitting together. "They've been wrecking my car; broke windows, scratched the paint. Did it twice."

Moran turned to hold the O'Rourke's with a withering stare, held out his arms in a 'what gives' gesture.

"Big man. College graduate, too good for his old chums," Devlin whined. "Wanted to teach him a lesson, is all. He should remember where he came from."

"The man is one of us, boyo," Moran said, shaking his head. "No matter where he lives, what he's done. I'm ashamed of ya."

Devlin, having been called out by the boss, hung his head, his mouth twisting into a snarl.

Callahan didn't want to raise the temperature in the room or get into a physical altercation. "Just want them to back off," he said, staring daggers at Devlin.

The younger O'Rourke didn't want to incur Moran's wrath either. He'd seen him beat a man to within an inch of his life. He changed his grimace to a smile.

"No hard feelings. Guess you got the message, though, huh?"

Callahan held back his urge to pummel the man, couldn't hold his tongue. "Got it, all right. That you're a chickenshit bastard." Devlin stood, balled his fists, prepared to strike. His brother wrapped him in a tight grip.

The last thing Bobby needed was a drunken brawl that would lead other members of the gang to join in. They had been guzzling beer since the place opened despite the early hour.

"This ends right now, right here," he said, shifting his eyes from Devlin to Callahan, then scanning the length of the room. Everyone nodded, even those uninvolved.

Moran, pleased, put his arm around Michael and walked him toward the door when the red warning light blinked.

Alerted to danger, all of the crew fingered weapons.

Callahan raised his hand in a stop signal. He hadn't expected Gallo to come into the saloon, not surprised that he did. He whispered, "That's probably a friend of mine; drove me here. Told him to wait in the car, guess he didn't listen."

Moran opened the door a crack and peeked out. The detective was gulping a beer. "That him," Bobby said in a low voice, measuring Gallo from head to foot as Callahan stepped beside him and peered out. "Yup," he said.

"Big guidh," Moran exclaimed, using the Irish word for man.

"Will you talk to him?"

"About what?"

"Don't get mad. He's an MDC cop investigating the murder of a guy named Mitch Smith. Wants to eliminate your boys as suspects."

Moran wrapped an arm around Callahan, pulled him close to murmur in his ear. "Don't need cops breathing down my neck, boyo. I called off Shamus who wanted to make an example of that schmuck Smith who lost some product—couldn't make good. Tell your cop friend to look elsewhere. None of my guys was involved. I swear on my mother's grave."

"You should tell him yourself. Doesn't hurt to make a friend in law enforcement."

The Mafia boss sneered. "Already have some cop chums, boyo. You tell him what I said." He paused, then whispered in a threatening tone, "And maybe you shouldn't come back here anytime soon."

Callahan stepped away. "Got the message. You watch your back."

"Always do, Mikey. Always do."

Callahan exited the back room, walked by Gallo without acknowledging him and left the Shamrock. AJ waited five minutes, paid his tab, nodded to the bartender/waiter and strolled out into the sunlight, all eyes on his back. He joined Callahan in the car, which he had left unlocked, and slid into the driver's seat. He pulled away from the curb before speaking.

"Didn't hear any smashed furniture or shouting."

"All's good. I don't expect more attacks on my Impala."

After a deafening silence, Michael said, "Bobby swears they didn't kill your man Smith. Says one of his men wanted to make an example of him for welching on his debt, but he backed him off."

"You trust him?"

"With my life, strange as that may seem."

"You grew up together; were friends. Loyalty should count for something. Kind of like the Marines; you serve with a guy in combat, you develop a bond. Once a Marine, always a Marine."

"I bailed on the gang, turned my back on them, as guys like Devlin O'Rourke see it. And Bobby made it clear I shouldn't come around anymore."

"That bother you?"

"Nope. Left that life long ago. Have no desire to return to it. Plan to start a new life with Susan, have a family."

Gallo peered out the window to conceal a frown that creased his face, his stomach queasy. Callahan was a good guy. Susan could do worse. Time he let go of his fantasy of reuniting with her. He turned back towards him. "Good luck. And thanks for sticking your neck out with the Mafia boys. Makes our investigation easier."

"Coming here worked out for both of us. Time to move on."

Gallo winced. The words Susan used to tell him it was over.

When Callahan left the back room of the Shamrock Bar, Moran walked back to his gang and stood before them, arms folded. "Cops were looking at us for the killing of that loser, Smith. They won't be doing that no more."

"Who was the flatfoot?" Shamus O'Rourke asked, anger reflected in his tone.

"Mets guy. I convinced Mikey we had nothing to do with it, right?" he said, staring down Shamus and eyeballing Devlin.

"Not us," Shamus said. "You ordered us to back off and we did."

"Okay. Drink up boyos. We got too much going on to do something stupid."

Everyone seemed relieved and chatted among themselves. Shamus leaned into his brother and whispered, "Let's find out why those fuzz bastards are looking into us and who they are. We should 'a never let that idiot Smith deal for us. Whitey vouched for him and now he's in a lock-up."

Devlin tilted his head back, guzzled his beer in one long gulp. "We got to send a real message to those pigs," he said; "a real message." He swiped his mouth with his shirtsleeve.

Bodies would drop.

CHAPTER 40

At 10:00 p.m. on Thursday, the day before Memorial Day this year, the robbery crew parked in a deserted lot behind the Quincy Savings & Loan. They came in two vehicles. One, a 1957 De Soto two-tone green Fire-flite station wagon, was laden with power tools and safety gear, and driven by Shamus O'Rourke with Patrick Duffy riding shotgun. Buster Grimes, "White Shoes" Dolan and Frankie O'Brien occupied the other car, a Nash Rambler. The tension among the would-be thieves was palpable. Grimes kept cracking his knuckles. Dolan grabbed him by the neck and shook him until his teeth rattled. "Knock it off, you dumb shit," he snarled.

Once the equipment was unloaded, the cars would be taken to a residential area to blend in. Lieutenant Newman, of the Quincy PD, their look-out, would pick the men up and drop them back behind the Savings and Loan to minimize the danger of a nosy patrolman getting suspicious.

Roger Newman, like most lawmen drawn to the dark side, needed money. He saw this scheme as a way to extricate himself from growing debt. He had three adolescent daughters and a wife who couldn't overlook a bargain; a constant point of irritation between them that threatened the viability of their marriage. The robbery promised to be his ticket to a better life.

The first step in the plan was to access Detulio's Watch Repair shop whose south wall abutted the Savings and Loan, while Grimes installed his homemade electrical device to jam the alarm system.

Patrick Duffy studied the store layout a month earlier and figured they could enter the bank from Detulio's. They'd breach the store's lathe and plaster walls, then pound through the bank's concrete. No problem for Duffy, who had worked for a construction company. The repair shop's small upstairs office would take them in over the bank vault's steel reinforced concrete walls, considered impenetrable.

Once inside the repair shop, the team shut all blinds to block prying eyes from looking in. The also hung canvas tarps to minimize noise from their power tools. Since the next day was a holiday, foot and vehicle traffic would be minimal. All stores would be closed and Lieutenant Newman would steer patrols away from the area.

Duffy, the experienced safe cracker and contractor, would do most of the work to breach the walls leading to the vault. He rented the required equipment in three different cities and had retained other gear from prior construction jobs.

Starting the job, he used an angle grinder to hack through the plaster of the repair shop. He marked off the zone to be cut, large enough for a man to crawl through, with masking tape to reinforce the surface and drew cut lines over the tape. He donned goggles and pulled a mask over his nose and mouth—cutting plaster generated considerable dust. The beauty of the angle grinder was that it didn't generate much vibration and noise, making it easier to maneuver and less likely to be heard from the outside.

When through the wall, Duffy dispensed with the wood lath behind it, leaving a square hole suitable for their purpose. The next obstacle, however, was more difficult; the steel reinforced concrete wall of the adjacent Savings & Loan which relied on its massive thickness for strength.

Duffy, prepared for the task, rented a circular saw with a diamond blade. It had an inlet to attach a garden hose to reduce dust, but Duffy opted to make the cuts dry. He didn't want water to inundate the repair shop and seep through to the street. He and the rest of the crew wore goggles and face masks to deal with the fine powder and ear plugs to minimize noise.

He again used a pencil to mark the cut area, set the blade to a depth of two inches and began. The wall was at least a foot thick, so he made several cuts before having one of his guys wield a sledgehammer to finish the job.

The work was tedious; the saw heavy when held horizontal to the floor, taxing arm muscles; breaks were needed. Duffy outfitted "White

Shoes" Dolan with the proper protective gear and employed him to help with the cutting. He had packed sandwiches and soft drinks for the men to provide nourishment.

After three hours, Duffy ordered O'Rourke to use the sledge. He broke through and opened a four-by-four hole wide enough for a man and equipment to snake through. Duffy took a flashlight, crawled in and smiled. He was on top of the vault. Satisfied, but exhausted, he told the men to quit for the night. He called Lieutenant Newman on his hand-held radio and requested pick up. They'd complete the job the next day; Memorial Day.

Newman picked up the crew and ferried them back to their vehicles, unaware that they were being watched from behind several bushes across the bank parking lot.

"When are we going to take them, Turk?" Jimmy Aslam said to AJ Gallo. Jimmy's given name was Yusuf. He came to the United States in 1938 with his family who feared the coming war. His Turkish parents often regaled him about the formation of the Republic of Turkey by Mustafa Kemal Ataturk, who became a hero to young Yusuf.

His Marine buddies called him "Jimmy" as more befitting an American. In Korea, he humped ammunition for Gallo's .50 caliber and started calling him "Turk" because he reminded him of his "old country" idol. The name stuck, at least within their unit.

"Take it easy," AJ cautioned. "This is a recon mission. We need to find out what we're up against before we move."

Disillusioned, AJ didn't know when or if they would intervene. Even if he broke up the robbery, that might not help Wilkinson in the long run unless they took down some of the bigwigs with their hands in the till and their heads in the sand.

"These boys will be back tomorrow. We may come back then. Maybe not. I know where they're going after the heist."

"So, we'll pop them then?"

AJ, amused by Jimmy's use of the term "pop them," shook his head.

Duffy's team returned to the Savings & Loan the afternoon of Memorial Day, May 30th. There had been a celebratory parade at 9:00 a.m. down Hancock Street with high school marching bands, drill teams, cheerleaders and the national guard. Mini-flags were in abundance and spectators threw confetti at the marchers. The Grand Marshall was a young wounded army Korean War veteran from the city. The festivities were long over by the time Duffy and his gang rolled up. All shops were closed. Most families were home barbecuing on patios or back yards, draining bottles of beer; others took brief vacations.

Again, Lieutenant Newman of the Quincy PD escorted the drivers and their vehicles to a side street. He taxied the men back to the repair shop where Patrick Duffy continued his work. The expert safe-cracker donned pigskin gloves, a thick pigskin welding apron, boots, goggles and a face shield.

He wiggled through the hole in the wall to the top of the vault and was handed two steel cylinders of oxygen and acetylene gases. Burning together they would spew a flame reaching three-thousand degrees centigrade, hot enough to melt metal and cut through steel.

The blow torch concentrated the gases into a pinpoint flame that melted the metal, turning it into a molten slurry. Duffy then pulled the trigger to activate the oxygen jet, blowing the slurry out of the way, creating a path for him into the vault.

When the metal cooled, the team dropped one end of a flexible rope ladder down to the vault floor and secured the other to a heavy oak desk in the repair shop. Grimes, Dolan and Duffy climbed down the ladder, which stopped about two feet from the vault floor. Sheamus O'Rourke stayed topside to respond in case problems developed.

At first, they were disappointed. Only about a $100,000 in stacked bills lined the shelves. While not insignificant, not worth the effort and expense to break in. But the next phase of their operation proved more than fruitful. Duffy wielded a crowbar to smash the locks on the hundreds of built-in safe deposit boxes loaded with valuables: pearls, diamonds, gold coins, expensive watches, cash and packages of what appeared to be drugs.

The abundance of cash and the drugs gave the men pause. They might have stumbled onto a stash from a gang; no way of telling. But mesmerized by their bonanza, they didn't care. No mob group would come forward to report their losses. They either used innocent dupes to rent the boxes, for a fee, or their own people adopted fictitious identities to do so.

Too bad for them.

The robbers stuffed jewelry into two duffel bags and the money in another to be hidden at Duffy's Whitfield home. He warned his co-conspirators to lie low until they could safely divide the loot. Grimes protested, but Duffy informed him that their benefactors, the Irish Mafia, and some high-ranking cops in on the scheme, wanted it that way.

They didn't, but Duffy, a criminal con all his life, figured he could sell the plan to Bobby Moran and Captain Kellum. He'd skim several thousand bucks from the take and spread it around to satisfy his men in the short term. The best part was that they didn't, and wouldn't, take an inventory of the valuables as long as he guarded them—no one would know if he cheated them.

When they finished, Duffy called Lieutenant Newman on his hand-held radio to pick them up. Newman received the call as he was sitting outside of a Howard Johnson's slurping on a black and white Frappe he'd just purchased. He'd needed a break from the boredom of the constant patrolling of the area around the Savings and Loan. He told Duffy he'd be delayed about ten-minutes taking care of police business.

His blunder endangered the whole operation.

While the robbery crew assembled their equipment at the back door waiting for Newman, store owner Dominick DeTullio returned to pick up an expensive Girard Perregaux men's stainless steel manual wind watch he had promised to deliver to a wealthy client the next day. He kept the prized possession in his safe.

DeTullio was a happy man. His wife had fixed the family his favorite eggplant parmesan and desert had been ricotta filled Cannoli with dark chocolate chips purchased from a storefront Italian pastry shop in Boston's North End. He topped the meal off with a glass of Bellini Chianti from their famous straw bottle.

He was whistling the tune from Volare when he parked behind his store, exited his Crown Victoria and opened the back door to a sight that stopped him cold. Men with saws and other equipment were poised by the exit. He managed to stammer, "What, who are you?" before O'Rourke grabbed a crowbar and smashed it on the side of the sixty-year old's head.

"Jesus H. Christ, Shamus," Duffy screamed as he leaned over the crumpled proprietor. "Ya killed him."

O'Rourke stood paralyzed holding the crowbar, blood dripping from the curved end. "He could recognize us, had to shut him up," he declared, shaking.

The crew stayed motionless—eyes fixed on the fallen man.

Lieutenant Newman arrived minutes later. He stormed in after seeing DeTullio's Crown Victoria parked in the lot, no other cars nearby. He stumbled over DeTullio's body, staggering into the assembled equipment, cursing. Losing his composure, he roared, "what the fuck happened, Duffy?"

Duffy reddened, went on the offensive. "You were supposed to stop anyone from coming in here. It's your damn fault."

O'Rourke, still gripping the bloody weapon, stared down Newman and in a shaky voice asked, "What are we gonna do?"

"How about we take his wallet, dump him at a hospital. They won't know who it is," Dolan said. "By the time they figure it out, we'll be long gone."

The group began talking over each other, proposing different options. Chaos reigned until Newman shouted, "Shut the Fuck up."

Having gotten the group's attention, he explained, "We can't take him anywhere, particularly a hospital; too risky. We could be seen. We leave him. Let the cops find him when they discover the robbery and trace the entry point here."

He looked around. "Everyone's wearing gloves. Wipe the place down just in case." He reached into DeTullio's pocket and flipped his keys to Duffy. "Drive his car to our rendezvous spot. We'll carry on as planned," he ordered.

Shaken, the crew did as Newman directed. They waited until Duffy, having ditched DeTullio's Crown Vic, returned, then lugged their equipment out of the repair shop and stored it again in the back of the station wagon. Duffy had slipped $2000 of the stolen cash to Newman and would do so to the others when they got back to his house to satisfy them for the time being.

Duffy had never been involved in a murder and was already planning to flee Massachusetts with the loot.

MDC Detective AJ Gallo and his Marine partner, Jimmy Aslam, did not return the second day of the robbery, aware of the gang's Whitfield destination. Torn between Bill Wilkinson's entreaties to help, and the need to alert the authorities, AJ resolved to notify the FBI. He believed he could convince them Wilkinson was an unwilling pawn.

His call to the Feds would prove to be a fatal mistake putting himself and others in jeopardy. Kellum's tentacles spread far and wide. And the FBI didn't require his "heads up." They had their own inside man. They knew everything about the heist: who was going to pull it off and what law enforcement officers were involved.

At home, Patrick Duffy pushed aside thoughts of the murdered owner of the watch repair shop and marveled at the satchels stuffed with cash, jewelry, gold coins and watches, much of which he planned to skim for himself.

The stacks of fifty and hundred-dollar bills, close to a million bucks, he guessed, came from the safe deposit boxes, that both captivated and frightened him. He suspected most was stashed by a mob. If they found out who stole it, his life wouldn't be worth a plug nickel as they always said in western movies—he laughed nervously.

Of course, some of the money came from wealthy people, survivors of the bank failures of the Great Depression, who thought deposit boxes safer than trusting the bank to use it wisely. Problem was, Duffy had no way of separating mob money from that of innocent patrons.

He counted out a hundred thousand dollars, put it in the bottom of a used tool box and placed it with two similar boxes in his garage—

safe until he figured out how much of the loot he could pilfer without raising suspicion.

Again, none of the guys who participated in the robbery knew what their split would be. But he couldn't stall for long. He knew several "fences" who would appraise what he had and give him a dollar amount. He'd use that process as leverage to delay splitting the take and make plans to disappear.

CHAPTER 41

On the day after the Memorial Day weekend, employees of the Savings & Loan reporting to work were astonished to discover the vault breach and every safety deposit box smashed open. At the sight of the devastation, the bank manager, sixty-five-year-old Harold Robbins, suffered a heart attack and was rushed to the city hospital, placed on life-support.

Confusion reigned among the staff who were sent home by Assistant Manager, Michael Woodleaf. Quincy Police officers, under the supervision of Lieutenant, Roger Newman, swarmed over the premises and the watch repair shop next door.

Newman, first to enter, "discovered" the owner lying in a pool of blood, moaning. His head wound had bled profusely but was not fatal. Newman was both astonished and relieved. He helped place DeTullio into an ambulance to be transported to the same hospital as the bank manager.

The FBI was called in.

The headline in that evening's Patriot Ledger blared: **Quincy Savings robbed; unknown amount taken.** The article, written by crime reporter Bert Jones, mentioned the manager's medical emergency and the attack on the repair shop owner and reported the FBI had been alerted. Lieutenant, Roger Newman, pledged that every resource would be used to bring the thieves to justice.

Some distraught safety deposit box owners descended on the bank demanding to be reimbursed for any losses. They lamented the theft of hundreds of valuables and priceless family heirlooms and had lists of estimated values. One customer claimed that two Rolexes, the new Explorer and Submariner, had been stolen, each valued at $150.00.

The next day, The Boston Globe and Herald Examiner ran the story with headlines similar to that of the Patriot Ledger, under the fold of the front page. These stories included interviews with the FBI Special Agent in Charge (SAC) of the Boston Division, S.V. Peterson.

Peterson, cocky and confident, had reason to be. Two years earlier, the FBI, in cooperation with the Massachusetts State Police and the Boston Police, had cracked the notorious Brinks Robbery of 1950, heralded in the press at the time as "the crime of the century," and the "perfect crime."

Thieves wearing dark clothing and Halloween masks lugged off $1.2 million in cash and $1.5 million in checks, in laundry bags. It took six years of diligent investigative work to break open the case. Eight men were caught, convicted and sent to prison. Peterson headed the multi-agency task force.

For the Globe article, Peterson was interviewed and photographed in front of the FBI Office, which occupied five floors of the Boston Trust Building at 100 Milk Street. The SAC stood a slender six feet tall, had cropped silver hair and wore a black suit, white shirt and red tie. He had a bemused expression on his face. His words were brief. "We will apprehend these people no matter how long it takes. Agents will be on the scene and cooperate with the Quincy Police Department."

He didn't say it, because he believed in cooperation with local law enforcement, but his men would lead the investigation, mindful that local cops didn't always trust the Feds. He was confident in solving the case because he had a secret—a mole in the Winter Hill Gang.

Captain Kellum digested the articles in both the Globe and Herald with mixed emotions; happy that the robbery succeeded, afraid too many people were involved and appalled at the assault of a businessman almost killed. He never anticipated that. He didn't condone violence against innocents. For the first time, he thought of ratcheting back his criminal activities. He could only hope everyone would keep quiet.

He knew Duffy, an old hand, wouldn't crack. The others were unpredictable. Newman would help by keeping tabs on the Feds progress and do his best to undermine the investigation—steer it in a different direction if necessary. But some of the agents would be men who worked the Brinks robbery; tough to fool.

Bill Wilkinson, distraught, left Captain Kellum's office under instructions to liaison with Patrick Duffy to ensure they got their share of what was stolen. Wilkinson was terrified the FBI would solve the case and he would be dragged in as a co-conspirator though he hadn't done anything. His defense, following orders, wouldn't cut it as the Nazi's discovered at the Nuremberg Trials after World War II. He thought about running, had nowhere to go and a family to support. He sensed doom unless he took unprecedented measures.

At 10:00 a.m., he called the MDC Station in Nantasket to notify AJ Gallo he was on his way to see him. He got to the peninsula by noon, and walked Gallo out on the pier again. AJ, who read the newspapers and had spied on the robbers with his pal Jimmy Aslam, anticipated what his lieutenant wanted to talk about.

Although it was June 3rd, frigid winds swept across the empty Nantasket wharf giving the lawmen the privacy they sought. Both shivered and leaned into the gusts to keep from being knocked off their feet. Wilkinson began without preamble. "You're aware they got away with it, right?"

"Yeah! And almost killed someone in the process."

Wilkinson looked away, visibly shaken. "That was never in the plan. I swear I would never have participated if I thought it was a possibility."

Gallo, unmoved by Wilkinson's statement; kept silent.

"I've been ordered to meet with them, get my share of the take."

Gallo remained mute.

Wilkinson, frustrated by the silence, raised his voice; sounded hysterical. "I can't do it. My life will be ruined. I've got a wife and sons."

"Go to the FBI. Tell them everything. Ask for a deal."

"You don't understand. They'll kill me."

"The Feds can protect you."

"Not my whole family, man. I can't risk it. But I've got a plan."

Gallo shook his head. "And it involves me, right?"

With a hang dog expression, Wilkinson bowed his head.

After his meeting with Wilkinson, and without his knowledge, AJ contacted the Boston Office of the FBI, fearing members of his own organization, the Mets, were compromised. Despite his partner's pleading and vulnerability, he didn't see how he could intervene to save him.

Gallo believed the FBI couldn't be corrupted. Their Director, J. Edgar Hoover, was a fervent anti-communist, a crusader for Democracy and a leader in combating organized crime. When he took over the agency in the 1920s, he weeded out political appointees and incompetents, instituted a strict code of conduct, and implemented a rigorous hiring practice including background checks and personal interviews. His hand-picked and trained agents were considered incorruptible. It was unthinkable that bad guys could slip into that outfit.

Gallo was wrong, of course.

Greed is a dominant human characteristic. Most men could be bought, even those at the highest levels of law enforcement. Gallo's call was routed to Special Agent Arthur Fitzpatrick, who assured him the department would follow up on his incredible story. Righteous when he made contact, Gallo's gut churned as soon as he hung up.

Agent Fitzpatrick's partner, Steve Slauson, listened in on the call from the Mets Detective as he frequently did at Fitzpatrick's request. The FBI often received unsolicited and unauthenticated tips requiring verification. Many were dismissed as being without merit; others, like this one, coming from a lawman and implicating other officers in a nefarious scheme, could not be shunted aside. Slauson said he'd look into the allegations.

"Thanks Steve," Fitzpatrick said as he turned the inquiry over to him. "Could be a break in the robbery case. Check out this guy. See if he has an ax to grind."

"Will do," Slauson answered, pleased to be able to contact Captain Kellum under the pretext of following up Detective Gallo's phone message at a senior agent's request. He kept his call to Kellum brief. "Quincy Market" his only words.

Quincy Market, officially Faneuil Hall Market, consisted of three massive buildings housing fish and produce distributors. It replaced ramshackle wooden sheds when it was built in 1826, but was now in such disrepair some city officials recommended tearing it down. Slauson and Kellum did not plan to go inside, only to use it as a landmark for their meeting. They met at the site and walked down to the harbor for privacy.

"You have a problem," the federal cop said. "One of your guys, an Anthony Gallo, called our office to report lawmen were involved in the Quincy bank robbery."

Kellum stunned, blurted, "Shit. Was my name mentioned?"

"No. But a Lieutenant Wilkinson's was."

"What about the Irish?"

"Yup."

The Mets Chief of Detectives folded his arms across his chest and stared into Boston Harbor, deep in thought. He shifted his look to the crumbling Rose Wharf. This whole section of the city was decaying. He hoped it wasn't a harbinger of the collapse of his criminal enterprise.

He turned back to Slauson who transferred his weight from one leg to the other, his face a mask of concern.

"What are you going to do?" Kellum probed, worried.

"What can I do?" the agent responded. "Cover my ass. I'm going to talk with your guy. Report my findings. We're talking about attempted murder in the commission of a federal crime."

"Can you stall that?"

"A day or two. You know S.V.'s reputation."

"Okay. Contact Gallo. Tell him you can meet with him in a couple of days. Meantime, I'll clean up things on my end."

"What's that mean?" Slauson said, his expression deepening from concern to fear. He regretted getting involved with Kellum. He feared his career was about to implode. He might have to execute his escape plan.

Kellum tried to placate him. "Don't worry about it. I'll convince the detective to back off."

"How?"

"Leave that to me."

Slauson left the meeting unappeased and fearing the worst. Events would prove he had reason to be afraid.

CHAPTER 42

Captain Kellum, spooked by the report from FBI Special Agent Slauson, called Bobby Moran from a telephone booth a block from the Metro office to ensure privacy. Shamus O'Rourke answered. "Yeah!" was all he said.

"This is a friend," Kellum said, always paranoid using the phone.

O'Rourke knew who it was, stuck to "yeah" as his response.

"Need to speak to the boss."

"Ain't here."

"When will he be in?"

"Don't know."

"Who is this?"

"Shamus."

Nervous and frustrated, Kellum gave O'Rourke the info about his detectives sniffing around the Mafia. He named Wilkinson and Gallo; told him to pass it on and hung up, unwilling to listen to another ridiculous retort.

He took deep breaths to calm his nerves. Compromising one's values was a slippery slope, like losing your balance while skiing and crashing into a tree. Once you pushed off at the top of the hill, you were at the mercy of your skill, geography and the elements. He slid down that grade many times, hadn't wanted to stop, couldn't even if he desired.

He knew his warning to O'Rourke endangered two of his men—so be it. Cops risked death every day. They should be prepared for anything. Even for betrayal by their boss. He laughed nervously knowing how ridiculous that sounded.

Kellum stepped out of the phone booth, lit up a Chesterfield and watched the smoke dissipate in the air. Life was like those fumes, he thought, fleeting. He strode back to his office confident he'd survive another day regardless of what havoc he may have unleashed.

Despite his bravado, events would soon spiral out of his control and that slippery slope became even more dangerous—for him.

Bill Wilkinson lived on Greenleaf Street, west of the Southern Artery in Quincy. His was a modest one story, three-bedroom house, his lawn weed infested, the concrete walkway leading to the front door, cracked. He refused to hire anyone to mow the grass or repair the walk. Promises to his wife do the work himself were shunted aside in favor of his job.

He parked his blue Dodge Coronet at the curb at 5:00 p.m., snatched his brown briefcase from the passenger seat, locked the car, skirted around it, and sauntered toward the house. He smiled anticipating the Martini his wife would have waiting; a daily ritual. The Mets job had become an albatross and it was dragging him deeper into the depths of depression.

As he prepared to enter his home, a black Buick Roadmaster crawled by, its rear window opened, the barrel of a Thompson submachine gun protruding. Oblivious to the danger, Wilkinson fumbled with the lock on his front door as a rapid burst of gunfire ripped through his torso, shattered windows, and splintered the door. He jerked uncontrollably as his briefcase flew from his hand and he crumpled to the ground; eyes wide but not seeing.

Errant bullets lodged in his living room wall, knocking a family picture from its perch and smashing a vase of flowers on a table, yet no one inside was hurt, despite screams which resonated throughout the neighborhood.

The Buick jackknifed down the street as the gunman sneered.

Detective Anthony Gallo exited the MDC Police Station on Nantasket Avenue in Hull within minutes of Lieutenant Bill Wilkinson being gunned down. He had received a call from an FBI Agent requesting to meet in two days. Though glad they responded to his warning about the Savings and Loan robbery, he thought putting off the meeting reflected skepticism of his story. He shook his head, deep in thought. He turned south on the sidewalk to circle the building planning to pick up his Ford coupe parked in the rear.

Mid walk, he stopped, startled by Quincy Ledger reporter Bert Jones striding toward him, grinning. Jones planned to question Gallo about the suicide/murder of Mitchel Smith, proud he uncovered that secret by dogged investigative research. Brimming with confidence, he waved as he glimpsed Gallo. AJ gave a half-wave back.

About ten feet from the detective, Jones' flicked his eyes at an approaching vehicle, his expression turning from joy to alarm. From an innate sense—a gut feeling—Gallo whipped his head to his left as a 1940 black Mercedes-Benz bore down on him, the barrel of a gun extending from the rear passenger window. Without hesitation, the former Marine rolled to his left yanking his Colt .38 Special revolver from his shoulder holster.

The move caught his assailants by surprise. The staccato volley from the Thompson submachine gun went awry, slamming into the MDC Station and clipping Jones in the neck as he remained riveted to his spot.

Unaware Jones had been struck, Gallo popped into a kneeling position and pumped four shots into the Benz striking the driver and obliterating the face of the machine gunner, whose weapon clanked to the pavement.

A third person in the front passenger seat grabbed the steering wheel preventing the car from careening off the road. The wheel-man, not mortally wounded, used his companion's help to maintain control as they sped out of town, tires squealing.

The MDC desk sergeant stunned by the fusillade of bullets smashing into the stucco wall of the building, dashed outside with a shotgun too late to fire at the Benz as it rocketed away. He uttered an expletive before realizing Gallo was lying on his side, blood gushing from a head wound—another man lay face down, a jagged gash where his ear had once been.

Not all of the gunman's shots missed.

A mile out of Hull, the driver of the attack car steered it to the roadside and exchanged places with his mate in the front passenger seat. A quick glance into the back revealed the shooter was dead. They would dump his body in Boston Harbor and dismantle the Mercedes-Benz in a "chop shop" run by confederates. A sympathetic doctor on the payroll would tend to the wounded man.

The ambulance attendants who treated AJ Gallo on the lawn of the MDC Substation believed his head wound to be superficial despite the abundance of blood. They bandaged the abrasion while transporting him to South Shore Hospital for treatment and observation. Those attending Jones in the other transport were not optimistic—his injuries appeared life threatening.

Two Hull patrol cars and an MDC cruiser escorted the ambulances to Weymouth. The MDC patrolman planned to stand guard outside Gallo's room to deter any assailants who might try again. The doctors ignored Gallo's entreaties to be released just before he lost consciousness. Jones remained in the operating room, staff struggling to save his life.

Hingham Detective McCrory and Cohasset Officer Caruso showed up two hours after their colleague and friend was admitted; neither on duty. They had been alerted by their departments of the shootings of a civilian and two Mets detectives, one in Quincy, one in Nantasket.

McCrory, although fearful the news would distress Gallo, passed on the information that Wilkinson was dead, cut down on his front doorstep. He didn't report on Jones condition.

Gallo fumed at learning his partner had been assassinated. "The sons-of bitches picked on the wrong guys this time. They'll pay for this" he bellowed, smacking his right hand into his left palm repeatedly until Caruso stopped him by touching his arm.

He was still agitated when Hingham Chief Taylor joined the group. "What's all the shouting about," he asked.

"Just letting off some steam, Chief," Gallo said, mortified. Regaining his composure and shaking off his brain fog, he asked about Jones; hadn't seen him go down.

Taylor grimaced and shook his head. "Doesn't look good. He's still being operated on."

Gallo closed eyes; anger etched on his face as he passed out a second time.

The MDC chain of command alerted Captain Kellum of the attacks. He was unnerved, worried he had set the shootings in motion when he contacted the Irish gang and spoke to that idiot, O'Rourke. Murder of his men was never part of his thinking, though he was cavalier about that possibility earlier when he made his call.

Assaults on law enforcement officers would draw a massive response, unlike stealing exams, falsifying records and even committing a bank heist. He knew from his conversation with Agent Slauson on the waterfront that Wilkinson told Gallo about the robbery plan, but maybe not his, Kellum's, involvement. If he did; he would tough it out. Play the solicitous commanding officer; turn the internal investigation over to men he could trust. There was no evidence to implicate him. They couldn't find any without cooperation from those officers indebted to him. They'd ruin their own careers by turning on him. He would show his concern by visiting Gallo in the hospital as would be expected of the Chief of Detectives.

Kellum didn't count on the fury of his rabbi.

He received a sealed envelope carried to his office by a secretary he didn't recognize. The note inside ordered him to meet within the hour at the Warren Tavern in Charlestown. The pub was one of the most historic in America built in 1780. It was named after Doctor Joseph Warren, one of Boston's patriot leaders, who died during the Battle of Bunker Hill. Two of its most famous patrons were George Washington and Paul Revere.

Kellum knew it well.

When he arrived, he made his way to a private booth in the rear shielded from locals and tourists. He wore a blue blazer, white turtle-neck and grey slacks. His mentor looked dapper in a three-piece grey/brown herringbone suit with a dark brown tie.

Neither looked like a cop.

While the Patriots may have plotted the revolution in this pub, these two had less lofty goals—self-preservation. The look on his mentor's face gave Kellum chills. "What the fuck is going on Marty?" the man demanded. "Are we killing our own officers now?"

A waiter poked his head behind the lattice wall that separated the booth from general seating inquiring about drinks but was waved off.

Kellum could only lie. "I knew nothing about this, sir. Would never have approved it."

"You better ensure nothing like this happens again. I can't protect you if it does. The troops are restless and with good cause."

"You can count on me, sir. I'll find out who the perpetrators were and hold them accountable."

"Do it fast, Marty, do it fast," the man said and left abruptly.

When the waiter peeked in again, Kellum ordered a Budweiser and sat for a half-hour sipping his beverage and thinking over his next move; his nerves rattled.

FBI Special Agent Steve Slauson grabbed his briefcase on the way out of his office when stopped by his boss, senior Special Agent Arthur Fitzpatrick. "Steve," he said, "did you hear about the shooting of the two Mets detectives earlier today? One was Gallo, the guy who called us."

Slauson, surprised and frightened, shook his head. *"What had he done?"*

He knew the SAC, S.V. Peterson, would unleash the full power of the organization to apprehend the perpetrators. He needed another meeting with Kellum.

The next morning, all the local newspapers carried front page articles on the attacks. The Boston Globe ran a story on the heroics of AJ Gallo during the Korean War headlined: **War Hero Attacked.** The article read:

On the night of November 27th, 1950, 12,000 men of the First Marine Division, in snowy, below-zero temperatures, were attacked without warning and surrounded by an overwhelming force of Chinese Communist soldiers at the Chosin Reservoir. Second Platoon, "C" Company, 1st Battalion, 7th Marines came under withering small arms, grenade, machine gun and mortar fire.

Although wounded, Corporal Anthony Gallo, wielding his .50 caliber machine gun, led a counteroffensive as Marines around him fell. Out of ammunition, he engaged in hand-to-hand combat with the attackers killing more than twenty enemy soldiers and helping to blunt the attack. When reinforcements arrived, he refused evacuation until other men in his unit were treated by Corpsmen. For this gallantry in action, Gallo was awarded the Navy Cross, second to the Medal of Honor, on the hierarchy of U.S. military decorations.

Bill Wilkinson became a footnote in the dramatic story.

McCrory and Caruso stayed overnight in Gallo's hospital room, taking turns to sit by his side while trying to catch some shut-eye in uncomfortable straight-backed chairs.

When morning dawned, AJ received an unexpected but welcome visitor: Susan Lawrence. She went to AJ's bed, kissed him on the cheek and took his hand. The two lawmen glanced at each other and slinked into the corridor to allow them privacy.

Overwhelmed, Gallo blurted, "I, I, didn't expect you."

"We're still friends, aren't we? I care about you, always will."

Gallo eyes welled up. He turned away to brush away the moisture with the sleeve of his hospital gown."

Susan gripped his hand. "Are you okay? Really?"

"Yes. I swear. I've had worse."

Lawrence smiled as AJ's mother and father came into the room followed by Captain Kellum, who stood aside in deference to the parents.

AJ gave Kellum a quick glare as he suffered the hugs and kisses of his mother and his father's firm grip on his hand. Neither asked the obvious question about his health, happy he survived. His mother, a devoted Catholic, believed the lord protected him. How else would he have survived Korea and now this? She would pray a Novena for him over the next nine days to ensure Jesus would continue to shield him from harm.

Kellum backed out of the room and engaged McCrory and Caruso in conversation after shaking the hand of the MDC Officer who stood guard overnight.

"I've been working with AJ on the Paragon Park murders and the subsequent killings in my town," McCrory explained.

"I know. Bill kept me informed and I read Gallo's updates."

At the mention of Wilkinson each lawman dipped his head.

"Gotta be related to our investigation," McCrory said. "We believe Mitch Smith got cocaine from the Irish mob. Maybe they thought we were getting too close."

Gallo hadn't yet filled him in on the meeting between Mike Callahan and Moran.

"Any proof? I didn't see any in the reports," Kellum probed, without emotion.

"Unfortunately, no. We intended to question Jerry Morris, the gas station attendant who worked with Smith and knew about the drugs. He's lied to us before, though, and his testimony wouldn't carry much weight in court, I'm afraid."

Kellum concealed his relief. "Okay, but he may be able to offer a lead or two to follow up."

"That's what we counted on."

"Good. We'll provide you support as needed. We can't tolerate attacks on our people."

McCrory stepped aside to let him in to see his detective as Mr. and Mrs. Gallo and Susan Lawrence came out of the room. The parents held hands and Lawrence draped her arm around Mrs. Gallo's shoulders.

Gallo kept his face neutral as his Chief approached. Wilkinson never mentioned him in the corruption scheme—no reason to accuse him now. He struggled to understand why his partner was attacked. It had to be the Irish gangsters, but what prompted them to act? Callahan got an assurance from Moran that his boys didn't take out Mitch Smith. And he in turn assured Bobby the cops wouldn't pursue evidence to implicate them.

As competing theories bombarded his brain, he settled on his call to the FBI about the impending bank robbery as the catalyst that provoked some Mafioso to action. Agent Slauson put off their meeting for two days. Why the delay? Was his trust in the FBI misplaced? Did the agent tip off the Mafia about their knowledge of the scheme? In inimitable Gung Ho fashion, he promised himself to pay Slauson a visit.

When Captain Kellum stepped up to his bedside, Gallo greeted him with a nod and a handshake. He would reserve judgement about him for now. But if Bill's blood was on Kellum's hands, there would be more than one visit to make.

Kellum, unaware of Gallo's thoughts, of course, mirrored concern as he moved closer to the bed. "I won't take up much of your time, son," he said. "You need to rest. I want you to take the next week off. Spend time with your folks. Your girlfriend. Then we'll talk."

"I'm fine, sir."

"That's not a request, son. It's an order."

Seething inside, Gallo replied as required: "Yes, sir."

CHAPTER 43

Gallo, exhausted by the visitors and well-wishers, closed his eyes for a nap, but a heated exchange outside his room interrupted the effort. Within a minute or two, John Lynch, the MDC guard, who relieved his colleague who spent the night, stuck his head into the room. "Detective," he said, "A Mr. Jones is here. Says he's the father of that Patriot Ledger reporter got shot the same time as you. Wants to see you. Didn't know if I should let him?"

"It's okay, Johnny. I'll see him."

Lynch nodded. As he left, a tall man, at least six-two, entered. He wore a dark blue, fitted pin-striped suit. With a prominent jaw, hazel eyes and a full head of neatly trimmed brown hair, he carried himself like someone used to being in charge. He strode to Gallo's bedside, hand outstretched. AJ took it and noticed the strong grip.

"Detective, I'm Alan Jones. Bert's my son. Nice to meet you but certainly not under these circumstances. How are you?"

"A little woozy from a head wound. I'll be fine."

Jones smiled. "Glad to hear it. You're my son's hero, you know. Couldn't stop talking about you and the case he was working with you."

Gallo frowned, but before he could respond, the elder Jones interrupted. "I know he wasn't working with you. He was thrilled thinking he might be helping out."

AJ laughed, but winced when a sharp pain pierced his skull.

Jones recognized his distress and apologized for bothering him. He pivoted to leave when Gallo's voice stopped him. "Wait! How is Bert doing? Nobody tells me anything around here."

Jones turned back, shook his head as tears flowed down his cheeks. He dabbed them with a white handkerchief he pulled from his jacket pocket. "A bullet perforated his carotid artery; he bled out. Everyone did their best…" He choked up, then blurted. "He's gone."

Gallo received similar news often during his combat days, never easy to have an appropriate response. He felt himself choking up but managed, "I'm very sorry, sir. Very sorry."

Jones frowned, dipped his head. He strode out of the room, unable to maintain his former regal bearing, his shoulders convulsing—a broken man.

As he shouted once before, Gallo mouthed to the empty room, "We'll get them Bert. I swear."

He leaned his head back on the pillow and fell asleep.

Bobby Moran, furious about the hits on Wilkinson and Gallo, did not authorize them; never would have. He, like his mentor Buddy McClain, nurtured relationships in the Boston PD and the Mets, precarious links at best that would collapse if cops thought the Mafia had slaughtered their colleagues. He would have to find out who carried out the attacks—better still, who ordered them.

He was baffled about why it was done, though. His boys swore they did not kill that Mitch Smith dude and he believed them. He considered taking out the guy himself, but made a promise to his "special benefactors" to abstain from murder. He worried the same people who attacked the two coppers also took out Smith—reckless members of his own gang. Guys who wanted him out as honcho and who would do anything to further that end. If one of his own free-lanced it, he would make him, or them, pay.

Gallo welcomed McCrory and Caruso into his room after Kellum and Alan Jones left. Informed them of the captain's order for him to rest.

"He's right man," McCrory said. "Take some time off. Looks like your old girlfriend is still interested."

Gallo ignored the comment about Susan. "They killed my partner, Jeff. Tried to kill me. And caught that poor bastard Bert Jones in the crossfire. That's bullshit. Time will give those bastards leeway to regroup; cover up. Can't let them do that."

McCrory crossed his arms. "What are you going to do?"

"Round up some friends; pay the mob a visit."

"Are you crazy?" the two lawmen shouted in unison.

"Kellum didn't say what I had to do while resting," Gallo said, a smirk creasing his face.

"You're serious, aren't you?" Caruso said, shaking his head.

"Damn right. I didn't fight Commies in Korea to put up with this shit."

"This isn't Korea, AJ. They won't pin any medals on your chest for doing something stupid."

"Who says it's stupid?"

"We do," they both chimed in.

Gallo pushed a button next to his bed and summoned a nurse. "When can I check out?" he demanded, when she arrived.

Susan Lawrence left the South Shore Hospital, torn by conflicting thoughts. Seeing AJ lying on his back in bed, head bandaged, looking forlorn, her heart skipped a beat. For a moment she toyed with the idea of a reunion with him. But ten years was a long time, he deserted her for the Marines without a word. Didn't contact her when he came back from Korea.

Her fiancé, Mike, a colleague, was a dependable, sensitive man. They planned to marry in June. Harboring romantic feelings for AJ betrayed him. She had to shake them.

Could she?

She'd pray on it.

She still attended Church, believed in most, not all of Catholic doctrine; discarded those tenets she thought absurd or out of touch with reality in the 20th Century.

AJ was a sweet man but when she thought about it, she had so much more with Mike. Best to move on. No going back to a time—and a boy—that didn't exist anymore.

She chastised herself for even thinking about it.

CHAPTER 44

Gallo's stay in the hospital and his bravado about seeking revenge on the shooters, led him to think about his boyhood chum, Lenny Pierce, and the agony he must be enduring since being paralyzed in Korea. Gallo had shied away from visiting Lenny, didn't want to see him in a wheelchair.

Lying in bed now, he understood his reluctance was about himself, not Lenny. He was that frightened boy on Forrest Avenue again, running away from his responsibilities as a friend.

He vowed to visit Lenny as soon as able; felt better thinking about it.

They held a wake for Bill Wilkinson at the Keohane Funeral Home on Hancock Street, Quincy, four days after his murder. The casket would be closed.

The funeral parlor was a three-story, white clapboard building with an overhang above a circular driveway to shield people exiting a hearse or vehicles as they drove up in inclement weather. The stars and stripes flew on a twenty-foot pole located on a strip of grass across from the entrance.

Two MDC officers in dress uniforms flanked the door as mourners filed in. Fifteen rows of ten chairs were set up facing the casket in a reception room that seated one-hundred people. An eight by eleven photo of Wilkinson in his uniform and a collage of other pictures of him with his wife and kids adorned a small table adjacent to the coffin.

The MDC hierarchy filled the second row of seats, leaving the front for family. Captain Martin Kellum sat next to Superintendent Fisk. Uniformed lawmen from several local departments, including the Hull Chief, Daniel Short, occupied chairs in other rows.

The family planned no official program according to pamphlets distributed by a funeral home representative at the door. Bill Jr. was expected to make informal remarks at 7:00 p.m., about halfway between the viewing hours of six to nine. He stood in a receiving line on the right-hand side of the room. He and his younger brother flanked their mother. Bill's sister and brother-in-law filled out the queue. Gallo had never met any of them.

At 6:30 p.m., Gallo and Jeff McCrory, both in formal dress, walked into the room. Hesitant, Gallo stepped over to meet the first family member who turned out to be William Francis Jr. at least four inches taller than his dad and heavier. His hair was cut short. He dressed in black from his suit, to his tie to his shoes. Gallo introduced himself and McCrory. "I know who you are, sir," Junior announced. "My father spoke of you often. Said you were a great detective."

AJ was surprised the sergeant cum lieutenant mentioned him at all, let alone in glowing terms. Loathe to extol Bill's virtues, Gallo said as enthusiastically as he could, "I learned a lot from him."

The younger Wilkinson presented his mother next in line; a petite woman, thin, eyes red from sobbing. She held a white handkerchief in her hand that she used often.

As Gallo faced her and extended his hand, she ignored it and hugged him. Her face pressed into his chest; her arms didn't make it around his bulk. Her tears moistened his shirt. She stepped back after a minute or two and beckoned with her finger for him to lean down. When he did, she whispered, "Promise me to find out who killed my husband. Promise me."

He assured her he would and sidestepped to meet the others waiting to greet him, followed by McCrory, who felt out of place. He'd met Wilkinson once that he could recall when they went to talk with Mitch Smith.

Concealing his disdain, Gallo went over to shake hands with the MDC brass, including Captain Kellum, who he suspected of blackmailing Wilkinson into participating in the Savings and Loan fiasco. He may also have had something to do with his assassination.

That ritual over, the two detectives left the building slinking along a far wall, not wishing to offend the family, who were engrossed meeting other well-wishers. Outside, both men lit up cigarettes, though neither smoked heavily like many of their colleagues. Gallo laughed, then said, "With his cough, Bill probably wouldn't have made it to old age."

McCrory eyed his Marlboro. "Then why are we doing this?"

"Could be we're stupid."

McCrory raised his eyebrows. "By the way. What did Bill's wife say to you?"

"She wanted me to promise to find out who murdered him."

"Did you?"

"Damn right."

"I'll help in any way I can, but that's a tall order, man."

Gallo nodded and said, "I need a drink."

They drove to the Jolly Roger in Wollaston Beach. The twin roofed blue and white building, advertised as a bar and nightclub, stood across the highway from the Yacht Club pier; not far from where Captain Kellum met with his co-conspirators to plan the Quincy bank heist. Gallo found a parking spot in a gravel lot behind the club.

He and McCrory walked to the street and entered through the awning covered entrance.

They emerged into a banquet room with tables draped in blue cloths. A mahogany bar was on their right. In keeping with the club's motif, a flag with skull and crossbones was fastened on the back wall. The smiling skull sported a red bandana and black eyepatch.

Between the dining area and a two-foot-high stage was a buffed wooden dance floor. A slender woman, perhaps in her early twenties, lips painted deep red and wearing phony eyelashes, crooned onstage. A young man in a frilly white open-necked shirt, black pants and scuffed matching shoes, accompanied her on piano. His unkempt dark hair flopped over his face as his fingers danced across the keys—reminded Gallo of Jerry Lee Lewis.

The girl sang Sinatra's "Fly me to the Moon." The lyrics struck a chord with AJ. He blanched and stood mesmerized as she bellowed out:

You are all I long for,

All I worship and adore,
In other words, please be true,
In other words, I love you.

A server interrupted Gallo's reverie and directed them to a table near the dance floor. They ordered Budweiser on tap. Four couples occupying tables nearby, enthralled by the song and the singer's heartfelt rendition, swayed to the beat.

Vivian, according to her name tag, dressed in a thigh high blue skirt, with a tiny white apron, delivered their beer within three minutes. She smiled and took their order of fried clams—a marketed house specialty. Both men eyed the girl's backside as she sauntered away.

They sipped their drinks in silence until their food arrived and the waitress returned to the bar area. In their dress uniforms, they drew furtive glances from the other diners, but they acted oblivious.

"What are we doing here, AJ?"

"I needed a Bud."

"I've never seen you drink."

"I do after two friends are gunned down."

McCrory grimaced. "You didn't like Wilkinson; hardly knew Jones."

"They got killed because of me."

"Feeling sorry for yourself?"

Gallo raised his glass in answer.

McCrory, who didn't know how he would have handled the situation, didn't press further. He pulled a pack of Marlboros from his pocket, gave one to AJ. He lit them with a gold, flip-topped Ronson lighter and asked, "So, what's next?"

Gallo took a deep drag, tilted his head back and blew rings toward the ceiling, where it mingled with the residue sent aloft by others. The haze created by everyone puffing away, Gallo thought, hovered over the room like an artillery barrage obscuring a battlefield—both deadly—but no one knew it at the time. The cigarette companies quashed any research that labelled smoking dangerous.

"I've been invited to a memorial service for Bert Jones," AJ said, laying his cigarette on an ashtray and signaling the waitress for another drink.

The Hingham detective raised his eyebrows in surprise. "You gonna go?"

"Wasn't going to, but they killed him coming to see me. Wouldn't have been there if not for me, feel obligated."

"Doing his job. Not your fault," McCrory said. He paused then added, "Hear his dad's a big wig; hob-knobs with politicians."

"Not going for that reason, pal," AJ said, annoyed. "Same gang that murdered Bill took out Jones. Had to be. I get one, I get 'em all. And I will get 'em."

They clinked glasses as the singer began another Sinatra favorite, "The Lady is a Tramp."

Two beers and three shots of whisky later, Gallo was reeling. McCrory signaled the waitress, settled the tab and helped his friend stagger out of the lounge. They resembled two drunks leaning on each other for support, the smaller man grimacing in pain.

McCrory snatched the big man's car keys, dumped his carcass in the back seat and drove back to his place in Hingham. His parents were out of town. He stretched his pal out on the living room couch, covered him with a blanket and went to bed.

Gallo slept late although in an uncomfortable position on the sofa. His stockinged feet dangled over the arm; his back ached from sinking into the sagging cushions as his full weight crushed them. He got a crick in his neck despite having been provided a pillow.

The aroma of brewing coffee awakened him. He rubbed the sleep from his eyes as McCrory came into the room with two steaming cups of the brew and placed them on a low, mahogany table between he and AJ.

McCrory studied his disheveled colleague; bloodshot eyes, wrinkled clothes, mussed hair. "You look like shit, Gallo," he said.

AJ screwed his face up in pain and pressed his fingers to the side of his head. "Feels like a platoon in combat boots stomping through my head."

McCrory laughed. "Want aspirin to go with the java?"

Gallo shook his head, winced in agony.

"This may ease the sting," McCrory said, and pushed a folded piece of paper across the table.

Gallo forced himself to focus on what appeared to be a handwritten note signed Vivian. "Call me," it said, with a phone number under her name.

McCrory guffawed, a sound that reverberated through Gallo's brain. "Looks like you got more out of last night than a hangover."

AJ closed his eyes and moaned.

McCrory persisted. "You gonna call her? Seemed like a nice girl."

Gallo sipped his coffee then managed a weak, "Too young."

"What are you, twenty-eight, twenty-nine. She's two or three years younger at most. Perfect match."

AJ took another sip of the hot liquid, put the cup down on the table and fell back on the cushions; didn't respond.

"You're stalling," McCrory challenged. "Phone her. Have some fun. Forget the high school chick. That's going nowhere."

Deep down, AJ knew McCrory was right about Susan, couldn't admit it yet. He struggled to his feet. "Not ready to move on. But I'll keep the note just in case. Gotta clean-up for the Bert Jones Memorial tomorrow. Let me have the keys to the unmarked."

McCrory handed them over. "Okay. Don't wait too long. That girl's not going to wait forever."

AJ forced a smile, made a quick bathroom stop, and left the house.

CHAPTER 45

Bert Jones had been buried in a private cemetery in Hingham the same day of Wilkinson's wake. The burial was a family only affair noted in the Patriot Ledger obituaries and in a single column in the local news section. A memorial was to be held at the Jones Mansion on Main Street, Hingham, two days later.

Bert's father, Alan, owned the largest construction firm in the Bay State. His trucks rumbled on the roadways from Boston north to Springfield and south to Cape Cod. His company paved roads, built bridges and erected public buildings in Brockton, Quincy, Worcester, Lynn, New Bedford and elsewhere.

In addition, he was a major contributor to the Massachusetts Democratic party. As a result of this largess, he counted numerous politicians among his friends. The ceremony for his son Bert attracted the scion of the Kennedy Clan, Joseph P. Kennedy, his wife, Rose, and sons, Senator, John Fitzgerald Kennedy, and Robert F. Kennedy, Governor Foster Furcolo—though there was animosity between the Kennedy's and the Governor—Mayor John Hynes of Boston and Richard Cushing, Archbishop of Boston.

The Jones home, located on Main Street, Hingham, dubbed the "most beautiful roadway in America" by Eleanor Roosevelt, was a three-story gray structure with blue shutters flanking banks of windows facing the road. A semi-circular drive cut through the grass in front while a long asphalt private driveway on the right led to a four-car garage in back. Cadillac and Chrysler limousines were stacked nose to rear along the side drive. Other vehicles crammed the road with state troopers on foot and motorcycles directing traffic. It resembled a gathering of royalty, which it was.

When Gallo drove up to the house, his Ford coupe became sandwiched between two sleek limos. Two men in their late twenties or early thirties, dressed in black suits, matching ties, and wing-tips, directed Gallo to find a place on the street. With the help of a cop, he found a spot ten cars down on the right and walked back to the house.

He ascended the stairs and the two men told him to go straight through the living room to the back. A roll of plastic sheeting covered the carpeting as he marched through. His head was on a swivel as he noted the hand-crafted woodwork, two stone fireplaces and landscape paintings adorning the walls. He suspected the canvases were expensive and by acclaimed artists he wouldn't have recognized.

Two white tents, bumped together, sheltered the backyard which Gallo estimated to be the length and width of a quarter of a football field. Pine, spruce, beech and oak trees surrounded the yard blocking out the view of neighbors—an idyllic setting.

Two buffet tables were set up under the tents. One held sandwiches, fruit and bowls of punch, the other, manned by men in chef's hats, doled out hot food.

Gallo, sensing he was out of place, turned to leave, when Alan Jones rushed up to shake his hand. He guided the detective to a small, round white table and introduced him to the Governor of Massachusetts and Mayor of Boston and their wives.

Jones then signaled a young waiter, whose build and rough hands pegged him as a construction worker, to bring the detective a plate of hot food and glass of iced tea; no alcohol was served.

When the food and drink came, Jones sat next to Gallo and extoled his virtues to those seated and to others who dropped by to offer condolences and stories of Bert as a precocious child. AJ kept his head down for most of the meal, did engage in small talk with the mayor and his wife.

JFK stopped by to whisper in Jones' ear then moved on to Gallo who stood up to shake hands. The senator, though six-feet tall, was dwarfed by Gallo's bulk. JFK praised him for his heroism in combat and his swift action in Nantasket when ambushed.

Gallo, impressed that the senator knew of his military service, said, "Not fast enough to save Bert, I'm afraid, sir."

Kennedy produced the smile that captivated men and women on the campaign trail. "You did your best detective; all we can ask when under fire."

Kennedy's words weren't a politician's empty platitudes. He displayed courage and grit in the Pacific, saving his crew when a Japanese destroyer sank their PT boat. It was an act that helped propel his career but saddled him with back pain the rest of his life.

"Thank you, sir," Gallo said.

JFK tapped him on the shoulder and moved on to schmooze with other guests, conscious he'd need their votes and financial support in his upcoming run for the presidency.

An hour later, Archbishop Cushing stood behind a makeshift podium and thanked everyone for honoring young Bert. He offered words of praise to the intrepid reporter who gave his life in the interests of freedom of the press. That was a stretch, but no one was going to challenge the statement. The archbishop concluded with a benediction.

Alan Jones did not speak other than to offer his heartfelt thanks to all those present for taking time from their busy schedules to honor his son. He had spoken one-on-one with each attendee beforehand.

As the group broke up, Jones slid in beside Gallo, put his arm around him and said, "My son held you in the highest regard, idolized you. If you ever need anything, and I mean anything, you contact me." He slipped his business card into Gallo's sports jacket pocket and teared up.

After leaving the ceremony, AJ sat in his car and reflected on the scene he just experienced. Doubted he'd tell anyone about who was there—didn't want to appear to be bragging. He'd make an exception for his parents, of course.

They would tell their friends. Susan would hear.

CHAPTER 46

The day following the memorial for Bert Jones, Jimmy Aslam and AJ sat at a table in the Gallo kitchen after finishing a huge plate of spaghetti and meatballs and fending off Mrs. Gallo's entreaties to have seconds. They opted for black coffee and apple pie.

AJ took a sip of his hot brew, put it down on the table and leaned toward his Marine pal. His mother knitted in their living room, out of earshot.

"I got my lieutenant killed," he said, in a voice just above a whisper. "He warned me our law enforcement agencies were riddled with corruption. I thought the FBI was untouchable. I was wrong—cost him his life."

"You couldn't have known Turk. Not your fault. They almost took you out too, don't forget."

"Doesn't make it easier. He had a family."

"What are we going to do about it?"

Gallo balled his fists. "Make them pay."

Aslam smiled, eager to do battle again. "Got a plan?"

"Working on it. How many guys from the Frozen Chosin are in the area?"

"Three that I know of."

"Okay. Contact them. Find out if they can get their hands on weapons."

Jimmy sat back, devoured the remainder of his pie, washed it down with coffee and stood. "Thanks for the meal, Mrs. G.," he shouted to Gallo's mother as he turned and walked out the front door.

"Such a nice, polite boy," Mrs. Gallo said to AJ when she returned to the kitchen to pick up the dirty plates.

AJ smiled. "Yes, he is mom."

Jimmy Aslam, a "nice, polite boy" and one hell of a Marine, didn't look the part. A knuckle shy of six feet, he weighed one-hundred-sixty pounds, wiry, dark skin, dark eyes, short black hair, glasses. Could have been a college professor or encyclopedia salesman.

But at the battle of the Chosin Reservoir, he humped ammunition for AJ's .50 caliber machine gun. When the ammo ran out, he fought hand-to-hand with the enemy. Twice wounded, he stayed by AJ's side until the Chinese had been beaten back and they hopped on an M-26 Pershing Tank to evacuate the battlefield. Jimmy now lived with his parents in Plymouth, Massachusetts, and managed an auto accessories store in Hanover.

AJ helped clear the table, strolled outside to the porch and sat in the rocker his father used in the evening to smoke his cigar. His mother refused to allow smoking inside.

Many of the houses in his Kenberma neighborhood were summer cottages boarded up for the winter. The area took on the appearance of a ghost town. AJ liked the solitude. He lit up a Marlboro and heard the ocean waves breaking on the beach not far away. Water was ever present in this narrow peninsula. He rocked back and forth and thought about his next moves. His partner had been killed, he believed, by other lawmen or their gangster confederates. He couldn't let that act of cowardice stand. Even the FBI had been infiltrated, though he had no proof of that.

As he rocked, he was having second thoughts about going rogue. Was it right to involve Jimmy Aslam and other buddies in a personal vendetta? Not their fight; they could be hurt, killed or arrested and jailed. AJ, sworn to uphold the law, wouldn't honor Wilkinson or other officers who toiled every day to do their jobs with integrity, by breaking the law.

Must be another way. After all, Jimmy Aslam was a "very nice boy."

And so was Lenny Pierce, his boyhood pal. Gallo stopped rocking, got in his Ford Coupe, drove to the package store at the bottom of Atlantic Ave and picked up a six pack of Budweiser. When he returned, he parked in front of his parent's house and walked to the Pierce's. He hoped during the short distance he'd figure out what to say to his friend and how to apologize for avoiding him until now.

Nervous, he climbed the inclined ramp and knocked on the door, shifting his weight from one leg to the other. Lenny's mom, a fifties-something lady, answered the knock. She wore a flowered smock with a bluish apron. Her hair, sprinkled with gray, was pulled back in a bun. Her face was still unlined, though dark circles encased her eyes. At first stunned to see him, she broke into a warm smile.

"My lord, AJ," she said, "you look wonderful. Read you were shot. Couldn't believe it. You look none the worse for wear." She paused then said, "Foolish me. Come in, come in. And let me take that beer, put it in the fridge."

AJ handed her the six-pack and stepped into a familiar modest parlor, with a sofa and two chairs draped by homemade blue dusk-covers. To his astonishment, a boy of about two stood in the center of the room holding a red firetruck, awestruck, looking him up and down. "You're big," he said.

"Mind your manners, Georgie," Mrs. Pierce said, as the youngster ran to her and buried his face in her middle.

Gallo knelt down and put his arm around the toddler. "Bet you'll grow to be as tall as me someday, maybe even taller."

Mrs. Pierce laughed, hugged the lad, and said, "Yes. And eat us out of house and home like you and Lennie and your friends did."

"Did they really do that grandma, did they, eat all your food?" the boy asked, his face screwed up in wonder.

"They surely did, Georgie and I'd guess you'd like some of my famous chocolate chip cookies, right now, too?"

The boy took her hand as she walked him to the kitchen. "Are they really famous, grandma?" he squealed.

A toilet flushed and moments later Lennie Pierce wheeled himself into the room. His face registered surprise and a hint of anger "Been a long-time man," he said.

AJ, though having rehearsed his response, failed to come up with a wise-crack to lighten the moment. He mumbled, "My fault Len. My fault."

Pierce glared at him before his expression softened. He opened his arms for a hug, something they would never have done as kids—too girlie.

AJ relieved, didn't hesitate, wrapped his boyhood chum in a bear hug and held the embrace for two or three minutes. Mrs. Pierce watched from the kitchen doorway, tears streaking down her cheeks.

"Sit-down, sit down, pal," Lennie said. "We have a lot of catching up to do."

"I have a better idea," AJ said. "I bought some Bud. How about we go to the beach, sip a few and watch the tide come in, or go out, whatever the hell it's going to do now?"

Lenny jerked his head toward his wheelchair and raised his eyes in a question.

"I'll maneuver that machine there if you trust me to push you down that ramp without dumping you on your head."

Pierce laughed as his mom brought them the beer, having listened in on their conversation, which surprised neither man.

AJ finessed the wheelchair to the beach weaving back and forth down the streets, making noises like a car engine as the childhood chums hooted like loons. A wooden plank leading from Beach Avenue extended about five yards into the sand. Gallo stopped at the end of the walkway and sat down as the two friends guzzled beer and talked about old times until darkness descended. The tide was coming in although the expanse of white sand kept it from reaching them.

Rejuvenated, they returned to the Pierce house with a promise from AJ to return soon to meet Lennie's wife. They had adopted Georgie, Lennie said, and couldn't be happier. Diane was a nurse. They planned to find a place of their own with her income and his military disability check.

AJ hoped it would work out for them and made a pledge to himself to keep in touch, amazed their reunion, of sorts, turned out so well. He determined not to let time intercede again but sometimes fate has other ideas.

CHAPTER 47

At 6:30 a.m., Shamus O'Rourke sat with his brother Devlin in a Buick sedan in a parking lot at Revere Beach, about five miles from downtown Boston. The city of Revere was renowned for its Wonderland Greyhound Racetrack and to a lesser extent for Kelly's Roast Beef eatery; neither was open this time of day, nor were there many beachgoers although two surfers in wetsuits struggled to ride the feeble waves splashing onto the mud.

Shamus, in the driver's seat, craned his neck to look around and ensure their privacy. "Your boys fucked up trying to take down that MDC copper in Hull," he said. With his accent, the word "fucked" sounded more like "fooked."

Devlin grimaced. "My guys said he reacted before they got a bead on him—fucking war hero."

"No excuses man. Now we're the ones who may be fucked."

"Why? Doesn't change anything. Bobby will be blamed. The cops will be on him like a swarm of bees."

"Maybe. But if Bobby goes on high alert to fend off the police, it will be more difficult for us to take him out."

"So, we make our move now. We got a couple boys close to him, loyal to us."

Shamus forced a laugh. "That worries me man. We paid them off big time. Promised more influence in the gang. The messed-up hit shows our weakness. They won't stay with us for long. They know Bobby's reputation first hand. We may have lost them already."

"All the more reason to act now. Got to happen in the next twenty-four hours or we're dead men."

Bobby Moran was indeed on high alert. Despite his friendly law enforcement connections, who else would they expect to have the balls to assassinate two detectives? Nervous and enraged, he risked a direct call from the Shamrock Bar to Captain Kellum who picked up on the second ring. When he did, Moran blurted, "Marty, I had nothing to do with the attacks on your people."

Kellum, shaken by the incidents, his less than cordial meeting with his rabbi and his funeral home visit with Wilkinson's bereaved family, was still wary about answering the phone. He intended to keep the call short.

"Who then?" he mumbled.

"I aim to find out."

"You better do it fast. I won't be able to hold my guys off for long or the Boston PD and the Feds, for that matter. They figure your boys did the shooting."

"I'm working on it; have my suspicions."

"Okay. But don't contact me again until you find out."

"Understood," said Moran, and hung up.

He didn't realize he was now a target.

Moran kept his family away from anything illegal—conducted no business at his home. No body guards patrolled his residence. Two German Shepard's roaming the grounds served as his lone nod to security.

He had struggled sleeping since the assaults on the Mets detectives. His contacts in ten police agencies couldn't hold back colleagues bent on revenge. An attack on one cop was an attack on all.

Lying in bed thinking about how to repair his damaged relationships with the law, barking dogs warned him of imminent danger. Grabbing his sawed-off shotgun standing by the bedside table, he raced into the living room and pulled back the drapes. He spied two men, one stood guard while the other was doing something under his parked car. He couldn't make out who they were.

Enraged, he stormed out the front door cursing as he ran. Startled, the would-be assassins scurried to a waiting black sedan. It roared off, wheels squealing. Moran held his fire for fear of hitting a neighbor's house, although the effective range of his sawed-off was twenty yards tops.

Fuming, Moran inspected the underside of his car and found a plastic explosive wired to the ignition. He shook with rage. Surely, whoever did it expected him to seek revenge now that they knew their assassination plan failed. They would try again. He vowed to beat them to it. But first he needed to find out who had the audacity to attack him in his home.

He ran through the list of possibilities in his mind. He dismissed the Italians in Boston as culprits. They controlled their own territory, wouldn't start a needless war. Rival gangs would be happy to muscle in on his rackets, but he doubted they would go into his neighborhood. Their rules were the same as his; family was off limits.

The only option, he believed, was a rogue group of his own gang bent on a takeover—specifically, the O'Rourke's, who chafed under his tight control. They didn't like it that he was temporary boss while Buddy McClean was in prison. They had acted restless since the attack on the coppers.

Moran, no less dangerous than his predecessor, bristled at the disrespect of those who wanted to take him out. He'd strike back but didn't know who to trust? Even his own men were now suspect. He needed to go outside his organization to recruit soldiers loyal to him.

Desperate, he considered a group known for viciousness. But if they agreed to help him, and something went wrong, it could trigger an international incident.

The Irish Republican Army (IRA) was a paramilitary group seeking the end of British rule in Northern Ireland and the reunification of the country. The Somerville mob, along with other Irish immigrants, contributed to that cause.

Bobby's appeal to them, though, was doomed to fail. They kept their activities out of the United States to not offend the American government which turned a blind eye to their attacks on the British and the money that flowed into their coffers from loyalists in the states. Their crusade was a more important issue than one man's safety—even a staunch supporter.

Moran had an alternate plan, but chaos might reign within his gang if he implemented it. Without allies, he would have no choice.

CHAPTER 48

Patrick Duffy lived in a quiet neighborhood on Chestnut Drive in Whitfield, ironically, less than two miles from the police department. He stayed to himself; neighbors unaware the bachelor in their midst was a notorious criminal. But no killer, he was relieved when the watch repair shop owner survived the blow to his head by Shamus O'Rourke.

Rethinking his association with the mob, the ringing doorbell startled him. When he answered it, Bobby Moran and "White Shoes" Dolan were standing there. He forced a smile and invited them inside.

"Hey boss. Just going to call you." he said.

Bobby knew the comment was bullshit. Duffy, ever the con, fidgeting and shifting his weight from one foot to the other, appeared up to something, but Bobby didn't have time to waste to find out. Another attack on his life could happen anytime. He smiled to put the man at ease then said, "Patrick, my boyo, I want my share of the bank take, now."

Duffy recoiled before regaining his composure; tried to stall. "Much of the loot is in valuables like jewelry and gold coins. I'm having a fence evaluate it to determine what it's worth, could be hundreds of thousands."

Seething inside, Moran kept the smile on his face. "You did get some cash right?"

Duffy felt Dolan's glare boring into him. "Yeah. Haven't counted it all."

"That's okay, boyo. Billy and I will help you."

Duffy grasped that to delay longer endangered his life. "You got it boss. I'll take you to it."

While Moran put the screws to Patrick Duffy, S.V. Peterson, the FBI Special Agent in Charge (SAC), Boston, met with his two subordinates—Special Agents, Arthur Fitzpatrick and Steve Slauson. They sat at the end of a ten-foot-long mahogany conference table in Peterson's spacious but austere office. His desk was clear save for a phone, an in-out box and a black and white photo of his wife and son. A single picture of Dwight Eisenhower adorned one wall. The President had called S.V. to congratulate him on solving the Brinks robbery.

"This attack on the MDC cops is bad business," Peterson said, by way of opening the conversation. "And Arthur, you said it might be related to our Quincy Savings & Loan investigation?"

"Yes, sir," Fitzpatrick acknowledged. "One of the men attacked, a Detective Gallo, phoned our office to report people affiliated with the Somerville Irish Mafia, and aided by local police, planned the caper. He didn't know any names, although he said his partner, Bill Wilkinson, drawn into the scheme against his will, might be able to identify the players."

"Did this story seem credible?"

"I asked Steve to check it out."

Both Peterson and Fitzpatrick swung their attention to Slauson, who shifted in his chair.

"I did contact Gallo, sir," Slauson said. "He agreed to meet with me two days later. The attack occurred before that could take place."

"Did he request the delay?" Peterson asked.

"No sir, I did," he confessed. "In hindsight, wish I hadn't. I postponed it to follow up some other leads on the robbery, didn't think the meeting was urgent."

To Slauson's relief, the boss didn't query him further. "Okay," Peterson said, "we need to question Gallo when he recovers from his wounds."

Fitzpatrick jumped in. "Yes, sir. I understand he's been released from the hospital. I'll conference with him in Nantasket as soon as I can arrange it."

"Good, and send a couple of agents there ASAP for his protection. His assailants may try again."

"Already done."

"That's why I keep you around, Arthur," the SAC joked. They all laughed.

Agent Slauson left the meeting with his boss unnerved. His fingerprints were not on the Quincy affair or the attempted assassination of the MDC detectives. Although he warned Captain Kellum of Gallo's call, he never expected a hit on the lawmen. Savvy enough to realize that was sufficient to indict him for conspiracy, he continued to delude himself.

He acted as a minor player in Kellum's corruption schemes; pocketed bribes for providing information on the Feds activities involving organized crime. He took cash as payment stashing it in deposit boxes in separate banks using phony identification. He believed he was safe as long as Kellum escaped scrutiny and kept his mouth shut. No proof tied him to anything unlawful.

He was wrong.

Unknown to Steve Slauson, Bobby Moran was an FBI informant. His tips led to the arrest of two participants in the Brinks robbery enhancing S.V. Peterson's reputation. According to policy, when the FBI secured moles from within the ranks of mobsters, they could continue their illegal activities, short of murder.

Peterson and Fitzpatrick knew beforehand of the planned Quincy Savings & Loan caper. They didn't stop it because not all of the gangsters or leaders, like Kellum, would be there. They wanted to ensnare everyone from top to bottom. If Dominick DeTullio hadn't survived, their thinking would have been altered.

The SAC's bravado in front of the press was for show and to protect Moran. In time, the valuables taken would be returned to their owners and as much of the cash as possible. This wasn't as critical as it once might have been; banks had been federally insured since 1934 with the creation of the Federal Deposit Insurance Corporation (FDIC).

Patrick Duffy had been under surveillance since the heist. Jewelry he tried to fence would be confiscated.

After his conference with Fitzpatrick and Slauson, S.V. walked down the hall to his deputy's office and closed the door. "Do you think

Moran's gone off the rails with the attacks on the two Mets detectives and the assault on the watch repair shop owner?" he asked Fitzpatrick.

"That's troubling, sir, but Moran's too smart to do that. I'll meet with him to find out what's going on."

"Set it up please, Arthur."

Patrick Duffy had shown Moran and "White Shoes" the cash he stowed in duffel bags in his garage. They counted out five-hundred thousand in fifty and one-hundred-dollar bills and, to Duffy's relief, left without demanding to see the rest of the loot. During the counting, Dolan fixed Patrick with a withering stare. Duffy shivered, almost soiled himself.

Later, Duffy contacted two shysters in Boston who would fence the valuables. He arranged to show them the goods the next day. The intrusion by the two Irish thugs shook him up as did the near murder at the robbery. He considered disappearing until things cooled off.

The IRA, upholding its policy of refraining from acting on American soil, rejected Moran's effort to recruit some of its soldiers for protection against a splinter group of his own gang who, Moran suspected, carried out the attacks on the two MDC detectives and tried to kill him.

Bobby wrestled with his options when he got a call on his home phone. The caller didn't identify himself and kept his message short: "South Station, 9:00 a.m. tomorrow."

South Station served as Boston's main transit hub for trains and busses. Thousands of passengers streamed through each day. It was easy to get lost in the throngs. Moran and Arthur Fitzpatrick met in a vacant office once the domain of the station master, a site they had used several times since their association began. S.V., a recognizable public figure, did not take the chance of a rendezvous even in a venue where he could lose himself in the crowd.

Fitzpatrick and Moran stood in the ten-by-ten room cluttered with discarded furniture. The FBI agent spoke first: "What the hell's going on, Bobby? An attack on police officers?"

Moran put up his hand in a stop signal. "Didn't have nothing to do with that. Ya know I wouldn't."

"Who then?"

"Not sure. But I suspect some of my guys want me out—tried to kill me a couple days ago."

The agent showed no compassion for the man's plight. He chose his way of life. "You better find out fast, 'boyo'," he said, using one of Moran's favorite expressions. "We can't hold back the troops for long. Everyone has your gang pegged as the shooters. And when bullets fly, they can hit anyone."

Moran recognized the threat, smiled. "I have a plan."

He was not familiar with Murphy's Law.

CHAPTER 49

Bobby's plan was simple and dangerous. He would call a meeting of those involved in the Quincy robbery, ostensibly to divvy up the spoils. The conspirators would include Captain Martin Kellum, the Quincy Chief, Lieutenant Roger Newman, Patrick Duffy and Shamus O'Rourke.

Moran would notify the FBI of the date and time of the gathering. Everyone would be scooped up in a lightning strike including him, to protect his identity as an informant. He assured Peterson and Fitzpatrick that members of his gang, under threat of extended prison sentences, would rat out their pals who had attacked the Mets detectives.

S.V. Peterson understood the strategy would take careful planning. A raid at the Irish center of operations in downtown Somerville would put civilians at risk—those who patronized the saloon and those strolling the streets near the building; bullets weren't selective in who they killed or maimed. Caution was necessary, but he couldn't delay long. If a disloyal faction was conspiring to take control of the mob, they might succeed in killing Moran before the FBI acted. He also wanted to make sure Detective AJ Gallo participated. They owed him.

Shamus O'Rourke, his brother Devlin and the third conspirator in their little scheme to take over the Winter Hill crew, Frankie O'Brien, met at their usual rendezvous at Revere Beach at 6:00 a.m. O'Brien parked next to O'Rourke, got out and slipped into the back seat of the Buick Sedan.

"Bobby escaped our hit," Shamus said, when Francis X closed the door. "We used a couple of boys from the 'Dogs' in Roxbury. Same gang we hired to attack the two MDC detectives."

"Didn't do such a great job on that either," O'Brien grumbled.

Devlin ignored the jab and jumped in. "Too dangerous to try to recruit our own guys. Most are loyal to Moran."

"What now?" O'Brien asked.

"Bobby is calling a meeting of the gang to split the take from the Quincy robbery," Shamus answered. "We can strike then. Catch him by surprise. We've made contact with some bangers from 'The Three' in Dorchester. Tough bastards."

"But why'd you attack the Mets cops?" Francis asked.

"We got a tip their investigation into the murder of one of our dealers, a Mitch Smith, was getting close to us. Might bring in the Feds."

He didn't tell O'Brien that Moran assured the cops the gang had nothing to do with Smith's killing and the lawmen agreed to drop them as suspects. Nor did he tell him he intercepted Kellum's call to Bobby alerting him Gallo tipped off the FBI about Wilkinson trying to weasel out of being involved in the Quincy scheme. The veteran detective represented a liability, he saw, who might blow up the whole operation if he panicked. Gallo was a bonus.

What was two less cops?

O'Brien shook his head. "Great idea, genius," he said, his voice dripping with sarcasm. "Now the FBI and every copper from Boston to the South Shore is itching to pounce on us."

Shamus swiveled to face Frankie; face contorted in anger. "You want out?"

Frankie recoiled. "Nope," he said, aware the O'Rourke brothers would kill him on the spot if his answer had been different.

"OK," Shamus said. "As soon as Bobby calls the meeting to split the robbery take, we'll be ready."

O'Brien left the Buick and got into his two-tone blue and white Ford Skyliner. He made an abrupt U-turn and sped out of the beach parking lot peeling rubber.

"I don't trust that guy," Devlin said.

"Don't worry. A stray bullet may find him during the get-together with our dear leader."

Devlin scoffed.

CHAPTER 50

In any decision, plan or scheme, something will go wrong—the concept known as Murphy's Law. Simply put, the Law states: "What can go wrong will go wrong." In some forms it is extended to: "Anything that can go wrong, will go wrong and at the worst possible time."

Neither Moran, who didn't know about the law, nor the FBI agents who did, heeded its ramifications.

At the last minute, Bobby dropped the idea that the raid should happen in downtown Somerville in favor of Patrick Duffy's place in Whitfield. Not all gang members were involved in the robbery scheme so it was natural to exclude non-participants. An attack on their command center would rope in everyone and spur jealousy in those left out of the heist.

Peterson and Fitzpatrick supported the change despite the fact their assault would occur in a residential neighborhood. They thought it easier to control than in a business district where many shoppers and bar patrons could be injured. They didn't account for one nosy, seventy-eight-year-old neighbor and an unwise operational decision.

For security reasons, the FBI did not notify the Whitfield PD of their raid, though its headquarters was less than five minutes from Patrick Duffy's. That omission coupled with an old lady's snooping put everyone at risk; not to mention that those armed Dorchester gangsters hired by Shamus O'Rourke were scheduled to hit Moran on the same day as the raid.

Murphy's Law personified.

Three days before the planned bust, AJ Gallo received a double dose of bad news. The first was delivered by Special Agent Arthur

Fitzpatrick, who met him at the MDC Building, Nantasket. He gave Gallo the details of the raid and informed him the SAC, Boston, wanted him to participate since the murderers of his partner were expected to be there.

"Great," AJ said. "I promised his wife we'd get those guys."

Fitzpatrick shook his head, put his hands on his hips. "Not good. We disillusion the family when we can't deliver…and sometimes we can't."

"She caught me at a vulnerable time at the wake."

"Understood. My advice—never do that again."

"Got it."

"Good. Be at the FBI, Boston Office at 5:00 a.m., June 19th, for a briefing. It'll take an hour to get to the target."

The words 'target' and 'briefing' reminded Gallo of his Marine Corps days. He also remembered when bullets started flying most plans went to hell and people, even friendlies, died.

He dismissed the thought as negative Karma and as Fitzpatrick stood to leave, he asked, "What about Hingham Detective, Jeff McCrory? He's been working on my investigations and knew Bill. He'd want to be involved."

"No can do, orders from the top; just you."

It was a gut punch, but AJ feared if he protested too much, they might exclude him too.

He kept silent.

He received the second dose of bad news by phone. Captain Kellum advised him that as of that moment, he was off the ongoing investigation of the murders of Bradley Evans and Mitch Smith.

"Let McCrory carry the ball, Gallo," Kellum said. "They're Hingham matters. I stretched the point to authorize you to continue working them. That's an order."

Gallo acknowledged the directive, clicked off, then threw the telephone against the wall and stormed out of his office, startling his FBI bodyguards.

CHAPTER 51

At 7:00 a.m. on a Wednesday morning, a caravan of seven unmarked cars left the FBI Office, Boston, on the way to Whitfield. The car models varied from Fords to Chevys to Chryslers so as not to draw attention in rural neighborhoods. The occupants carried Thompson submachine guns, Browning and Winchester shotguns, Colt revolvers, Smith & Wesson 357 Magnum revolvers and M1911 Colt 45s. No one donned a nylon bullet proof vest believing them ineffective.

The normal one-hour trip to Whitfield took thirty-minutes longer, slowed by an unexpected thunderstorm that pummeled windshields, obscured visibility and unnerved agents as the metallic sound of hail battering car roofs reverberated inside the vehicles.

In an earlier briefing, the SAC outlined the plan. Peterson stood ramrod straight in his black suit, red tie and spit-shined Florsheim shoes in front of the seated agents—the strike force. His eyes bored into every man. No one turned away; eager to go to battle.

Mounted on a tripod to the left of Peterson, was a hand drawn map of Whitfield, created using blue markers. It showed Chestnut Drive, the target road, on the east of Pleasant Street which formed the stem of a crooked "T" heading south. In a costly mistake, the abbreviated map did not show the terminus of each road.

"Gentleman," the SAC began, "this will be a lightning-fast operation which will catch the mob by surprise." He pointed to the rough drawing. "Two cars will seal off Chestnut from the east and two from the west, cutting of any escape attempt. Two others will rush the Mafia members huddled in Duffy's house expecting to share the cash and valuables stolen from the Quincy Savings and Loan."

He paused looking into the eager faces hanging on his every word. "Unfortunately," he said, "neighbors could not be evacuated since such an act might alert the gangsters inside."

After another pause, he continued. "We also didn't warn the Whitfield PD to prevent any leak of our impending action."

Peterson ignored the expressions of concern displayed by some agents and Detective Gallo's shake of his head. The former Marine believed there were too many possible glitches in the plan.

He was proved right.

Moran set his meeting with the robbery gang for 8:00 a.m. The FBI would sweep in at 8:30 a.m. giving the slow-pokes time to arrive. Bobby, who would be scooped up with everyone else, was given a hand-held radio for the occasion. He would click the receiver three times to signal the strike team to move in.

The plan immediately unraveled when a carload of Dorchester mobsters rolled to a stop in front of Patrick Duffy's at 8:15 a.m. As they did, seventy-eight-year-old Audrey Meadows pulled the curtains back on her bay window; a ritual she performed frequently to safeguard "her neighborhood" from annoying children traipsing on her lawn, loud parties or cars parked too long in front of her house. Considered a busy-body and nuisance, the police often ignored her grievances.

Audrey's heart raced when she spied men with guns across the street. She'd purchased an extension cord for her phone to make it easier than going back and forth to a wall outlet. Without hesitating, she dialed the Whitfield PD.

The veteran dispatcher, familiar with the woman's rants, sensed fear in her voice instead of her usual outrage. Torn between dismissing her warning as the bluster of a paranoid old busy-body—low priority—or treating it as a legitimate alert of an impending violent crime, he opted for the latter and sent two patrol cars, lights flashing, sirens wailing, to the location.

A critical mistake.

Chestnut Drive was in a middle-class neighborhood of single and two-story homes. Duffy's was a low-slung brick, three-bedroom residence with two front doors and a picture window facing the street.

The five gangsters leaping from their Buick sedan to attack the conspirators gathered inside froze, stunned to hear sirens of approaching police cruisers, torn between running or carrying out their hit.

The Whitfield officers in their one-man vehicles turning on to Chestnut, not expecting a violent encounter, were wiped out by a fusillade of machine-gun fire. One car veered onto the lawn of Duffy's neighbor to the east and plowed into a tree. The other continued on a collision path with the attackers and slammed into their Buick—the cop at the wheel slumping forward, his foot still on the gas pedal. The smell of cordite and rubber filled the air.

Alerted by the commotion outside, Moran signaled the FBI to move in. Two cars positioned a minute away, charged ahead and confronted the gangsters hiding behind their wrecked sedan.

The hoodlums raked the oncoming FBI cars with withering fire as they swerved to block the street. The driver of one was wounded and pulled to safety by AJ Gallo, who leaped from the back seat as bullets ripped through the windows. The man hit had jabbered all the way to Whitfield about the exhilaration of going into battle. Gallo suspected he had never been in combat. Most men who had, stayed silent or prayed as they prepared to attack an enemy.

"Sorry," the agent said as he gripped Gallo's forearm. "I was stupid." He grimaced and passed out.

Special Agent Arthur Fitzpatrick, in the adjacent car, radioed to the blockading vehicles on the west end of Chestnut to forget their mission and join them. But in another Murphy's Law gaffe, those agents lost precious time circling the area having discovered Chestnut was not a through street. It took them ten minutes, and many mis-turns, to reunite with their comrades.

Audrey Meadows fell to the floor when the shooting started, afraid she would be hit by a stray bullet. Her body shook and tears flowed but she managed to phone the Whitfield PD while lying on her back. She screamed, "God help us. Your boys have been killed. Murdered. It's bedlam here. Blood everywhere. Those poor boys. Please help us. Please."

Her anguished plea unleashed another round of confusion at police headquarters. The dispatcher, though a veteran of twenty-five years, hadn't been confronted by such a situation. He heard the sound of staccato gunfire during Audrey's call and without consulting his chief, ordered all remaining cars on patrol to the scene.

Inside Duffy's, Shamus O'Rourke, taking advantage of the turmoil outside, pulled his gun and shot Bobby Moran and his right-hand man, "White Shoes" Dolan.

"I'm in charge now," he shouted, pointing his Glock at the startled men. "Anyone object?"

No one did.

He disarmed the law enforcement officers present, all involved in the Savings & Loan heist. His co-conspirators, brother Devlin and Francis X, "Frankie," O'Brien, collected the weapons and herded the group into a back bedroom leaving Moran and Dolan lying in pools of blood on the living room carpet.

Though he exuded an outward confidence, the collapse of his scheme rattled O'Rourke. The Dorchester gunmen were embroiled in a gunfight with the cops who blocked one end of the street. He fled to the back room and ordered Duffy to bring him a canvas bag from the robbery and fill it with cash and valuables. "You better stuff it full," he threatened, "or the next bullet will be for you."

Terrified, Duffy stumbled into the garage, jammed an empty sack with as many bills and jewels as he could, and dragged it back to O'Rourke. While Duffy was gone, O'Rourke saw an opportunity to break out. His car, parked near the second front door in the house, faced away from the police blockade. He, Francis X. and Devlin could bolt out that door, jump in his vehicle and scram.

Murphy would have been laughing.

The FBI plan was a disaster.

The two bureau vehicles returning from their odyssey to block the non-existent end of Chestnut, roared up to the scene at the same moment Whitfield patrol cars turned up. A sergeant and a rookie manned one cruiser, while single officers drove the other three—none possessed high powered weapons.

The local cops, seeing the unmarked Fed autos filled with armed men, obstructed their movement and scrambled from their cruisers, guns drawn. Arthur Fitzpatrick grabbed a bull horn from the front seat of his Chevy Fleetline. He bellowed, "Don't shoot. Don't shoot, Federal agents." He held up his badge to corroborate his statement. The Whitfield sergeant still wary, ordered his troopers to stand down but not holster their weapons. They did so with unease.

The Dorchester bangers, at first distracted by the arrival of the local cops, resumed firing, hitting agent Steve Slauson, who stood up when the confrontation with the Whitfield officers began. Other agents, along with the police, took cover and returned fire. The racket sounded like an invasion and three other panicked stay-at-home moms called Whitfield Police Headquarters, jamming the switchboard.

AJ Gallo, a veteran of many firefights, concealed behind one of the FBI vehicles, saw that the mobsters, focused on the lawmen in front of them, could be outflanked. He grabbed a Thompson from the fallen Slauson and scampered toward a car opposite Duffy's house. Fitzpatrick's call for him to stop went unheeded.

Most residents in the neighborhood, lacking garages, parked on the street providing plenty of cover if Gallo could reach their cars. A volley of gunfire erupted and bullets strafed the ground as he zigzagged like a running back avoiding tacklers and dove behind a green Mercury

Montclair. A sting and moisture on his thigh revealed he had been hit. But his adrenaline kicked in, his heart raced and his sympathetic nervous system over-rode the pain. He figured that if he could reach two other vehicles about ten yards ahead, he could outflank the gangsters.

Taking a deep breath, he shed his cover and unleashed a burst at the Dorchester gang. FBI agents and cops, seeing his maneuver, provided covering fire. With a forward roll, Gallo reached his destination but not before a round clipped his shoulder. Shaking off the discomfort, he popped up and took down two exposed mobsters late ducking behind their Buick.

Next, in a move everyone present would talk about for years, Gallo jumped up, and firing from the hip, screaming like a banshee, rushed headlong toward his adversaries. Stunned by this audacious act, the three bangers left standing threw down their weapons and raised their hands above their heads.

They couldn't fight a crazy man.

Seeing the cops and agents preoccupied apprehending the mobsters, Shamus O'Rourke, his brother Devlin and Francis X. O'Brien, dashed out the far front door of Duffy's, leaped into Shamus's car and peeled off west on Chestnut.

An unwelcome surprise awaited. Like the FBI agents earlier discovered, Chestnut Drive ended in a cul de sac.

Gallo disarmed the men who surrendered as other lawmen ran past him into Duffy's to arrest those inside. They found Bobby Moran and "White Shoes" Dolan lying on the blood-soaked living room floor and the others face down in a back bedroom unaware that the O'Rourke's and O'Brien had fled.

Multiple ambulances were summoned to remove the dead and wounded. Dolan died instantly from his chest wound; Moran held on. The two officers who had been first on the scene were dead as was Agent Slauson who stood up when the Whitfield cops arrived. Agent Fitzpatrick running up to Duffy's, noticed Galo's wounds and retrieved a first aid kit from his vehicle and wrapped them as best he could until medical staff came. "Never seen anything like your one-man attack on those killers," Fitzpatrick said, awe struck.

Gallo kept silent, seething inside at the ineptitude of the assault plan. Men died needlessly. He wished he had spoken up when S. V. Peterson presented it.

Vans transported those arrested back to Boston for interrogation. The Whitfield Chief was livid, when he surveyed the site of mayhem where he lost two officers. He and Agent Fitzpatrick faced off nose to nose. "You dumb shits," the Chief ranted, jutting his jaw as close to Fitzpatrick's as he could without making contact. "High and mighty Feds, know everything. Couldn't stoop to let us lowly locals in on your plans. Oh, no! We might screw it up."

His near deranged laugh echoed through the now quiet neighborhood. "Couldn't mess it up worse than you, pal," he continued. "You cost the lives of good men with your carelessness and bravado. Hope you can sleep tonight."

He turned to leave then pivoted back, "On second thought, rot in hell."

The Chief's withering tirade shook Fitzpatrick to his core. He knew the man was right. So did Gallo, who lowered his head and shuffled away.

The fleeing O'Rourke's and Frankie O'Brien, found Chestnut Drive to be a dead end. Cornered by Whitfield cops, O'Brien surrendered without a fight, while Shamus and Devlin ran; Shamus dragging a satchel full of cash and jewelry. A young officer chased him down in the backyard of a house fronting the street. The cop pummeled his face as he lay handcuffed on the grass until pulled off by a colleague. Devlin, trapped by a fence he couldn't scale, gave up.

The neighborhood resembled a war zone. An anticipated straightforward operation turned into a nightmare. The architect of Murphy's Law might have smiled if the chaos and death had not been so horrifying.

First responders rushed Bobby Moran, not expected to survive, to Whitfield Hospital's new trauma center fifteen minutes away—his outlook bleak. Gallo went to the hospital to be checked. His wounds proved superficial. He was released after nurses changed his bandages.

In the late afternoon, the day of the raid, the SAC, Boston, S.V. Peterson stood at a wooden podium in front of the press in a conference room at FBI Headquarters to provide an update.

"This morning," he began, "agents from this office conducted an assault on a private residence in Whitfield, Massachusetts, and apprehended members of the gang who organized and participated in the robbery of the Quincy Savings & Loan. Sadly, among those arrested, were law enforcement officers who violated their oaths to protect and serve their communities—and held greed above honor."

He declined to name them.

Ignoring raised hands, he continued. "We are also pleased to announce that, we believe, two of the mobsters taken into custody ordered the murderous attack on two Mets detectives over a week ago."

Deluged with questions he chose not to answer, Peterson stepped aside to let Special Agent Arthur Fitzpatrick, who commanded the operation, relate further details.

"The assault on the mob, while successful," he reported, "was not without loss. I'm sad to report that two brave Whitfield officers lost their lives along with one of our agents. We will honor them all as soon as possible."

He did not name names.

His remarks finished; Peterson joined him to field queries. The back and forth did not go well. Inquiries like: "How did they know which house to hit?" "Who ordered the raid?" "Did you brief Director Hoover beforehand?" "Can you identify the law enforcement officers arrested?" "Did you loop in local police?" were met with a standard response: "That's confidential at this time."

Somehow Gallo's one-man assault leaked. Fitzpatrick fielded the question. "As you may have heard, Metro Detective Anthony Gallo, a former decorated combat Marine, and one of the men wounded in an earlier attack by Mafia hoodlums, received injuries today. He requested to participate in the operation. His bravery, which, again, I cannot describe for confidential reasons, surfaced in the face of withering automatic weapons fire and, without doubt, saved lives."

Fitzpatrick and Peterson stepped away from the podium and left the room still being grilled by reporters. They retreated to the SAC's office where they slumped into two padded chairs, exhausted, reeling from the disastrous outcome of the plan. One, or both, of their heads likely to roll.

When notified of the debacle, Director of the FBI, J. Edgar Hoover, ordered them to Washington to provide details and to answer the same questions posed by the newsmen.

The Whitfield Chief of Police remained inconsolable. No officer under his command had lost his life in his twenty years on the job. Ignoring advice from the mayor, he publicly criticized the FBI for withholding information about the raid. He inferred that the oversight, or deliberate act, caused the death of his troopers. Speaking before reporters in a cramped conference room adjacent to his office, he unloaded: "This operation was a fiasco planned and carried out by the incompetent Boston FBI leadership. They need to be held accountable by the highest authority in that organization."

The distraught families of the slain men threatened legal action.

In the aftermath of the debacle, a search of MDC Captain Kellum's Office, agents uncovered a hidden list of lawmen on his payroll or beholden to him for providing stolen tests. The officers, in several different organizations, were suspended pending dismissal. A debriefing of Kellum determined he played no role in the attacks on Wilkinson and Gallo, but helped organize the Quincy Savings & Loan robbery.

Kellum kept no record of his relationship with his rabbi, who was aware of the Savings and Loan heist and who expected to benefit from it. Kellum stayed silent in the hope his mentor would find some way to get him out of his dilemma.

Shamus O'Rourke, withstanding intense interrogation, refused to admit he ordered the hits on the MDC detectives. But as the Mafia boss predicted, his men turned on each other. Frankie O'Brien confessed to agents that both O'Rourke's told him, after the fact, details of the attacks. He swore Moran had no prior knowledge of the assassination attempts.

O'Rourke admitted shooting Moran and Dolan in an attempt to take control of the gang. He denied any involvement in the murder of Mitchel Smith, the dealer who lost some cocaine intended for sale. He thought about killing him but backed off after a warning from Moran.

Now expected to recover, Moran lingered in intensive care facing a long recuperation. His status as an FBI informant remained secret. No one as yet stepped up to fill the leadership void in the Winter Hill mob. Buddy McClean, the gang's founder was rotting in jail and not due to be released for another year. The FBI was tracking an up-and-coming gangster who, they thought, could also turn into an informant—guy named Whitey Bulger.

CHAPTER 53

Captain Kellum's downfall shook the MDC, the Boston PD and other police agencies throughout the greater Boston area. Officers in Kellum's network in Quincy, Needham, Milton, Newton and Watertown, were arrested and banished from those departments. Patrolman, sergeants, lieutenants and captains were indicted and faced criminal conspiracy charges—among them Lieutenant Roger Newman.

The state police and the FBI participated in the purge which lasted two months and in some municipalities was still ongoing. Detectives Hogan and Hawkins were recalled to Boston after being vetted by internal affairs and state investigators and absolved of any wrongdoing. Six of their colleagues, ensnared in Kellum's web, were fired and awaited trial. The Massachusetts Attorney General, George Finegold, placed watchdogs in the MDC organization empowered to root out any additional malfeasance. Morale plummeted with the detective bureau at a standstill.

MDC Superintendent Bob Fisk escaped the Attorney General's ax but received a written reprimand for lax oversight. He considered retirement but opted not to leave under the circumstances—abandoning ship, as it were, as he told staff.

He was kidding himself and lying to them.

He couldn't retire. He owed serious money to the mob. While maintaining the façade of a respected leader—tough on crime and corruption—he dropped thousands of dollars betting on the horses. This brought him into contact with James "Buddy" McLean—and now Bobby Moran—whose Winter Hill outfit controlled the races; fixed many.

As Martin Kellum's rabbi, Fisk shielded Kellum as the captain built his criminal empire inside and outside the MDC organization. Kellum's schemes and shakedown of crooks filled his pockets as well. He expected the proceeds from the Savings and Loan theft would allow him to pay off his debt to the mob and get out from under their control.

With that prospect now unavailable, he faced another quandary. Kellum, awaiting sentencing in the Suffolk County House of Corrections for his part in the bank robbery and accessary to murder charges over the deaths of the law enforcement officers killed in the Whitfield FBI raid, now threatened to expose Fisk if he didn't help him.

Fisk, shaken by Kellum's threat, sat in his spacious office on the top floor of the MDC Headquarters Building. His teak desk and leather swivel chair occupied one end of the room and overlooked the Boston skyline.

Other furnishings included a blue Canal Sofa and four matching chairs, a teak credenza with pictures of his wife and children resting on top and a Crawford maple coffee table positioned in front of the sofa—all expensive and paid for by graft.

Fisk began pacing the room, hands behind his back. At once, he quickened his pace, then slowed; his footprints imprinted in the plush carpet. He stopped at the window and peered out; the view almost hypnotic. He stood there fixated considering his options.

Finally, he returned to his chair, his decision made. A gambling man, he chose not to be intimidated by Kellum's threats; no one would believe them. There were no written communications between the two. His reputation remained impeccable—no reason for the Irish to give him up. They would relish having a high placed lawman under their thumb. He opted to try to repair the damage done to the Mets organization by staying at his post. He convinced himself future good deeds would outweigh past transgressions.

To begin the recovery, he appointed Major, Nick Osterman, as the Chief of Detectives. Osterman, a gray haired, bespectacled man of fifty-five, served as an army captain in World War II. He had piercing hazel eyes, a strong jaw and the glare of a man who brooked no disobedience. He always wore his trademark tailored blue striped suit and red tie with a combat infantry pin in his left lapel.

Once Osterman was ensconced in his position—he'd been in the white-collar crimes division—Fisk summoned AJ Gallo to meet his new boss. Gallo saluted both superior officers as he stood before them.

"Have a seat, detective," Fisk said and introduced the new man who smiled and offered his hand. Gallo took it and said, "Look forward to working with you, sir."

"As do I son. You're a legend in this organization."

Here we go again with the "son" stuff, Gallo thought, but kept silent, not acknowledging the praise. He didn't want to start off on the wrong side of the new Chief of Detectives, an outstanding, honest leader according to bureau scuttlebutt. For the present, he'd suffer any name he called him.

Fisk interrupted the exchange between the two men. "You're going to get a Medal of Valor for your action in the FBI raid, son."

Gallo shook his head, set his jaw. "Thank you, superintendent, but no thanks. Just doing my job."

"You don't have a choice, detective," Fisk said, annoyed. "This recognition will bring honor to the organization and is much-needed in view of recent events."

"You deserve it," Osterman said, breaking into the conversation. "It will lift the morale of your colleagues going forward."

Gallo, outnumbered, agreed to accept the award under one condition. When he told them what he wanted, Fisk and Osterman eye-balled each other and nodded.

When Fisk left the office, Gallo, arm in a sling and standing on crutches, requested to rejoin Hingham Detective Jeff McCrory in the probe of the murders of Bradley Evans and Mitch Smith.

He shared with the new Chief of Detectives that he received assurances from Bobby Moran, through Mike Callahan, that his gang did not kill Smith. And Shamus O'Rourke verified this during his FBI interrogation.

Osterman leaned back in his chair and lit up a Camel cigarette. His stare fell on the wall behind Gallo and remained there for two or three minutes. When he returned to face Gallo, he said, "Detective, I'm not up to speed on much of what's been going on in the unit. We're shorthanded as you might expect. It doesn't make sense from an operational standpoint. Let me review the situation. I'll get back to you, I promise, and you need to shed those crutches and sling before resuming work."

"Please consider my request, sir. We have some viable suspects. I'd sure like to bring my first case to a successful conclusion."

"Noted, but my understanding is that your first investigation succeeded. You solved the murders in Paragon Park. Finding out who murdered the killer will be icing on the cake; officially the job of the Hingham PD."

AJ acknowledged that was true, yet he still wanted to tie up everything connected to those killings. As he got up to leave and fumbled with his "support sticks" as he named them, he said, "Sir. May I take a few days off to attend to a personal matter? I know that's an awkward request to make at this time."

Without hesitation, Osterman agreed. "Take all the time you need, detective. I expect you to stay out until you're recovered. I won't clear you for duty till that happens."

On his drive back to Hull, Gallo felt guilty about abandoning his colleagues but doubted he'd be much help hobbling around. His thoughts turned to one idea; how to win Susan Lawrence back. He liked her fiancé, Michael Callahan, who had helped find out the Mafia didn't murder Mitch Smith.

But Gallo decided to take up McCrory's challenge to fight for Susan. After another brush with death, he believed he had no choice.

Gallo, unfamiliar with the tale of Don Quixote, was tilting at windmills.

Gallo took fifteen days to recuperate under the watchful eye of his mother who fed him chicken soup, pasta and pastries. His father, who worked for the water company, took time off to sit with his son. They spent hours on the porch reminiscing about high school football and talking about AJ's plans for the future. His former sweetheart did not enter their conversations.

Once recovered, Gallo persuaded Susan Lawrence to meet at Abbadessas pizza parlor in West Corner, also known as "Four Corners." It served as the intersection of four roads, two from Cohasset and one each from Hull and Hingham. Gallo chose a lunch to make it appear less like a date than an evening meal would at an upscale place like the Red Lion in Cohasset.

When they were seated, having ordered a pepperoni pizza and a pitcher of draft beer, Lawrence said. "So, you did it again, huh?"

Gallo, confused, asked," What do you mean?"

"Became a hero."

"Just doing my job. My partner deserved justice."

"From our conversations, I gathered you didn't even like the guy."

Gallo's jaw hardened. "He was a cop, a detective, had a wife and kids, didn't deserve to be shot down in front of his home and family."

Susan, embarrassed, said, "Sorry. Didn't intend to minimize the impact of his death."

A waitress interrupted the conversation by delivering the beer and two mugs. AJ filled them and raised his in a "toast" gesture.

Susan, surprised, clinked his, but glowered when he said, "To us."

She slammed her mug down, folded her arms across her chest. "There is no us AJ. I'm engaged to a man I love. I'm happy. Won't deny you and I spent a wonderful time together as teenagers. But we're not children anymore."

About to interrupt, she silenced him by raising her hand in a stop motion. "Don't please. We will always be friends, but I've moved on. I hope you can too."

The waitress returned with their pizza and the conversation stalled as they each sampled a piece.

Finishing his slice, AJ quaffed a long gulp of beer and said, "Okay. Got the message through this thick skull."

He lifted his mug again. "Friends always."

She reciprocated this time. "Always," she said, wiped away a tear, got up, pecked him on the cheek and left, leaving him like she did at their first meeting at Darcy's Bar.

Distraught, he filled his mug two more times, devoured another slice of pizza, and sat back, fighting tears.

After sitting for five minutes staring at the high back of the mahogany booth vacated by Lawrence, he got up, dropped a ten-dollar bill on the table and shuffled out of the restaurant.

On the street, he clenched his teeth and admitted to himself that his "infatuation fantasy" was history. Time to refocus; catch the killer of Bradley Evans and Mitch Smith. Get back to work.

In his car after his catastrophic reunion with Susan, his radio station jolted him by playing the latest hit by the Everly Brothers, "All I HAVE TO DO IS DREAM."

The boys sang about a young man in love, who, when away from his girl, brought her to him by dreaming. Lyrics like: "Whenever I want you, all I have to do is dream," reduced the former war hero, now police detective, to tears. His shoulders shook and he sat, unable to drive off until the song finished.

Swiping his eyes with his right sleeve, he engaged the car's clutch, shifted into first gear and pulled away from the curb determined not to be the lad, as the Everly's declared, "dreaming my life away."

CHAPTER 54

Needing a shoulder to cry on, Gallo phoned his old pal Lenny and asked if he'd like to drink some beer and watch the sun go down at the beach. Pierce agreed if they could bring Georgie.

Gallo wheeled them to the beach with Lenny's son sitting in his lap and giggling all the way. When they stopped on the wooden planks in the sand, Georgie, pail in hand, raced to the water's edge. He began digging and throwing mud over his shoulder, much of it falling on his head.

"Great kid, Len," AJ said. "Lots of energy."

"Like we used to have," Pierce said.

Gallo sat beside the wheelchair as both men watched the toddler scurry into the waves, fill his bucket, and splash back to fill the hole he dug. He then plunked himself down in it and poured water on his head with his pail, laughing and shivering.

The old friends chuckled, watching the boy's antics, then gulped some brew.

"So, what's up, AJ? Haven't seen you in ages and suddenly we're bosom buddies again."

"Can't fool you, huh?"

"Nope."

"Susan dumped me."

Pierce downed more beer and looked AJ in the eyes. "You're an idiot, pal. That was over when you took off without a word, like leaving the bride at the altar. Never going to forgive you."

Gallo finished his beer, stuck the can in the sand, and gazed out into the Atlantic. "She's engaged."

"Good for her."

Gallo cranked his head toward Pierce, eyeballed him for a minute or two, then emitted a guttural sound, intended as a laugh that came out as a harsh expletive. "Time to move on like she keeps telling me."

"Sage advice, man. Look, I learned something about relationships in therapy when recovering from my wounds."

"You saw a shrink?"

"You don't think being paralyzed doesn't play with your mind?"

"Of course, it does. I'm stupid."

"Not stupid. Oblivious sometimes. Well! Most of the time."

AJ laughed. "Okay. I deserved that. What do I need to know?"

His pal shook his head. "Everything, man, but let me fill you in on the basics. And this relates to you and Susan."

Gallo raised his hands in surrender, so Lenny proceeded to give him a relationship lesson: "My therapist explained that people enter our lives for a reason, a season, or a lifetime. Your dalliance with Susan falls into the "season" category. It happened at a certain time of your life, lasted for a minute, brought you joy, then ended."

AJ listened intently; didn't interrupt.

"You guys were children. You've outgrown each other, though you don't want to accept it. You influenced each other in a positive way; but that "season" is over."

"So where do you and me fall in your scenario's?"

Pierce took a gulp of beer, then said. "Lifetime, man. We've gone through different stages. Our time as kids cemented a bond that will last, if you want it to?"

AJ teared up, moved by Lenny's passion in pronouncing their connection as lasting for a lifetime. Before he could respond, little Georgie came running back to them holding a starfish in his hand. "Look daddy, a star from the sky. Can I keep it, please, please?"

Lenny hugged the boy. "Sure, you can. And you know what?"

"What daddy?"

"Lots of people think a starfish brings good luck."

The boy's smile widened and he jumped up and down. "Good luck for me," he shouted.

AJ wiped the tear from his eye, something he had been doing a lot of lately, glanced at Pierce and said, "Georgie. Can you find another one for me? I could use some good luck."

The boy handed his treasure to his dad and waddled back to the ocean to search for another starfish for his new friend.

"Luck," Pierce exclaimed, "says the guy who keeps getting shot and walking away—well limping away."

Gallo felt like an ass looking at his paralyzed pal.

Lenny picked up on the pitiable expression. "Don't you pity me, AJ. Don't you dare. I have a son and a wife who loves me. It is what it is. I'm going to be all right."

AJ, feeling miserable, dropped his eyes to the sand. "I know you are, Len. Didn't mean to be a jerk. And I plan to be around you and your family for a lifetime."

Before Lenny responded, Georgie came skipping back screaming with excitement. "I found one for you mister. Now we can both have good luck."

Gallo took the starfish and engulfed the startled boy in a bear hug. "Yes, we can, Georgie. We sure can."

AJ and Pierce looked at each other and AJ mouthed, "We sure can."

The old friends left the beach on an emotional high; one that didn't last.

CHAPTER 55

In a two-hundred square foot conference room on the second floor of MDC Headquarters used for department meetings, fifty people were in attendance for an awards ceremony including the Mayor of Boston, the FBI Special Agent in Charge (SAC) Boston, and Gallo's colleagues Brian Hogan, Christopher Hawkins and Jeff McCrory.

The Gallo and Wilkinson families were honored guests along with businessman Alan Jones. The presence of Mrs. Wilkinson and her sons to receive a commendation for Bill was the condition AJ set to accept a Medal of Valor for his actions in the raid on the Irish Mafia.

Since the exposure of Captain Kellum's nefarious criminal network, he rethought his opinion of his veteran partner. Still disappointed in the man's behavior, he recognized the lieutenant was trapped between the proverbial rock and a hard place.

Yes! His acceptance of a copy of the lieutenant's exam prior to the test was a mistake, but to defy Kellum meant the end of his career and at the worse, endangered his life. His family deserved a final tribute to his mostly honorable work as a peace officer.

Superintendent Fisk stepped to the wooden podium and adjusted the microphone so that it came within inches of his mouth. He looked around the room and smiled. "Today," he began, "we are gathered to recognize heroism and dedication to service of two of our own. This is a bright light in an otherwise dark period in our history. I'm not going to dwell on that except to say that those lawmen in this room and others on duty elsewhere plan to move forward to once again bring honor to our organization."

He paused to take a drink from a glass of water, then beckoned Bill Wilkinson's family and Anthony James Gallo to the front of the room. "I'd like Bill's partner to make this presentation."

Gallo smiled and accepted a plaque with the inscription: "To Lieutenant William "Bill" Wilkinson, for exemplary service and dedication to the highest level of police standards." An MDC lieutenants badge was affixed to the award.

Gallo read the message aloud and handed it to Mrs. Wilkinson along with a hug. He shook hands with the sons and clapped each on the shoulder. Their mother chocked up and was unable to speak. Junior stepped in, thanked the superintendent and gushed how proud his father was to have served as a lawman.

The family returned to their seats as AJ's parents were summoned to the front. They stood on either side of their son as he was presented with a plaque and a medal for conspicuous bravery above and beyond the call of duty. Fisk bestowed the medal to Mama Gallo who, standing on tiptoes, placed it around her son's neck and bussed him on the cheek. His dad shook his hand.

Gallo, ever shy, thanked Fisk and accepted the award on behalf of all law enforcement officers who do their best to keep the streets safe from criminals.

Fisk then encouraged everyone to move to the back of the room to sample assorted cookies and cakes, coffee, tea and soft drinks. Wilkinson's wife intercepted AJ and his parents and hugged all of them. She heaped praise on Gallo and whispered her thanks; she knew he was responsible for this ceremony which meant so much to her sons.

Mr. Jones and S.V. Peterson, FBI SAC (Special Agent in Charge,) Boston, came by to offer their congratulations.

Gallo, embarrassed by all of the attention—one reason he at first declined the valor award—ushered his parents out of the room after he spoke a final time to the Wilkinson's. He praised Bill as decent man and mentor. He felt awkward saying that, but thought it would do no harm and would help Bill's family overcome their grief.

He wondered if he was being a hypocrite.

Later, he began to speculate on why Superintendent Fisk agreed to the commendation for Bill Wilkinson so fast. A troublesome idea had been forming in his mind. He asked Hogan and Hawkins what they thought of their leader.

"Good man. Doing his best to right the ship," Hawkins said. "He didn't totally escape punishment for what happened. The grapevine Tom Toms report he got a letter of reprimand from the Attorney General for careless oversight."

"That's a career killer," Hogan added. "He could have retired with no one the wiser."

"Just wondering why Captain Kellum was allowed to operate so freely," Gallo said.

"Dah! Careless oversight," said Hawkins, raising his eyebrows. "What are you getting at?"

"I think it was more than that," Gallo persisted.

"Like what?" Hawkins challenged.

"Like he knew what was going on; may even have been in on it or, at the least, looked the other way."

Hawkins shook his head in disbelief, his face flushed. "That's nuts. Got any proof?"

"No, but I think I know where I can get some."

"You're way off base, rookie," Hogan said emphasizing the word rookie. "He's a great boss; great man. Always been tough on crime and corruption. It's been his hallmark."

"I know it's hard to believe but something smells. How do you explain Kellum? It goes beyond negligent leadership. Kellum's got this corrupt team within our ranks and Fisk has no idea?"

"Did you?"

"No. But I'm just a lowly rook as everyone points out. I think you guys may have suspected something was going on. You had to."

Hogan bristled with anger; pointed his finger at Gallo and stuck out his jaw. "Are you accusing us of something?"

"No. But tell me you had no suspicions."

His two colleagues, red faced, kept silent.

"I know you guys," Gallo said. "You're honest, hard-working cops. Will you help me uncover the truth?"

The two men glanced at each other. Hawkins spoke for them. "No way, man. This is your show."

Gallo was disappointed, but determined to get proof of his accusation on his own. He'd start at the Suffolk County House of Corrections where his former boss was a resident.

He looked at his colleagues and sighed. "Okay" was all he said.

Gallo met disgraced Captain Martin Kellum in an interrogation room at the Suffolk County House of Corrections. The captain was unshaven, had dark circles under his eyes and appeared to have lost at least ten pounds.

"What can I do for you detective?" Kellum said. "Come to gloat."

Gallo shook his head, remained professional. "No, sir. Just have a few questions about the Savings and Loan robbery and how you were able to get so many of our guys involved in criminal acts?"

Kellum stifled a laugh. "You really are a rookie, son. Did you think I would answer that? I haven't had my day in court. Haven't pleaded guilty to anything."

"They caught you red handed, sir."

This time Kellum emitted a guffaw that reverberated through the small room. "There are always deals to be made, son. The justice system isn't necessarily about justice."

Gallo was irritated by Kellum calling him son—like everyone seemed to be doing these days—but didn't go there; not the right time. "Just need to know one thing, sir."

"And what might that be?"

"Did the superintendent know what was going on?"

Kellum blinked twice and looked away—a tell that he was lying. "You're way off base, son. Way off base."

Kellum stood and shouted for the guard, signaling the meeting was over.

Gallo got what he sought even though Kellum stonewalled him. He would confront Fisk himself.

When Gallo left the House of Corrections, Martin Kellum—who used his connections in the prison to get access to a private phone—dialed a familiar number answered on the third ring by MDC Superintendent, Bob Fisk.

"Yes," he said, thinking the call came from inside the building; few outsiders had his direct line.

Without identifying himself, Kellum said but four words: "Gallo's coming for you."

Fisk didn't ask him to elaborate. He had feared exposure ever since the FBI raid netted Kellum and others within the department.

He didn't expect it to come from the rookie.

He opened the right-hand drawer of his desk and fingered his .38 Special. His eyes moistened and he sighed. He then pulled over the lined tablet on his desk-top used to write down messages received or things to do.

He addressed a note to his wife, Carol, and apologized for what he was about to do. He slipped the note into an envelope, sealed it, and left it on the middle of the desk-top.

That finished, he got up, went to the credenza where he kept his liquor, poured himself a shot glass, filled it to the brim, and took it to the window where he gazed over the Boston skyline.

The last thing he would see, he thought.

CHAPTER 56

The killer of Bradley Evans and Mitch Smith sat in his car two houses down and across the street from the home of Jerry Morris. In his warped mind, he held all three accountable for his brother's murder: Evans because he did the actual killing; Smith and Morris because they provided him with drugs. He believed his twin never would have joined in something as stupid as a gas station robbery unless under the influence.

He was done trying to make Morris' death seem like an accident. The cops wouldn't buy it. Next time the bastard left his house, he'd gun him down. He took a swig of whisky from a metal flask and stowed it in the glove compartment to bolster his courage.

Gallo was greeted with handshakes and backslaps when he entered the Hingham PD sans limp. Even the taciturn desk officer came from behind the counter to offer congratulations. He escorted AJ down the hall to the conference room where a reception awaited: Chief Taylor, Jeff McCrory and MDC Detectives Hogan and Hawkins down for the welcome back only. They were ordered to return to Boston as cases piled up. They were still somewhat irked by Gallo's intention to go after Superintendent Fisk.

AJ called ahead a day before to say he received permission to rejoin the investigation. Taylor had released a sergeant, Peter Burbank, to replace the MDC lawmen. Burbank, a twenty-year veteran, had been an acting detective year's earlier, but preferred patrol. A squat, sturdy man in his forties, hair cut military style and greying at the temples, he presented a no-nonsense appearance, someone you didn't want to tangle with. His rugged exterior belied his intelligence.

They were examining the lists of drug clients retrieved from Mitch Smith's when Gallo entered the room. After another round of handshakes and congratulations, Chief Taylor reviewed their progress. He stopped when AJ informed them that the Irish Mafia was off the table as suspects in the slayings of Evans or Smith. He believed, as did the FBI brass, the claims of Moran, O'Rourke, Frankie O'Brien and other gang members when they swore they were not involved. Mike Callahan had been given the same assurances when he met face to face with the Winter Hill thugs.

"Seemed like a long shot," McCrory said.

"Where does that leave us?" the Chief asked.

"Right here," AJ said, holding up one of the lists of Smith's clients. He put the paper back on the table, underlined a name and passed it around.

Everyone shouted at once. "D. Rose."

"Jeff and I talked about this when considering suspects in the Evans and Smith killings. We opted to focus on the Mafia because of the drug connection."

McCrory interrupted. "I pushed for that. AJ thought we should look at Rose."

"A joint decision," Gallo said. "We planned to investigate Dustin's twin if the gang link didn't pan out."

"Makes sense," Taylor agreed. "David is ticked off when he finds out Evans killed his brother and holds Smith responsible for getting his twin hooked. Thinks he wouldn't have participated in the robbery without that influence."

"That's my thinking," AJ said. "His sister told us that David knew Dustin was meeting up with Bradley the night of the gas station heist. When Dustin was slain, he suspected Evans. That's why he ran him down before we announced he was the killer. At first, I feared a leak. With Linda's information, I'm convinced David's our man, and I'm sure he also took out Smith."

"He's our lone option now in both slayings," Chief Taylor agreed. "I'll get a warrant to search his house. Haul him in."

"Can we get that today?" Burbank asked.

Taylor smiled. "I know a guy, as they say."

Everyone laughed. All they could do now was wait for a judge to act.

Seizing the moment, Hogan and Hawkins took their leave, expressing their gratitude at being allowed to join in the investigation and at having worked with such honorable men—a backhanded slap at their former boss. After another round of handshakes, they left.

No one thought Jerry Morris might also be a target.

David Rose was impatient. He'd staked out Morris' place for two hours; it was past time for his walk. Rose sipped Jim Beam from his flask. The liquid courage warmed him. He was sweating and rubbing his hands on his thighs. No more stalking the asshole. He was going to get him today if he had to storm the house, take out his wife and the other lady if it came to that. He took another swig of whisky. Agitated, unable to stay seated, and seeing no one out and about in the neighborhood, he got out of his car.

A mistake.

As he paced back and forth on the dirt and grass—no sidewalks in this area—Morris' wife, Sheila, looked out the window to verify the day's forecast of rain. She thought about warning her husband to forego his walk. Of course, in New England, the weather was fickle and one couldn't survive taking predictions as gospel. Heck, he had a raincoat and hat. Why worry about him?

Pulling the drapes closed, she glimpsed the man across the street who looked familiar. After a moment's reflection, she recognized it was the man Jerry met at the country club. In the gloom of the day, he was wearing his Calloway golf cap and wraparound sunglasses. That was odd. She waved Jerry to the window. "Isn't that the fellow who wanted to give you a ride at the country club?"

"Yeah! Nice guy. What's he doing here?"

"How should I know? He's your friend."

Morris started to open the door to waive the man in, paused, then shut and locked it. He had seen the dude three or four times, but never saw him on the course or carrying a set of clubs. Then again, he didn't golf either. He laughed; thought he was being paranoid.

He opened the door, stood outside, and motioned him over. David waved, then reached into his car to retrieve his Colt. That move, for some reason, spooked Morris. He turned to go back into the house when a bullet caught his left shoulder, spinning him around and dropping him to the cement stoop. Two more shots buzzed over his head as he crawled into the house.

His wife, still peering outside, was astonished. She rushed to pull Jerry inside and shouted to her mother-in-law to call the police.

"Someone's trying to kill Jerry," she yelled, her voice cracking. She set the door lock, and dragged a chair over to prop it under the doorknob.

Jerry, moaning and bleeding from his wound, was in shock as David Rose pounded on the door. He didn't yet have the presence of mind to break a window to gain access to the house. He was ranting and raving on the stoop, demanding Morris come outside.

The ruckus attracted the attention of a neighbor who called the HPD. The desk sergeant took the calls from Jerry's mother, and the neighbor, and raced down to the conference room.

"Someone's trying to kill Jerry Morris," he bellowed.

Gallo and McCrory looked at each other. "Rose," they shouted in unison and ran to get into Gallo's Plymouth. Burbank slid into the back seat.

The dispatcher requested patrol cars in the vicinity to rush to Beal Street, warning them of shots fired.

David Rose continued to pound on the door, then stepped back and put two rounds into the lock, blasting it off its screws.

While Jerry moaned and Sheila wailed, Estelle Morris scurried to a hall closet to retrieve a Remington shotgun. It had been stored there since her late husband, Lloyd, purchased it five years ago. He showed her how to use it once in the woods. Lloyd acquired the weapon to fend off the aliens everyone said would try to take over the United States. A flying saucer had landed in Roswell, New Mexico, he reasoned. Hingham could be next.

Estelle hefted the gun, released the safety as her husband had shown her, and pointed it at the door. She didn't know if it was loaded. Sirens screeched as police cruisers sped to the scene.

Jolted by the sound of the cops approaching, Rose drove his shoulder into the door. The chair Sheila had propped up against it gave way. Rose stumbled inside. As he straightened up, a shotgun blast hit him center mass, propelling him backwards. He landed on the stoop, blood gushing from his chest, his Colt .45 flying from his hand.

Two patrol cars skidded to a stop, followed by Gallo's Plymouth with McCrory and Burbank. On his home turf, Detective McCrory took charge. He ordered the patrolmen to call for ambulances and to stand guard to discourage looky-loos from getting too close.

Gallo ran to the house and checked Jerry; fluid oozed from his shoulder. AJ asked Sheila to get some towels to staunch the bleeding. He showed her how to put pressure on the wound and hold it until the medics arrived.

Sergeant Burbank trailed Gallo and found Estelle Morris in shock, still holding the shotgun. He managed to pry it from her grip, helped her to a couch to sit down and propped the Remington against a wall. He went to the kitchen, fetched a glass of water and brought it back to the distraught woman.

Two ambulances barreled in soon after. Attendants patched Jerry's abrasion and loaded him into the back of their van. Sheila jumped in and accompanied her husband to the hospital.

Gallo dove into the other ambulance to ride with David Rose, eager to talk to him although his condition appeared grave .

Chief Taylor drove up as the ambulances weaved by him. He exited his car and approached McCrory. Blood was on the stoop and inside the home. "What the hell happened?" he asked, his tone incredulous.

"Don't know for sure," McCrory said. "Appears that David Rose shot Jerry and stormed the house to finish him off. Mrs. Morris— Jerry's mother, not the wife—grabbed a shotgun and blasted him as he tried to force his way in."

Taylor shook his head. "Jesus. What a mess. Why was he going after Morris?"

"No clue."

Rose fought for his life as the ambulance sped to the South Shore Hospital in Weymouth. Gallo, realizing he might not make it, bent over and whispered: "David. Did you kill Brad Evans and Mitch Smith?"

David didn't respond. His eyes were open, staring upward. His chest heaved as he choked, blood dribbling from his mouth.

Gallo glanced at the attendant, who shook his head, indicating he didn't think the guy would survive. Gallo, not ready to concede, had seen many wounds on the battlefield that presented as bad as this where the Marine survived. He leaned in again and asked the same question. Rose didn't speak but nodded in the affirmative; admitting he killed Evans and Smith.

"You saw that, right?" Gallo pressed the attendant. "He confessed."

The young man nodded in agreement but Gallo wasn't satisfied. "I need you to say it out loud and testify in court if you have to."

The man hesitated, then said, "Yes! He answered your question by nodding. He killed the two guys you asked him about."

"Good. Good," AJ said. He would later have him sign an affidavit as a witness to Rose's confession, which would have been difficult to hold up in court.

That wouldn't be necessary.

CHAPTER 57

The day after the incident at the Morris home—a Saturday— Chief Taylor scheduled a meeting of the group, minus Hogan and Hawkins, that investigated the murders of Bradley Evans and Mitch Smith. AJ had been contacted at the hospital and notified of the morning gathering.

At eight a.m., the detectives and Sergeant Burbank assembled in the conference room. A dozen donuts rested on the table along with a carafe of coffee.

"Nice to see you all, bright eyed and bushy tailed," Taylor said, using the well-worn cliché to open the meeting. McCrory and Gallo groaned.

"Okay," the Chief began, ignoring their reaction. "Not to be a wet rag. I want to review where we're at before I talk to the press this afternoon. Tell us what you learned, AJ."

Gallo took a sip of coffee, then responded. "As you know by now, David Rose, in a dying declaration on the way to the hospital, confessed to killing Bradley Evans and Mitch Smith. I guess he blamed them both for his brother's death even though Evans pulled the trigger, in self-defense, I believe."

Burbank, new to the investigation, asked, "Why go after Morris?"

"Not certain. He wasn't in his right mind. I assume he lumped Jerry in with Evans and Smith for getting his brother hooked on coke. Afraid we'll never know."

"Not to be a party-pooper," Burbank interrupted, "are we positive about this? Seems like a lot of guessing and assuming."

"Yes," Gallo replied. "The ambulance attendant witnessed David's confession and agreed to furnish a written statement to that affect. We all saw the results of his attack on Morris. We can only speculate as to why, like I said. He died before I could push him on that. I barely got a nod when I asked him about Evans and Smith. Have to admit, a crafty lawyer might have gotten him off if he survived and it went to court."

"We don't need to worry about his reasoning," Taylor said. "We were investigating the killing of Evans and Smith and got our man. Case closed. Thanks to all of you for laboring so hard to bring the killer to justice."

He grabbed a glazed donut, sat back in his chair and sipped his coffee, relief on his face.

After a brief pause while everyone savored the refreshments, Taylor directed his question to Gallo. "What's next for you?"

"Probably back to the grind. I'll be reassigned to the detective unit in Boston, I suspect. They're short-handed. Nantasket will return to its image of a sleepy village in winter and playground in summer."

"Okay. Stick around for the press conference this afternoon at one o'clock please; help with questions I can't answer."

Back in his office at the MDC Substation, Gallo reflected on Chief Taylor's news session. It was masterful. Taylor linked the deaths of Berger and Rose in Paragon Park to those of Evans and Smith using the evidence collected. He praised the work of his own man, McCrory, and gave accolades to the Mets detectives. He threw a bone to the reporters present by mentioning the murder of Patriot Ledger reporter, Bert Jones, in the performance of his investigative reporting.

Gallo smiled to himself. Taylor, an excellent lawman and leader, also displayed pollical savvy. He leaned back in his swivel chair, eyes closed until an intercom buzz interrupted his reverie.

He pushed the button on his phone and answered.

"Detective," the desk sergeant reported, "there's a gentleman here to see you, a Stephen Evans."

Surprised, Gallo clomped down the steep stairs in deference to the old man who appeared older than when they first met; his face pale, dark rings circling his deep-set eyes, Boston Bruins sweater buttoned all the way to the top. "May I have a moment of your time, detective," he asked, in a quavering voice.

"Of course, sir. Let's go outside."

They walked across Nantasket Ave to a bench on the concrete boardwalk bordering the Atlantic.

"What can I do for you?" Gallo asked, once they were seated.

Evans, distracted by a flock of gulls swooping down on the beach, stared at them without speaking for what seemed like an eternity to Gallo but he gave the man time.

"I read the papers, listen to the radio and watch TV, you know," he said, turning toward Gallo who wondered where the old timer was going with this.

"Every time they mention the Paragon Park deaths of those two men, they call Bradley a murderer. He wasn't. You know that. He defended himself. They were after him. Tried to kill him—a gentle boy. A nice boy." Tears flowed down his cheeks.

Here we go again with the nice boy thing, AJ thought, didn't say. He handed Evans a handkerchief.

"I believe it was self-defense, sir. I put that in my reports. The evidence shows the men he killed pursued him."

"Then why don't they say that, instead of besmirching his name. Why don't they say that?"

The old man's shoulders shook. He bent at the waist as he dabbed at his eyes and wordlessly vented his frustration.

When he regained his composure, Gallo didn't try to explain that the reporters were trying to sell newspapers or attract listeners on the radio and viewers on television. He changed the subject. "How is Mrs. Evans doing?"

"She's not upset like me. Doesn't read the papers or watch TV news. She likes the Danny Thomas Show, Red Skelton, Leave it to Beaver, Lawrence Welk. Sometimes Gunsmoke and Wagon Train"

"I admit, I prefer those shows, too," Gallo said. "So do my mom and dad."

Evans forced a smile. "Anything you can do about them people calling my nephew a murderer?"

"Afraid not, sir. We know the truth. We can live with that."

The man absently studied the gulls again, then stood up and led the way to his car in the beach parking lot, his gait unsteady.

"Thanks for listening," were his last words as he drove off.

As he jogged back across Nantasket Ave to the stationhouse, Gallo felt sorry for Stephen Evans. The man wanted to clear his nephew's name, and that wasn't going to happen. Reporters had already moved on. One might write a retrospective this year or the next about the Paragon Park murders but it wouldn't change who they identified as the killer; his motive and the circumstances lost until someone set them straight.

He decided that person would be him.

At his desk, he fished the business card out of his wallet that Alan Jones slipped him at the memorial service for his son Bert and dialed the number. A secretary answered in a practiced, professional tone; "ABJ Construction. How may I help you?"

"I'd like to speak with Mr. Jones please. This is Detective Gallo."

After a brief pause, the woman said excitedly. "Detective. I know he would like to talk with you. He mentions you often and how Bert, rest his soul, admired you. He's in a meeting right now, though, and can't be interrupted. May I have him phone you as soon as he's free?"

Gallo didn't expect to connect with an important executive on his first attempt. "Yes, ma'am," he replied. He gave her the stationhouse number as well as his home phone.

Two hours later, he prepared to leave the station when the intercom buzzed. "Detective. A Mr. Jones is on the line."

Gallo answered with a note of surprise in his voice. He didn't anticipate such a quick response.

"Detective. Sorry I missed your call. I'm heading to another conference. I'm available most of the day Monday. Can you come to my office? Say 10:00 a.m."

"Yes, sir. I'll be there. Thanks for seeing me."

Jones clicked off before AJ could explain why he wanted an appointment.

CHAPTER 58

The drive from Nantasket to Quincy took forty-five minutes and required Gallo to cross the vertical lift bridge spanning the Weymouth Fore River. It opened to permit ships from the adjacent shipyard to pass out into the Atlantic. The yard, one of the busiest in the country during World War II, built carriers, battleships and destroyers. Gallo's father worked there alongside a contingent of other Hull men. That knowledge led him to smile with each crossing of the bridge—and enhanced his pride in his dad.

The ABJ Construction Company, a two-story red-brick structure on Hancock Street, displayed the firm name emblazoned on the front in glistening, polished steel letters. Gallo entered through double glass doors into a large room filled with a maze of cubicles. An army of women pounded away on typewriters. A thirty-something receptionist directed him to take the elevator to the second-floor.

Once there, he walked through another labyrinth of worker bees and found his destination at the end of a narrow, tiled corridor. The reception area, an expansive, well-appointed suite, with white cushioned leather chairs and couches, could accommodate four offices the size of Gallo's Nantasket cubbyhole. Expensive looking paintings of old Quincy adorned the walls. Gallo introduced himself to the secretary who told him to take a seat. Mr. Jones would see him shortly.

"Shortly" turned out to be about thirty-five minutes. While waiting, Gallo thumbed through construction journals displayed on an end-table next to his chair. The array of equipment pictured: front-loaders, back loaders, trucks of all shapes and sizes, drills, acetylene-torches, caterpillar tractors, road pavers, and cranes fascinated him. The cost of running a construction company must be outrageous, he thought.

Alan Jones came out to greet him in person. He wore a starched white shirt, sleeves rolled up, gray slacks and a maroon tie; the top two buttons of his shirt undone, tie askew—a man in work mode.

He guided AJ into his spacious office. Like the reception room, a sofa with comfortable chairs arranged next to it occupied one wall, with a six-foot conference table on the right; seven padded, black Naugahyde chairs surrounding it. A carafe of coffee rested on a glass topped table in front of the couch where Jones steered Gallo.

"Can I offer you coffee?" Jones asked.

AJ, having skipped breakfast to ensure he arrived on time, accepted.

"How about some Dunkin' Donuts?"

"You trying to bribe me, sir?" Gallo said, a smile creasing his face.

Jones returned the smile, used the intercom to ask his assistant to bring in the refreshments, then said, "Perhaps."

The answer caught Gallo off-balance. He gave the man a quizzical glance.

"Saw you perusing the journals on the table next to you in the waiting room."

"Owning a construction company seems like a pricey business," Gallo said in awe.

"It is. Which leads to the reason for my bribe, as you called it."

AJ raised his eyebrows.

"Thieves raid our sites daily. Despite our best efforts, they often succeed in stealing expensive equipment, even lost a bulldozer once."

"Why are you telling me this, sir?"

"I want you to become my head of security. I'll double what the Mets are paying you. You'll have free reign to organize staff any way you want. You're a man of integrity and skill, unafraid to take risks when necessary. I trust you."

The offer blew Gallo away.

Jones recognized he caught the detective off-guard. "I know this is a big decision, son. And I can assure you it's life-changing; one you shouldn't take without serious thought. I can give you a week or two to decide. After that, I'll need to move on. Choose someone else."

Gallo took a sip of coffee and a bite of jelly donut to buy time thinking about the offer. The law enforcement agency he'd joined in an effort to serve the community turned out to be riddled with corruption, including the FBI. Should he continue to work to change that, or take a job that promised freedom to act and financial security?

"That's an intriguing proposition, sir," he said. "As you point out, I'll need time to consider it."

"Can't ask for more than that, son. I know this wasn't what you planned by coming here. What can I do for you?"

Still rattled, Gallo pressed Jones to use his influence on the Patriot Ledger board of directors to get a retrospective article printed about the Paragon Park murders. He wanted the story to emphasize Bradley Evans killed Dustin Rose and Donald Berger in self-defense. It would ease the feelings of an old man and not change the big picture. Evans would still be viewed by the general public as a murderer.

Jones made no commitment. Said he'd think about it.

Gallo left the office of Alan Jones, hungry, hadn't eaten breakfast before leaving Hull—the donuts only a stop-gap. He thought about grabbing a bite in Quincy, then realized he was close to Wollaston Beach. He fished the slip of paper from his wallet with the name and number of the waitress from the Jolly Rodger—Vivian.

He found a nearby phone booth, put ten cents in the slot and dialed. Nervous, he shuffled his feet as he waited for the call to be answered. When she didn't answer after four rings, he figured she might be sleeping late after a long night shift. About to hang up, a sleepy voice stopped him. "Yes."

Torn between answering and hanging up, he screwed up his courage and said, "Sorry if I woke you. I'll try some other time."

"Hold on," she protested. "Now that you did get me up, who is this?"

"Uh," he stammered. "Uh. Detective Anthony Gallo. You served my friend and me at the Jolly Rodger a while ago. We attracted stares because we wore uniforms. Probably won't remember me. Didn't mean to intrude. I'll try again some other time."

"Wait a minute, Gallo, I remember. We don't get many cops in uniform as customers. Thought detectives didn't wear them? You're six-feet a hundred inches tall."

Gallo laughed. "We'd just come from a funeral."

"Oh! Now I'm sorry," she said. "Is that why you tied one on? You didn't look so good leaving the place. Your pal struggled to hold you up."

"Wanted to forget a few things, I guess. A friend had been killed. Two friends actually."

After a long silence, AJ thought they might have been disconnected until she said, "I heard that on the radio. You were attacked too."

"Lucked out."

"Not what the reporter said."

"You believe everything you hear on the news?"

She laughed again. "What can I do for you detective?"

"Hoped you'd have breakfast with me. Attended a meeting in Quincy." He paused, then said, "Sorry if I woke you. Some other time."

"Oh, no, Mr. detective. You're not getting out of buying me breakfast that easy. Meet you at Fails Café on Washington Street in about half an hour."

She clicked off without waiting for his response.

Gallo arrived at Fails Café first. He took a window seat, ordered coffee and told the waitress a lady would be joining him.

The young girl returned with his coffee and two menus when Vivian, so far, no last name, walked in, caught his eye and waived. Her dark hair cut short, she wore a white blouse, sleeves rolled up, a striped red bandana, and a gray flared skirt with a wide matching belt and black flats. Her skin was unblemished, her eyes mischievous, something he missed in the darkness of the Jolly Roger.

She took the bench seat opposite AJ and extended her hand. "Nice to meet you again, detective."

He took her hand, careful not to crush it in his over-sized mitt. He said, "Same here. Vivian, uh?"

She presented a warm smile. "Hunter. Vivian Hunter."

He returned the smile. "Pleased to officially meet you, Vivian Hunter."

She giggled as they perused the menu and both ordered French toast. They spent the rest of the morning kibitzing about where they went to high school, teachers they liked or didn't like, same with foods, their current jobs. In addition to waitressing, she was enrolled in the elementary teacher education program at Northeastern University. She adored the Everly Brothers and thought Elvis sexy when he gyrated those hips.

AJ blanched at that revelation, admitted he too enjoyed the Everly's. He deflected questions about Korea.

The meal flew by and ended with AJ promising to contact her again soon.

One week after his breakfast with Vivian Hunter and his appointment with Alan Jones, Gallo received a call from a Patriot Ledger reporter developing a follow up article on the Paragon Park murders. He planned to include the subsequent killings of Mitch Smith, Bradley Evans and the capture of David Rose. The newsman didn't reveal his editors ordered the piece at the suggestion of a board member; he didn't need to. AJ pressured the man to emphasize that Evans had killed the men in self-defense. The guy promised but AJ didn't know if he'd come through.

Gallo called Alan Jones to express his gratitude and asked for an additional week to consider the security job offer. Jones agreed but emphasized the time constraint on the proposal. He needed to fill the position to stem the series of thefts ruining his company. AJ, faced with making the decision alone, chose to enlist the help of those he trusted: his parents, the new Chief of Detectives, Lenny Pierce; didn't include Susan Lawrence.

Gallo's feelings about Vivian Hunter surprised him; a bright, funny woman easy to talk to. He held fond memories of their breakfast meeting and considered the likelihood of his calling her again. He hoped he and Susan Lawrence could remain friends, but now accepted he couldn't rekindle their adolescent romance. She moved on and so would he.

His parents were torn when AJ told them of his opportunity. His father liked the accolades his son received as a detective. He reveled in the praise of old pals when they greeted him in a store or on the street. His mother felt relief that her boy might take a less stressful and dangerous job. Though she took pride in his career as a lawman, she worried every time he left the house. They offered no clear advice.

When AJ met with the new Chief of D's, Nick Osterman, he wrestled with mixed emotions. On the one hand, satisfaction in having solved the Paragon Park and related murders, on the other, concern that turning down a lucrative job opportunity could be a catastrophic mistake.

Osterman had re-arranged his predecessor's office. He swapped the desk which Kellum altered to his advantage to peer down on those who sat before him, for a round table and four chairs. The set-up facilitated conversations rather than dictates from the boss. He replaced portraits of state and national politicians with paintings of Fenway Park, Boston Commons and the Old North Church. A couch and padded chairs replaced the conference table.

"So," Osterman said, after AJ recounted the offer made to him by Alan Jones. "You considering it?"

"I am, sir. Tired of getting shot at."

"Can't blame you there, son."

AJ stifled a laugh. Now everyone was calling him son. Alan Jones; Osterman, Fisk.

"The money's great, can set my own hours, organize the department as I see fit."

The Chief sat back, clasped both hands behind his head as his chair tottered on two legs. "I expect you'll make sergeant soon, if that's any incentive, comes with a pay raise."

AJ, worried that Osterman might topple backwards, asked, "Any advice, sir?"

To AJ's relief, the man dropped his chair back onto the floor. "We need you here, son. Your reputation alone has raised that of the entire organization after the recent scandals. You'll sit in my place sooner rather than later."

He paused, ran both hands through his thinning hair. "Having said that, I cannot in good conscience encourage you to stay. You have to make that decision yourself without undue influence. I want you here, of course. Know that."

Gallo left the office no closer to a choice than when he entered; Lenny Pierce his last hope for clarity. He picked up a six pack of Bud, helped Lenny into the front seat of his Ford coupe and drove to the top of Allerton Hill, the highest of the seven hills comprising the town.

The houses, browned shingled two-story structures with open porches, sported expansive lawns. JFK's grandfather, "Honey Fitz" Fitzgerald, a mayor of Boston and member of the House of Representatives, once owned a home on the hill.

Their vantage point displayed a panoramic view of the Atlantic Ocean, Boston Light and Fort Warren—an abandoned fortress that housed confederate prisoners during the Civil War—and the silhouette of the Boston skyline. Gallo parked on a steep grade that required the emergency brake, something he seldom used.

The former classmates drank beer, enjoyed the sights and stayed silent for about twenty minutes before AJ broached the subject of his working for ABJ Construction.

"What do you think, man?" AJ asked.

Pierce took a long pull of his drink, then said, "I think in your heart and your gut you know what you're going to do, pal."

AJ, caught off guard, didn't know how to respond. He procrastinated by taking his time to sip his beer and by commenting on the view.

"It's a tough choice, Len. Could make me financially independent, help my parents buy a bigger place, and let me stop dodging bullets."

"I stick by my comment."

"No advice. No weighing the pros and cons?"

"Nope. Waste of time."

Their tete-a-tete over, they rode down the hill and back to their Kenberma neighborhood in silence—no further dialogue about the job or his options. Gallo resented Lenny's certainty that he had made his decision. But he could read AJ's mind even as a kid.

Was he right? He spent the night tossing and turning without resolution.

CHAPTER 59

The Dorchester gangsters, members of "The Three," had surveilled AJ Galo for weeks. The son-of-a-bitch detective killed one of their own and arrested two others in that FBI raid in Whitfield. They overlooked the fact that their brethren had been on a mission of murder; didn't matter—only payback did. If they didn't act, rivals would view their inaction as weakness, use it as a reason to make a move on their territory.

The gang bangers rode in two cars, a four-door Chevy Two-Ten and a mint green Oldsmobile 98. Four men, armed with automatic weapons, occupied each.

Gallo never varied from his route to work. He took Samoset Ave to Phipps Street behind the War Memorial. Today was his last day in Nantasket. The Chief of Detectives recalled him to Boston. With the Paragon Park murders resolved, the small town with minimal crime didn't need a detective.

At 7:45 a.m., he encountered few other vehicles. In deep thought about his recall and the construction job offer, he wasn't aware of the Chevy Two-Ten trailing at a respectful distance. Chevys were among the most popular cars sold in 1958. Even if he caught a glimpse of one in his rear-view mirror, it wouldn't raise concern. He sensed danger only when behind the War Memorial. An Oldsmobile veered off Nantasket Avenue blocking his progress. The Chevy following him cut off any effort to retreat. Men with guns leaped from both vehicles and assumed firing positions.

AJ sighed; would it never end? Though trapped, he was better prepared than in the FBI Whitfield raid. At that time, he carried only an M1911, Colt .45 semi-automatic pistol. Now, a loaded Winchester

Model 50, three shot, 20 gage shotgun lay wrapped in a blanket under his front seat in addition to the M1911 in his shoulder holster.

Still outgunned by the gangsters, who all toted Thompson's, they didn't learn their lesson from Whitfield. Gallo did not play defense. Offense was his game, had been since high school when he rumbled through the line carrying the football, bulling over defenders.

He shifted the coupe into first gear, ducked below the windshield, and inched forward. The nervous gunman did not notice until too late. When he guessed he was close enough, he jumped back up behind the wheel, floored the coupe's engine and plowed into the Oldsmobile. The startled assassins fired wildly, but not without effect as it turned out. Two were pinned under the coupe's front end and the crumpled side of the Old's, forcing two others to leap aside.

Though hit twice, Gallo rolled out of his door with the shotgun, blasting one of the hoodlums sprawled on the grass. He pivoted and took out the other on the right who lay on the asphalt, stunned. He seized a Thompson from one of the downed attackers and took up a position behind his car waiting for the gangsters poised around the blocking Chevy to charge. Instead, seeing their pals overwhelmed and hearing distant sirens, they sped off, going the wrong way on Samoset Ave.

Patrons in a nearby diner, alerted to gunshots outside, had called the Hull PD who corralled the fleeing mobsters on Nantasket Ave without shots being fired. Gallo made sure the two bangers caught beneath his car were immobilized, then staggered over the grass of the War Memorial toward the onlookers across the street. Blood dripping from a head wound blurred his vision and a gash in his side seeped down his leg. He lost consciousness and fell face down on the manicured lawn, his badge clutched in his left hand.

Ambulances arrived in minutes and rushed Gallo and the injured gangbangers to the South Shore Hospital. Motorcycle officers led the way, sirens blaring, lights flashing. Ambulance attendants treating Gallo shook their heads, skeptical the detective would make it.

CHAPTER 60

The funeral procession snaked through Hull Village cemetery passing a grave whose headstone read: Strangers Corner. It contained the remains of one-hundred men, woman and children, victims of shipwrecks from 1860 to 1898. The town gained notoriety during that time for its lifesaving efforts spearheaded by the famous coast guardsman, Joshua James.

Those in the current motorcade took no notice of this historical marker. The vehicles halted at the top of a small rise, located below the vine covered walls of Fort Revere, a Revolutionary era fortress. Two hundred French soldiers died there of smallpox and were buried outside the Fort's walls. This has led visitors over the years to claim sightings and sounds of the spirits of those men roaming the dark passageways of the fortress.

On this gloomy, overcast day, with no eerie noises in the air, black clad friends and relatives of the deceased sat graveside near a flag-draped coffin. Father Robert Turner of Saint Mary's Parish read from scripture and offered words of comfort and encouragement to the family. Two Marines folded the flag covering the casket and presented it to the deceased's mother. The seven-member honor guard from Camp Lejeune then fired a twenty-one-gun salute followed by the playing of taps. On the first note of the distinctive melody, active and retired service men came to attention and saluted.

Everyone is familiar with the bugle rendition of the song, but few know its lyrics. The tall former Marine, supported by a cane, wearing dress blues, Navy Cross, Purple Heart and Silver Star with oak leaf clusters pinned to his left breast, did. He had heard it played many times. He whispered the words as the bugler blasted them out:

Day is done, gone the sun,

From the hills, from the lake, from the skies,
All is well, safely rest, God is nigh.

Tears flowed as the bugler finished:

Day is gone, night is on, thanks and praise
For our days, neath the sun, neath the stars, neath the sky,
As we go, this we know, God is nigh.

AJ Gallo snapped off the salute and crouched over, leaning on his cane, made his way to Lenny Pierce's mother to offer his condolences. Lenny's wife and son attended the church service but Diane didn't want to expose their child to the trauma of witnessing a military burial. A sensible decision since the three rifle volleys from the honor guard unnerved adult mourners shaken by the noise and repetition.

In a cruel act of fate, an embolism had felled Lenny Pierce while giving Georgie a wheelchair ride down the ramp from their front door. A clot in his leg blocked the pulmonary artery and he died of a heart attack before he could receive treatment.

The irony nearly destroyed AJ. He survived multiple attempts on his life and injuries that would have killed many others. Lenny endured the loss of his legs and dies when playing with his son.

With the service concluded, a wave of mourners dispersed to their cars, as if fleeing a disaster. Gallo stayed behind, removed his Navy Cross and placed it atop the casket. He saluted, fighting back tears.

Vivian Hunter joined him, clutching his free arm and laying her head on his chest. Gallo kissed her forehead before guiding her toward his car as a cold wind and dark clouds swept in from the Atlantic. They reached the car and slipped in as rain sounded a drumbeat on the roof.

A fitting end to a tragic event, Gallo thought.

Two days after the burial of his friend, AJ sat alone on the sand at Kenberma sipping a Bud; an illegal act but no one was around to chastise him. He watched the waves crest and marveled how some crept up on the beach and died, while the remnants of others retreated as if pulled back by an unseen hand.

He divided his attention between the breakers and the gulls circling overhead. They spread their wings, as they glided down, turning on their side like Marine Corsairs preparing for a strafing run. They retracted their wings when they alighted on the wet sand, some dipping their feet in the water when white capped waves overtook them. Others scurried toward shore as if being chased.

The ritual played out over and over as the gulls took to the air, joined their companions in formation then landed again. Gallo wondered if the actions of the birds and cresting surf carried a message—that life followed an endless series of routines till the end.

Did a God orchestrate this?

He had abandoned his religious upbringing on the slopes of Korea, rejecting the notion of a Supreme Being who would allow such slaughter. He couldn't lead his life in pursuit of some hoped for salvation he rejected. But where did that leave him?

He had no answer, drank his last beer, laid back and dozed off.

Gallo moped around his parent's house using the rocker on the front porch until he regained his strength and shed the cane. He walked to the Pierce home a couple of times, picked up little Georgie, put him on his shoulders and carried him to the beach, whinnying like a horse as he plunged them into the ocean. Georgie laughed like only a two-year old could and called him Uncle AJ.

On her days off, Vivian came to Hull and Gallo often took her to dinner at the Red Lion, in Cohasset, an upscale Colonial Inn used for weddings and other special occasions. They dined on steaks, sipped wine, shared a truffle for dessert, then strolled through downtown gazing in shop windows, some displaying New England landscape paintings for sale.

They frequently wandered all the way to the common and rested on a bench overlooking the man-made lake—a post-card setting with the white clapboard first parish meeting house, its spire and gigantic clock.

Vivian would lean her head on AJ's shoulder and they sat unmoving sometimes for fifteen minutes or so enjoying the solace and the view. Later they walked arm-in-arm past St. Stephens Episcopal Church with its steep stone stairs and stone façade dating back to 1900.

When their sojourns were finished, they returned to the Red Lion for a night-cap. AJ rented a room for privacy, away from the close quarters of his parent's house. They drank and talked until exhausted and retired to their room.

Once there, Vivian changed into a modest gray flannel nightgown in the spacious bathroom. While waiting, Gallo sat in a stuffed chair next to a floor lamp glancing through a tourist brochure extolling the many attractions in Cohasset.

When Vivian came into the room, Gallo brightened; he thought she could be listed as one of the town's charms. Her face was scrubbed, her cheeks a light pink and her lips, without lipstick, alluring.

She was beautiful.

Their eyes locked; the desire reflected in them, unmistakable. AJ sprang toward her in one swift motion picked her up and twirled around as they both laughed. He placed her gently on the bed, shrugged off his clothes and pulled her gown up and over her head.

Lying in a naked embrace, their body heat smoldered like the logs in the room's stone fireplace, their hands explored each other; their kisses hard and soft at the same time. They moved as one and both shuddered as they released months of longing.

They slept with Vivian's head resting on his chest, their legs entwined; AJ's arms wrapped around her protectively.

In the morning, they strolled arm-in-arm to a small bakery/café in the center of town. They both had blueberry muffins and black coffee—AJ adding bacon and scrambled eggs. They weren't sure what last night's intimacy meant for the long term but basked in its glow.

Over several cups of coffee, they discussed Vivian's work and college preparation for a teaching credential. They did not chat about AJ's impending decision to continue as a lawman or enter the private sector.

She did not attempt to influence him.

CHAPTER 61

Aweek after his visit to Cohasset with Vivian Hunter, on a Saturday, AJ attended the wedding of Susan Lawrence and Mike Callahan in Saint Mary's of the Assumption Church, Green Hill. He sat with his mother and father in a pew midway between the front and back of the church.

He did not go to the reception at the Surf Ballroom despite the urging of his parents. He accepted the fact he and Susan didn't have a future together. He admired her husband Mike for his tenacity in breaking away from a gang that threatened to tear him down. That said, he couldn't face a raucous party where everyone enjoyed themselves and where he might be encouraged to say a few words; didn't know if he could pull that off.

At any rate, it was time for a decision on his future.

As he often did, he walked along the beach from Kenberma toward the base of Allerton Hill letting the waves wash across his bare feet. He took his time weighing in his mind the pros and cons of returning to the Mets or starting a new career as a security chief with a construction company.

He loved law enforcement in the beginning, but the whole affair with Wilkinson, Captain Kellum, the FBI and the Irish mobsters destroyed his idealism—even more than Korea. He still believed men like Jeff McCrory and Vince Russo could make a difference, but he felt tired; drained.

He had recovered from his physical wounds but the mental toll wore him down. He walked back along the water and through the sand to his parent's house, sat at the kitchen table, and reached for the phone. He dialed the number of the ABJ Construction firm.

His decision made.

If he returned to the MDC or joined another police force, there would always be bad guys with guns; and he would never retreat from danger but would, in fact, embrace it; put himself in harm's way. He thought of Vivian and the possibility of marriage and a family. When the phone was answered at ABJ Construction, the secretary connected him to CEO, Alan Jones.

"That job still open, sir?" he asked, when Jones picked up.

After a brief pause, Jones said, "Welcome aboard, son."

AJ laughed. He would have to break his new boss of referring to him as "son."

EPILOGUE

The killing of two men in Paragon Park, Nantasket Beach, in the winter of 1957, had far reaching consequences. David Rose, seeking revenge for his murdered brother, killed two men and was himself slain attempting to kill a third. He didn't survive the chest wound inflicted by the mother of his intended victim. His dying confession wrapped up the investigation into the murders of Bradley Evans and Mitch Smith.

Jerry Morris survived the attack by Rose although he spent three weeks in the hospital recovering. During that time, his wife, Sheila, moved out of her mother-in law's home and back with her own parents in Hanover, Massachusetts. She filed for divorce a month later.

Devastated, Jerry's drinking increased. One afternoon, stumbling back from the country club, he strayed into traffic, was hit and died at the scene. The driver of the car that struck him swore to officers that he jumped in front of his vehicle. An investigation deemed his death an accident.

Bobby Moran, temporary boss of the Winter Hill Gang, survived the wound inflicted by one of his own men; a traitor who sought to oust him during the ill-fated FBI bust. Moran ran the gang until supplanted by the true leader, Buddy McClean, when he was released from prison. McClean's tenure ended in 1963 when he was shot by a rival gangster as he left the 381 club on Broadway, in Winter Hill, Massachusetts.

Captain Martin Kellum, who developed a network of police officers willing to do his bidding in illegal ventures, served fifteen years of a forty-year sentence for these acts. Abandoned by his family, he walked into the surf at Wollaston Beach and was never found.

Kellum's rabbi, Superintendent Bob Fisk, did not commit suicide as he had planned. Sitting at his desk fingering his .38, he snapped out of his melancholy. Taking his own life was a coward's way out not befitting a decorated soldier and longtime lawman. He resigned and turned himself over to the FBI.

Lieutenant Roger Newman of the Quincy PD served ten years in prison for bank robbery and accessary to attempted murder. His wife divorced him while he was away. He moved to Florida and started a private investigator firm; some of his clients were reputed mobsters.

Shamus O'Rourke and his brother, Devlin, were convicted of murder in the deaths of Metro Lieutenant, Bill Wilkinson, gang member, "White Shoes" Dolan, and the attempted murder of Bobby Moran. They were sentenced to life imprisonment.

Francis X. "Frankie" O'Brien was convicted of being an accessory to the murder of Dolan and the attempted murder of Moran and served twenty of a thirty-year verdict. He left the gang life upon his release and moved to California.

The Special Agent in Charge, Boston, S.V. Peterson, summoned to Washington by J. Edgar Hoover, received a written reprimand for his part in planning the disastrous raid in Whitfield that cost the lives of two Whitfield officers and an FBI Special Agent. The rebuke was kept secret. He retained his position as SAC, Boston.

Special Agent Arthur Fitzpatrick, also reprimanded by Hoover and facing a transfer to the FBI office in Grand Forks, North Dakota, chose to resign. He later became a police chief in a small Massachusetts town.

Cohasset Officer, Vincent Russo, waited a year and began dating the former wife of Donald Berger, murdered in Paragon Park. They married and had two children, both girls. AJ Gallo served as "Best Man" at the wedding.

Hingham Detective Jeff McCrory, was promoted to sergeant and received a commendation for his role in the investigation of the murders of Brad Evans and Mitch Smith. Five years later, he parlayed that recognition into becoming police chief in Duxbury, Massachusetts. Gallo pinned the gold stars on the collar of his uniform during his induction ceremony.

AJ Gallo retired from the Mets and became head of security for the ABJ Construction company. He established procedures that cut the company's theft losses by eighty-percent. After ten years in that position, he became executive vice-president.

Gallo and Vivian Hunter, who graduated from Northeastern University and joined the ranks of elementary teachers in Quincy, were engaged. But after six years, the relationship foundered and they went their separate ways; still friends.

Gallo relished his role as "Uncle AJ" to young Georgie Pierce. The two were inseparable, attended football and baseball games, and held family barbecues at the beach although Lenny's wife re-married and moved to Hingham. Georgie received a scholarship to Harvard. His close bond with AJ gave way to his connection with his college classmates, though they still kept in touch.

AJ retired and bought a home on Allerton Hill with the same ocean view he and Lenny enjoyed. With a ghost writer, he published a memoir of his wartime exploits and his Mets career which became a bestseller.

The "Hull Boy" truly made good.

Acknowledgements

I grew up in Hull in the 1950s and worked at Paragon Park as a teenager. To my knowledge, there has never been a murder within the park's confines. Many people who lived in the Boston metropolitan area knew the town only as Nantasket primarily as a result of Paragon Park and the beach. The Nantasket Reservation is only a mile strip of land within Hull.

Hullonians in the 1950s knew the police agency that patrolled the beach area as the MDC while outside the town, the organization was frequently referred to as the Mets. Hence I used the names MDC and Mets interchangeably.

I relied on Dr. William Bergen, Hull's unofficial historian, for much of the history of Paragon Park and that of the town. His book, <u>Old Nantasket</u> is filled with humorous personal anecdotes. He served as a Hull selectman—the town's governing body—for several years.

The bank robbery was based on an actual incident in 1980. It took place in Medford, Massachusetts. The caper was masterminded by Gerald Clemente, a captain in the MDC and involved lawmen from several different cities. Clemente went to prison and eventually wrote a book entitled <u>The Cops Are Robbers</u>.

Bobby Moran is a fictitious character. The real leader of the Somerville Irish Mafia was James "Buddy" McClean who founded the group. The gang was dubbed "The Winter Hill" mob in the 1970s by journalists from the Boston Herald.

A couple of "real" people made cameo appearances in this novel. Larry Stone owned Paragon Park until it was sold in 1986 to developers who built condos on the site.

Leonard Damon was my eighth-grade principal at the Memorial School. As graduating seniors at Hull High School in 1960, we dedicated our yearbook to him. He was characterized as a patient and understanding leader.

I want to thank all of you who have read this book. All of the proceeds—like those of my other books—go to help fund two scholarships for graduating seniors at Hull High School.

No book is the result of the work of one person, though I take responsibility for any mistakes in the final product. Those who helped immensely with ideas, recommendations and the elimination of grammatical errors are: Alan Tubman, Pat Laramee, Jeanie Conway, Tom Gibbons, Bill Wallace, Debbie Pavich and Carol and Jack Curtiss.

Special thanks to my wife Carol, who has always encouraged me to write.

www.ingramcontent.com/pod-product-compliance
Lightning Source LLC
Chambersburg PA
CBHW030645260626
47157CB00007B/2501